JOAN

LINDEN PRESS/SIMON & SCHUSTER

COLLINS

Prime Time

A NOVEL

NEW YORK · LONDON · TORONTO · SYDNEY · TOKYO

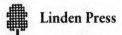 **Linden Press**

Simon & Schuster Building
Rockefeller Center
1230 Avenue of the Americas
New York, New York 10020

This book is a work of fiction. The characters are fictional and created out of the imagination of the author. When reference is made to individuals whose names are identifiable and recognizable by the public, it is because they are prominent in their respective fields and mentioning them is intended to convey a sense of verisimilitude to this fictional work.

Designed by Eve Metz
Manufactured in the United States of America

10   9   8   7   6   5   4   3   2   1

Library of Congress Cataloging in Publication Data
Collins, Joan, date.
  Prime time.

  I. Title.
PR6053.0426P75   1988   823'.914   88-11579
ISBN 0-671-61885-7

I would like to thank—

Michael Korda and Nancy Nicholas, my editors,
for their encouragement and wonderfully
constructive criticism...

Irving Lazar, for believing I could do it...

Cindy Franke, who tirelessly deciphered my
complicated shorthand with accuracy
and devotion...

And Judy Bryer, for her loving support.

For every actress
who has ever suffered the slings and arrows
of outrageous fortune
that are such a part of all our lives...
and for Daddy, who was
such a part of mine.

Prime Time

Part One

Part One

1

Chloe Carriere strode swiftly through the Heathrow departure lounge, trying with little success to escape the inquisitive lenses of the familiar throng of paparazzi. As photographers and reporters buzzed around her, several businessmen waiting for flights lowered their morning newspapers to stare at one of Britain's most famous and sexiest singing stars. "How long will you be in Hollywood, Chloe?" demanded the hack with acne from the *Sun*.

Chloe smiled, increasing her pace. Her sable-lined trench coat billowed gracefully around her newly slimmed figure. She had spent a grueling week at a health farm in Wales trying to erase the combined ravages of Josh, a demanding six-month tour of the provinces, and her first acting role in a BBC docudrama about women in prison. It had brought her down to fighting weight, and now she looked and felt great—better now in 1982 than she had in years.

"What kind of a part are you testing for?" grinned the one with the green teeth from the *Mirror*. "Is it a new television soap opera, then?"

"I don't really know too much about it yet," she hedged. "Other than that it's based on a best-selling novel called *Saga.*"

"Do you want the part?" asked the one from Reuters with the adenoids and the bulging Adam's apple.

Did she want the part? What a stupid question! Of *course* she wanted the damn part. After more than twenty years of singing gigs in Britain, Europe and the States, she ached for it but she answered their questions casually: *if* she was lucky enough to be chosen for the role of Miranda Hamilton, it could turn her career around, make her a big name, maybe even a superstar. But she didn't want these little bastards—and those bigger bastards —waiting in Hollywood to look her over to know just how much she cared, how desperately she needed this role, particularly when she was only one of four or five actresses who were testing for it.

Testing for it! Demeaning, but what the hell. She knew this business was no fairy godmother. She had been up and down in it, then up and then down again, like a Yo-Yo for years. Seven hit records in two and a half decades. A fixture in the Top Ten, now suddenly, in 1982, she couldn't even make *Billboard*'s Top 100. Twenty-five years of performing, but still surviving and still sane, thank God. She gave the reporters and the photographers a smile and a friendly wave as she reached the departure gate, and as they snapped a few more frames for good measure, she hoped the photographs would be kind in tomorrow's tabloids.

In the first-class comfort of the British Airways cabin she relaxed, accepted a Buck's Fizz from the smiling steward, then changed her mind in anticipation of the forthcoming scrutiny of studio moguls, asking instead for Evian water. She waved away cashew nuts and caviar, accepted the *Herald Tribune* and the *Daily Express,* removed her cream kid boots and belt, reclined her seat to its maximum, and thought about this irresistible role.

Miranda Hamilton, in *Saga.* A story of intrigue, corruption, betrayal, ambition and lust, set against a background of great wealth amidst the opulent estates, luxurious yachts and ultra-modern skyscraper offices of Newport Beach, California. A tale of men and women who loved and hated with passions larger than life. The book had been on *The New York Times* best-seller list for six months, and now they were casting for the television series. According to Chloe's agent, Jasper Swanson, they had already cast several familiar television names for various roles, but had not yet found their bitch-goddess villainess Miranda. The network wanted a glamorous manipulating bitch, a rotten-to-the-core heartless tramp, a deviously ambitious but sexily elegant woman of the world, a female so mean and gorgeous that every man watching would either want to make love to her or give her a taste of her own medicine, and whom every woman would either envy or emulate. If the show were a hit, the actress who would play her could be catapulted to ephemeral television fame, glory, and the eventual megabucks that went with that success.

But Miranda Hamilton *couldn't* be the average Hollywood blond bimbo. She had to be at least forty, preferably closer to forty-five. Survivor of three or four marriages and three or four dozen affairs, she had borne three or four children, owned three or four estates scattered throughout the world, had three or four million dollars' worth of jewels, not to mention two or three hundred million dollars in the bank. The actress picked for this plum part would certainly have to have enough in common with Miranda to be believable to the audience. They would have to hate her, and they would have to love her. Not an easy combination to achieve. She had to be a bitch, but she had to be vulnerable. She had to have fire, but she had to be warm. She had to be dominating, yet men must feel they could be the one to dominate her. And last week the producers, dynamic Abby Arafat and his partner, the equally dynamic Gertrude Greenbloom, had come up with the idea of testing Chloe.

Chloe had attracted Abby Arafat's interest at a cocktail party at Lady Sarah Cranleigh's Eaton Square flat. Just returned from a tour of Scandinavia, Chloe, unable to decide whether to reconcile with her husband, Josh, in L.A., had lingered for a few days in London, where the other person dearest to her heart lived.

She felt there was very little hope of patching things up with Josh. There was no question that she had been a loving, faithful wife to him. Yet he seemed unable to control his sexual drive with other women. He was lukewarm with her, whined if she wasn't around, yet nagged her if she was. He was a man who had almost ruined his career with his volatile temperament so much so that record companies had been canceling contracts, and his tours were drying up. Often he would sulk for days, refusing to talk to Chloe, locking himself into his personalized state-of-the-art recording studio and mixing his own records hour after hour, day after day, week after week, blocking out everyone else around him.

The day before she had left, walking past his bathroom she saw him masturbating over a copy of a men's magazine. It had nauseated her, but she had not let him know she had seen him. If he could become aroused by a picture in a cheap magazine, why couldn't he make love to *her* properly any more? It had been weeks—no—months now since they had. Ever the optimist, she had hoped things would be different after this last separation. Obviously she had been wrong.

Chloe sighed, coming out of her reverie as the Fasten Seat Belt sign went off. Carrying her beige crocodile Morabito overnight bag, she walked to the plane's cramped toilet. Why, she wondered, with so much effort expended on design, are the toilets not big enough even to brush one's hair without fracturing an elbow? She slipped off her Gianni Versace cream silk blouse and skirt and pulled on a blue velour track suit. She ran a comb through her luxuriant black curly hair and removed her makeup to let her skin breathe, then slathered moisturizer on lavishly— flying ruined her complexion, there was no doubt about that— and strolled back to her seat.

Although aware that several of the women passengers had noticed the transformation and were checking her for cracks, Chloe didn't care. She had little vanity about her looks. She thought she looked fine without makeup, casually dressed. Not for her the elaborate lengths to which many female entertainers went to prevent the world from seeing their real faces. She smiled as she thought of her co-star in the BBC TV play she had just finished. Pandora King was a seldom-out-of-work American actress who had been appearing in supporting roles in series and movies of the week for the past ten years. Although the public never really knew her name, they always recognized her attractively foxy face and glamorous auburn hair. Pandora would arrive in a full, light makeup at six every morning, completely done, even to false lashes, and wearing one of her many Kanekolan wigs which she possessed in several styles. She would be swathed in her mink of the day, which she had in all colors, and would then disappear into her dressing room for three hours. Her makeup box was the size of a compact car and contained every device known to drugstore and cosmetic counter, from plastic fingernails to vaginal jelly. Only God and her makeup man knew what she did in that room, because when she eventually surfaced she looked little different from when she went in.

The two women had spent an amusing lunch hour going through the contents of "Pandora's box," as she called it, on a rare day when Pandora's frosty attitude toward the world, and especially toward other actresses, had thawed slightly.

19

Chloe wondered if a question one of the journalists had asked was true: Was Pandora also testing for Miranda? If so, Pandora herself would be the last person to reveal *that* bit of news to Chloe. She believed in giving nothing away, particularly information of a professional kind.

Arriving at Los Angeles Airport ten hours later, Chloe was whisked by limousine to the endless freeways of Los Angeles.

She grimaced as she observed the repetitive and unattractive streets and boulevards that passed endlessly. Gray smog hung heavily over the city, stinging her eyes and throat, even though the windows of the Cadillac were closed and the air-conditioning turned on full blast.

Chloe had spent a great deal of time in the past two decades living in L.A., but she still disliked the look of the city. It was so ugly, almost sordid in places, and inhabited by people who seemed to exist solely on hamburgers, doughnuts and diet sodas judging by the number of establishments that were selling those substances. New health clubs, gyms and fitness centers sprouted like mushrooms. She counted sixteen new ones. The residents obviously needed them to balance their ruinous eating habits.

Rows of faded buildings, their signs proclaiming the delights of "Yoghurt City," "The Popcorn Palace," and "Chuck's Chili Dogs," passed by. Chloe sighed. Nothing had changed in the six months she had been away. There just seemed to be more smog.

She snuggled deeper into her sable-lined coat, shivering although it was seventy degrees. She was in Los Angeles, coming home to face Josh, hoping to salvage something of their years of magic together.

When the limousine came to the end of the interweaving freeway, turning right onto the straight Pacific Coast Highway at Sunset Boulevard, Chloe relaxed, loosened her coat and opened the window to feel the cool sea breeze on her face. She loved the ocean, the mystery and power of it. She never tired of watching the greenish gray flatness of the Pacific crest into thick fierce white waves as she sat on the beach.

When they had first bought the house in a secluded part of Trancas Beach, beyond Malibu, she and Josh spent early mornings and most evenings walking along the caramel sands dodging the tide, talking about everything under the sun, laughing at the baby sandpipers, breathing the salty pure air, so different from the smoggy atmosphere that passed for oxygen in the city. They had been so happy that Chloe thought that no married couple could ever have been as gloriously and passionately devoted to each other. But that was then, and this was now, and it was time to find out if he had changed his tune in the six months they had been apart.

He was watching the box as usual, slumped in his favorite suede comfortable armchair. They kissed abstractedly, lovers whose lust for each other had lost its luster. He was dressed in rumpled navy blue cords and a V-neck cashmere sweater. His black hair was untidy and flecked with gray. Although he had known she was coming home, he hadn't bothered to shave, and she felt his splintery stubble against her soft cheek.

"I brought you some special honey from Fortnum's. It's new from Devon—they say it's wonderful." He ignored her, his body loose and relaxed as she hugged him tightly.

Was it too late for them now? she wondered, as she held the face she had adored for so many years between her hands and kissed his cool lips. In spite of his waning interest in her and his womanizing, she still couldn't believe this was happening to them. *Why* was he turning off her. After six months apart, why did he make no effort? Not even a pretense of delight in her homecoming. He didn't even bother to stand up. What had she done to make him so indifferent? Even before she went on tour, there had been too many moments in bed, their usual arena of compatibility, when she had had to coax him to make love to her. She felt like a cheap tart. Was this what ten years of mar-

21

riage did to a man's libido? she wondered bitterly, as she pressed her body seductively close to his. She felt nothing. Not a bump, not a lump, not a twitch. This from a man who had a worldwide reputation as a great lover. Maybe still did. But not with her.

She turned away, pretending to busy herself with a pile of mail. Hot tears pricked the back of her lids and her throat felt constricted. How long could this continue? It was a farce. Without comedy.

"Your agent called," Josh said coolly, turning up the volume on the TV. Eyes glued to Clint Eastwood, "Call him back, says it's *important*." The last word sounded almost like a sneer. She ignored his tone, smiled too brightly. Went to the antique wooden bar to fix a forbidden vodka and ice. The health farm had said no liquor for at least a week. To hell with them.

She called Jasper from the bedroom, not wanting Josh to hear. The slightest thing set him off these days. She wanted to try and keep the peace as long as she could.

"Dear heart, I'm so glad you called," Jasper sounded pleased. "It's looking good for 'Saga,' looking very good indeed for you, dear."

"Wonderful." Chloe smiled, the vodka giving her an excited buzz.

"They will probably shoot six or seven days a month in Newport Beach," she heard Jasper saying. "The rest of the filming will be at one of the studios. Possibly Metro, maybe Fox."

"That's great, Newport is beautiful. Will we be shooting on any boats?"

"Yes, yes, dear." Jasper was often impatient with his clients' desire for details. "Listen to me, Chloe, on the twenty-fifth you're on display. Abby and Maud Arafat are giving one of their casual little dinners, just twenty or thirty of the most important people in this town. They want you there, dear girl. Best bib and tucker on. You have twelve days to prepare, so get out your new

Bob Mackie. I *hope* you lost all that bloat at the fat farm, dear, bellies don't look good in Mackies."

"Yes, Jasper, I lost every ounce," she said obediently. "I won't let you down. I promise."

"You better not, dear. This one's a biggie, believe me. Could make you HUGE, dear, really huge."

"I know, Jasper. I know."

She knew what a casual little dinner for twenty or thirty meant. There were no casual little dinners in Hollywood any more. Every meeting in LaLa Land was business. Whether spoken or unspoken, potential deals simmered beneath the surface of even the simplest lunch. A gathering of twenty or thirty of the town's finest citizens at an important producer's house was often the equivalent of a summit meeting in Washington.

Knowing Abby and his partner, Gertrude Greenbloom, who would unquestionably be present too, Chloe surmised that the three or four other potential candidates for Miranda would also be attending. She knew she was only included as the lucky result of the recent fortunate meeting in London.

The slit of Chloe's black silk Valentino skirt had been just high enough to glimpse a firm, elegant thigh. Her chiseled features had a look of abandon, her hair was an aureole of black curls, and her figure was slim but voluptuous.

Abby had downed two martinis, and holding back had never been his forte. "How would you like to play Miranda? I hear you could do with a job and you've certainly got all her attributes from where I stand." His eyes scanned her body and face like a laser beam.

Chloe laughed. "Abby, you know I'm just a saloon singer."

Although she was aware that Hollywood's search for "Saga's" leading roles was a hot show business topic, she was too canny to be taken in by Abby's pitch, and yet—and yet—why not?

Singing had not been satisfying for some time. The young Stevie Nickses and Pat Benatars had more appeal to the public today than a forty-year-old singer, and God knows touring was becoming more and more grueling. Maybe settling down again in California with a steady job would bring her and Josh closer together.

"Streisand said that, Garland said it, so did Liza." Abby smiled approvingly as he surveyed her. She certainly was a gorgeous woman, five feet six to his six feet two, but in three-inch black satin Maud Frizon sandals she met his eyes with ease. "They thought they were just singers too."

"I'm not really an actress, Abby. I just did one play for the Beeb, that's all." She sipped her kir while surveying him through a forest of real eyelashes. "I did get good reviews, though I'm sure you read them." She smiled a catlike beam that was one of her stocks in trade.

He started to melt. Abby was that rare Hollywood phenomenon, a producer who actually *liked* and admired actresses. He puffed on his cigar, scrutinizing her from top to toe. She had class—there was no doubt about that. And beauty, sex appeal and glamour.

"Who cares about acting? It's presence, charisma, pulling power, that's what we need for Miranda. Most of the old-time screen greats couldn't act their way out of a McDonald's hamburger bag. Look at Hayworth, Grable, Bardot, Ava Gardner. None of 'em could *act*, for Christ's sake, but they had *it*. And I think *you've* got *it*, kid, in spades—so let's give it a whirl. Come to California and we'll test you, honey. You'll be great, I know you will."

"Let me think about it, Abby—truly I will consider it." Chloe suspected that Abby's pitch, enthusiastic as it was, was probably equally strong to the other actresses he was considering. "Doesn't Miranda have to age from twenty to some ancient age? Mind you, I could probably play *that* end," she joked.

"Yes, yes," Abby said eagerly. "That will be in the four-hour movie of the week we shoot before the series starts. When first we see the young Miranda she's eighteen, and a virgin."

"Oh, no *way!*" cried Chloe with a chuckle. "I couldn't look eighteen!"

"Of course you could." He laughed at her protestations. "We've got Lazlo Dominick doing the lighting. He could make Bette Davis look twenty, for Christ's sake. You've got the aura, you've got the looks and the sex appeal. I think you've got the talent. Test for us, sweetheart, please. You won't be sorry."

"All right, Abby," Chloe had agreed. "All right. I'll test but I warn you, I'll be terrified."

"Wonderful," Abby had wheezed. "Olivier's always terrified —sign of great talent. You'll hear from us next week, sweetheart, and don't be frightened—you'll be terrific, I can feel it in my bones."

"So who else is testing?" she asked Jasper a mite too casually.

"Some of the suggestions are *insane.* Simply *mad.*" Jasper laughed. "I know it's a peach of a part, dear, and this town has gone wild about the casting. There hasn't been anything as exciting since Selznick was searching for Scarlett O'Hara, but listen to the other contenders."

"Who are they?" Chloe's voice wasn't casual now. She needed this information.

"Sissy Sharp. Now we all know she hasn't had a hit in years, needs the part badly. Wonderful actress. Zero sex appeal but she's an Oscar winner, of course."

"I know," Chloe said ruefully. "I was there, Jasper, remember? I sang the winning song. Whatever was it called?"

"Who cares?" Jasper said testily. "Nobody remembers the names of who won *last* year, let alone fifteen years ago! Sissy is hungry, dear—hungry as hell for that role. Hungry enough to test, but she's pretending she's not interested in TV, only the big

25

screen, and they don't give a fuck about her these days. However, the good news is that Abby and Gertrude don't think she's right."

"She's not looking too good these days, is she?" said Chloe. "I don't mean to be bitchy, but I saw her on 'Lifestyles' last week; she looked, well, ravaged—like a fugitive from Belsen."

"Diets like an anorexic teenager," Jasper said bluntly. "She's crazy, she thinks she constantly rejuvenates herself with all those fad diets—not to mention the surgery. She must have had her face and her tits lifted at least three times in the past five years."

Chloe shuddered. The idea of a knife near her body terrified her.

"Then we have Emerald," said Jasper smoothly. "Now *she* is definitely a contender, Chloe, and don't underestimate her."

Emerald Barrymore. No star had ever been bigger. Not Brando, not Kelly, not even Monroe. And no one had sunk to the depths she had. Drugs, alcohol, men and scandal, all had contributed to her downfall.

"She has been the subject of more front page headlines than you have had hot dinners, my dear," Jasper continued. "But *what* a survivor. The ultimate. And the public adore her."

"And she is still a major star." Chloe heard a reverence in her voice that the mention of Emerald's name often caused.

"So's Kim Novak, dear," said Jasper snidely, "and she can't get a job either. Emerald really needs bread now. She's been desperate for cash ever since her last lover fleeced her. She wants that part desperately, and she's using all of her influence."

"Who else, Jasper?"

"Rosalinde Lamaze. Lamaze is somewhat of a slut, as we all know," purred Jasper in his smoothest English tones. "But the public love her—especially males. They would all like to fuck her tiny brains out. She's possibly a little too Latin, too ethnic for Miranda, but she has a huge fan following, even though her last three films didn't even recoup their negative costs."

Chloe took a gulp of vodka. This was indeed tough competition. Why she was even included with this group she couldn't imagine. She realized television was constantly searching for new, fresh faces—maybe that was the reason. She was virtually unknown in America now. She'd been gone so long from the charts. She could be a new face yet!

"Help!" Chloe gulped the last of the vodka. "Jasper, I'll be the *last* of that group the producers would want."

"Nonsense," the old man countered swiftly. "You actually have most of the attributes needed for the role. There are several other actresses Abby wants to test, but I assure you that Meryl Streep, Jackie Bisset and Sabrina Jones will not be interested, even though there will be a great deal of fanfare about them being considered. Now get some rest, dear. Don't worry and remember *always:* Think positively. Banish those negative vibrations."

He hung up, leaving Chloe trying to "Think positively," but still thinking her chances were slim. In the living room Josh still sat glued to the tube, oozing "negative vibrations." She poured herself another vodka. Some of his mates were on "Hollywood Squares," so he *shsshd* Chloe as she tried to tell him about her conversation with Jasper. She wanted him to cheer her up, joke with her as he used to, but he was like stone. Tears filled her eyes as she walked into the bathroom and turned on the taps in the big marble Jacuzzi tub. It had been built for the two of them. Now Chloe lay there alone, the bubbles tingling her flesh as she stared out into the beauty of the ocean and the cresting waves and wondered if she could make it work with Josh. How many more separations and reconciliations would it take before she stopped fighting for their marriage and gave them both their freedom? This had been their third separation in as many years. She remembered the first one. Two years ago. . . .

2

For eight years they had reigned as one of show business's happiest and most successful couples. But in the past year, as Josh's last three singles plummeted, Josh's behavior had finally become so outrageous and intolerable that she had to get away from him, hoping that a trial separation would make him see reason—make him see what he was losing by losing her.

Raindrops slid across the windows of the first-class railway carriage taking her to Scotland.

It was a bleak January day. Sleet scudded onto the roofs of identically dun-colored houses as Chloe's train approached the suburbs of Edinburgh. Everything looked as gray and dismal as

28

she felt. Sheep huddled together for comfort, and the sodden meadows seemed to echo her misery.

As she poured the last of the Liebfraumilch into a thick British Rail glass, her feeling of guilt was quickly replaced by a feeling of security as the wine warmed her.

She was getting away from it all. Getting away from Josh. From his lies, his drinking, his drugs and his philandering. Getting away from her stepdaughter, Sally, a willful Beverly Hills brat, whose blazing love for her father was matched by an equally blazing dislike for her stepmother.

Chloe could never understand why Sally hated her so much. God knows, she had bent over backward to be as good a stepmother as she could, understanding only too well what effect it must have had on the little girl to watch her own mother's slow death from cancer. But in spite of her attempts to fill the maternal void in Sally's life, she only seemed to hate her more.

Sally was nearly eight when Chloe had married Joshua Brown in 1972. A scrawny, sullen-looking wisp with mousy braids, her grape-green eyes dominated a tiny, strangely adult face. She seemed to magically appear from around corners surreptitiously whenever Josh and Chloe were cuddled up on the couch watching TV, eating the lavish high teas they loved of brown bread and butter with the crusts cut off, covered with honey, being particularly cozy and affectionate with each other.

Silently the tiny child would stand, unnoticed by the lovers staring stonily at their newlywed happiness. Josh had not always been an affectionate father to Sally, so Chloe was not taking anything away from her. But in Sally's mind Chloe was the rival for her daddy's love. Her jealousy for her stepmother turned to hatred as the years went by, and Sally grew to realize that the more she misbehaved and insulted Chloe, the more attention she received from her father.

29

Their houseman, Roberto, had addressed Chloe as Mrs. Brown the first week of the marriage, as they were discussing menus. Sally, who had been engrossed in a comic book, suddenly whirled violently on the frightened Filipino and screamed, *"Don't* call her Mrs. Brown! There's only one Mrs. Brown, and that's my mother!"

Sobbing, she scurried to her bedroom and locked the door, oblivious to the entreaties of everyone except Josh, who, summoned from the recording studio, arrived and finally placated the hysterical child with cuddles and as much fatherly affection as he could.

When Josh first married Chloe, to appease Sally he started to get the little girl involved in his music. She lapped it up. She took guitar lessons at eight, trumpet lessons at nine. She already played the piano, and had started singing lessons at five. Josh discussed many aspects of his music with her. She was a stern, knowledgeable critic: he had a certain respect for her ideas and opinions, and she worshipped him.

God knows there had been enough romping and giggling and wrestling and climbing on Daddy's knees and cuddling in the eight years since Chloe and Josh had married. Sally did it to distract her father from Chloe—she did everything she could to antagonize Chloe. Often she succeeded.

Chloe had tried from the beginning to conceive a child with Josh. She felt a baby would make their life together complete. But try as they might, it didn't happen. Chloe went to the top gynecologists from all over the world. There seemed to be no physical reason why she couldn't conceive; they should "just relax and keep trying," was the advice given.

She had thought that if only she could have given Josh a child, their marriage would have been better, but she knew why she couldn't. Even though her doctors said she was perfectly fine physically, she knew that something had gone wrong when she had given birth to Annabel. Chloe had been in labor for twelve hours, nearly out of her mind with pain, and the postnatal care she had received in the clinic had been minimal.

Chloe had never told Josh about her baby. At first she was afraid he would disapprove because she had given her away. Then, as time passed, she thought it best to keep the truth from him as the realization she could not have another child might have been blamed on Annabel's difficult birth.

Chloe had been twenty-one when Annabel was born. With the resilience of youth she recovered quickly from the ordeal, but the physical scars left by the pain of the difficult delivery and the anguish of having to give up her baby—her beautiful little Annabel, so close to Sally in age, but so different from her in temperament—would never disappear.

Now it was too late. Annabel had been brought up by Chloe's brother and his wife in their little red bungalow in Barnes. And nobody ever suspected. Nobody. Not the slimy Fleet Street reptiles, nor the staff at the clinic. Annabel herself didn't even know. Chloe sadly lit a cigarette in defiance of the "No Smoking" sign. No one other than her brother and sister-in-law knew about her secret child and the deep devotion she had for her.

Chloe never stopped loving Annabel. Throughout the years, whenever she saw another woman with a baby, she felt pain and bitterness that she couldn't see her lovely little girl growing up. Susan and Richard sent photographs regularly, which only made her feel worse as she saw the sweet little face, dark-eyed, like Matt, curly-haired like Chloe, laughing out at her from brief moments captured in time. On the pebbles at Brighton beach, in the family garden in Sussex, standing with Richard and some of his friends dressed in cricket clothes outside a pub, Richard proudly holding the little girl on his knee. Annabel with her favorite doll, Annabel with a kitten, Annabel with her new best friend, Annabel with her two older brothers. And growing... all the time growing up. Without her real mother.

Chloe kept a scrapbook of her child. Lovingly she pasted in the mementos, the photos, all the tiny notes in a childish scrawl that dutiful Susan had made the child write. Chloe sent her gifts from all over the world, and always received a grateful letter. Toys, clothes, books, souvenirs. Wherever she toured, Chloe was passionate about buying something wonderful or unusual for Annabel.

She realized that Annabel had become almost an obsession with her—and Sally noticed it. The chant of "Not *another* special present for your niece! Anyone would think she was *your* kid" made Chloe flinch.

As Sally approached her teens and became aware of Chloe's thwarted desire for a baby she often needled her with it. "You're *barren*, aren't you?" she gloated at Chloe one day as they lay by the pool trying to tan under a sun almost obliterated by a thick pall of smog. Sally was studying Elizabethan history. "Just like Henry the Eighth's daughter Mary. Barren!" She chortled gleefully, "Barren, barren, barren!" and dived into the pool, drenching the novel Chloe was reading. Eventually Chloe gave up all pretense of friendliness, and their relationship became a minor battlefield.

One spring when Chloe and Sally were in Paris, where Josh was playing at the Olympia to packed houses, Chloe had gone to Galeries Lafayette to shop, and Sally, her instinct telling her this was another chance to antagonize her stepmother, had cajoled Chloe into taking her too. Chloe picked out matching shirts and sweaters for her nephews, and then carefully chose a Christian Dior burgundy coat with a velvet collar and hat, and a matching dress, for Annabel. She was off to London to visit her brother, and was filled with excitement at the prospect of seeing her daughter. Sally, now that she was a teenager, was wearing a collection of tattered rags that were the "in" thing in Beverly Hills prep schools this year. She had sneered at Chloe's choice. "Square—*yuuck*—what a *nerd* Annabel must be," she said, examining a pile of socks in bright neon colors and stuffing a couple of pairs into the pocket of her oversized jacket while no one was looking. No matter that her father could have bought her a crate of socks—Sally loved to do the forbidden.

Annabel was a typically well-behaved, nicely brought-up English schoolgirl, the complete opposite of Sally. She had loved the outfit. She was charming, delightful and shy. After lunch as she and Chloe had walked along a leafy English lane, she confided in her "aunt" that she too wanted to be a singer one day, and had started taking guitar lessons as well.

"But you're so young," demurred Chloe. She wanted something better for her daughter than the tough life that she had chosen.

"Oh, Auntie Chloe, I love the guitar and I love singing. I love it so much." The girl had jumped up and down, her cheeks flushed, her deep green eyes sparkling.

"I play your albums all the time, Auntie Chloe. I *love* how you sing. I've never told you this..." She blushed and looked away.

"What, what, darling?" Chloe's throat tightened with the effort of holding back the tears. This darling girl, this sweet lovely child was her own and only baby. If only she could be with her. But she couldn't. Stop it, Chloe, she told herself. Don't rock the boat. Let's not have a True Confessions here, it will wreck everyone's life—especially Annabel's.

She listened carefully as the girl breathlessly confided her secret hero worship and admiration for her "aunt."

"When I grow up, Aunt Chloe, I want to be just like you," she chirped, her little face alive with animation.

"Oh, Annabel darling, oh, baby." Chloe couldn't stop her tears now as she knelt in the Sussex lane and hugged her daughter to her fiercely. "Darling Annabel, I will do anything I can to help you, I promise I will."

"I'm so proud you're my aunt." Annabel wondered why Auntie Chloe, normally so cool, was drowning her in tears. It was embarrassing, but grown-up people were often weird.

The sudden acceleration of the train jolted Chloe back to the present. She sighed, removing her dark glasses, which had not protected her from stares of recognition from waiters and several passengers. She looked a wreck. Two bottles of wine each evening, followed by sleepless Seconal-filled nights and a difficult tour, did not for beauty make. A week at the fat farm would take care of that. The health farm was her yearly savior. With luck, she would look five years younger again. Her cheekbones would emerge from their cocoon of bloat, her turquoise eyes, no longer dimmed with inevitable red threads of too much vodka, would brighten again, and the waistbands of her clothes would regain a comfortable ease.

She sipped her wine, trying not to feel bitter. Sally would be thrilled she was away. She could have her father all to herself. Perhaps they could share a joint and listen to his latest single, turning up the volume so loud that the Labrador whined and sought refuge in the wine cellar. Oh, they were so alike, father and daughter, two peas in a pod. Both Scorpio, both selfish, scornful, beautiful and arrogant. He was forty, she was sixteen, and they understood each other perfectly. Their close relationship made her longing for her own daughter only more intense.

3

*I*n 1964, to have given birth to an illegitimate child could have wrecked Chloe's blossoming career. She was just beginning to make it as a singer; moving up from workingmen's clubs to "Top of the Pops" with new jazzed-up renditions of old Cole Porter standbys had taken her barely five years. Five years of fierce determined dedicated work on her voice, of studying Ella Fitzgerald for the phrasing, Sinatra for the nuances, Peggy Lee's husky sensual overtones. She managed to instill sexuality and meaning into the most mundane lyrics.

Every night since Chloe was still in her teens, waiting on tables, singing the occasional song when they would let her, she had gone to sleep, no matter how exhausted, to the sounds of one of her three favorite performers lulling her into the dreamless eight hours necessary for the maintenance of her second best asset, her face—hours spent applying and reapplying lipsticks, eye shadows, brow shapers, analyzing—re-restructuring with cosmetic witchery a pleasing proportion of wide innocent eyes, upturned nose, slanting cheekbones and full lips into a seductive exotic face that would not have been out of place in the fashion magazines.

She accepted any one-night gig anywhere in the British Isles, watching, learning, imitating and discarding. Eventually her talent and burning ambition to succeed turned her into a successful and popular singer, famed for her sensuality and elegance.

She had no time for men. Certainly those she met in Leeds, Glasgow or Birmingham were so dotish that rejecting their advances required little effort. But there was the occasional crooner on the same tour. Usually married, usually on the way down, whereas Chloe was—she knew it—on the way up. There was the occasional young drummer with the band and the occasional saxophonist or clarinet player, and once even the Maestro himself, the leader of the band. But all in all they were a sorry lot and in no way conformed to Chloe's ideals.

She had observed Susan, her best friend since school, now married to Chloe's brother, Richard, weighed down with the responsibility of shopping, cooking, cleaning and taking care of a toddler while pregnant again. Susan was already losing the bloom of youth and vitality that had made them the two most popular girls at school. No man was worth it, thought Chloe, worth the effort, worth the pain. And no one *had* been—until she met Matthew Sullivan.

Matt was a newspaperman. He worked for the *Daily Chronicle* as a show business journalist, interviewing has-been American stars who were flocking to London to peddle their fading wares in the thriving British film industry of the early 1960s. He drank whiskey, flirted with anything in a miniskirt and told outrageous jokes. He was a half-Irish, half-Jewish rogue, charm personified, cynical, hard drinking and careless about with whom he dallied. More often than not he could be found propping up the bar at any Fleet Street pub regaling his mates with anecdotes, rather than in his family nest in Shepherds Bush with his plain wife and their twins. His reputation as an inveterate womanizer, wastrel and life-of-the-party raconteur was well known to everyone. Except Chloe.

With fame and success on her mind, and men low on her list of priorities, Chloe, bright-eyed, full of life and twenty-one years old, was performing at the Cavern, a dingy but extremely popular disco in downtown Liverpool, much publicized recently for discovering four local lads known as the Beatles.

She had met Matt several times before at clubs up and down the less salubrious parts of northern England. He was writing about the rock scene, as his readers were interested in many of the new groups. The Beatles. The Stones. The Animals. Herman's Hermits. Chloe had been aware of his interest in her the last time they met, although he had been with his wife. They had all gone for drinks to an after-hours drinking club. Chloe was with her current clarinetist, Rick. But her interest in him was on the wane. Rick knew, and was already casting his eyes to new pastures.

Matt made Chloe laugh with juicy gossip and outrageous jokes. When she stopped laughing, she found him staring at her. Their eyes locked; he was giving her a clear message. She found herself blushing as he gestured to the dance floor.

Vic Damone was singing—something mellow and sultry. The smoky club had an aura of sexuality. Bodies swayed together, warm—sweating—moist. Matt held her confidently. Not the usual groper, she thought gratefully, although his arms around her were possessive. He had the assurance that came from knowing he was attractive, desirable, and could probably have any woman he wanted.

His arms tightened as the music slowed, their bodies molded even closer. She was aware of his excitement now. She was also aware of hers. An unusual feeling for Chloe, to want a man. To really desire him. She shivered, gazing into his black eyes again. His message was clear. She felt a total melting new to her, and it frightened her. Mesmerized, she continued gazing into his eyes, holding him closer to her until his wife tapped him on the shoulder to tell him the baby-sitter had to go by twelve-thirty and they must leave.

Matt telephoned three days later. He was back in Liverpool again, minus wife. Did she feel like a drink at the Cavern after the show?

Chloe didn't hesitate. She had found herself thinking too often about his face, his hard body, his black hair—his heavy-lidded black eyes, his aggressively curved mouth. Goodbye, Rick.

Matt was pleasant and funny at the club, but they shared no meaningful looks. Chloe began to wonder if she had imagined the physical yearning he had conveyed to her last time they had met, as she asked him back for a coffee.

When they arrived at her digs she asked him to be as quiet as possible as they climbed the rickety stairs. Her landlady didn't approve of nocturnal gentlemen callers, often a good excuse for Chloe to get rid of overly ardent swains. This time she didn't want that excuse. She wanted Matt.

When Chloe awoke the next morning, he was gone. She felt unbelievably, glowingly wonderful. She had experienced inde-scribable sensations last night. He had stayed until dawn, and every minute he had been with her, Chloe fell more passionately in love with him.

At least it felt like love, she ruminated, running her hands over her body that still felt his caresses. She stretched deliciously. Was six or seven hours of the most heavenly lovemaking she had ever experienced love? If not, it was better than anything Cole

Porter had ever written about. At this moment, she couldn't, didn't, ever want to think about anyone but Matt. She felt vibrant, full. At twenty-one, she felt like a woman.

Annabel was conceived in London on the fine spring bank holiday weekend when Matt's wife and twins went to visit her mother in Bogner. Matt had an important article on the Beatles to finish. He asked Chloe if she wanted to stay with him for the weekend. She couldn't resist. She had fallen heavily for the irresistible combination of Irish charm and Jewish wit and wasn't about to lose any opportunity to be in his arms again for the whole weekend.

She could smell May blossom in the air as she rang the bell of the shabby front door in Shepherds Bush. In spite of herself, her breath caught in her throat when he came to the door. Although he was eighteen years older than she, Matt was an impressively handsome man. His black hair, touched with feather streaks of gray, curled carelessly around his face. His black eyes devoured her as she embraced him.

"Oh, darling, darling, I've missed you—how I've missed you," she breathed huskily, holding his body close to hers.

"It's only been a week, love, you couldn't have had time to miss me with that ball-breaking tour you've been on. Come in, come in—the neighbors will see us."

In the tiny front parlor he poured two generous helpings of whiskey into mismatched glasses and gestured to Chloe to sit down on the well-worn velveteen sofa. In a window, a yellow canary swung in its cage, the tray encrusted with droppings. Ashtrays were full of butts, files of discarded newspapers and magazines littered the floor. Take-out pizza moldered on a table next to an ancient typewriter, seven or eight half-empty mugs of congealed coffee were scattered around, and, she observed with a pang, on the piano reposed a large color photo of a plain woman and a pair of plain twins. Chloe pretended not to notice that.

39

"Matt, oh, Matt! It's so wonderful to see you again." She felt incredibly excited. She couldn't take her eyes off him, couldn't keep her hands off him.

"You look good, kid, you look fine." He squeezed her arms playfully and stroked the back of her neck, which sent shudders all over her body. She wanted him now—wanted him badly. But he was not ready yet.

"Ciggie?" he asked, lighting two Lucky Strikes and handing one to her.

"I'll share yours," she breathed, remembering the last time.

He took a puff of his cigarette, inhaled slightly and leaned toward her. With their lips slightly parted, hers soft and moist, new petals on a rose, his cool, yet sensual, they kissed—a kiss as soft as butterfly wings. She felt the acrid smoke filter into her mouth. She could feel, taste his lips, his tongue. He exuded a masculine smell of cigarettes, whiskey, faint sweat, but his breath smelled sweet to her. The taste of lust was in his mouth. His blazing black-fringed eyes gazed into hers as his tongue lazily traced the outline of her mouth. She saw his pupils dilate with desire. His hands softly touched her blouse, caressing the outline of her full breasts. He looked into her eyes the whole time, mesmerizing her, the fire in his eyes equaling the fire inside both of them.

"Oh, darling, darling," she breathed. "I want you so much."

"Not yet, baby, not yet." His experience made him able to hold back. She was so eager, just a kid in spite of her sophisticated songs, panting like a puppy, dying to feel him inside her. He could afford to take his time. He knew the longer he made her wait, want him, desire him totally, the better it would be for them both.

He played her like a Stradivarius. Slowly, with infinite patience, he unbuttoned her blouse and brushed first his fingers, then his mouth, against her eager nipples.

Finally, when her clothes were off, he laid her gently on the sofa, tracing a pattern of ecstasy all over her body with his tongue. She felt the hardness of him inside the corduroy of his trousers. She tried to free him, but he wouldn't let her.

Chloe thought she would die of pleasure. The only part of him he allowed her to touch was his mouth. He teased her clitoris with his tongue until she exploded. Every part of her body was afire with an intensity she had never felt before. She had never known a man to take this much time to give this much pleasure with his lips, his tongue, his fingertips.

When she felt she would go mad if he did not put himself inside her, when his touch on her clitoris made her dance to another orgasm, when she begged him, cried, pleaded, "Please darling, Matt, take me *now*, I *want* you darling, now! I want you! Please!" only then did he take off his clothes and fuse his body with hers.

It was a night unlike any Chloe had ever experienced. She had only known musicians and singers, whose chief aim was to get her pants off as quickly as possible, get themselves installed inside her immediately, pump away for a few minutes in a quick frenzy and then collapse. At best it had been only moderately exciting. She had never even approached the heights of rapture she did with Matt.

Hours later, she was limp, replete, surfeited, yet still wanting more of him as he carried her up to his tiny bedroom. There in the dark, he held her tightly, spoke to her lovingly, longingly, as he made love to her throughout the night. She clung to him, passionately whispering over and over how much she adored him, needed him, wanted him.

Unfortunately he no longer wanted or needed her six weeks later, when she informed him she was pregnant.

Chloe's obsession with Matthew had grown so much in the two months she had known him that she was now consumed by sexual passion. She could not stop thinking about his dark eyes, his body fusing with hers, his hands on her flesh, his lips bringing her to the heights of desire.

She knew his faults. Faults! There were few redeeming qualities in his character other than his extraordinary gift for lovemaking. He lied. She knew he lied all the time—to his wife, obviously, and to Chloe too. It was a way of life to him. Lies tripped more easily from his tongue than truths. Too much time spent in Fleet Street, no doubt. But she forgave him. She forgave him everything once he was in her bed. She could not get enough of him—but she saw him so rarely. Five times all told, including that incredible weekend. Five magical, wonderful nights that left her glowingly fulfilled, but the following day miserable with longing and the need for more of him.

But she was not to have more of him. That he made clear to her in his bluntest manner. He did not love her. He was completely honest about that, at least. He desired her sexually, he adored making love to her, but he knew himself only too well. He was nearly forty years old, he had no intention of ending his marriage; if Chloe left him, there would be other nubile young bodies around, other fish to fry. He had plenty of options and there was no way he could accept Chloe's having the baby.

In Chloe's naiveté she couldn't believe that he had made love with her so passionately and not fallen in love with her. She found it impossible to come to terms with his callousness. She cried herself to sleep for months on end.

She thought it a crime to abort their baby, their love child. Atavistic primal female instincts made her want to keep it. In spite of his denial and his dismissal, she went through to term, and in January of 1964, in a nursing home in Plymouth under an assumed name, she gave birth to a baby girl she called Annabel—it had been her grandmother's name.

She had made one difficult decision; now she had to make another. She knew she could never keep the baby. She had to earn her living, and the only way she knew how was by singing on the road again. No life for Annabel.

So Chloe's brother, Richard, and his wife, Susan, agreed to bring the baby up with their own two. They explained to nosy neighbors that Annabel was the daughter of Susan's cousin, sadly killed in a car crash in Australia. No questions were asked by the neighbors, and soon Chloe went back to work with a vengeance. She sang for her supper up and down the length and breadth of England, Ireland, Scotland and Wales. And in seven years she had risen to the top of her profession.

Chloe was an exciting singer of popular and standard songs, a performer who gave audiences more than their money's worth. And her indisputable talent, coupled with her undeniable sex appeal, enthralled audiences and critics alike. She had risen to the top in Britain, and now America was starting to make tentative overtures to her. She was considering an offer to play Las Vegas the night she first saw Josh.

4

She hadn't wanted to see the show. Having just finished a forty-city singing tour, she felt and looked exhausted. The realization had dawned on her that twenty-nine was no longer nineteen. Now she needed eight full hours of sleep every night, otherwise, goodbye face. She snapped open her compact in the warm darkness of the theater, glanced hastily at her almost flawless complexion, then looked back at Josh on stage. In spite of herself, she smiled. God, he was gorgeous!

Chloe had been instantly attracted to Josh. A surge of sexual excitement and interest she hadn't felt since Matt.

Joshua Brown was the show business king of "swinging London." Thirty years old, he was a brilliant, talented cock o' the walk and an *enfant terrible*. By virtue of his exceptional looks and innovative style, the West End was at his feet, and Chloe was no exception.

Thousands of men watching her sing her sultry songs had lusted after her, and now she was experiencing this feeling herself—lusting after the performer onstage. Why Josh Brown, of all people? This physical stirring she hadn't experienced for years—this was it. She reveled in it. She let herself bask in it. Sat back and drank him in.

Her enormous turquoise eyes widened with admiration at the athletic feats Josh performed. He was playing a 1920s silent movie star, a Douglas Fairbanks-type character. He leaped and danced about the stage and into the auditorium for nearly three hours, performing stunts of such virtuosity and sheer daring that the cheering audience gave him ovation after standing ovation.

Three days later Chloe went back again to see the show for the second time. This time, instead of being in the seventh row, she had deliberately chosen front row center. She had gone alone.

That's the man I will marry, she thought, her eyes never leaving his handsomely saturnine face, his powerful body. At the curtain call, when he stepped forward from the rest of the cast to receive a solo ovation and her palms were raw with clapping, she willed him to meet her eyes.

He bowed to the waves of applause, lapping it up, obviously loving his audience. His thick black hair fell over his tanned forehead, he was six feet tall, with a devilish face, and he personified masculinity, charm, humor and sex appeal. You name it, he had it. She could see the perfectly developed muscles of his chest ripple through his white cambric shirt open to the waist, and through his tight black trousers she could see the outline of his sex. A power bulge indeed. The cuffs of his shirt were ruffled and she noticed strong hands, hands she wanted to feel on her body. She thought about the rumors she had heard about him.

45

Supposedly not only difficult, but the biggest philanderer in London. Well, in this business, unless you were Julie Andrews the gossips wagged their tongues constantly. Maybe it was true, maybe it wasn't. Right now she didn't care. All she felt was an unbelievable physical and metaphysical attraction.

His eyes met hers finally. They looked at her appreciatively. A clear message of interest was shown, an imperceptible nod of his head, and she was winging her way giddily backstage to his dressing room. A fourteen-year-old with a crush on Elvis.

Perry, Josh's valet and man Friday, offered her a drink as she waited expectantly in the shabby anteroom, halfheartedly looking at faded portraits of Edmund Kean and Henry Irving that decorated the peeling yellow walls. She heard him humming opera—was it Verdi? *Aida?* Could this musical-comedy singer, composer, matinee idol, jack-of-all-show-business-trades aspire to the higher level of opera? Before her question could be answered, the scruffy green velveteen curtain was flung aside and he stood there. She knew immediately he was meant for her. Forever, a voice inside her said. *Forever.* His presence overwhelmed her.

"I've loved all of your records." He wasted no time in flattering her. "Especially 'I've Got a Crush on You.' We play it all the time, don't we, Perry?" His energy was a force Chloe could almost taste.

The young man smiled admiringly at Chloe as he motioned to a stack of LPs. "Sinatra, Ella, and *you,* Miss Carriere. They've always been the young master's faves."

"Thanks," murmured Chloe, more than overcome, yet trying to act the cool sophisticate. Why, oh why did she feel, in front of this man, so weak, so *feminine,* so—let's face it, dear, said the voice inside, horny? Just plain horny. Celibacy at your age is a bit much, don't you think? Go *get* him, girl!

"I don't suppose you're free for a bite of supper?" Josh asked diffidently. They both knew the answer to that.

During dinner at a tiny restaurant in Soho they laughed and joked. He regaled her with stories of the ill-fated tour of his show and the disasters that had befallen it before it hit the West End to become the biggest musical hit in England since *Oliver*. There was no question as to where the evening would end. He had a little flat in Fulham. She had a little flat in Chelsea. They tossed a coin for it. He won.

She had thought that no man could ever surpass Matt in her bed. She had attempted a few halfhearted affairs in the past seven years, but after a while decided it wasn't worth it. She would rather be in bed with a book, or playing cards with friends, than rolling around the sheets with a stranger, trying to simulate a lust she couldn't feel. So she hadn't bothered. Idly she had thought she had probably become frigid since Annabel's birth. Luckily she was wrong!

With Josh, she was turned on even before he touched her. His curved sensual mouth brushed her lips in the elevator going up to his flat. An experienced kisser, a gentle kisser—a man who knew women, who truly liked them—she could tell by his lips, by his hands tangled in her curls, no question about that. She felt his passion building as the ancient elevator shuddered to a halt. Slowly their lips parted from each other.

Apart from the furnishings in his bedroom, very dark plain furniture, *very* large four-poster bed, the only out-of-the-ordinary feature was a large mirror on the ceiling, attached to the chrome-and-mirrored posts at each corner of the bed, incongruously covered with a blue candlewick bedspread.

"A gift from the Empire Hotel in Las Vegas," he laughed, as she looked at it quizzically. "I broke the house record there last year. They asked me if I wanted a diamond-studded Rolex, but I said I preferred the bed, so they shipped it over. It's fun."

I bet it is, thought Chloe.

Five hours later, limping to the cramped untidy kitchen for a sustaining drink, she knew just how much fun it was. Her legs felt as if she had worked out for three hours at the gym. He certainly was a wonderfully exciting lover, but oh, what fun he was to talk to as well. In between bouts of lovemaking, which at the very least equaled anything she had experienced with Matt, they talked, laughed and joked. They were so easy with each other. After hours of exploring each other's bodies with lips, tongue, fingers, she had to beg him, "Take me, please, Josh, take me." He had kissed and teased her until she was at a pinnacle of ecstasy, thinking she would die if he did not enter her. The buildup of desire made her body feel as if it were one enormous battery—a million nerve endings waiting to be ignited by his body.

When he finally started to make love to her, the sensation was so exquisite that neither of them was able to hold back. Within seconds, they simultaneously reached a plateau of such intensity that Chloe almost fainted. Afterward, as he held her tightly against his warm, muscular chest, stroked her black curls, damp now with the sweat of their bodies, she knew that he was the one. The man she had always known she would meet one day. Her forever man.

She knew in her soul that this could be the start of something big. And it *was*. They were perfect for each other. The perfect couple. They had everything in common. Their courtship was swift, their marriage three months later an occasion to rejoice. They were both extremely popular, so they had a huge flashy show business wedding at the Dorchester, attended by everyone from Peter Sellers to Sir Lew Grade, and for their honeymoon they went to Capri, where, when they weren't swimming and sunbathing, they spent most of their time in bed.

From the start Josh insisted on being totally honest with Chloe. He had told her about his many girlfriends, confessed he had never been able to be faithful to a woman for longer than a few months, but he was going to have a damn good try with Chloe. He was thirty now—time to grow up at last. He even told her about the tiny amounts of white powder he occasionally had the need to sniff to get through the exhausting show. She didn't care. She loved him. Love would conquer all. Marriage would be forever. They were ecstatically happy together, in spite of his precocious daughter, who lived with them. Although, as in most marriages, the physical side became less important with time, they had tremendous camaraderie and rapport. They laughed, loved, argued, worked together. The perfect couple, everyone said. Chloe thought their bond was of iron and she worked at the marriage, worked at their love, and it flowered and prospered.

They hated to be apart. They needed each other's support, each other's presence. Often at parties the hostess became annoyed as Josh and Chloe, who had spent all day and night together, would sit together on a sofa laughing, holding hands, engrossed in each other, ignoring the rest of the guests. Their communication was total, their commitment to each other complete. Their only area of dissent was his cocaine habit. Sometimes he wouldn't touch the stuff for months on end—then, when the pressure of work became too much, he would be at it again.

"I've been doing it since I was eighteen, for Christ's sake," he would say angrily. "It's never hurt me yet."

"It's a *killer*, Josh." Chloe always became excited and angry whenever she caught him taking it. She had seen the ravages coke, smack and speed had caused several musician friends. She hated it. It destroyed lives.

Josh made no promises to stop—only to cut down. For now, that would have to suffice, Chloe realized. After all, he *had* given up all the women. No one was perfect. Least of all herself. And they had a good marriage. A wonderful marriage. Eight years of wedded bliss. She was a lucky woman.

Then one day, she came home to the sickening truth of his infidelity.

She had told him she was lunching at the Polo Lounge with a girlfriend and then would go shopping on Rodeo Drive. By this time they had bought a beautiful airy beach house in Malibu as well as a little town house in London. They managed to combine life on both continents with comparative ease, taking the best of what each continent had to offer.

After lunch, walking out to the forecourt of the Beverly Hills Hotel to get her Mercedes, Chloe decided that the heat was so intense she could not face a trip to Rodeo Drive. Besides, her period was five days late—maybe this time she and Josh had at last made the baby they wanted so much, and at thirty-seven her biological clock was running out of time fast. She decided to head for home.

She let herself into the sunlit house quietly. There was no sound from Josh's rehearsal room, where even through the soundproofed doors she could often hear the muffled sounds of his eight-track as he endlessly mixed his next single, hoping for a new hit. Sally was at school, the housekeeper at the market.

She kicked off her shoes and walked over the soft blue carpet to their cool bedroom. What she saw there made the bile rise in her throat.

Josh had insisted on keeping the mirrored canopy from Las Vegas, had shipped it back from London. On that bed, underneath the mirror, lay a very young blond girl. Her legs were spread-eagled, her long yellow hair fanned out on Chloe's blue satin sheets. Her eyes were open, staring up into the mirror with fascination.

Kneeling over her, his black curly head between her legs, was Josh. He was doing things to the girl that were causing her to spasm with delight as she watched herself. His strong muscular hands were caressing the young girl's breasts, his thumbs massaging her nipples. Chloe knew by the movements of his body, by his deepening moans low in his throat, how much he was enjoying this.

The girl was young, fifteen or sixteen, and inexperienced; Chloe noticed that her hands, although clutched around Josh's thick penis, were not stimulating him as she knew he liked. Motionless, she stood watching the sickening tableau, the two of them so intent that they did not notice her. With horror, Chloe realized the girl was coming, her husband's head thrusting faster between the child's thighs as she bucked and moaned with pleasure.

Chloe could not stop the cries that involuntarily rose from the depths of her being. The girl screamed, and Josh turned to her, shock and horror on his face. Chloe couldn't move. In a dream she watched as the girl ran whimpering into the bathroom, as Josh picked up his terry-cloth robe and almost too casually put it on after a few minutes. The girl, now in blue jeans and T-shirt, darted sobbing out of the bedroom.

Then Chloe ran into the bathroom and wept.

Later that night Josh begged her to forgive him. "I'll go down on my knees, Chloe," he sobbed.

"You were on your knees this afternoon, you *bastard.*" Chloe's throat was raw from screaming at him, her eyes swollen almost shut with tears. "In *my* bed, you pig. You disgusting pervert. *Our* bed. How? Why did you need to do it? What did I do wrong?" She couldn't stop weeping. Couldn't bear the betrayal, the disloyalty.

"Nothing, Chloe, nothing. Christ, I don't know why, Chloe. I'd been to the bar down at the beach with the boys—had a few drinks, you *know* how it is—Chlo—"

"Yes, I *know.* I *know.*" She couldn't keep the screech out of her voice as she opened drawers and closets, throwing clothes into a suitcase blindly. "The boys, the boys—you've always got to be one of the boys, haven't you? You *bastard.*" She tried to slam the case shut. "Is *that* why you need young girls?"

She had to get away—away from him. She couldn't bear to be near him.

Hearing the row, Sally, just home from school, came into the bedroom to watch. This was better than a TV sitcom.

"Bugger *off,*" her father had yelled, one of the few times he had ever raised his voice at her. Chloe knew the reason why, and it disgusted her even more—it was sick, perverted. She had recognized the blond girl as a school friend of Sally's. Sally had set the whole thing up. She knew her dad liked young "grumble," as he and his musician friends called it when there were no women around to call them male chauvinist pigs—"grumble and grunt," English rhyming slang for a particular part of the female anatomy. The girl probably had a crush on Josh. It must have been easy for Sally to arrange. She knew her father very well, knew his weaknesses. After all, he was only a man. Men were weak—Sally knew that already.

Josh continued trying to stop Chloe from leaving, but everything he said only angered Chloe even more. "Fuck you, Josh. Fuck you! Fuck you!! *Fuck you!!!*" she screamed, as she snapped the lid shut on the Vuitton case. "You *disgust* me! And I can't be with you any more—ever again." She wished she could stop weeping. "Get yourself to a shrink—you need help."

"Babe, babe, please listen—I couldn't help it. Christ, Chloe, I'm a *man,* you know—sometimes a man needs to..."

"Needs to what?" She turned to him, her turquoise eyes blazing with fury and hurt. "Screw a teenager? Make a groupie come? You make me sick, Josh. Sick to my stomach." She started to leave the room but he grabbed her arm and held her tight. His eyes were soft, sad—almost filled with tears. He never cried. He was a child of the Second World War years. You hardly ever cried, however much you hurt.

"I know I'm a shit, babe, but I love you. Remember that,

Chloe. I've always loved you. I want you—you're my woman and you always will be. Remember that, when you sleep by yourself in an empty double bed."

She began to interrupt, but he stopped her. "I *know* you, Chloe. You're not a bed-hopper, you don't go from man to man, you won't find another man who loves you like I do. All right— so I made a mistake. A bad one. Lots of men make mistakes. You found this one out. It's terrible, I know, Chloe...but don't leave me, Chloe—please, please *don't,* darling."

She sobbed uncontrollably, sobbed as he tried to take her in his arms, kiss her sodden cheeks, but she wouldn't, couldn't, let him.

She pulled away. The thought of his arms around that young girl...his mouth, his tongue—how many other girls had there been? She felt sick. She couldn't bear to be near him. Couldn't bear his hands on her ever again, his mouth on her mouth.... The thought of his mouth on the girl...

She pulled away from him, dragging the heavy suitcase with her. She ran to the front door, climbed into her silver Mercedes and, blinded by tears and the rain that fell from the Malibu sky, she drove off into the wet California night.

Chloe immediately accepted a six-month tour of the English provinces to try and forget him. But it was not easy to forget a man you had loved with such passion, although the pain started to fade. Josh continually called her. He pleaded. He begged her to forgive him. Finally he cried, he cajoled, he sent gifts and bombarded her with roses, with messages of love undying and adoration. Until she melted and eventually forgave him. She always forgave him. Would he have done the same for her?

That had been the first time she had caught him.

The last time had been a year ago. When she discovered this second infidelity she was so hurt and confused that she had gone on a drinking binge. Vodka healed. When she came to after a week of debauchery, she decided to go to a health farm in Scotland to recuperate.

Now, together again after a six-month absence, seeing his indifference, how distant he was, she finally admitted to herself that the marriage was over. As she watched the bath bubbles slowly going flat, she thought how sad it was, how terribly sad. There had been so much that was good between them. So much love—so much investment in laughter and fun.

That was all gone now. She had to get her mind onto other things. She had to think about her career—think positively, as Jasper had said. Miranda—Miranda Hamilton. She *had* to get that part. She needed it now more than ever.

Part Two

5

Sissy Sharp sank back onto her nest of pink satin and lace pillows and impatiently pushed away the head of the blond young Adonis from between her legs.

"Who?" Sissy screamed into the phone, her tiny boobs bouncing. "Luis who? He's not *right* to play my husband, for fuck's sake. You promised me it was going to be Pacino or Nicholson or that English actor—what the fuck is his name, Finney something or other—and now you tell me I'm playing opposite some fucking unknown Mexican greaseball?"

The vehemence of her yells caused the blond Adonis, whose name was Nick, to rise sulkily from the bed and skulk into a corner, where he slouched angrily in a pink art deco armchair covered with protective plastic and glared at her with ill-concealed fury.

He had been giving head to the bitch for over an hour, had her close to coming at least twice, and each time the phone rang and she picked it up. Picked it up! While his tongue was playing a concerto on her clit. This time it was her fucking agent talking about some new actor to star opposite her. Why not him?

Nick wasn't screwing Sissy for love—nor even a modicum of lust. Sissy's skinny frame, lack of frontal development and penchant for pills did not inspire him to great cocksmanship. But as the current teenager's TV delight, he was more than anxious to break into movies before he hit the advanced age of thirty. Screwing Sissy Sharp, the aging good old girl next door, was Nick's entree into the world of feature films. He hoped.

It had been Sam's idea. Sam Sharp had been married to Sissy for seventeen years, during which time they had convinced the American public that they had one of Hollywood's happiest marriages. Sam's preference for his own sex was well known in Hollywood circles, as was Sissy's sexual appetite for men twenty years her junior; but true to the Hollywood tradition of never sullying the images of their most prominent citizens, no publication had even hinted at anything untoward in the Sharp marriage. They went their merry way, a picture of marital togetherness in the eyes of their public, while continuing to compete for the favors of the young studs who proliferated in Hollywood.

Sam and Nick worked at the same studio, where Sam had been starring in movies for thirty years. He regularly made seven hundred and fifty thousand dollars a picture, and many of the aspiring young actors on the lot.

Nick was in his second TV season, riding high. As the star of a fast-paced sitcom in which he played an undercover cop, he had teenagers in heat over his blond hair and perfect face and body. He was on the cover of every TV magazine and supermarket scandal sheet, and his love life—a succession of gorgeous starlets and models—was well chronicled. But career advancement was uppermost in his mind. The transition from TV hunk to motion picture star was tough, particularly when the powers that be considered Nick's acting ability low on his list of assets.

He knew Sissy always made sure she had casting approval of her leading man, and of any female performer who might conceivably overshadow her. She was starting her new movie in two weeks. Rumors on the street had it that everybody who was anybody had turned it down. No well-respected leading man wanted to star opposite a has-been like Sissy. But it could be Nick's big chance.

He'd allowed Sam to chat him up in the commissary one lunchtime. He'd allowed Sam to invite him to his mammoth motor-home dressing room and to share a bottle of Dom Perignon after shooting. He'd allowed Sam to unzip his jeans and expertly suck his cock. He had not allowed Sam to kiss him on the mouth. Nor had he touched any part of Sam's body himself. He closed his eyes and imagined a beautiful girl was giving him head. Men were not his scene. But he was ambitious, and he needed to get invited to the Sharps' mansion in Bel Air for dinner one night. He had been—about three months ago.

And he met Sissy at last. She looked pretty good for forty-four: skinny and bejeweled, the lines of discontent and envy not apparent behind the heavy makeup until you got close. Really close. Which Nick intended to do.

He had been seated on Sissy's left during dinner. The table was crowded with the usual overdressed dinosaurs that the Sharps surrounded themselves with socially. Median age fifty-five, thought Nick. Not an attractive woman in sight. Unless you counted Lady Sarah Cranleigh, fifty if she was a day, so covered in frilly lace, pearl necklaces, ringlets and ruffles that all that was visible was a double chin and a pair of laughing eyes.

Known in England for her penchant for young men, Lady Sarah was having a delicious time in Los Angeles. Daily trips to the Santa Monica beach yielded her a quota of gorgeous young studs of a quality hard to find in Britain. Her latest conquest, who was barely nineteen, was seated next to her, in utter confusion as to which of the three golden forks he should use on his artichoke.

Nick found Lady Sarah extremely amusing, but quite unfanciable. A true Rabelaisian character, she was devouring her food with gusto, at the same time giving the beach boy a grope and rubbing one ample, satin-covered knee against Nick's. In contrast, Sissy, ever conscious of her weight, age and appearance, was picking at her food, her tiny birdlike hands reaching often for the Venetian goblet of champagne discreetly refilled by the butler.

Nick had concentrated his considerable magnetism and charm on Sissy, aware that, at twenty-nine, he was perhaps a bit too old for her taste. He noticed her locking eyes with Lady Sarah's beach boy, who was probably more her type.

Abby Arafat, one of Hollywood's most prolific producers, was talking about his latest project, a miniseries that would spin off into a series.

"It will make *Gone With the Wind* look like a B feature," he boasted. "The budget is going to be twenty million, we'll be shooting in London, Paris, the Caribbean and Newport Beach, and with Deane directing and the right actors to play Miranda, Sirope, Armando and Steve, we're gonna blow the ratings through the roof. I know we will."

"What is this property called?" asked Lady Sarah, delicately wiping up the last of her artichoke butter with a large piece of French bread and signaling to the butler for more champagne.

"The biggest goddamn blockbusting novel since *Taipan,*" bragged an excited Abby. "You must have heard of *Saga*—it's been on *The New York Times* best-seller list for six months now.

Cost us two million for the rights, but what the hell! Everyone wants to play Miranda: Dunaway, Streep, Streisand. What a part! It's the greatest goddamn woman's role since Scarlett O'Hara. Miranda Beaumont Duvall Hamilton. God, what a role—a real Emmy getter."

The attention of the table had left the artichokes, and Abby had his audience.

"For Steve, we want a major male star." He looked knowingly at Sam.

Sissy pricked up her ears. As hound smells fox, so she smelled a potential part for herself.

"I didn't know you'd bought the rights to that book, Abby, darling," she trilled sweetly across the table to him, cursing silently that she had not seated him on her left instead of the blond TV star, who was obviously after only one thing—her body. Sissy was convinced that most men who met her desired her body. She had a loyal coterie of sycophants and yes-men who assured her constantly how gorgeous and desirable she was while gleefully tearing her to pieces behind her back.

"I just *loved* that book—I couldn't put it down, could I, Sam?" She smiled at her husband, who dutifully chimed in on cue. The Sharps were completely in cahoots with each other. They cared very much about their careers. Strongly supportive of each other in this respect, they cared not at all about each other's sexual flings.

The fraction of a second Sam caught Sissy's eye was enough for him to realize she wanted that role.

"So who *is* going to play Miranda?" Sam asked casually.

"Who? Who? Aha, that is going to be *the* question from now on." Abby sat back complacently and lit a cigar despite the fact that the first course was not yet cleared and he knew Sissy loathed cigar smoke. He leaned confidentially across the table to Lady Sarah, who was far more interested in exploring Nick's thigh than hearing this boring Hollywood gossip. Really trite. So unlike London small talk. No one would ever dream of discussing his business affairs at a dinner party in England. But Americans were so crass, particularly Californians. She glanced at the young blond boy who looked totally baffled by the prospect of having to dismember the small but perfect squab just placed in front of him. She couldn't wait till dinner was over and she got him into her bungalow at the Beverly Hills Hotel. Meanwhile there was nothing to do but feign interest and enjoy the cuisine, which was not bad—not bad at all. She took a large bite of squab, oblivious to the juices that dropped onto her slightly soiled Emmanuelle dress, and leaned toward Abby, displaying a more than ample cleavage.

"Who—*do tell*—who is going to play the female lead?" she lisped eagerly. Abby drew on his cigar, aware of the interest he had created and milking it for all it was worth.

"Streisand's agent called this morning. But it's no good—as good as we could photograph her, Barbra's no beauty, and no chicken either. And if there's one thing that Miranda has to be, it is *gorgeous!*" He stabbed his squab for emphasis. "This role is too important. We can't give it to Streisand, star that she is. Miranda is a beauty—a raving beauty—and only a beautiful actress is going to play her. Maybe Brooke Shields."

"Forget her, Abby. Her mother's a pain in the ass," chimed in Arthur Van Dyk, executive vice-president of MCPC, the Makopolis Company Picture Corporation, one of the few remaining major studios in Hollywood. Founded by a shrewd Greek immigrant in 1911, it had reached its zenith in the thirties, forties, and fifties, thanks to the business acumen of its chairman, the austere Stanford Feldheimer, who had taken the studio into television production in the late fifties with great success. "Besides," he went on, "she's too young. Brooke could never age up to forty or forty-five." Sam and Sissy exchanged a fleeting glance. Although she was loath to admit her true age, nevertheless for the right role Sissy would play age sixty—or kill her grand-mother.

"What we're *really* going to do—to create maximum excite-ment and controversy about the four-hour miniseries—is to ask the public to vote for who they think could play Miranda," said Abby smoothly with the confidence of a man whose mistakes would be paid for with other people's money.

"The public will eat it up. Great, heh?" He looked to Lady Sarah for approval. Like so many Californians, he had a healthy respect for the British aristocracy. Weren't they all related to the Queen?

"But suppose the public decides that they want Barbra Strei-sand or Brooke What's-her-name or other equally unsuitable people—what then?" asked Lady Sarah, bored to tears by it all, but trained in the subtle art of polite dinner-table conversation. One hand held a squab leg, the other rested on the crotch of the beach boy.

"Unknowns. We test unknowns. Dozens of them," crowed Abby, spearing his squab triumphantly.

"And—" he winked—"we'll test established stars too. Great publicity. Can you imagine? We test Bisset, Streep, Lamaze! Christ, the publicity will be *dynamite.*"

Sissy's blood froze. Lamaze! They were thinking of testing that Mexican cooze! Were they mad?

For fifteen years Rosalinde and Sissy had been one of Holly-wood's favorite feuds. The thought of Rosalinde Lamaze even being considered for this plum role infuriated Sissy so much that she choked on her champagne. To control her anger she started to return the attentions of Nick's wandering fingers on her Bob Mackie beaded thigh, but her mind was elsewhere.

She wanted that role. She realized how it could revive her flagging career. All the couture clothes, the jewels, the flattery, the lavish Bel Air mansion and the ever-present sycophants could not disguise the fact that she was no longer young, no longer "hot," no longer considered for the top movies, which now mostly starred nineteen-year-olds on the heels of the hot triumvirate of Fonda, Streisand, and Lange. She tossed down another glass of champagne and gave Nick what once had been a golden smile but was now a rictus grin.

A dazzling miniseries, which would automatically spin off into a successful weekly series! It was too good to be true. She needed it, and she would do her damnedest to get it. God knows films of a decent caliber were becoming harder and harder to come by these days. Hardware films like the James Bond series, *Superman* and *E.T.* were the box-office blockbusters now. Or teenage horror and comedy films, made on low budgets and designed for the high school and juvenile college crowd, starring unknowns who looked as much like real movie stars as Lassie. The writing was on the wall. The glamorous romantic love stories she had made a career of in the sixties and seventies were finished; she must move with the times.

It was a similar story for Sam. The epic adventure stories he had made his forte in the fifties, sixties and seventies had run their course, and now were popular only with TV audiences. His last three features had been huge flops. Young audiences of today were not interested in a leading man nearly half a century old. O.K. for Newman, Redford and Nicholson—they were special. Different. Elevated super megastars. Sam was of the old school—the Cary Grant, Robert Montgomery, William Powell school of acting. Dry wit, innuendo, subtlety, glamour, romance and adventure. The kids today didn't want it. God knows, they were the only people supporting the cinema. Older folks stayed home to watch TV. And by older, that meant anyone over twenty-eight. It was too expensive to go out at night. If they had babies they had to get sitters, then buying dinner out, even if it was only hamburgers, parking and the tickets could cost close to fifty bucks for two. So they stayed home, watching the hot new TV shows like "Starsky and Hutch," "Charlie's Angels" and "Dallas," and their favorite stars of the sixties and seventies— like Sam Sharp—in the movie reruns on their own TV in their own living room.

Sam was astonished at how well his movies did in the TV ratings. The network put them on regularly in prime time opposite the rival networks' hottest shows, and invariably the Nielsen ratings proved Sam's popularity with the public. His TVQ, although he had never made a product specifically for the medium, was one of the hottest.

Although the networks and television producers always denied it, a TVQ was a popularity contest in which actors on TV were graded according to their likability quotient with the public. The public, amidst enormous secrecy, was secretly polled to name its favorites, as it was considered "unconstitutional" by the Screen Actors Guild to base hiring on the public's opinion. Nevertheless, the policy continued and those with the highest TVQ received the highest salaries. And the best parts.

Abby had made Sam a top secret hard-to-refuse offer to star in "Saga." Fifty grand an episode, thirteen episodes at least this year, and if the show was a hit, the network would guarantee twenty-three episodes next season. That was a cool million plus a year. Sam had been thinking about it but hadn't told Sissy yet.

He would play the patriarch of a large fashion manufacturing and designing family who lived in Newport Beach. They would shoot in Newport for several weeks, at least two or three times a season—a prospect most appealing to Sam, who adored the ocean and owned a ninety-five-foot sailboat. His character, Steve Hamilton, would have a devoted wife, two feuding ex-wives, and six children—a boy and a girl by each ex-wife, and a boy and a girl by the present one.

He would work a minimum of two days a week and a maximum of four. No more than ten hours of shooting a day. He would have perks galore. Approval of cast, director, scripts, his own stand-in, double, and full-time valet and cook at the studio, paid for by the company, a wardrobe of clothes made by his tailor, Doug Hayward of London, whom the studio would fly over twice a year for fittings. He would keep the clothes, naturally. There was also to be a chauffeur-driven Cadillac with smoked windows to drive to and from the studio, and his own makeup man and hairdresser to put on his pancake and his auburn toupee in the privacy of his luxurious motor home.

Yes, a veritable cornucopia of goodies. Certainly better than most actors were receiving in TV today. He was definitely considering it. Definitely. Too bad his father wasn't alive to see how big he had gotten. Not John Wayne, of course, but big.

John Wayne. "A 'real man,' " his father used to tell him on the Saturday afternoons when they would go to the cinema in Tulsa, where he had been born and raised. "That's a *man,* son. You watch how he walks and talks. He don't take no shit from no one, boy. That's what a real man is like. He's the boss—the chief, the breadwinner—everyone takes real good notice of him, you see."

Little Sam nodded, gazing in awe at the huge black-and-white cowboy up on the screen. John Wayne was a massive person, and the screen made him even more so. In fact, he did not look unlike Sam's own father, Hank. A towering granite-faced cowboy-looking man, who chewed tobacco and spat it on the sidewalk, and who got drunk with the boys in the bar every Saturday night. After he had a fight with one of them he went back to his tiny two-bedroom house, woke up Lizzie, Sam's mother, who was petrified of him, and without preamble, foreplay, kissing or hugging, fornicated with her with such grunts and groans and thumps and moans, that Sam's young ears heard everything. Heard his young mother's cries of "Oh, no, Hank, no, not tonight. I've got the curse." Heard his father's hoarse whiskey-thickened voice tell her to "shut up and raise yer night-gown, woman. I don't want to look at it, I just want to get me piece in it." Heard the stifled cries of his mother, then heard his father cursing, "Look at this, look what you've done to me, woman. Look at this blood. You're a filthy woman, and the Good Lord will punish you for having such filth between your legs."

Sam heard the slap, heard his mother's weeping long after his father's snores shook the house. He'd go sit with her in the kitchen, where, sobbing quietly to herself, she tried to hold ice on her swelling eyes.

"Don't cry, Mama—please don't cry," begged the little boy, holding his mother close.

"I'm not crying, dear." She tried to curb her tears as she held Sam close to her warmth and rocked him to her bosom. These were the tenderest moments in young Sam's life.

When Lizzie's second pregnancy was in an advanced stage, two or three weeks from delivery, Hank came home one night considerably drunker than usual.

In spite of the doctor's warning not to, he tried to have sex with Lizzie, who, after fighting him off, managed to escape next door to the sanctuary of their neighbor's house. Sam lay in his cot, scared for his mother, but relieved that tonight he wouldn't have to hear the usual panting and moaning. Suddenly, his door was pushed open and his father stood there, silhouetted against the dim yellow light.

"Wake up, son," snarled the huge man. "Wake up, I want to show you something."

Terrified, Sam pretended to be asleep.

"Wake up, I said," yelled his father. "Wake up, you little pisser."

He pulled all the bedclothes off Sam with a yank of his massive hand. Through half-closed eyes, Sam saw what his father held in the other hand. His ten-year-old senses screamed danger, but he still pretended to sleep. Anything rather than having to look at that huge red *thing* his father grasped.

"Wake up, son." Hank's whiskey breath came closer to his son's face. "I want to show you what a *real* man is like."

"Asleep are yer?—well, you won't sleep much longer now, sonny boy. I'm going to teach you the facts of life."

His huge hand lashed out. Sam jumped up to crouch, cowering, on his bed. He couldn't believe what his father was doing. His massive thing, as big as a hose pipe, red and swollen, was in his hand, and he was pulling it, pulling it hard.

"See, boy, this is a cock, boy. Look at it. This is what John Wayne and all of us *real* men have got between our legs. Let's see what you've got down there, son." With his other hand he grabbed Sam's flannel pajamas. "Well, look at that, I declare." He almost fell over laughing. "That's not a cock, boy, that's more like a little thimble, something your mother would use to sew with. *This* is a cock, boy, and if a man is not ramming it into some woman, then he's doing *this* with it." Sam watched in horror as his father jerked his hand harder and faster across himself until the boy thought it would burst. As he thought that, it did, and he watched in horror as his father let out what sounded like a wolf howl and slumped against the wall.

A few years later, a boy named Bobby took him into the boys' bathroom after school hours and, proudly bringing out a rather large thirteen-year-old penis, suggested to Sam that if Sam touched it, he would do the same for Sam. For the first time in Sam's short life, he experienced sexual fulfillment as both boys came together. He found it to be an experience of such excitement that he and Bobby met there twice a week for the next two years.

Even when Sam became a fully grown man of twenty, his penis never came even close to the size of his father's. He thought he was not a "real man" like John Wayne and his father, because, he realized reluctantly, he liked "doing it" with boys. Well, maybe he couldn't be a "real man" by his father's standards; but he soon had a chance to be a "real star."

Sam was a solid actor, one on whom the movie company could always rely. Not overly exciting, sometimes a little dull. After all, Sam had played some of the most solid citizens since God, starting off with George Washington and including Abraham Lincoln, General Eisenhower and Franklin D. Roosevelt. American heroes all. Fine upstanding gentlemen to boot. To some of the audience Sam *was* the President, so many had he portrayed.

Sam had interspersed these parts with lighter roles, for which he had been nominated for an Academy Award, though none had won. Four perma-plaqued certificates attesting to his Oscar nominations were displayed on his library walls, along with framed photos of him and Sissy with Nancy and Ronnie, Gerald and Betty, Rosalynn and Jimmy, and Jack and Jackie. A testament to almost but never. His agent had said the role of Steve Hamilton would be a shoo-in for an Emmy. It wasn't an Oscar, but it wouldn't be just a nomination this time. This time he'd have a real honest-to-goodness gold-plated statuette, almost as good as the kind he had craved all those years as he'd sat in the Santa Monica Auditorium, heard his name announced in ringing tones, and lost out with monotonous regularity to Jack Nicholson, Al Pacino, Ben Kingsley and Dustin Hoffman.

He was slightly bitter about never having won an Oscar, especially since Sissy had received one. Hers was prominently displayed on a red-and-gold boulle table in their marble entrance hall. She kept it there, she said, because the gold in the figurine matched the gold inlay of the table so well. He knew better. She kept it there so that every damn person who came to the house couldn't fail to see it. Naturally it had been stolen a couple of times being in such an accessible place, but each time Sissy just called the Academy and they sent her another. One of the statuettes had been recovered, but Sissy, instead of sending it back to the Academy, kept it. It resided in a rather less obvious place, on a shelf opposite the bidet in her bathroom. Now it appeared she had not one but two Oscars. Bitch. He frowned. He didn't often think of his wife of seventeen years as a bitch, although to many people she most certainly was.

He was loyal to her, they had an excellent marriage, but she could be an impossible cooze. This morning she had insisted on involving him in a fashion layout she was doing for a syndicate of European magazines. Running her hands through his hair—goddamn it, how he hated having to stick his hairpiece on by himself—using him as a backdrop for her newest Norells and Blasses. When he informed her he had a one o'clock call, she had pouted sulkily, as though they were the loving couple the public imagined.

Now that she realized the potential in the role of Miranda, if he accepted Abby's offer to play the lead he would have to do his husbandly duty and try to get her a test.

He groaned inwardly. She could be the grande dame diva to end them all, but still, she was his wife. He was a loyal husband. He would try to use his influence. Otherwise, his life could become unpleasant.

Sissy had a way of doing that to people.

Sissy and Sam's party broke up early, as all the best (and worst) Hollywood parties always do.

In spite of the general public's opinion that Hollywood was a place of fun, brilliance and glamour, filled with outrageously extroverted, gorgeous people, deliciously dressed and participating in scintillating conversation, the opposite was true. The truth was that Hollywood in the 1980s was dull. The glamour girls and boys of the thirties, forties and fifties no longer existed. It was a business town now, run by company men.

Paparazzi and reporters clustered outside Sissy and Sam's

home waiting to snap the stars and celebrities who were leaving were aware of this lack of star power today. That was why, when a star like Emerald Barrymore attended an event, flashbulbs exploded and the paparazzi knew they would make money tonight.

Calvin Foster waited quietly by himself, his heart pounding, but his demeanor expressionless. He would see *her* tonight. His idol, his queen: Emerald.

He was a slight young man with dirty blond hair and an absolutely forgettable face; people who met Calvin never seemed able to remember him—not even the paparazzi, with whom he spent hours, carrying a Nikon and pretending to be one of them. Only his eyes, cold, pale gray and secretive, would have attracted attention if anyone had looked closely. He knew that, which was why he usually wore mirror sunglasses.

He licked the sweat congealing on his upper lip.

The photographer from the *American Informer* was complaining that all the women had worn furs or wraps to the party and there wasn't a decent cleavage shot to be had.

"When Emerald comes out she'll have on a great dress, you'll see," volunteered Calvin, the excitement of this thought electrifying him.

"Shit—she ain't here, she's in South America or somethin'," replied the *Informer* guy.

"She's not here?" gulped Calvin. His information was usually flawless.

"Nope," said the *Informer*. "Her picture went over schedule. She ain't due back till next week."

Calvin felt emptiness engulf him. He hadn't seen Emerald for over two months now. It was true, she had been in South America recently making some low-budget adventure film with some unknown Spanish actor. The pang of disappointment was so intense that Calvin couldn't disguise it. He jabbed his fist in the air with frustration. The other paparazzo looked at him curiously as he loped off to his car, his camera bag flapping against his potbelly.

No Emerald! Damn. Damn. Damn...

He had been deprived of a glimpse of her beauty, her one-of-a-kind sexual glamour. No one else had it, had ever had it, like Emerald. She of the emerald eyes and the sea-green gowns. She of the golden curls and the tremulous upper lip. Emerald, the survivor of torrid love affairs with James Dean, John Garfield and Gary Cooper, among others. Close friend of Monroe, Garland and Clift—Hollywood survivor par excellence. Survivor of Valium and vodka, aspirin and anisette, casting couch and death. She'd looked them all in the face very often and said, "Fuck you." Survivor of two car crashes, one of them fatal to her husband, the other to her fiancé, six marriages, two abortions, nine miscarriages, fifty-seven mediocre movies, three Academy Award nominations, more than one hundred lovers, not all of them male, not all of them white, and numerous smear campaigns to blacken her name, starting with the one during the McCarthy era, when she was only a teenager and in no way interested in communist plots....

Star of stars, oh, how he loved her, wanted her, needed her! Calvin felt the familiar heat in his loins as he slid behind the wheel of his green Chevrolet—green in honor of Emerald. Her face was everywhere in his room. He must hurry home to her.

6

*L*uis Mendoza slammed the door of Rosalinde's house. Her three Persian cats rubbed themselves against his ankles as he crossed the garden. He kicked them away. Luis hated animals and children. In Luis's life, only two things were important—beautiful women to make love to and Luis himself. As far as narcissism went, he made Rosalinde look like Mother Teresa. Whereas she was shrewd enough to see herself objectively as a commodity, he saw himself as simply the most handsome, most talented, most *macho* man in the world.

"The male Bo Derek," his new manager, Irving Klinger, had assured him last month as Luis had scrawled his almost illegible signature across the all-encompassing management contracts in

73

which shrewd Irving had arranged that 40 percent of all Luis's earnings would go to him.

"The sex symbol of the eighties!" cried his new press agent, Johnny Swanson, an enthusiastic and brilliant manipulator of talent, which he brought to the attention of the world's media for only 5 percent of the talent's earnings.

"The most superb man in the world!" Rosalinde had sighed to Suzy after their first date five weeks ago. He hadn't really fancied Rosalinde—being Mexican too, she reminded him of one of his sisters. He adored blondes, but Luis Mendoza was nobody's fool. To be romantically linked with Rosalinde Lamaze was good for his image. When you were the middle son of a poor Mexican family, and from the time you could toddle had fought for pieces of tortilla with nine brothers and sisters, you grew up crafty and clever or you didn't grow up at all.

Luis Mendoza had done what most twelve-year-old boys in Tijuana did for a living. He parked cars for tourists, cleaned their car windows for the five or so pesos he was lucky to get, and sold matches, or gum, or straw bags if he had been really lucky and managed with some other hungry boys to break into a warehouse to steal a couple of cartons.

By the time his mother died he had secretly saved a thousand pesos, the equivalent of approximately eighty-four dollars, which he kept in an old sock at the back of a cupboard. It was 1968. Things were happening in the United States. Senator Robert Kennedy had just been assassinated. Luis had heard the news on the radio. The Who, a rock group from somewhere in England, were taking America by storm. A beautiful Latin girl called Rosalinde Lamaze smiled invitingly at him from billboards and newspapers all over Tijuana. She was twenty-two, ten years older than Luis, but his adolescent manhood grew hard at the thought of her juicy lips and plump round thighs. She was a girl you could dream of screwing, unlike the beautiful cool North

American blondes who were beyond his reach even in his dreams.

He wanted it all, even then. He wanted to go to the United States and become a big rock star like the Beatles and make love to gorgeous women like Rosalinde, and the other one—the classic blonde, Emerald Barrymore.

One day he would have fame, success and money and make love to Rosalinde and Emerald and all the rest of the gorgeous creatures he glimpsed in the pages of the men's magazines he scanned at the newsstand. Of this he was sure.

He had been his mother's favorite. *"Guapísimo,"* she would murmur, running careworn hands through his abundant black curls. *"Niño mío."* She snuggled Luis close to her skinny frame, bloated constantly with pregnancy, and whispered endearments to him to the jealousy of the rest of her brood.

Carmelita poured the love she had once had for Luis's father into the handsome young boy—the love of a beautiful young Mexican girl who year by year grew older and uglier while her husband no longer had any use for her except as a household serf and receptacle of his occasional lust. Year by year the family increased until the frail mother, worn out at the age of thirty-seven by the birth of ten children, the poverty of her life, and the lack of love from her husband, expired peacefully in her sleep. Carmelita gave Luis her strength. She gave him pride in himself. She made him believe that he could be a king—a god—a star. These hopes and dreams she whispered to young Luis throughout his formative years, building him up, making him believe in himself, giving him the inner strength and resilience he needed to survive.

When she died, three days before his thirteenth birthday, Luis wept for the last time in his life. Now he must follow the path his mother had prepared him for.

With his thousand pesos tucked safely into his worn sneakers, and wearing one of his three T-shirts, jeans and a raveled sweater, he tried to cross the Tijuana border into the States one cold February night. Unfortunately he chose a time when Immigration was on the rampage against wetbacks. Caught by a patrol guard, he ended up spending a night in jail with a bunch of drunken derelicts, pimps and thieves, who promptly relieved him not only of his precious thousand pesos but also of his virginity. For a macho Latin boy to be disgraced and abused by foul-smelling drunks and lecherous queers, to the jeers of the other vermin who inhabited the cell, was an indignity so barbaric that Luis had nightmares about it for years. He had never liked the company of men particularly. His father's treatment of his long-suffering mother had always disgusted him. Eventually his disgust for his own sex had turned him into a loner who loved and needed the company of women.

Thirteen-year-old Luis returned to the family home the following week a sadder and wiser boy. One year later, on his fourteenth birthday, he boarded a train to Mexico City with the money he had again managed to save. He never saw his family again.

Luis was tall for his age and immensely strong and agile. His looks were such that women of all ages were his for the asking. Since the night in jail, he had made it his business not only to make love to as many girls and women as possible but had developed a peculiar passion for sadistically beating up any boy he even suspected was homosexual. He developed an aversion that bordered on the psychotic to all forms of homosexuality.

By the time Luis was fifteen, he was working as a waiter in a Mexico City nightclub. By the time he was twenty, he was part of the band, singing Latin American ballads and oozing so much raw sex appeal that staid Mexican matrons groaned with ecstasy at the sight and sound of him. By the time he was twenty-two, he had conquered Mexico as Cortez had never dreamed of doing.

He was the most famous and successful singer of romantic

ballads in the country. In Spain and Italy too, his records outsold those of Julio Iglesias, and his face and body endorsed everything from jockey shorts to after-shave lotion.

Adolescent girls wept when they saw him on television. They huddled for hours outside the entrance to his grand apartment in Mexico City for a glimpse of him. Luis Mendoza fever swept Latin America. At twenty-four he started making movies and became even more popular. Latin America was at his feet. But North America, the America he strived to conquer, wasn't interested in him.

"Latins have never made it big on the screen," said Abby Arafat, the arbiter of taste at MCPC Studios.

"What about Valentino?" argued Irving Klinger. "And Ricardo Montalban, he was big in the movies too."

"Yeah, but he was a has-been until 'Fantasy Island.' And Valentino was Italian."

"Look at Fernando Lamas, Cesar Romero, Tony Quinn," persisted Irving.

"People don't want to *know* from spics," spat Abby, inspecting perfectly manicured nails. "Pacino and Travolta may look a little greasy, but the world knows they're Italian, right? And Italians are O.K. So are the frogs and the limeys. But spics! There's never been one that could make it in the movies unless it was character roles. Men resent a guy who's a Mexican getting the girl. They think he should be parking cars or pumping gas."

"I'll tell you what, Abby," said Irving. "I'll test the kid in Mexico City. I'll pay for the fucking test myself, and I'll eat my fucking hat if you don't think he's got the greatest potential since Brando."

Irving rarely backed losers, and Luis Mendoza arrived in Hollywood one month later on a warm April day. He had a three-picture deal in his pocket and he expected Hollywood to be at his feet.

When he left Mexico City, hopeful of never seeing it again, he was besieged by weeping fans, harassed paparazzi, and reporters, whom he brushed off with his usual charming civility. He arrived in Los Angeles wearing a white Armani suit, dark glasses and a tan. As he moved swiftly through Immigration and Customs, there was not even a hum of interest from passengers and airport personnel.

He was one of the biggest stars in the world in Latin America, but no one seemed to know or care in California.

The going in Hollywood proved tougher than Luis had ever imagined. They snubbed him; the goddamn fucking Hollywood *pigs* ignored him. Oh, he knew why, well enough. Because he was to them just a greaseball, a goddamn Mexican wetback. What an insult. He had a legitimate green card; he was here under the auspices of the American government. He had a movie contract. Why were they so disdainful of him? Even Lamaze, that cooze, had insulted him last night. He had only screwed her because Irving said they would make a hot twosome from which he would get publicity, which might make him more popular with the American public. Sure, oh, sure. What he realized bitterly was that it was better for her career than for his to be a gossip item.

Eventually Irving got him a starring role in a picture. It meant playing opposite that over-the-hill bag of bones Sissy Sharp, but it was an American feature film at last, even though the script was lousy.

He looked in the mirror and arranged his tousled black curls more artlessly. Richard Gere, eat your heart out! Here comes Mendoza. In terms of looks and sex appeal, Gere was zero compared to Luis. He was on his way now. Nothing could stop him.

There are two kinds of people in this world, Rosalinde Lamaze decided, gazing into her magnifying mirror in the harsh north light: those who screw, and those who get screwed. And last night, she thought gloomily, she was a front-runner in category number two.

Luis Mendoza made no pretense of being in love with her. If his prowess in the bedroom was anything to go by, she was just a receptacle for his well-formed cock. So what *was* the problem? Was she losing her charms? She studied her face in the magnifying mirror, peering closely with her shortsighted eyes to get a better view. She sighed and applied Dr. René Guinot's moisturizing cream for mature skin with even more abandon to the threadlike lines that were starting to appear beneath her chocolate-brown eyes.

She was a plumpish, short, pretty woman of thirty-six, who, with the expert application of myriad cosmetic devices, exotic outfits and a number of cleverly arranged postiches and nun's hair wigs, was regularly transformed into the fantasy woman of every truck driver and construction worker from Hoboken to Hollywood.

A million men had fantasized about Rosalinde Lamaze as they reached for their wives to take their conjugal rights, thoughts of Rosalinde's tawny limbs locked around them arousing their minds and their cocks. A million schoolboys had awakened from erotic dreams with the guilty evidence of their nocturnal fantasies of Rosalinde's creamy skin, taut tits and glistening lips —a sticky little mess on their pajamas, which would be hastily rinsed under the faucet before Mother discovered it.

For fifteen years now Rosalinde had thrived on her image as a saucy, sexy Latin American goddess. It was an image that had brought her much money and many men, both of which she had used with a voracious Latin appetite.

But was she fading now? She frowned as she thought of last night, then quickly stopped as she caught sight of the furrows in her magnifying mirror. She was a study in beiges and browns. Pollen-colored skin deepened to a dark amber on her body, for she had kept her face from the sun as much as possible in the past several years. She had observed the skin disasters of women who littered the beaches and pools of Southern California like shipwrecked debris.

Her hair was as dark a brown as possible without veering to black. Her eyes were chocolate almonds and her nipples...She slipped the silk pareu she was wearing off her shoulders to her waist to observe the perfection of her perfectly formed, delicately tanned breasts with their thick brown nipples.

As she looked, she imagined Luis's lips on them last night, licking them to a fever before he entered her, and then a quick thrust or two and it was over. He had rolled off her, reached for a cigarette and turned his back and *gone to sleep!* He had used her like a *puta*—a whore. Her mother had been a *puta*. Some people thought of Rosalinde as one.

Unconsciously her hand reached for and cupped her left breast. It was still oily from Dr. Guinot's nourishing lotion, and the sensation was decidedly pleasant. As she caressed herself, she saw in the magnifying mirror her brown nipple hardening until it looked like a bud about to burst. In spite of her anger and sexual frustration from last night, Rosalinde felt her breathing sharpen.

To watch herself caressing herself in the privacy of her luxurious marble bathroom was a good deal more thrilling than the wham-bam-thank-you-ma'am that Luis had served her last night without a thought for her satisfaction. Angrily, she stroked herself more sensually. What would they think now, those millions of men who had lusted after her for all these years, if they could see her like this?

Suddenly she paused in the middle of arousing herself in the mirror. She left the dressing table and, stalking to her closet, took out an exquisite white ermine cloak. Throwing it on the bathroom floor she lay on top of it and looked into the mirrored ceiling of her bathroom.

She feasted her eyes on a sight most men in America would harden for. Amber skin, plump but exquisitely firm arms and legs. The face and hair were not so good, but with her short-sightedness, she neither saw nor cared; and running her hands over her own body, using the moisturizer of Dr. Guinot at two hundred dollars an ounce (an extravagance indeed), she made herself come as only she knew how to do with exquisite pleasure. She moaned, gazing at herself in the mirror as she climaxed. It excited her tremendously, and Luis was forgotten. The narcissistic pleasure she took in her body banished other thoughts. Even the ringing of the telephone did not stop her delicious frenzy. Once, twice, four, five times—the divine agony. Finally, exhausted and infinitely more satisfied than she had been for weeks, she rolled over, threw the fur wrap on the chair and answered the phone.

"How was it?" It was Polly, her agent and best friend.

"What a *disaster!*" Rosalinde was almost screaming as she reapplied the precious moisturizer to the sensitive skin under her eyes. "That bastard could barely get it up, and when he finally did, it was all over in two minutes. *Cabrón!* What a *putz!*"

"No no no, you little idiot," Polly said exasperatedly. Did Rosalinde ever think about *anything* except sex? "How was the *meeting,* dummy? Did you make a good impression on Abby and Gertrude?"

"Oh, that—oh yeah." Rosalinde slumped back in her cream satin chair, admiring her left breast as it escaped from her kimono. She grabbed a cigarette and tried to concentrate on her career, which had always come in second to her primary interest.

"Did you discuss the part with Gertrude or Abby?" Polly enunciated her words carefully, realizing that her friend and client's attention was still more concentrated on her woeful sexual fling with Luis than on an exceedingly important role.

"Oooh, yes—I did—I did make a good impression. Gertrude thinks I'm wonderful!" She beamed. "She loved me in *That Girl from Acapulco.*"

Polly groaned. "The character you played in that turkey was about as much like Miranda Hamilton as Juliet is to Blanche du Bois."

"No, no—I forgot. She saw *The Mistress*—the one I did in London."

"Ah, good, good, you were *great* in that, honey, great."

"Thanks." Rosalinde squinted, peering closely into the mirror as she found yet *another* line beneath her chocolate-colored eyes. Did they *never* stop arriving?

"Did she mention the test, honey?"

"What?" asked Rosalinde.

"The test—the test for 'Saga.'"

"Yes, she sort of did." Rosalinde was vague. She had sampled two of Luis's fine Mexican joints last night, and her mind was still hazy. The professional in her suddenly snapped back to attention. "Don't fret, Polly. Don't worry. I have an idea, *querida*. I have *every* intention of getting that part, and I *will*. I want it, and what Rosalinde wants Rosalinde *gets.*"

"Good girl." Polly knew that when Rosalinde was motivated nothing could stop her. She could be tough and strong as an ox when her mind was focused on something other than sex. In fact, when it was focused on sex she was usually stronger. "So what's your plan, honey?"

"Why *can't* you get me a fucking test for fuck's sake!" screamed Sissy Sharp over the phone to her agent.

"If you can't even get *me* a test, Dougie, I swear I'll go to the Morris office. I mean it, Doug! I truly mean it. First you get me this—this lousy Luis Mendoza, to play opposite me in this piece of shit film." She started coughing and her ever-watchful butler hastily filled her plastic patio glass with more white wine.

"Then I hear that everyone in town, I mean *everyone* except me, is testing for Miranda. You better do something fast, Dougie. I want that role. Otherwise I'm defecting to the Morris boys."

She slammed down the phone and glared into the black onyx pool where Sam was doing his usual forty laps. Part of her observed the rippling muscles of his admittedly well-shaped fifty-year-old back as he butterflied down the length. She wished she was in as good shape as he was. Maybe that's why they wouldn't test her. Too old. They thought she was too old. And I am, she thought sorrowfully to herself, allowing a tear to course down her overly tanned leathery skin. Forty-four. Shit. Even though her public relations people constantly told everyone that she was thirty-eight, the town knew the truth. Everyone always knew the truth in this town: how old you were, how much you made, how greatly in demand you were. They all knew. Jungle drums. No secrets.

Fuck this town, she told herself. There had to be a way to test! Had to. She poured more wine and stared at Sam's muscles until the phone rang. Sam had said he was going to do his best to get her a test, but he was not being assertive enough. She had to try, herself, subtly.

"Sissy, darling, have you heard the news?" purred her closest friend and confidante, Daphne Swanson.

"What news?" growled Sissy, knowing full well it had something to do with *her* part.

"They're going to test Chloe Carriere for the part—can you *believe* it, darling? A *singer* playing Miranda, and British to boot. It's too too hilarious!" Her well-modulated English diction trilled off into gales of girlish laughter.

"Who told you?" barked Sissy, rage enveloping her to such an extent that she seized a handful of Sam's cashew nut-and-raisin health mix and, throwing caution to the winds, shoved it in her mouth. She would do penance for that later, she realized—she would have to make herself do one hundred extra sit-ups. The nuts contained more calories than she usually ate all day. Sissy prided herself on weighing ninety-eight pounds. Many people said it made her look younger. Most thought she looked like a cross between a sparrow and a hawk.

"Johnny told me, darling," said Daphne, complacently munching a Godiva chocolate at her end of the telephone. She had no weight worries. Red-haired, zaftig, and at sixtyish still active in the sack. Two of her old suitors, Frank Tillie and Richard Hurrel, still were regular nocturnal visitors to her house. She was a lady at peace with herself. Her son Johnny filled her in on all the town's gossip, some of which he got directly from his agent father, Daphne's ex-husband, Jasper Swanson. "Can you *believe* it, darling?"

Sissy ground her teeth and stuffed some more health mix in her mouth. "Why her?" she sniffed. "She's not an actress. She's just a saloon singer and she's British—why would Abby want her?"

"Certainly not to screw her." Daphne laughed. "But even you must admit she's quite attractive, darling."

"Abby told me he was maybe going to test Bisset, Candy Bergen, Emerald, and maybe Sabrina Jones—what else have you heard? Who else?"

"Well," said Daphne, lowering her voice and her body into her imported downy-soft eiderdown comforter from Ireland, and dipping again into the Godiva chocolate box, "Johnny told me that Rosalinde Lamaze is *very* interested in testing."

"That Mexican trash basket," sneered Sissy. "She would be useless—hopeless. She has no class at all. What does Abby say? Have you talked to him yet?"

Daphne's mornings were always spent on the phone, where she became au courant with every piece of news, gossip and scandal from L.A., New York and London. Truly the eyes, ears and mouth of Hollywood, she was thinking of turning her expertise into something lucrative. She would, of course, continue to impart this information free to her friends, but she was considering an offer to write a gossip column in a trade paper.

"Of *course* I did. But, darling, his lips are sealed tighter than Tut's tomb. Other than Jackie, Candy, Emerald and Sabrina, he will *not* tell me who else is testing."

"Well, they've already announced *them* in the trades, so that's no news. I thought Abby told you *everything,* Daphne," Sissy said accusingly.

"He does—but, darling—" she lowered her voice—"he says he needs a star name for Miranda, so he wants the press to get really hot on this. He talks to Liz Smith and Suzy every day, darling. I'll put in a good word for you, poppet. I promise. I'll remind him you've got two Oscars." She giggled.

Sissy replaced the receiver and stared stonily at her husband, who emerged smiling and wet from the pool. He laughingly ruffled her hair, which irritated her. "You'll do anything to get that part, won't you, honey?" he joked.

"Anything," said Sissy grimly, "absolutely anything, Sam. I'd even fuck you for it." They both laughed hollowly.

The amazing thing about Sissy was that, like Rosalinde Lamaze, when she put her mind to something—really went 100 percent for it—she usually got what she wanted. She had wanted Sam all those years ago, and she had got him, even though he had seldom shared her bed even in the early days. She had wanted fame and success, and she had achieved those too.

Now the role of Miranda was her top priority and she would pull out all stops to get it.

7

Sabrina Jones lay on the beach and looked at the camera with an enchanting smile. The camera loved her. Everyone loved Sabrina.

She was America's newest golden girl. And golden she was. She had been renamed Sabrina by a shrewd network executive who had adored Audrey Hepburn in *Sabrina*. When she had walked into his office three years ago, she was immediately given one of the three leads in a new cops-and-robbers TV series. She didn't even have to test. Her five-foot-eight, one-hundred-ten-pound body was honey-tanned and flawless. Her tawny blond hair, the envy of every actress in Hollywood, was thick, shoulder-length, and fell into natural waves and curls without the necessity of hot rollers. She was clad in a golden mesh evening gown, which skimmed her sensational body. As she lay on the sand gazing into the camera lens the photographer shook his head in awe. There hadn't been anyone this gorgeous in town since Ava Gardner had hit it. She was sheer perfection. Those eyes! Those legs! Those breasts!

In "Danger—Girls Working," Sabrina zoomed to immediate TV superstardom. Instead of asking, as most overnight TV successes do, for more money and more perks, she had been perfectly content to stay in the series with the other two girls, accepting the reasonable increases in salary her eager bosses bestowed upon her. She was never demanding, never difficult. She loved the series, loved the crew, adored Patty and Sue Ellen, her co-stars, and had a wonderful life. She even liked giving interviews and posing for stills—a press agent's delight.

Sabrina was that rare creature, a truly happy actress, happy with her life, happy with her career, full of joie de vivre and love. A secure and loving family had given her a solid foundation for life, but at twenty-three there was one thing that had eluded her thus far—megastardom. Well, testing for "Saga" could change all that, now that her series had finished.

She turned and gave the photographer her most seductive gaze. He gulped again, clicked and immortalized her for her fiftieth magazine cover.

Sue Jacobs, her agent, was waiting for the photo session to end. "Get yourself dressed and then let's go someplace quiet for a drink," Sue said, brushing past the crewmen who were still ogling Sabrina. "We've got lots to talk about."

"How about the Polo Lounge?" Sabrina said. "I just love the Polo Lounge."

Clad in a raw silk Brioni jacket, a black silk shirt and black pants, Luis strolled into the Polo Lounge and stopped dead in his tracks as he came face to face with the most beautiful girl he had ever seen in his life.

Long, blond hair, perfect golden skin, sweet innocence in her eyes, she was in deep conversation with an older woman. Luis didn't even pause. He made straight for their table.

"*Señorita,*" he said, waving away the waiter, "allow me to introduce myself. Luis Mendoza, at your service, *señorita.* You are simply the most beautiful woman I have ever seen in my life. I am stunned by your beauty. Would you share a bottle of Dom Perignon with me, *señorita*—please?"

It was not an original approach; he had used it before, but due to his magnetic looks he was seldom turned down. Few women could resist being called the most beautiful woman in the world. Sabrina Jones was no exception.

"It would be my pleasure." She smiled at him invitingly, to the annoyance of Sue, who was in the middle of trying to convince Sabrina to take a three-picture deal at Universal instead of testing for "Saga."

Half an hour later, Sue toddled home muttering, "Cock, cock, that's all they think about today." She had realized after observing the way they gazed at each other that the force of their mutual attraction was too strong to fight. She was right.

The next day Luis arrived on the set exhausted. He felt as if he had already put in a full day's work. The crew bustled around him, setting up the lights and equipment for his big love scene with Ms. Sissy Sharp. His Latin temperament was tickled by the "Ms." that Sissy insisted upon. Who was she but some over-the-hill hag, obviously so ashamed of her femininity that she couldn't be called Mrs. or Miss. "Ms." indeed. A smile crossed his handsome face as he thought of last night and Sabrina. Sabrina. What a name. What a dame. He felt his balls tighten at the thought of her. Sabrina Jones, *the* female sex symbol of the

eighties. So gorgeous, so sexy, so young—every man's sublimated desire.

But not his—oh, no, indeed. No sublimated desire existed for
Luis Mendoza. Sabrina was his—she belonged to him now. His
Latin pride swelled at the thought of her firm tanned body close
to his. They had made love for hours, their physical attraction
for each other so mutual and strong that sex became ecstasy.
Experience had taught him what turned a woman on, but with
Sabrina lovemaking was so natural, so free, so *loving,* he didn't
need any tricks. Maybe he thought he was truly in love for the
first time in his life. Luis woke from his daydream with a smile
as the assistant director called him to rehearse. Sissy was waiting. She looked chic. Hard and chic. Probably women all over
America would copy what she was wearing in this scene. She
was a clotheshorse and about as fuckable as—Luis sought the
metaphor, then burst out laughing—a horse! That was what she
looked like. A racehorse in drag.

Sissy frowned at him. She was a total professional, and she
hadn't been in this business since she was sixteen years old without knowing it inside and out. She loathed Luis. Detested everything about him. Certainly he was handsome, and not a bad
actor, but she disliked foreigners in general. That included Jews,
Germans, French and Italians. About the only non-Americans
she tolerated were the British, but there were so many of them
around now, it would be like not accepting smog. They were
there, like it or not.

She sighed and tried to smile at Luis, who strolled over cock-
ily as the director called for a rehearsal. With thoughts of testing
for "Saga" whirling around in her mind, she had difficulty remembering her lines.

"Stop it, Sissy," she said to herself sternly. "You are a star—a
professional. Behave like one."

She *had* to have that goddamn part. Had to!

89

8

"*T*he search is on!" blazed the front page of the *American Informer.* "Biggest talent hunt since *Gone With the Wind,*" screamed *USA Today.* "Who will play Miranda?" demanded *Time,* which had photographs of Sabrina Jones, Jacqueline Bisset, Emerald Barrymore, Raquel Welch, Chloe Carriere and Rosalinde Lamaze splashed across its "People" section.

Sissy was having another one of her turns. Screams of pent-up rage, long-suppressed feelings of self-doubt, were released in a frenzy of hysterics. She lay on her velvet coverlet with the three heraldic S's intertwined in elaborate Gallic gold embroidery in the middle and sobbed her heart out. Not, thought her unsympathetic maid, Bonita, that she had a heart at all, nasty bitch.

Bonita bustled about dispensing Kleenex, aspirin, vodka and a stream of comforting Spanish words, while her mistress thrashed about on the coverlet, her big black mascara tears falling onto the lavender velvet.

Sam, downstairs in the study, listened with a mixture of concern and indifference. Concern, because he knew what playing Miranda could do for her career, which was definitely on a downward spiral in spite of the many movies-of-the-week she was offered by the networks, and this cheapie potboiler she was making with Luis Mendoza. Indifference, because he was finally becoming fed up with her constant hysterical, demanding and selfish outbursts.

Was she going through early menopause perhaps? he wondered, clicking a channel on his remote-control TV. She had certainly looked like hell recently—thin as a rail, dark as a prune, and with skin of the same consistency. He stopped his clicker at Channel 13 and admired the roguish looks and physique of the young Rod Dimbleby in a syndicated rerun of an old series. He certainly had what it takes in every department. Even this five-year-old rerun showed the twenty-four-year-old fledgling actor's promise. He was definitely gorgeous and charismatic. Sam felt a twinge of desire, remembering their passionate encounter in his trailer on the lot a few days before.

Sure, he realized that Rod was only doing it as a favor given for a favor gained. He wanted the role of Sam's second son in "Saga" and would at this moment turn every trick in the book he could.

Sam was aware that he could hardly enthrall for long a young man of Rod's obvious heterosexuality and sex appeal—nevertheless, he was interested enough to tell "Saga's" casting director, Dale Zimmerman, that Rod was right for the second son.

"Saaam!" screamed Sissy from her boudoir, arousing him from his reverie. "Come here, *Saam!*" Her voice rose to a crescendo of despair. Sighing, he clicked off the TV and loped into

his wife's purple sanctuary. She was sprawled in her mauve negligeé across the bed gazing with horrified fascination at the six photographs in the magazine.

"Look," she shrieked, her frizzed blond bouffant hair standing on end around her tear-bloated face. "Spic *bitch,* how could she ever be considered for *my* part?" She hurled the magazine to the floor and pressed the number 5 button of her automatic dial phone.

"Hello," said the clipped voice of Daphne Swanson.

"Did you see *Time?*" hissed Sissy. "Did you *see* it? I can't believe that spic slut is *actually testing!* Is it true? Tell me it's a lie, Daphne, for God's sake."

"I'm sorry, darling," breathed Daphne, and in spite of her close friendship with Sissy rather enjoying her misery. "It *is* true. I don't know what she must have done to Abby—but I spoke to him ten minutes ago to confirm it for my new column. It's true, darling. She's testing. I'm *so* sorry."

She smiled in spite of herself. As a former actress, she sympathized with the grueling in-fighting that one had to be involved in to crawl up the ladder of fame and success. Such miserable bedfellows really. She was delighted she'd given it all up. None of the Swansons were actors anymore, but they were all definitely Hollywood's in crowd.

Daphne and Jasper Swanson had been stars of the British silver screen following World War Two. When this electric twosome was imported to the USA in the late 1940s, Daphne, redheaded and reckless, launched herself into a series of sizzling affairs, in some part to emulate a notorious raven-haired English duchess whom she greatly admired.

Among those with whom she had cuckolded the hapless, handsome Jasper were: Richard Hurrel, the prominent attorney, of whom it was said he bedded only major stars or the wives of close friends; Lawrence Huntington, the celebrated Scottish Shakespearean actor, who on arriving in Hollywood proceeded

to cut a sexual swath through the ranks of the young and beautiful, the like of which had not been seen since the heyday of Errol
Flynn; and Frank Tillie, the witty, peripatetic producer of radio
soap operas. It was to Daphne's great credit that thirty years
later two of the men were still her lovers.

Jasper Swanson's smoldering sensuality fired the lusts of a
million Yankee virgins, and his CinemaScope career was off and
running. Off and running in another direction flew the dainty
Daphne. Frank, Lawrence, Richard and occasionally—very occasionally—Jasper shared the delights of her connubial bed until
eventually (or was it by design?) she became pregnant and a son,
Johnny, entered the world on a warm Christmas day in 1952,
screaming his lungs out. Nearby, a doting father and three
more-than-doting godfathers stood. Hollywood money was on
Frank Tillie but no one actually knew for sure who Johnny's
father really was.

When the boy was fifteen his mother, Daphne, was playing
the part of the mistress of King Charles II in a boisterous Resto-
ration comedy at MGM. It would be her last American film,
even though at forty-five she was still lusty, red-haired, sexy and
delectable, with a rapier wit to augment her charms. But this
was 1967 and full blown forty-five-year-olds had not yet come
into vogue. Johnny, however, thought otherwise, deflowered one
dusty sunlit lunch hour on the Metro backlot by his mother's
stand-in, Cathleen. An equally lusty, if not so tasty, forty-five-
year-old, Cathleen taught him the infinite pleasures of the flesh,
taught him how to please a woman as only an older woman was
bold enough to demonstrate. How to kiss, to fondle—to caress.
Cathleen was a fine teacher and Johnny an excellent
pupil. He continued these fascinating studies, unbeknownst to
his mother, for the remainder of his school holidays. He dallied
with Cathleen, who with a true generosity of spirit introduced
him to the likes of Deirdre, thirty-six, Maureen, thirty-nine, and
Kate, forty-one. Lovely ladies all, and more than willing to play

sexual coach to this precocious, erotic fifteen-year-old lad already equipped with the endowments of a full-grown man.

So Johnny had been well spoiled by these ladies, and when he came to manhood, sex was only exciting for him with mature women. Many a budding starlet and bright-eyed secretary had batted their eyelashes at handsome Johnny, but to no avail. With girls under thirty he couldn't even be *bothered* to get it up.

Daphne didn't exactly disapprove. Johnny dutifully came to dinner three times a week at her home, either before or after his current dalliance, and so there was, thank God, fat chance of her becoming —*quel horreur*— a grandmother, even though she was over sixty.

Daphne turned and smiled at Richard Hurrel, lying like a beached whale on her Irish linen and lace pillowcases. He was panting. A night with Daphne usually left him wondering if his heart would last through the next day. Even after thirty years of intermittent fornication, she was still the hottest number he'd ever had, and he'd certainly had a few, and still had, even at the age of sixty-three.

Her tumbling red curls—out of a bottle or not, he neither knew nor cared—creamy Irish skin, never abused by the California sun because, as she said, "I refuse to look like a crocodile" and abundant Rubenesque curves, coupled with a zest for life unsurpassed by many a third her age, made Daphne quite a woman. A constant parade of faithful lovers who kept coming back for more proved it.

Richard was glad of the phone break. She had been about to make a morning onslaught on him, and he knew his heart couldn't take it this time. He bounded out of bed with as much agility as a man his age could muster and, watched appreciatively by Daphne out of the corner of her eye, staggered into her marble bathroom.

"Darling," Daphne hissed into the phone, "I know the truth. I know why Lamaze is testing, but it *must* be between us."

"Why? How? What did she do—*fuck* the old fart? You know that's impossible, Daphne. If it wasn't, I would have tried."

"I can't talk now," said Daphne as Richard came into the room shaving himself with the portable shaver he always kept in his briefcase. "Let's meet for lunch—are you free?"

"Yes, of course, yes," said Sissy, mentally canceling her lunchtime exercise session.

"One o'clock, Ma Maison—I'll book."

Sissy slammed down the receiver and burst into tears. "I'm the only actress in town who's not been announced to test," she wailed to Sam. "It's so humiliating...I could kill myself," she sobbed as she rocked in his capable homosexual arms while he whispered comforting brotherly words in her ear.

"You'll get your test, darling. I promise you. I've spoken to Abby, I know you'll get it, as soon as the network approves."

"But suppose they *don't*," sobbed Sissy. "Then I'm truly *ruined*."

Calvin's heart pumped fit to burst. She had *smiled* at him! Emerald Barrymore had actually smiled.

She looked past the diehard fans and the rest of the eager paparazzi pressing in on her in the parking lot of Ma Maison and smiled at *him*. He was sure of it!

When Emerald had emerged from Ma Maison, clutching the arm of that old Italian actor Vittorio somebody, Calvin's breath had caught in his throat. His hands trembled so violently that he had difficulty in adjusting the focus on his camera. She was so sexy, so beautiful, so lushly undulating, so free. He almost swooned with excitement when she turned and when, for a fraction of a second, her emerald eyes made contact with his flat gray ones. Then the other photographers got in his way, pushing, shouting, yelling, *"Emerald, Emerald,* here, here, Emerald. Turn to me, *please,* Emerald! I love you, Emerald. Emerald, just one more! Please!" She had posed and preened for the appropriate amount of time, tossing her golden curls, enjoying the attention, then jumped quickly into her limo, a glimpse of perfect leg and golden ankle-strap shoe leaving an indelible memory on his mind.

Calvin thought about the first time he'd heard of Emerald. At sixteen he had a crush on a pretty blond girl called Jenny. Everyone at high school said that Jenny was the image of Emerald Barrymore, the big Hollywood movie star. Calvin had not been aware of Emerald up to then, as he was a staunch John Wayne—Randolph Scott fan. Calvin's awkward shyness had appealed to Jenny; after he plucked up the courage to ask her, she agreed to go out with him. On their first date they went to a movie to see her favorite star—Emerald Barrymore—in *The Princess and the Pauper.*

Emerald's beautiful Technicolor face appeared on the screen, and Calvin saw the resemblance immediately. He watched her voluptuous body, clad in seductive nineteenth-century underwear—white frilly bloomers, tightly corseted waist with blue rosebuds embroidered on the bodice—and felt his adolescent cock harden. As Emerald's magnificent powdered white breasts spilled out of her lacy camisole, close enough to touch, Calvin could contain himself no longer. His sweaty, trembling hand began to inch up Jenny's thigh. She pushed him away. He tried again, nature driving him. She pushed him away again. He became more aggressive. He had heard that Jenny let other guys do it. Why not him?

Finally Jenny had enough of his insistent groping. She got up. "Creep!" she hissed, as she left the theater.

Alone, sitting in the dark, he watched Emerald's vermilion lips fill the screen and felt his cock burst in his pants.

He started spending a great deal of time locked in his bedroom, his heart pounding, his palpitating cock in one hand, a photograph of Emerald from a magazine in the other.

His infatuation with the screen goddess grew, as did his collection of her photographs, which now almost covered all the walls of his room. Eventually he plucked up courage to write to her. Within a week the dutiful studio fan-mail department sent him a glossy eight-by-ten of Emerald wearing lace décolletage, her tumbling blond tresses beautifully backlit, the photo inscribed in green ink "To Calvin, affectionately, Emerald."

Calvin, unaware that her secretary wrote the inscriptions on Emerald's photos, was overcome. Three months later he sent in another request for a picture. This time it arrived in color—Emerald in a long green satin dress slit to the thigh, her blond hair shorn in a twenties bob, a cigarette dangling smokily from her carmine lips, eyes half-closed, sheathed in mystery. "To Calvin, with all my love, Emerald" was scribbled across one milky thigh.

Calvin was never the same again.

Calvin carefully tore the "People" section from *Time*—"Who will play Miranda?" screeched the heading—and analyzed the photographs of the six beautiful women.

Saga had been America's best-selling novel for months now, rivaling *Valley of the Dolls* in sales and popularity. Miranda was a peach of a part. It could not possibly go to any of those five sluts. To Calvin, all women except Emerald were sluts. A great role like Miranda should be—must be—was destined to be—played by the greatest of all actresses, Emerald Barrymore. *She* was the only woman who could play Miranda. Emerald Barrymore, superstar, his idol, his love. No one must get in her way.

He picked up the *Hollywood Reporter.*

"Who has the inside track to play the part of Miranda Hamilton in 'Saga'? *Tout* Hollywood is talking about Rosalinde Lamaze. This columnist believes she is the only actress right for the role," glowed Hank Grant.

Calvin placed the periodical carefully on top of his desk. He took out a fresh white pad, a new ballpoint pen, and wrote carefully at the top of the page: "Project Miranda." Number One: Eliminate negative factors."

He believed in planning. He was going to make sure Emerald got that role.

9

When Rosalinde wasn't working, she lay around her house all day wearing nothing but her ex-husband's pajama top and a torn, stained silk bathrobe. Both had seen better days, years, actually, but it was hard for Rosalinde to throw anything out. The bathrobe had adorned her lush body in *Latin Lover*, a film made in the golden Technicolor days of the late sixties when she was a big star—which she would be again when she got the part of Miranda.

Just the night before, she had been given a lecture about her image by her sister, Maria, who was very socially attuned—much more so than Rosalinde.

"Look at Sissy," Maria had commanded as the two women

sat on Maria's fern-filled patio watching "Entertainment To-night" and sipping margaritas.

Sissy appeared on the TV screen in the lobby of the Hilton on her way to a charity gala for the Princess Grace Foundation, attended by the cream of the Hollywood crop. The families of Sinatra, Stewart, Peck, Douglas and Moore were well represented. Sissy was a vision in black Balenciaga with the yellow diamond necklace from the estate of Merle Oberon clasped around her stringy neck. Sam was clasped to her left arm as she gushingly told the interviewer how thrilled she was to support this great cause.

"You should be there, it's good for your image," Maria nagged, but Rosalinde, eating taco chips and guacamole, laughed, "Why? I don't need that sort of thing. In fact I hate it."

No, Rosalinde thought, when she became Miranda, then she would start socializing again. Meanwhile, she lay on her un-made king-size bed amidst cushions stained with the residue of last night's makeup and littered with orange peel, trade papers and nail paraphernalia. She had vainly attempted to give herself a manicure, but had dumped that in favor of an intriguing movie that had just started on Channel Z. Curling up like a kitten, sucking an orange with gusto, Rosalinde was barely recognizable as the divine diva beloved throughout North and Latin America. The phone rang several times, but she ignored it. What was an answering service for?

Rosa, her maid and also an aunt once or twice removed, knocked respectfully on the door. "What do you want?" Rosa-linde snapped petulantly, her eyes pivoted to the planes of Mont-gomery Clift's profile as he clasped Elizabeth Taylor to his chest.

"*Por favor, señorita.*" In spite of Rosa's being distant family, Rosalinde insisted on monarchlike respect. Rosa was weighed down with an ivory tray, a gift from a Far Eastern admirer, on which reposed Rosalinde's brunch: *huevos rancheros* covered with hot sauce, half a dozen Oreo cookies and a diet Coke.

"What's the problem?" Rosalinde sighed, glued to the couple as the camera lovingly made an eighty-degree slow pan around their rapturous faces. "If only I could be photographed like that," she sighed, and then remembered that she just had been in the new photos she had had taken for Miranda.

"The service called," Rosa wheezed, thankfully depositing the heavy tray and catching her breath. "They say they have had several nasty calls."

"So what!" snapped Rosalinde. "I'm a star, not everyone can adore me." Rosalinde's eyes never moved from the television screen.

Rosa looked frightened. "But, *señorita,* the service say, they say thees man, he want to keel you." There, she'd said it. Her obligation to the fat cow was done. Eat your Oreos and *huevos rancheros, puta,* and gain another three pounds.

Rosalinde drank the Coke from the can, ignoring the wineglass Rosa was always instructed to bring. Her eyes left the screen long enough to feast upon the steaming plate of eggs.

"Who is he, this man?"

"The service, they don't know nothing. They only want to warn you. Maybe we should call the police. He sounds like a crazy man. He calls six or seven times."

Rosalinde shrugged again. "The usual crap. Don't worry." She turned back to Liz and Monty only to find Shelley Winters's young but already pudgy face filling the screen.

"But Miss Angelica, she away, and I go off tonight to see my gran'son. Are you sure you are fine alone here?" Not that she gave a damn, but she didn't want to get fired for lack of solicitousness.

"Yes, yes, yes." Impatiently Rosalinde spooned up her eggs. "Now go away, Rosa, and leave me alone. I want to *relax.* Can't I ever relax, damn it?"

Silently Rosa left, cursing the cow. What a pig. It was bad enough when she had two or three men a week and lay in bed half the day moaning and groaning like a bitch in heat; but now men were *out* and lovely little innocent Angelica was *in*—for how long, God knows. Now Rosalinde lay in bed longer and her moans were less frantic, more like the purring of a satisfied cat.

She knew what they did. Overcome with curiosity about the moans and screams of ecstasy, she had crept up the stairs one afternoon and applied a practiced eye to the keyhole. At first it was difficult to make out what was happening in the dim light; eventually she realized that the two women had stuck their faces into each other's most private parts and were licking and kissing each other with enthusiasm. No crevice seemed to be unexplored, and their bodies, shiny with sweat, bucked in multiple orgasms. This Rosa had only read about in the pages of Spanish *Cosmopolitan,* her mistress's favorite magazine, and she was deeply shocked and became quite faint, needing a large brandy before feeling fit enough to prepare dinner.

Her mistress was sex-mad, there was no doubt about that. A sex-mad slut. What the public saw in her Rosa could not fathom.

The following day, Rosalinde was over the moon. She'd done it! She was going to be tested! Along with five or six of the most important actresses in Hollywood. The photographs had worked. She was a genius, and so was the photographer.

She pranced around her bedroom in a paroxysm of joy as she planned the outfit in which she would lunch at Ma Maison. It was to be a celebration. A triumph of sheer cunning and audacity over established stars like Sissy Sharp, who, she knew through the grapevine, was not yet on the test list, yet desperately trying to be.

She considered the advantages of her gray silk Adolfo, very Washington working woman, against a new Saint Laurent burgundy bolero with cream silk blouse and skirt. Perhaps rhinestone buttons were a trifle much for Southern California at high noon, so she discarded both of them and decided to revert to type. It had made her millions, after all. She threw on a striped orange-and-white off-the-shoulder cotton peasant dress, several rows of chunky coral beads, and a wide-brimmed straw hat heavy with spring flowers.

In the hall she paused to tuck a celebratory white gardenia behind her ear, and with a gay "See you later, Rosa" to the maid, jumped into her red convertible and sped off down Benedict Canyon toward Melrose.

The man in the green Chevrolet followed her.

Ma Maison on a sunny Friday in early June was jumping. At the round table in the center of the patio dining area sat "The Boys." Although the cast of characters changed weekly, today most of the main protagonists were present. Richard Hurrel, having recovered from his heavy night of love with Daphne, looked dashing in a brown blazer and a brown-and-cream Cardin shirt with white collar and brown silk tie. It set off his snow-white hair and deep tan. He felt pretty good. Daphne usually had a rejuvenating effect on him—made him look and feel young again. Frank Tillie was regaling the group with hilarious stories of the latest antics of the gay male lead on one of his top seven soap opera series.

Johnny Swanson sat listening with admiration and amusement to the man who, some people surmised, could be his real father.

At the entrance, seated at a small table for two, sat Sabrina Jones and Luis Mendoza, who in a short time had fallen madly in love. They were truly a dazzling couple. Sabrina had a day off, as did Luis. She was ravishing as usual in a simple white cotton shirt and a khaki miniskirt that showed off her long, tanned legs to perfection. In her ears were tiny gold-and-diamond studs, a recent gift from Luis; around her waist she wore a thick tan leather belt with an elaborate enamel and gold buckle.

Luis wore cream linen pants and a dark blue silk shirt, open to his waist to reveal a smoothly muscled tanned chest. Several gold chains of various lengths and thicknesses, upon which dangled the talismans of superstition and virility beloved by Latin American men, glinted in the afternoon sunshine.

They were engrossed in each other—he swimming in the jade depths of her eyes, and she in the bottomless black of his.

"They seem *so* in love," sighed Lady Sarah Cranleigh, spearing the last of her asparagus, careless of the melted butter dripping onto her Victor Edelstein floral silk blouse.

"Bullshit," sneered Sissy, observing them from three tables away. "Take my word, Sarah, Luis Mendoza lives for one thing and one thing only—and that's himself." She reflected with faint nostalgia on their two-night stand during the location shooting of their movie. Brief it had been, but exciting. Luis was a thrilling lover and had been able to supply for an hour or two the sexual ecstasy she craved, but seldom received, from the post-adolescent, lackadaisical beach boys she usually sampled in bed.

But she had better things to discuss than the love life of Sabrina and Luis. She was irked that Daphne had brought along her undeniably amusing house guest, Lady Sarah. It was difficult to plot and plan with that overdressed lump of lard guzzling everything in sight. Lady Sarah had already devoured two rolls of French bread and four pieces of garlic toast with her asparagus hollandaise and was now deftly stealing croutons from Daphne's spinach salad.

Throwing pride and caution in the direction of La Cienega Boulevard, Sissy plunged in at the deep end. "How did she do it, Daphne?"

"Darling, I never would have believed that the trash basket could be so smart," said Daphne, spearing a crouton hastily, ahead of Lady Sarah's eager fork.

"Well, what? What did she do?" Sissy almost screamed, downing her vodka and Evian water and trying to remain calm.

"She went to Hana, spent thousands, poppet—absolute *thou-*

sands, having a series of photographs taken of herself as Miranda. Brilliant photos they were, too, of course. You know Hana's work, he's the absolute best. He actually made her look nineteen. I mean, he had to put a mohair blanket over the lens, but, my God, he *did* it."

"Brilliant," agreed Sissy through gritted teeth, cursing Rosalinde's cleverness. Why hadn't she thought of that? Come to think of it why didn't her fucking PR people think of it? Four grand a month plus expenses, and they couldn't even keep her name out of the fucking *National Enquirer.* She made a mental note to fire them and hire Rogers & Cowan.

"One photo was of her as a teenaged Miranda—she looked eighteen, I swear."

"Impossible," snapped Sissy.

"Not with Hana's lighting, duckie. He took other photos of her looking twenty-five, thirty-five, that was easy—because of course she is thirty-five." "Oh, really" sneered Sissy angrily, stuffing a large mouthful of garlic toast in her mouth. "She'll never see forty again and you know it, Daph." "Will you *listen?*" Daphne snapped. "Then forty-five, then fifty-five, and— listen to this—in the last one of the set she has been made up to look *eighty,* and that's what really sold Abby on the idea. He was so impressed with the presentation, he promised her agent, who just happens to be my ex-husband, darling, that he would definitely test her.

"And, petal—" Daphne fished in her capacious handbag and brought out an eight-by-ten envelope which she slid over to Sissy—"one of my sources managed to get hold of the photos. I thought you might be interested. Oh, but don't look at them *here,* dear."

Sissy snatched the brown manila envelope from her friend and stuffed it into her large Chanel bag. She glared at Daphne, who smiled blandly and looked around the restaurant, nodding at various acquaintances. Lady Sarah stared at Sissy with ill-disguised contempt. What a rude woman. In England she would simply not be invited anywhere.

As soon as she got home Sissy inspected the photographs. In spite of herself, she felt a grudging admiration for Rosalinde. She looked luminously young and fresh in the early photos, even if Hana had used his encyclopedia of camera tricks to make her so. And the brilliance of her attitude in the photos of Miranda at forty-five verged on sheer genius. It was a clever scheme, and there was no question in Sissy's mind that Rosalinde had leaped ahead in the Miranda Hamilton stakes.

It was so expertly simple, so obvious, so fucking clever, *goddamn* the bitch! Sissy knocked back another vodka. Bloody brilliant. It was, yes, brilliant, admit it. She, who had been in the business for twenty-seven years, should know how gullible people were. With enough chutzpah and assertiveness in this town, one could rule it easily. This round went to Rosalinde, but Sissy was not about to go down for the count just yet.

A life-sized nude of Sissy reclining on an eighteenth-century chaise à la Madame Récamier took pride of place above the gray suede couch in the combination gym and screening room.

As Sissy performed her morning workout to the music of Bob Dylan, she admired the soft angles and curves of this more than flattering picture of her painted fifteen years ago by a then unknown, but now much in demand, artist. The painting had the look to which Sissy aspired. Unfortunately, hard as she tried, the more she strove for the physical perfection of the portrait, the more it evaded her.

She was becoming dangerously anorexic-looking. Even her best friends were daring to criticize her. Her face, pulled taut from a recent trip to Rio and Dr. Pitanguy, was thin and gaunt, although there wasn't a line or wrinkle upon it. Somehow, instead of making her look more youthful, it seemed to age her. Sissy seemed not to notice. She clapped her hands with glee when she saw on her doctor's scale that her five-foot six-inch frame was down to ninety-seven pounds. She had to peer at the number with one of the thirty pairs of spectacles she left in every place where she could possibly need them.

"Perfect, perfect. Now I can wear the Grès for the test, and I won't look fat," she cried to no one in particular. She was testing for Miranda next week. Her husband had done it for her. The big pitch, and Abby had been unable to say no. Neither could the network. Sam was playing the male lead in "Saga." They could hardly not test his wife when he was so insistent. Of course she'd get the part. How could she not? After all, she was an Oscar-winning actress, star of some of the most successful films of the past fifteen years, and married to the leading man of the series. How could they not? The competition was negligible. She could beat them all, and she would—she had to!

Rosalinde Lamaze—no way. A trashy tramp, a lightweight, in spite of the amazing photographs. She was a workingman's wet dream—an aging sexpot. She couldn't be a serious contender. Emerald Barrymore? Certainly she was a legend in her own time, superstar, supercelebrity, but she was nowhere *near* the actress that Sissy was. She couldn't approach her for talent, and she was years older. Her applause and accolades had always been for her private life, which was far more interesting than the movies in which she had starred. That was what the public loved about her best—her men, her scandals, her suicide attempts. She was a tabloid celebrity, larger than life. She would overpower the rest of the cast. Surely the network was wise enough to see that?

The only fly in the ointment was that damned Chloe Carriere. She *was* a definite threat, no question about that. Sissy grudgingly had to admit that she was ideal for the role. She had the right look—that mixture of innocence and evil that everyone who discussed the part felt the actress who played it had to suggest. And she was a new face, even though she was forty—and everyone *loved* a new face. Sam tried to assuage Sissy's fears by saying that even if the network and Abby insisted on Chloe, *he* would then insist on Sissy playing ex-wife number one; he had made the network agree to that at least.

But Sissy knew that Sirope was not the plum part. Ex-wife number one was a dullard. A flaccid Goody Two-shoes role. It was Miranda Hamilton, wife number two, she wanted to play. Oh, how she wanted that role! The bitch. The wicked one. The manipulator, seductress, traitress, cunning, cool, yet with a heart of gold that she knew was buried in the pages of the "Saga" script. She could almost taste the character. Perhaps if she lost another pound?

It was the day of Abby and Maud Arafat's intimate dinner for all the contenders, and they were all rather concerned about it.

What to wear? What to wear? Chloe wondered what could she don that would knock 'em dead tonight?

Tonight, the producers—Abby and Gertrude—would see all their main contenders for the role together in one room. Comparisons could be odious, Chloe knew. Although she usually had no difficulty in choosing her outfits, tonight she was in a lather of indecisiveness. She had shopped feverishly for two days, systematically haunting Rodeo Drive and Sunset Boulevard boutiques. What facet of Miranda should she best exploit for this party?

The bitch? In that case, her high-necked black satin Valentino gown with a lace jacket sparkling with black-beaded jet bows and matching jet-and-crystal earrings should be the one.

The seductress? Ungaro's red chiffon, cut to the clavicle in front and to the tenth vertebra at the back. Clouds of red chiffon fanned seductively out from her knees to the floor, and matching red satin sandals with heels so high she could barely walk completed the ensemble. Sexy—yes—maybe too much so.

But perhaps she should just be herself, Chloe Carriere. Yes, why not? She would be just Chloe tonight. She would wear an old favorite, a gown she had worn several times before and felt at ease in. Cream silk jersey, cut on the bias, draped Grecian style over one tanned shoulder, leaving the other bare. She selected a forties faux diamond clip to fasten the draped fabric at her waist and small Bulgari diamond studs as her only jewelry. She would carry a cream enamel-and-rhinestone-studded Judith Leiber minaudière in the shape of a rabbit in her hand—a present from Josh on her last birthday, and a good luck mascot to boot. Luck! She needed it tonight.

Birthdays! She shuddered as she sat at her dressing table and swiftly applied myriad cosmetics to her face. She would be forty years old this year. Forty!!! It seemed so incredibly ancient. She couldn't believe her life had flown by so fast, her youth passed so soon. All those years so swiftly gone.

"It's not over yet, kid—not by a long shot," she admonished herself as she applied Dior lip gloss with a practiced hand. "There's life in the old girl yet." She brushed out her thick curly hair, sweeping it to one side with a tortoiseshell comb. Slipping cream grosgrain sandals, little more than tiny straps of ribbon, onto her silk-clad feet, she surveyed herself from every angle with a critically objective eye. In her three-way mirror she looked more than beautiful. She looked fabulous. Radiant. Everything was perfect tonight, except one thing was missing. Her man.

Chloe consulted her diamond Boucheron watch. He was late. Josh was recording again. He'd warned her that he might be late. The mixing of his new album was at the critical stage. Since it was already late for delivery, he *had* to get the last track finished, and he wanted it to be perfect. It was vital because this album was critical to his waning career. It had to be at least a minor hit, or, Josh knew, this time his career would be over. At his age, it *was* over as far as most of the kids who bought

109

albums were concerned anyway. They simply didn't care about someone old enough to be their father strutting his stuff on TV, video or stage. Offers for Josh to tread the boards in New York or London were thin on the ground, too. He was slipping fast, careerwise, and no one was more aware of it than he and Chloe.

The irony was that it had taken him years, decades, to become a star. The climb up had been much more difficult than the slide down. It crossed Chloe's mind that maybe, just maybe, he might be playing around again, but she dismissed the thought quickly. She had been absolutely final about what steps she would take if he started screwing underage bimbos again. No ifs, no buts, no maybes—she would divorce him instantly.

Forget. Forget all those times she had caught him. He had promised, hadn't he? Said that now that he was over forty he thought it undignified to pull young "grumble." Told Chloe he really cared, wanted the marriage to work. He'd promised, hadn't he? The limo was waiting. He *was* mixing his tracks. It was party time. She sprayed herself with *Bal à Versailles* and left for Abby and Maud's party in an optimistic mood and a cloud of fragrance.

It definitely was one of Tinsel Town's more up-market parties, Chloe realized, as the polite young man with "Chuck's Parking" embroidered on his red jacket opened the car door for her and she glimpsed the front hall of the Arafat mansion awash with true Old World Hollywood glamour.

No photographers, either unofficial or official, were allowed inside or outside the house. This was a sure sign of social superiority. Not even George Christy from the *Hollywood Reporter* had been invited. The more important the party, the less press. It was the golden rule of Hollywood. Premieres, publicity parties, launches, wrap parties, the more press at those the merrier, but on this occasion the press was conspicuous by its absence.

The entrance hall was vast. Polished gray marble terrazzo imported from Montecatini was barely visible beneath the hems of the designer gowns of the women and the impeccably creased black trousers of the men. The seventy-five distinguished guests who sipped Cristal champagne or Perrier water ignored the lacquered eggshell walls on which hung more than fifteen million dollars' worth of paintings. They had seen it before; industry talk was far more entrancing.

An eclectic group of paintings ranging from Renoir to Fischl was displayed to perfection on walls which had been sanded a dozen times and then had seven coats of lacquer applied to create a flawless matte finish. The guests also ignored the black onyx Corinthian columns placed at four-foot intervals throughout the hallway on top of which reposed priceless Roman marble busts from the fifth and sixth centuries.

Chloe, however, could not quite ignore any of it. She found it fascinating. She had never seen such opulent grandeur. She and Josh, although they had been on the Hollywood scene for years, had not been invited to this house before. Abby and Maud Arafat believed in putting their money where their friends could see it. Their home was clearly meant to look like that of a multimillionaire megaproducer. And see it they certainly could. Chloe gasped at the gorgeousness of the decor, the obvious value and beauty of the art. She accepted a glass of champagne from one of thirty liveried servants and strolled into the living room. The room was at least seventy-five feet long, dominated by a Picasso that was unfamiliar to Chloe. It was obviously from his blue period and portrayed two of his great sterile-looking athletes on the beach. The windows were over fifteen feet high, elaborately draped in cobalt blue brocade, heavy with fringe and tassels. The doors to the garden were open, and Chloe wandered onto the terrace. There, on a lawn so thick and green it resembled cut velvet, stood eight of the most exquisite and valuable Henry Moore sculptures in the world. Chloe was amazed that they should be placed so casually on the lawn.

Some of the guests were chatting on the lawn; it was a balmy California night with a light breeze blowing from the coast. Chloe thought about the letter she would write to Annabel describing the scene. She wrote to her at least once a week, describing with care interesting events that had happened, and places she had visited. In return she received little notes, for which she was grateful. Annabel, her baby. As usual, as soon as she started to think about her daughter, Chloe became sad. She took a gulp of champagne. "Stop it, Chlo," she said to herself. "This is business. Concentrate on it. Sparkle, girl—sparkle." So who was there? She couldn't help noticing that all the main contenders for Miranda were there, in the full flower of their elaborate toilettes.

Sissy Sharp had opted for red. Reagan Red, she trilled to all who were aware of the friendship, now, alas, long lapsed, that had existed between Nancy and Ronald and Sissy and Sam when Ronnie was president of the Screen Actors Guild, and Sam one of its officers. Sissy exaggerated the depth of the friendship, dropping the Reagan name with unerring consistency. She and Sam had, in fact, recently returned from a state dinner for the President of Yugoslavia, not one of Washington's top affairs, but newsworthy enough for a one-liner in *USA Today*. She had regaled everyone who would listen with amusing anecdotes about the doings of Nancy, and the funny sayings of "Dutch."

Rosalinde Lamaze, escorted by a languid stud, wore gold lamé from Lina Lee. Rosalinde looked satisfied, the stud, tired.

Rosalinde and Chloe exchanged glances, nodding brief hellos. Chloe thought the other woman's outfit looked cheap, but that Rosalinde herself was a remarkably attractive woman who certainly did not look her age. With her luxuriant dark hair caught at the side with a gardenia, and her vivacious smile, Rosalinde looked sexily gorgeous and no more than thirty.

There was a flurry of excitement when Emerald Barrymore

arrived. She was Hollywood's child. A major star since age three, she still managed to create excitement wherever she went. Not a decent movie under her belt in ten years, but her aura of stardom glowed undiminished.

No one loved a star more than those who lived and worked in Hollywood, and Emerald was soon surrounded by sycophants and worshippers, none of whom, however, was prepared to offer her a decent job, save for a guest stint on an episodic TV show or perhaps a supporting role in a miniseries.

She had arrived late, as usual, being unable to decide which one of her five fabulous necklaces to wear. Her jewelry was legendary, more so because people thought she had never bought a single piece of it herself. This was actually not true. She had bought most of it herself, jewelry was a passion with her—but she wanted the public to think she was always being showered with gifts by her many lovers, and her press agent worked hard on this image.

She was with her latest husband, Solomon Davidson, a New York suit manufacturer, out of his league but determined not to show it. She sported a cabochon emerald the size of a golf ball on her engagement finger and was wearing an ankle-length sable coat—even wholesale, as Solomon had managed to buy it, the $100,000 price tag was steep. The coat was a mite too long for Emerald's five feet two, but for what she lacked in stature she made up for in hair. Back-combed to within an inch of its life, her fine blond hair stuck out in dangerous punk-style spikes. She was sheathed in a silver Norell and looked, Chloe had to admit, glorious—a true superstar.

The two contenders who everyone agreed would turn Miranda down even if they were offered the role chatted amicably. Jacqueline Bisset and Meryl Streep were far too involved with the cinema to sacrifice their careers for a part in a TV soap opera. The general consensus was that Abby and his partner Gertrude Greenbloom, as co-owners of a studio and the creators of so many great films, were demeaning themselves by turning to TV. Snobbery was still rife about the relatively young medium—so far, in 1982, very few major stars had done a series. Those who did were looked down upon by their peers. Chloe didn't care. She was not a snob—TV or movies, it didn't matter. She needed a good job—and this was the one she wanted.

A few pretty young girls with names like Sharon, Tracey and Cindy wandered around with the fixed desperate smiles of those who feel they're out of place, but realize it's good for their careers to be there. They were starlets under contract to MCPC, outfitted in beaded dresses other stars had worn in last year's movies.

The old guard clung together, as usual: Edie and Lew Wasserman, Mary and Irving Lazar, Janet and Freddie de Cordova, and Billy and Audrey Wilder. How many parties had they attended throughout the decades? How many studio heads, how many up-and-coming actors, how many hot young directors had they seen come and seen go? Still they always seemed to enjoy themselves, and the fact that they were there tonight made it an "A" party.

Chloe felt confident, even in her two-year-old Bruce Oldfield. "Better under than over, m'dear," Lady Sarah had always told her. Lady Sarah, of course, had not listened to her own advice to underdress, and was festooned with ropes of pearls the size of garbanzos, mauve organza flounces and taffeta bows bouncing in her red curls as she chatted with Sissy. Chloe nodded to Sissy, who gave her an icy smile. They had never been friends, had little in common.

As the dinner hour approached, Chloe started to become nervous. Josh had promised to be with her tonight. She needed his moral support. It was nerve-racking enough to be at a huge formal Hollywood banquet, not to mention attending it alone. She nervously sipped her champagne, then put it down, realizing she was getting slightly high. She looked at her watch again. Ten to nine. Dinner was bound to be announced any minute. She was supposed to be seated at a table with Josh. It would be embarrassing if he didn't come. She crossed her fingers, willing him to arrive.

Another contender for Miranda, but in everyone's opinion a rank outsider because of her youth, lurked uncomfortably on the terrace, wishing she could go home.

"It's ridiculous," said Sabrina Jones to Johnny Swanson, her press agent. "I *know* I'll never get this part. I'm too young."

Johnny agreed. Twenty-three was much too young to play such a conniving woman of the world. "I'm sure Abby wants you to play one of the daughters. He knows a great hype and since you're so hot, your name means more interest in the columns." "Mmm," Sabrina said. She was miserable. She missed Luis, but Johnny had told her she couldn't bring him here. Too much emphasis on sex—not enough on career.

Chloe moved over to Sabrina and Johnny. The young man was friendly; he was witty and attractive, and, strangely, he seemed to want to pay more attention to Chloe than to his beautiful young client. Chloe enjoyed talking to him—he made her laugh in spite of her nervousness.

Johnny Swanson liked Chloe, had, in fact, fancied her for some time. She appeared to be in a daze, he thought. Was it because Josh wasn't with her? He felt sorry for her, but he admired how she was handling it. Lady Sarah approached and asked him to dance, her tongue too close to his ear for comfort. He disengaged himself in distaste. God, what a mass of amorphic flesh and frills! She didn't attract him in the slightest, even though she was the required age. "No, my little honeybunch," he said firmly. "Dance with the stallion in yonder corner who is giving you the once-over. My shoes aren't made to shuffle tonight, sugar." Lady Sarah raised penciled auburn eyebrows. "Honeybunch" indeed! She looked at the stallion, Alex. Mm, not bad, not bad at all.

Johnny moved away to continue studying Chloe. She was not easily had—the grapevine knew that. The boys lunching weekly at Ma Maison knew all about the sexual proclivities and preferences of "The Available 400," as they were called. Exchanging this information gave them many a clue as to what each lady preferred in bed. Johnny knew that Chloe's marriage had held up pretty well, but tonight it looked to be on its last legs. She was here alone. None of the boys had heard of her ever having an affair. A faithful wife was a rare bird in Hollywood. Particularly one who looked as good as Chloe. A one-man woman, faithful and around forty—just his type! She was leaning at the bar now, temporarily alone, sipping champagne, a frown between those ravishing turquoise eyes. She looked sad. Her facade was starting to crack.

"Champagne gives you nightmares," he cracked. "Hot milk's better for you. But then I suppose it depends on what you're doing in bed."

Chloe smiled faintly at his boyish charm, tried to banter back. "I hate hot milk," she said. "Reminds me of my childhood."

Before Johnny could continue his verbal foreplay the butler announced that dinner was served. The guests started to drift in from the marble hall, the manicured velvet lawn, and the Louis Fifteenth drawing room, and into the ballroom. The ceiling of the ballroom looked as if it had been painted by Michelangelo. Angels flew in formation against an azure sky with scudding white clouds. On the walls were eighteenth-century sconces in which beeswax candles burned. There was no electric light; only the hundreds of candles on the walls and on the ten tables which were set up symmetrically around the ballroom. In the center of each table reposed a Lalique bowl in which white roses, calla lilies and tiny fairy lights had been artfully arranged by Milton Williams. Liveried footmen helped the guests to find their tables.

Just as Chloe was in despair about Josh, he appeared at her side. "Hi, babe," he whispered, squeezing her arm and brushing his soft lips against her cheek. She smelled the faint aroma of tequila, and also the stronger smell of dope. "I didn't let you down, kid. I'm here—good old reliable."

"Darling, I'm so glad you came. I was getting worried." She smiled, touching the face she cared for so much.

"You knew I wouldn't let you down, Chloe." He wavered fractionally, and she knew he was high on something. His words were almost imperceptibly slurred. No one but Chloe would know he had been drinking or drugging; he was an expert at covering up, a true pro.

She did not reproach him. He had come to the party after all. For her. Don't make waves, Chloe, her inner voice said. He's here. He does love you. Be thankful.

The guests looked surreptitiously at their watches. It was ten-thirty. At ten forty-five it would be considered correct to split. Two and a half to three hours was the usual length of time guests stayed at a Hollywood party. Then they wanted to go home—watch Carson or a video, read a script, call a broad or smoke a joint. Few, other than those actors who arose at six to film, actually went to sleep at eleven, but it was such a perfect excuse to leave. There were so many parties—to stay longer than three hours would be a waste of time. Silver fork tapped against crystal goblet, and Abby had the guests' attention.

"Tonight is an important occasion for MCPC pictures," said Abby, reveling in the crowd's fickle attention focused on him.

"Our new show, 'The Great Conspirators,' has been very successful on network." Knowing looks were exchanged. A flop, everyone *knew* it was a flop, even at nine o'clock on Tuesday night when its only rivals were miserable sitcoms with appalling ratings. "The Great Conspirators" was the most dismal of failures, but Abby, a smart mover and shaker, was on to his next announcement, glossing over failure with practiced skill.

"I'm thrilled you're all here tonight, my dear friends, partners and co-workers." His eyes swept the room, meeting bland smiles, slight attention and fidgets.

"Get on with it, luv," muttered Lady Sarah, plump beringed hands tracing circles on the thighs of the hot young man she had pulled at the bus stop on Santa Monica Boulevard that morning.

"As you all know, TV is here to stay, and we're staying with it." Since the majority of his guests were motion-picture people, reaction was minimal. They still couldn't take television seriously. It was a medium for selling soap—for fading stars, and up-and-coming performers.

"We—" he nodded his head to his partner, Gertrude, who smiled encouragingly—"have decided to make *the* most exciting prime time long form series of the 1982 season. Of the next ten seasons, in fact, so successful do we think it will be!

"We have bought the book *Saga,* which as you know is the best-seller to end all best-sellers and we will start shooting the four-hour miniseries in three months, to be followed immediately by the series." He paused triumphantly to sparse applause. The guests were looking at their watches. "We are still in the process of casting, but we have some very exciting announcements to make. The part of Steve Hamilton, the Patriarch—a man of the people, a man of substance, integrity and true grit— will be played by America's favorite hero, Sam Sharp." Applause, applause. Sam was popular. Sam stood and made a self-deprecating bow, the kind that had endeared him to the American public for a quarter of a century. Sissy smiled a razor smile tinged with wifely pride.

"For the role of Miranda, the Scarlett O'Hara of the 1980s, we have narrowed our choice down to these five fabulous ladies. Please stand up, Miss Sabrina Jones." Weak applause. No one knew her here in spite of her moderately successful series. They would when her college movie was released. So far she was just hype. Sabrina looked flushed and embarrassed. Johnny gave her hand a comforting squeeze, wishing he could fancy her, but she was far too young.

"Miss Chloe Carriere!" Lukewarm applause. As Chloe took her bow in front of Hollywood's finest, she realized that she was not accepted by them at all. Certainly they would see her show in Las Vegas if they happened to be there. But she was of no real interest to them. She was just a singer. An English vocalist. Not famous. Not young. Not established. Just another performer.

"Miss Rosalinde Lamaze." More enthusiastic applause, a few murmurs of appreciation, as her bare thigh showed itself through the slit of her gold lamé skirt. Rosalinde had starred in many films that had made much money at the box office. She had been hot—could be again—so the applause was warm and almost sincere.

"Miss Sissy Sharp." Lots of applause, particularly from those who aspired to President Reagan's friendship. Sissy's flat eyes glittered triumphantly. If the reaction of her fellow guests was the criterion, she was a shoo-in! She milked it for all she could —aware that they all were pretending to love her tonight.

"And finally, Miss Emerald Barrymore." Vociferous, frenzied applause. Emerald was extremely popular, and her recent self-confessed struggle with drugs, her triumphant rehabilitation and physical metamorphosis, had touched the sympathy of the town. What difference did it make that she hadn't made an American movie in ten years? She was a survivor. A star with a capital S, and she would remain one for the rest of her life, even if she never worked again.

Josh squeezed Chloe's hand supportively. She squeezed his back and smiled. She saw by his pupils that he had been at the coke again. How long this time, O Lord? she thought. How long before his habits catch up with him and he goes off the rails and stabs me in the back again?

10

Calvin never made it to college. Not only could his parents not afford to send him, but his grades in high school were so bad that no self-respecting university would even consider his application.

At eighteen he decided to leave the sleepy Utah town where he had grown up and head west. California was his goal, and he felt that there he would eventually attain his ultimate dream: meeting Emerald Barrymore, his idol, in person.

He didn't find it difficult to get a job. His needs were simple, and he was prepared to work hard. He found work as a packer and loader at Thrifty Drug Store on Canyon Drive in Beverly Hills. Soon he was promoted to stock clerk, and finally after five

120

years he was allowed to deal with the public when he graduated to junior clerk behind the counter of the photography department.

There he daily came into contact with many stars of TV and the movie screen. Some of them even left their "happy snaps" to be developed, and once he had found some casual photographs of Emerald at a backyard barbecue at the home of superagent Sue Jacobs.

He bided his time. One day she would come in and he would serve her. They would become friends and then, who knows, perhaps lovers. All he had to do was wait.

When Josh was recording in L.A., he stayed in a room at the Beverly Wilshire. Watching the women on Rodeo Drive was his usual afternoon ritual. Then, trying to "pull" them. It was like big-game hunting or gambling, really, a fascinating game he never tired of. It bolstered his ego, and these days he needed that. He knew he was in a dance of death with Chloe but he couldn't help himself. It had become a sick obsession, and he knew it. In the ten days since the Arafats' party he had been snorting more cocaine than ever.

He'd woken up today at about 3 P.M. with a hangover as usual. Perry, his valet and Man Friday, had brought him the same breakfast he always had when Chloe wasn't around—a glass of Perrier and fresh lemon juice with three Alka-Seltzers fizzing in it, a cheese Danish warm with butter and blueberry jam, and half a gram of coke on a silver salver next to a fresh, neatly rolled hundred-dollar bill. The coke cleared his head. He had thought he would work today on the lyrics for the new song. But after three hours he gave up—ideas eluded him. He couldn't find words, let alone a tune, no matter how much he snorted.

He adjusted his telescope and, leaning on the penthouse windowsill, focused it on the south end of Rodeo Drive. It was just after lunch, and women and girls of all ages and sizes were spilling out of the nearby restaurants—the Bistro, the Bistro Gardens and La Scala—strolling down the elegant street, indulging in the Beverly Hills woman's favorite sport: shopping.

Josh became interested as he looked at a thirty-five-year-old Chinese woman and her adolescent daughter. They were waiting to cross the road, headed for Bonwit's. They looked around vaguely. Out-of-town from where? Hong Kong? Singapore? Not important. He grew hard as he looked at the pubescent girl's tiny nipples under her T-shirt. Her mother's were nice too. A pair of tiny Oriental porcelain dollies. He nodded to Perry. Perry was no slouch at picking up women. Over the years of soliciting for Josh, he had racked up a 75 percent success ratio, and he had a smooth line of chat.

"See the chink and the chinkette, Perry?" Josh said. "Get 'em."

From across the street where she was about to enter the Saint Laurent Boutique, Chloe stopped as she saw Perry approach two Chinese women. She felt a wave of nausea as she realized that Josh was up to his old tricks again. She could almost read Perry's lips and see the bemused expression on the women's faces as he chatted them up.

Disgusted, she turned to cross the road to the parking complex. Forget the new dress for their party tonight—they had decided to celebrate their tenth anniversary in spite of their problems.

Where did she go wrong? Was Josh just a conniving faithless philanderer, had he always been a philanderer, all through the first eight years? Had she been blind? Could he never be faithful? Or was he just bolstering his male ego? Was it because his career was on the wane, because he was frightened of getting old? Or was it drugs? Did cocaine cause him to behave in this sickening way? A forty-year-old man with the morals of a seventeen-year-old slum boy. She had wanted to understand, to forgive, but she couldn't any longer. Yes, things were looking up for her career, just as his was on the wane. But she couldn't let him destroy her now—destroy her ego along with his. How dare men think they were the only ones with a fragile ego. What presumption made them feel that women had no claims to one?

In the early months of their marriage, she had put her own career on hold. She had busied herself with newfound domesticity: cooking for her man, shopping for his favorite foods, filling his closet and hers with outfits in which they could relax around their sprawling estate in Malibu. One of their favorite pastimes was to ride around the countryside—he on his Arabian stallion, she on her favorite English mare. They would often ride through the dunes at dawn after a night of partying or abandoned lovemaking.

She collected records for him. He had a supercilious dislike for the efforts of Tom Jones, Rod Stewart and even Mick Jagger, all of whom he had at various times been likened to, so Chloe kept her antennae out, searching for long-lost recordings of Billie Holiday, Fats Waller and other greats of the past. Josh could listen to them all day.

He loved being cuddled as she caressed him, calling him endearing names, holding him like a baby. His eyes closed, his black tousled head would nestle between her breasts, a smile of satisfaction on his face. Her fingertips would trace a pattern across his body, touching him skillfully here, there, everywhere. Sometimes, wickedly, her expert fingers touched him intimately, transforming his soft innocence into her shaft of pleasure.

He never failed to thrill her. In all of the years of marriage she never tired of the feel of his thighs between hers, his tongue exploring her mouth, his muscular hands palpating where she liked it most, always bringing her to fulfillment.

"I want you so much, babe," he would whisper into her hair. As they entwined, all of his customary crudeness of speech disappeared in the act of love with Chloe. With her Josh became a tender, demonstrative, affectionate lover. No one was more amazed by this transformation than he—he who had never given a damn for any of the women from his indiscriminate past. For Chloe now only endearments issued from his lips. Terms of love, sweet talk, tender, loving, sincere. Chloe loved it. She loved him so much. Forever. It could only be forever.

"Stop it, Chloe," she said to herself, thoughts of their love-making now hopelessly interwoven with thoughts of him fucking the two Chinese women she had seen being escorted by Perry to the Wilshire. "Stop it *now*, girl. It's over. You know what you have to do. It's finished. It has been finished for years."

She drove her silver Mercedes back to Malibu, her eyes stinging with salty tears that coursed down her face. She had to get ready for the party tonight. Their anniversary party. She felt numb. Was this what a broken heart felt like?

It was four o'clock when she got home. Pop music blared from the kitchen where the Mexican staff was preparing a feast for the party. She walked to the beach and stared bleakly at the ocean. Her marriage was cracked. Josh didn't love her. She had subordinated her career, encouraged his flagging one. She had tried to breathe new life and respectability into his hell-raising image; he had not responded to her care. He was a wastrel and an ingrate.

Deny it as he might, he was a slipping, aging rock star. It didn't matter that he still looked sexy, tough and confident with his tumbling black curls, tinged faintly with gray—and only the tiniest hint of a gut, which he dieted and sweated off before each tour. No, the fourteen-year-olds *knew* he was hitting forty when they saw his face on an album cover, no matter how much re-touching from the experts. Their eager hands picked at the new Michael Jackson or Rick Springfield album, ignoring Joshua

Brown—he was yesterday's news, their mama's idol.

"We can't all be young forever, darling," Chloe had soothed and comforted him as he raged at the injustice of it, his insecurities mounting as his hairline receded. Try as she might, Chloe could no longer assuage Josh's self-doubt with her love. It wasn't enough for him any more. He needed fresh game to stalk. New pussy. The chase. Ah, the thrill of the hunt! He never tired of it now.

Although Josh had been notoriously successful with women, he had tried to be true to Chloe during their marriage. Chloe, loving, caring, demonstrably sexy, gave him neither reason nor motivation to stray in the early years of their marriage. But a stiff prick no conscience hath, and now he needed more reassurance that he was up to it twice, thrice, sometimes four times a session. He became petrified by his waning sexuality, a normal thing for most men his age. He had to prove himself again and again—perhaps not the same way as when he was a kid on tour with groupies—but certainly he needed to feel he was still desired by other women. His sexual interest in Chloe waned. Her all-consuming love began to smother him. Sure he loved cuddles —"the goodies" he called them—adored lying close to her as she caressed him, sang to him. She even sang *his* hits! Clever girl. He loved that. But she was too damn clingy, too damn wifely-womanly-motherly. She was smothering. Suddenly he wanted new game to hunt.

He thinks I'm his goddamned mother, she fretted, as she strode the Malibu sands in a flowing white cotton Laize Adler. Her painted toenails crunching and popping the seaweed that encrusted the shore, she puffed nervously on a cigarette, a habit she had quit a year ago.

"Damn him!" she thought two hours later as she lay back in the black marble Jacuzzi, so often the scene of their lovemaking. Only last week he had "taken" her there as she lay mesmerized listening to Lena Horne wailing "Love Me or Leave Me." It had been the first time other than an occasional "duty fuck" in six months that they had made love joyously and spontaneously. Covered with bubbles they had embraced each other in the hot foaming Jacuzzi. It was almost like the old days. Almost.

That had been a week ago. Remembering a time when they felt deprived if they had not made love once in the morning and once at night, at least, Chloe felt bitter sadness at the thought of him with the two Chinese women. What was he doing with them? She couldn't bear to think about it.

Love dies, passion erodes. The opposite of love is not hate—it is indifference. She groaned inwardly, trying to think about to-night's party, wishing she could feel indifferent toward Josh instead of this jealous sexual angst. She loved him still, she could not help herself. Oh stop it, girl—get it *together* now, get out of the bath. Think about the damn guests. Could she cancel the party now? Impossible. Half of them were home in Beverly Hills preparing their toilettes, painting their faces and nails, having their chauffeurs spit-polish the Silver Spirit or the Porsche. No, she must brazen it out tonight. There were problems with Josh's recording session, she would tell the guests with a smile. He's still at the studio. Deadlines. You know how it is. They would nod wisely. Of course they knew how it was. They were all in the business so they knew only too well.

Rosalinde Lamaze and Johnny Swanson were the first to arrive. She had dressed casually—tight white leather pants were tucked into seven-hundred-dollar Di Fabrizio cowboy boots inlaid with turquoise leather; her turquoise silk cowboy blouse was slashed to the navel; around her neck cascaded the spoils of some long-forgotten Navajo tribe, a silver, turquoise and mother-of-pearl squash-blossom necklace. A silver belt encircled her twenty-three-inch waist, and several turquoise rings adorned her dusky fingers.

Johnny and Rosalinde had been friends for years, relying on

each other for "escort duty" when no one more exciting was on
the horizon. Johnny was twenty-nine to Rosalinde's thirty-six,
and six feet to her five feet two. He was good-looking and slim
in a suave boyish way, and his cutting wit gave him a special
brand of charm. For one so young, he had more than a way with
both words and women. "If it moves, fondle it," was his motto.
His prowess as a "stick man" preceded him, along with his colorful family history.

Rosalinde rearranged her silver neckwear and surveyed the
room. Featured tonight were several bit players in both her life
and Johnny's. But Eureka! There he was again, fat old Abby
Arafat. The man who held the key to her future. She oozed
beguilingly over to Abby, voluptuous hips performing a melody
of their own as she played the game of "Oh I'm bored—I've got
sooo many movie offers but nothing turns me on. What shall I
do, Abby darling?" She didn't want him to know she was eager
for Miranda, although she had agreed to test. She who plays it
the coolest shall win the first prize. American phrase much in
vogue recently.

Abby chomped on his cigar and half-listened with amusement
as he surveyed the other woman he was going to test next week
for Miranda. That Chloe. She was beautiful and charismatic.
His eyes narrowed as he watched her in a clinging white silk
Azzedine Alaïa dress, her black curls tumbling artlessly, and the
definition of a well-formed breast visible as she threw back her
head and laughed with Alex Andrews. Where was her hubby,
Abby wondered? Why wasn't he keeping an eye on this hot
number?

Alex Andrews was the latest hunk in town. Gorgeous, young,
sexy, blond, virile, intelligent, he possessed every one of the
qualities necessary for big screen appeal. However, it just wasn't
enough to be gorgeous and young, etcetera, today, mused Abby.
That had been sufficient in the thirties, forties and fifties to
guarantee movie stardom; then in the sixties, those attributes

127

almost became impediments to an actor's career. Were Dustin Hoffman, Michael Caine and Jack Nicholson gorgeous and young? No. They were actors, artists, thespians who had perfected their craft. They had charisma as well as talent. Intelligence as well as interesting looks. In the eighties you had to have it all. The public was too demanding. Gorgeous, young and sexy were minor requirements. Essential were talent, personality, intelligence and uniqueness.

Alex, studying hard with his acting coach, strived to acquire all these. But tonight he was working in a different way on Rosalinde, flashing his hooded hazel eyes in her direction, turning to give her a fine view of his twenty-five-year-old black-leather-covered buns. Alex was a pure soul, a cowboy from Indiana, with all the accompanying naiveté. "The great open spaces are in his head," quipped Johnny, ever vigilant to spot an upstart trying to break into the rarefied ranks of the "in" crowd.

Johnny was totally accepted everywhere in Hollywood: at A parties, B parties, orgies, stuffy charity affairs he was ever welcome. He wasn't an actor, and he was from a fine family, even if no one was quite sure who had sired him. But Alex was an outsider. A climber. All curls and cock. No family. No background. He had far to go, even if his agent claimed that he had the part of Steve's son on "Saga" all but sewn up.

Alex chatted eagerly with Rosalinde, trying to spark her feminine interest in him. He realized that although she was a big star, and he the male equivalent of a starlet, they were both playing the same game. He felt she was hungry. He could sense her sexual hunger in the way her round brown eyes admired the contours of his high-cheekboned face. Her plump, beringed fingers had started to flutter gently, skimming over his black silk shirt. A delicate butterfly touch. Little did he know she wasn't thinking of him. Rosalinde had Angelica on her mind. God forbid this crowd should ever find out she was a dyke. She'd be finished in this town. Men could get away with being gay; it was a man's world, let's face it—but a woman—a sex symbol be a lesbian? Perish the thought. She'd never get another job.

Abby Arafat moved smoothly through the crowd, talking to everyone. Smiling, nodding, charm personified, he was fully aware of his power tonight. Who wouldn't be? He had the crème de la crème of the acting profession at his feet, all dying to play one of the six or seven wonderful roles in "Saga."

Abby mourned the long-gone era of the true movie stars. The Hedy Lamarrs, Ava Gardners, Lana Turners and Rita Hayworths. Nubile, tender wisps of sixteen or seventeen summers plucked from high school or the cosmetic counters of the local drugstores, adored and worshiped for a few years by an adulatory yet fickle public who soon glorified another new face. That same public was unaware that the stars they paid homage to were merely the products of a slick studio build-up. Many of them were plastic models, with no heart, no guts, no reality— robots who lived by the studio's rules and behaved themselves. So they should, thought Abby. Do what the studio said. Enough already with these coozes with brains, these Glenda Jacksons, Vanessa Redgraves and Shirley MacLaines. They thought they had ideas. They wanted to produce, to direct, to have a say in their work. They couldn't be manipulated, cajoled or flattered.

None of *them* would ever play Miranda, or even Sirope. He wasn't even considering them. He needed a dame with oomph —vulnerable, soft, beautifully dressed, who oozed sex appeal— all those qualities that were unfashionable in these emancipated days of 1982. A woman of sensitivity and sex appeal who appealed to the basics in a man. A woman like...Chloe. His eyes glimpsed her curves again through the silky stretch fabric of her gown. Her sultry face, knowing, yet young-looking. Why not Chloe? He chomped on his cigar. Sure, she's really a saloon singer, but who says singers can't act? Look at Streisand, Minnelli, Cher. On second thought, don't, he groaned. Streisand gave him heartburn.

He moved to where Chloe was talking animatedly to Johnny. She knew she was giving off good vibes tonight. She was amusedly aware of her power over men who were attracted by her aura of vulnerable little girl, but one who knows the ropes. Several men at the party were vying for her attention as she fumed inwardly over Josh's nonappearance but desperately tried not to show it. She knew what she wanted to do, what she *had* to do for the sake of her self-respect. Dump him. End the marriage. Get the part of Miranda and ta-ta, Josh.

"Great party, Chloe," Abby intruded, reeking of cigar and goodwill. Johnny melted away. He had nothing to gain from chitchatting with this ancient relic of Hollywood about whom his dear mother, Daphne, often fondly reminisced. Aware that his dear mother had bedded half of Hollywood, Johnny was shrewd enough not to let it bother him—in fact, he joked about it, so that Daphne's escapades in bed became part of his own repertoire of anecdotes. Often he recounted a tale of Mummy and a swain with minor embellishments at the exclusive men-only Friday lunches at Ma Maison.

Suddenly Chloe saw her husband stumble in through the Aztec-carved front door. He was supported on each side by an Oriental female, and the crowd engulfed him in a shower of bonhomie as he disappeared toward the bar. He was drunk—very drunk. Probably stoned, too.

"Darling," Chloe cooed, pressing her silken body close to his. "You're just a tiny bit late, darling. Did the session go well?" She managed to combine wifely concern with womanly understanding, while squeezing his cheek hard.

"Yeah, babe, went late, real late." He pinched her perfumed ivory cheek gently. He wasn't about to tell her about his afternoon at the Beverly Wilshire. He realized he'd made a mistake. A bad one. He hadn't fucked the Orientals, although they clung to him like lint. As his head cleared and the room came into focus, the realization of the magnitude of his mistake in bringing them here hit him. Christ, if Chloe should suspect, she'd be bloody furious! She didn't seem to be.

"Why don't you have a quick shower and freshen up, *darling?*" Chloe used her sweetest tone, aware of forty pairs of potentially gossiping eyes viewing their reunion. Rumors were already rife that Josh had started catting around—and he and Chloe were, after all, on their third reconciliation in less than two years. Everyone knew Josh possessed a roving eye, and many people were surprised that Chloe had kept him by the home fires all these years. "A leopard never changes its spots," observed Abby sagely. "Never."

After Josh's arrival the party proceeded smoothly. A tiered mocha cake from the X-Rated Cake Shoppe, featuring a couple in pink-and-brown icing suggestively entwined, was served. A trio of singing telegramettes arrived and sang "Happy Anniversary" while stripping to approving cheers from the crowd. Toasts were drunk to the happy couple who had survived ten years of marriage, a record by many Hollywood standards. Chloe watched Josh with impassive eyes that hid her pain as she realized it was finally over. Goodbye and farewell to her "forever marriage." There was no use prolonging the agony. She glimpsed his tongue playfully teasing the ear of one of the women he'd arrived with, saw her stroke the bulge in his jeans, observed his hand try to sneak up the skirt of the other. Saw—and died inside.

Sally saw it all, too, and, daughterly devotion aside, felt sorry for her father. But she did enjoy seeing Chloe squirm. She could read the pain in her eyes. She saw the glances Chloe stole at Josh. She realized how it must hurt her to watch him with the two women. She didn't care. Maybe they would get a divorce and she would never have to see Chloe again. "Miserable old cow," she said, downing a beer and throwing back a tequila after it, as she had seen her father do.

Chloe circulated among her guests, laughing, charming, playing her part. Josh stayed at the other end of the stadium-sized living room, surrounded by his buddies and the two women. As he drank more, he became more raucous, more aggressive and, Chloe noticed, more unattractive. An aging, graying, middle-aged rock star trying to remain young. It was pathetic. He had been smoking dope and drinking tequila—he looked out of it. He looked over the hill, tired and unsuccessful. "He's wrong for you, darling," Daphne whispered. "Wrong, wrong, wrong. He's a lout, and a drunk and a wastrel." And a loser too, she thought, behaving like this in front of everyone.

Chloe was beyond humiliation. The embarrassment of seeing her husband in her living room with those two strange women, his obvious fascination with this Chinese mother-and-daughter act, made her ill. She felt as if she were observing everything in slow motion. One of the waiters continuously refilled her glass with champagne. She floated through the room, watching everything objectively, not caring any more about anything or anyone. She realized that Abby had left. She was thankful that a potential boss was not a witness to her humiliation. As for the other guests, she simply didn't give a damn what they thought.

"Where's the wife? Where is she then?" Josh suddenly called out, whirling on the tinier of his tiny strumpets, slapping her hands away from where they were toying with his chest hair. "C'mon, Chloe, give us a song," he bawled, grabbing Chloe's hand in his bear grip and pulling her over to the piano.

"No, Josh, no." Chloe tried to pull away from him. "No duets tonight. I can't. Don't do this, Josh, *please.*"

Josh seemed oblivious to her distress. He shrugged and beckoned to the teenage Chinese girl, who came to his side with a sly Oriental smile.

Chloe desperately wished everyone would leave. Finally, as if reading her thoughts, they started to.

Rosalinde threw back her sixth Bailey's Irish Cream and smiled at Alex. "Let's get out of here, honey pie. It's a bore," she murmured. "Got wheels?"

"Sure, sure," Alex said happily. His manager had lent him his Cadillac, not wanting his latest client to be seen at an important party in a clapped-out Mustang. Alex realized that leaving this party with Rosalinde Lamaze was quite a coup. Even if she was a decade older than he, she was a big star. He hoped there would be paparazzi outside the house, ready to take a happy snap for the *National Enquirer*. He made a mental note to have his press agent call Army and Hank tomorrow, to give them the exclusive scoop about this new hot twosome. Maybe even Liz Smith or Suzy would run it in New York. What would the folks in Indiana think!

Johnny hadn't scored tonight. Not that it bothered him. Scoring was too easy in this town. By the time a good-looking guy was twenty-nine he had usually scored so much easy pussy that, if he didn't start playing the marriage-and-divorce game, only challenges could excite him. Chloe Carriere, for instance, was quite a challenge, and Johnny thought he might throw down his gauntlet for her.

Calvin, from his hiding place, outside the house, saw Rosalinde leaving the party with Alex. He sneered to himself. What a slut! Hanging on to a stud at least ten years her junior, stroking his long blond hair, fondling him in places that Calvin knew were dirty. Filthy whore! She was scum.

Where was Emerald? Why wasn't she at this party? Many others of importance seemed to be. He had been told she was coming, but perhaps Chloe hadn't invited her—out of jealousy, no doubt. A jealous British bitch. They were all jealous of Emerald—she was so ravishing, so sweet. Vulnerable yet glamorous. None of these over-the-hill spic sluts or limey cows was in her league. None of them was fit to lick her size three satin-shod feet. She was the Queen. The Goddess. The Best.

He looked at his watch. Twelve-thirty. He saw that the Mexican tramp and the stud toy-boy were locked in an embrace in the front seat of a Cadillac.

An unaccustomed excitement suddenly engulfed him as he watched the couple fondling each other. Even though he despised Rosalinde, watching her hands roam over Alex's body aroused Calvin tremendously. As Alex finally disengaged himself from Rosalinde's hot hands, put the car in gear and moved into the highway, Calvin followed in his green Chevrolet.

After the guests had left, Chloe confronted Josh. "This was the last straw tonight, Josh. I want a divorce, and I mean it this time. How *dare* you bring those women to our house?"

"No, babe, please, *no*. Chloe, I love you, you know I do. It's always been you, babe. Always, you know it, babe." His words were erratic.

"Oh, stop it, Josh—you sound like a broken record. I can't take your cheating any more." She tried to keep the pain out of her voice. It hurt to swallow, her throat was so constricted. He had wounded her too many times now with his playing around. She had tried to pretend to herself it didn't really matter, it was just sport fucking—nothing serious. Had tried many times to forgive him. But tonight she had run out of forgiveness. "I *won't* stand for it any more, Josh," she said wearily. "We've come to the end of the road. You know we have. We *must* divorce, or I'll go mad, because I think *you* are, Josh."

"No, Chloe, no. I can't make it without you," he had begged her, gone on his knees, tears streaming down his face. He used every trick in his book to persuade her not to end their marriage. But bringing up old times only made her think of old injuries and convinced her more than ever that the marriage was over. The Oriental women were the end. It was intolerable. Whether or not he had made love to them made no difference. The fact that he *wanted* to was enough. In front of their guests, at their anniversary party, he had humiliated her terribly. Insulted their marriage. Disgraced them both. "This isn't *love* any more, Josh," she screamed, all control suddenly evaporating. "It's war —it's sick—it's horrible. The whole goddamn party saw it, and I *won't* stand for it. It's an *illness*, Josh."

She'd drunk a lot of champagne. Now it released her, released the pain. She locked the bedroom door, took two Valium, ripped off her clothes, letting them lie on the floor, and, without removing her makeup, fell into a dreamless slumber.

Josh zoomed down the Pacific Coast Highway at 75 mph in his Cadillac convertible. He didn't notice the police car behind him. His stereo was turned on full blast to his latest track, and he had just taken a swig of tequila from his leather Gucci flask. The booze and the joint he had smoked earlier were making him feel slightly better. Chloe would eventually come to her senses. She had to. He needed her. They were the forever couple, weren't they?

Then as the flashing lights of the police car pulled in front of him and the sound of the siren finally penetrated his consciousness, he realized that he was in more trouble.

He woke up covered with sweat. His black silk shirt was sodden, his gray slacks oozed moisture. Where the hell was he? His bewildered brain waves tried to connect. Was he in jail? But for chrissake, why? How dare they put him, Joshua Brown, superstar, behind bars. He started sweating even more; he needed a snort badly. He reached into his pocket for the leather pouch in which he kept his paraphernalia—the brown cube of "downtown," the glass phial of "uptown," the solid-gold razor blade, the platinum straw. Gone. Frantically he felt in his other pockets and then scrabbled on the filthy floor. "Hey, you motherfuckers," he screamed, the tendons standing out on his neck. "Bring me back my stuff, you shit-eaters!"

A black guard appeared, opened the hatch and looked at him coldly. "Shut your mouth, junkie, or we shut it for you," he spat, and slammed the hatch shut.

Josh started to tremble. He hadn't had a fix since...when was it? Two or three o'clock this morning—after Chloe had gone to bed and left him alone. It was now—he looked at the clock on the wall outside his cell—9 A.M.

Shit. He started to tremble violently, waves of nausea rocking him. He threw up into a bucket, then, weakened and disoriented, fell back onto the filthy bunk again. Staring at the ceiling and walls encrusted with the graffiti of a thousand derelicts, he dropped off to sleep. The pain in his head and chest faded as his dreams took over. He was a star once more. A superstar. Caesars Palace in Vegas...the London Palladium...Olympia in Paris. He had packed them to the rafters all over the world. Standing room only. Josh Brown, the most charismatic English performer the world had ever seen. He could have had any woman he wanted, and he did. But eventually he wanted only one—only Chloe. And he wanted it to last forever. The others never mattered. Why couldn't Chloe realize that? He loved her —he would always love her. He groaned.

He was allowed one phone call from jail. He called his agent, who immediately sped down to the county court with bail money. Josh was released in a blaze of bad publicity.

In the days that followed, Josh tried to contact Chloe, but she insisted the marriage was finished and she wanted out. With a heavy heart, he moved into the Beverly Wilshire, and she sent his belongings over with Perry. Chloe filed for divorce two days later on the grounds of irreconcilable differences.

Josh threw himself into finishing the album while he consumed huge amounts of tequila and cocaine and made frantic love to as many under-age girls as he could. When the album was nearly finished, his agent called and told Josh he had an interesting job for him. He could and should go back into the theater. A major English impresario wanted him to write and star in a musical version of *Cyrano de Bergerac*. It was a wonderful opportunity, one he had wanted for years, for the theater had always been his first, his true love.

Two weeks after he and Chloe separated, Josh packed his bags and left for London.

Part Three

11

They sat in the number one booth at the Polo Lounge drinking Dom Perignon and exchanging information.

Solomon Davidson, Sol to his many acquaintances, was telling Chloe about the events at the end of his recent marriage to Emerald. Sol and Emerald had indulged in a rapid tabloid-style romantic affair, culminating after a few months in a quick engagement, a short marriage and a fast separation last week.

"Why did you wear that color?" he asked her accusingly, eying her jade-green Halston dress.

"Why—don't you like green? Don't tell me you're superstitious?" Chloe murmured, as she sipped her champagne, watching him with amused eyes.

Solomon, bon vivant and friend to the stars, and Chloe had been good friends for years. They had laughed and joked through many evenings together, and Chloe was sorry to see him still clearly obsessed with Emerald.

When Emerald divorced for the fifth time, she had immediately turned her sea-green eyes, the light in them undimmed, even though she was approaching her half century, in Sol's direction. Oh, lucky man! Oh, foolish and vain man! She had eventually crucified him on the altar of the trash magazines. He had been made to look like a bumbling fool—a poor peasant not fit to slip a bangle on Emerald's slim wrist.

Poor Sol, who reveled in his role as confidant and gofer to the famous, lost both his credibility and his lady to the snide sniggerings of supermarket pulp. But he had swallowed his pride, picked himself up, dusted himself off and ventured back into the Los Angeles social scene again.

"I want her back," Sol confided to Chloe. "I still love her."

Chloe sympathized. Josh-less now for over a month, she had shed many tears and soaked many pillowcases every night as she yearned to have him beside her.

Emerald read Army Archerd's column with growing concern: "Chloe Carriere, one of the main contenders for the coveted Miranda role in 'Saga,' and Solomon Davidson, Emerald Barrymore's soon-to-be ex, had more to discuss than the heat wave in the Polo Lounge last week. Is that the love light in their eyes?"

She threw down the paper, lit a Sherman with a green malachite lighter, and with remarkably steady hands inserted it into a pale emerald holder.

Chloe was a parvenu, a Johnny-come-lately. She didn't belong. First of all, not only was she British, but she was not even an actress. She was a singer—a singer who had a couple of hits in the sixties and seventies, and then faded out. Now she had reemerged as a more-than-serious contender for her, Emerald's, role. When Emerald first heard that Chloe was testing, she thought it was a joke. Now the joke was turning out to be a serious threat not only to her part, but to her nearly-ex-husband. Not that she wanted Sol, but she didn't want Chloe to have him either.

Emerald crunched the pale emerald holder between her tiny, perfectly capped teeth. It was essential to her career that she get this role. She was no longer hot in movies. She needed this part. Doing this commercial in Australia was not a great career move.

In spite of her many marriages, her drinking problem and a penchant for carelessly throwing away her hard-earned cash on her friends and husbands, she was a true child of Hollywood, and it still loved her. She had thrived in the era in which she had grown up, become Hollywood royalty, and the ultimate symbol of survival. Many of her contemporaries had succumbed to drugs, drink, suicide or illness. How much of it caused by career failure, no one could know, or even guess.

Marilyn Monroe. Poor Norma Jean—she had never believed in herself, and it had destroyed her. Emerald and Marilyn had studied at the Actors Studio together. Milton Greene, their feisty mentor and glamour photographer par excellence, brash, knowledgeable, and crafty, had guided both their careers simultaneously in the early sixties. The girls had been close friends. Shared gowns, men, and laughs. Emerald had been devastated when Marilyn had died.

James Dean—Jimmy—darling Jimmy—her first lover. No matter that Pier Angeli, Ursula Andress, and countless others were on his fishing line that long hot summer of 1955. She had given herself to him—totally. Emerald Barrymore, eighteen years old, gorgeous, sexy, idol of millions of youngsters, had allowed James Dean, moody, unpredictable and intense, to take her much-discussed virginity.

143

She had adored him passionately until his death a few months later. A shortish period of mourning—after all, she was only eighteen—then Emerald was in love again. This one was more dependable, and the studio breathed a sigh of relief when they married. A young actor, up-and-coming. Unfortunately for Emerald, he was not able to come up often enough to satisfy her. And when she discovered him in bed with another man, he had to go. Divorce, more tears, more mourning. Then into her life came Stanley O'Herlihy. How destructive can one man be to himself? Maybe Irishmen have a death wish, but Stanley carried it to new heights. He was short, middle-aged and ugly, with a thirst for whiskey and women that was practically unquenchable. Writing was the driving force of his life, and he devoted most of his waking hours to it.

He was fifty to her twenty when they wed for the first time. His lovemaking left a lot to be desired: two bottles of Irish whiskey a day did not a stallion make. After brief, unsatisfactory couplings he would retire to his desk and his fountain pen and write far into the night, leaving his radiant young bride alone and unfulfilled. He gave her a vibrator for her twenty-first birthday, with a sarcastic note. She took it to the studio and her latest leading man showed her what to do with it—and him.

For some reason, Stanley's obvious lack of interest in her charms captivated Emerald further, making her more determined to make him love her. He had told her he had never truly loved a woman in his life, and that if he did, she would certainly not be the one, as she was nowhere near intellectual and intelligent enough for him; the more he insulted her, the more besotted with him she became.

Twice she left him in frustrated rage for younger, handsomer, wealthier and more caring men—men who satisfied her sexually, who complimented and praised her, who wanted to marry her. But they were never enough for Emerald. They represented

only convenient arm decorations and temporary sexual passion
—they meant nothing.

She yearned for Stan O'Herlihy, who, knowing a good thing
when he saw it, allowed Emerald to move back into his life time
and again. She put up with his drunken rages, his foul Irish
temper and his indiscriminate fornication with the trashiest of
waitresses and prostitutes, women he seemed to find far more
exciting than he did her. He craved kinky sex: three-
somes, orgies, S and M. She put up with it until finally after two
marriages and divorces and ten years of on-again, off-again connubial non-bliss, Stanley drove his Porsche into a tree, instantly
killing himself and the black prostitute with him.

Emerald mourned long and loud. It was 1970; she was at the
peak of her beauty and sexuality, yet now she couldn't get arrested as far as movies were concerned. Studios considered her a
celebrity, no longer a serious actress, in spite of having made
fifty films. After decades of success, suddenly she was considered
box-office poison.

In Hollywood, socially she was still the crème de la crème, but
to new hot young directors and producers she was yesterday's
news. She was, after all, well into her thirties, even though her
smashing blond beauty showed none of the wear and tear expected.

Eventually Emerald philosophically accepted that Hollywood
had turned its back on her and she went to live in Italy. There
she learned the language, starred in some low-budget but com-
pelling Italian and French program fillers throughout the decade, married a couple of times, traveled, spent every cent she
earned, and waited for the day when she would return in
triumph to Hollywood.

Now as she sat in her Sydney hotel room, watching the sunset
behind the facade of the beautiful white opera house shining off
the harbor waters and reading a week-old copy of *Daily Variety,*

she knew she *must* pull out all the stops to get this part. She would call in every one of her markers. She would do anything to get it. *Anything.*

A week later, back in her Hollywood apartment, she reclined on soft green towels and let Sven do his damnedest to her vertebrae. "God, vat kinks," he said, enthusiastically pummeling her with firm Scandinavian hands. Emerald's eyes were alight in her middle-aged, still-beautiful face. More than four decades a star and now reborn, thanks to the miracles of South American plastic surgery and a Midwestern alcohol-and-drug rehabilitation clinic. She had lost more than thirty pounds in the past year thanks to a restrictive diet of zucchini, broiled chicken and Evian water. A major consumer of alcohol all her life, she had completely cleaned out her system of the poisons and toxins that had accumulated over the years, and was now determined to conquer the new and exciting world of prime time TV.

She balanced a pale green phone on the pillow. "You know I'll test," she said. "I don't have any false pride about that, darling." Her agent, Eddie De Levigne—a diminutive, elflike figure who had been around since the days of Swanson, and whose legendary career and monetary accomplishments for his clients always paid off so handsomely that his nickname in the business was Fast Eddie—was pleased. Emerald was a smart cookie. The smartest thing she'd done recently was to fire the Morris boys and hire him. In this town where fledgling actresses become prima donnas in less time than you could say, "Who won last year's Oscar?" her attitude was refreshing. Throughout her bouts with alcoholism and drug addiction and her mistakes with men, Fast Eddie had waited in the wings for her to come to her senses so that he could pick up her pieces and put them together again, as only he knew how. He was an agent in the proper sense of the word, not a faceless gray-flannel-suited cipher like so many of the boys at the conglomerates. Fast Eddie cared—and he got results.

Sven finished kneading her back, packed up his equipment and left. With a groan of pleasure, she strolled, unself-consciously naked, into her mirrored closet to survey her dozens of green outfits.

Emerald almost exclusively wore green, and, occasionally, white. For films she wore other colors, but in private life, all she ever wore was pistachio green, grass green, pea green, or olive green—every imaginable shade of green hung in the hundred feet of her spacious walk-in closet. She selected a mint-green Ungaro blouse with matching gabardine culottes, clasped her everyday emerald pendant around her reconstructed throat and left for Eddie's office to discuss strategy.

Fast Eddie did not mince words. Although Emerald was at the moment his favorite client, he always called a spade a spade. "This Carriere dame is the favorite, kid," he rasped. "No doubt about it. I talked to Gertrude today and she gave it to me straight. Abby loves her, so does the network, and they always have the final say, as you know."

"Shit." Emerald sat up straight, her gorgeous eyes flashing. "That English nobody. How *can* they prefer her to me? I'm a *star*. She's a nightclub singer. What can we *do*, Eddie?"

"The best we can, kid, the best we can," said the little man wisely, frowning through his massive spectacles. "Listen, kiddo, we've just gotta persevere. I've told 'em you're the best, the biggest star, the most gorgeous and the most talented. I'm gonna give 'em all I can, kid, and you've gotta help me."

"Oh, I will, you know I will, Eddie darling."

"Give 'em your best shot on the test. You're a damn fine actress kiddo, in spite of all your rotten movies and your stupid marriages."

Emerald winced. True, the critics didn't love her, but the fans

147

did. They adored her. Producers and directors loved her too, but didn't give her jobs. They gave them to Anne Bancroft, Sally Field and Jessica Lange. "Saga's" Miranda Hamilton was the key to a whole new career for Emerald, and she was determined to get it.

The network, Abby, and Gertrude finally decided on a date to test their finalists for Miranda. Scripts were sent. Wardrobe women went on the hunt for costumes. Early nights for the five actresses became de rigueur. The town waited for the results eagerly.

The day of the test dawned to uncharacteristic California weather. Rain in great gray sheets had bucketed down on the highways and boulevards all night, leaving the Los Angeles area sodden and drab.

Chloe was awake at 5 A.M. She gazed with alarm at the six-foot waves pounding the foundations of her Trancas house and wondered if, as usual, the hills around Malibu Canyon had collapsed under the weight of the rain and become impassable. What then? Maybe she could make it over the Ventura freeway and cut through to Hollywood Boulevard via Franklin Avenue. She wasn't due at the studio until seven-thirty. Throwing on an old chenille robe and snuggling her feet into oversized bunny slippers, she went down to the kitchen. As she waited for the coffee to percolate and the Highway Patrol to answer the phone, she inspected again the call sheet for today's test.

There they all were, the final *six* names that had been approved by the network, by Abby and by Gertrude.

So Pandora had managed to get a test, too, Chloe mused. Or was she going to play the other ex-wife? Either way it was not a bad idea. She had a sharp, dark, foxy face, was a good actress, the right age—oh, dear, more competition for Miranda.

As she sipped coffee, then showered, she mulled over her chances compared to the other five actresses.

Sabrina Jones was no competition. Everyone including Sabrina knew she was wrong. She was a red herring. A publicity shill used by Abby to garner media coverage and hype the public's interest.

Pandora King? She would probably get the other role of the first wife, since according to the call sheet she was testing for both roles. She was a respected actress, but a second-stringer, and always would be.

Rosalinde Lamaze? Too ethnic. Whatever the networks might say, however much the producers denied it, it was doubtful that this very important leading role would go to Rosalinde, because of her Mexican origin. It wouldn't jell with the total Anglo-Saxon feeling and look that Chloe knew Abby and Gertrude wanted for the show.

Chloe's main competitors were Sissy and Emerald—she had absolutely no doubt about that. Sissy was the better actress, plus being married to Sam would give her a strong edge. But Emerald was still such a megastar that Chloe was surprised she had agreed to test. Still, what the hell—they were all only actresses, weren't they? Bakers must bake, painters must paint, and actresses must act. That was their life.

Ah, well, may the best woman win, she thought as she dressed in jeans, a flannel plaid shirt of Josh's, and her Burberry raincoat that had seen many a rainy day in the provinces of England. She drove her silver Mercedes swiftly through the pouring rain without encountering anything other than the occasional stalled car. Highway Patrol had managed to keep Malibu Canyon open, thank God. Huge men, sweating in spite of the freezing rain, shoveled the sliding mud as it threatened to cover the Pacific Coast Highway. Once on the Hollywood freeway, she relaxed and put the tape of the scene that she had committed to memory into her tape deck.

The English-accented voices, hers and that of Lawrence Dillinger, her acting coach, filled the Mercedes. Chloe listened objectively. Would she be too British for the network? There seemed to be no foreigners on prime time TV right now except Ricardo Montalban, and he was a character actor. The darlings of the tube were all-American as apple pie and very *young*. Charlie's Angels were all in their twenties—and the Dallas Dollies were certainly a lot younger than the group who would assemble on Stage 5 today.

True, Suzanne Pleshette, Stefanie Powers and Angie Dickinson had all starred in prime time shows recently. They were close to, if not over, forty, but they were also 100 percent American. Chloe wondered for the umpteenth time if her British accent would hamper her chances.

She rolled down the window as she approached the guard at the studio gate. He wore a clear plastic cover over his policeman's hat, and barked at her in an unfriendly way, "Name?"

"Carriere," said Chloe. "I'm here to test for 'Saga.' "

"Oh, yes—report to makeup, Stage Five." He peered into Chloe's face, letting raindrops drip from his visor down her neck. "Don't I know you? Didn't you used to be Chloe Carriere, the singer?"

"I still am," said Chloe calmly, having endured this type of conversation with strangers for the past six or seven years.

"Well, I'll be damned," said the cop, smiling now. "I used to *love* your records, Miss Carriere—played them all the time when I was in high school." Chloe winced. *High school!* The man was at least forty-five judging from his weatherbeaten face; he was older than *her* high school!

"How do I get to Stage Five?" she asked, politely cutting him off before he had a chance to get effusive.

"Turn left at Ladies' Wardrobe...see that cross light?...then make a right at Stage Seven and then another right past the Administration Building and you'll run right into it. Good luck,

Miss Carriere." He saluted her goodbye and Chloe, obeying the five m.p.h. speed limit, drove to Stage 5.

She parked in a visitors' parking space as a young girl with waist-length blond hair ran eagerly up to her. "Hi, I'm Debbie Drake, the trainee second assistant director on 'Saga.' If you'll just follow me, I'll show you to your dressing room, they're not quite ready for you in makeup yet."

In a seven-by-seven-foot shoe box called a dressing room Chloe regarded the lilac satin peignoir in a clear plastic bag hanging on one of the metal hooks hammered inexpertly into thin, cracked plywood. A pair of satin shoes dyed to match was placed carefully on the one piece of furniture, a brown couch. Next to the shoes lay two envelopes of Caress panty hose, one Beige Glow, the other Tawny Tan, and three pairs of rhinestone earrings of various sizes. They winked at her in the light from the flyspecked lightbulb hanging shadeless from the ceiling of this cell. There was a tiny dressing table with a cracked mirror in which she could see herself only if she hunched down two feet. There was a rickety chair, and covering the yellow-and-black linoleum a threadbare rug with "Property of MCPC Studio" stenciled on it in fading black.

What a dump, thought Chloe à la Bette Davis, hanging her raincoat on the one other hook behind the door. But you've seen worse, she said to herself. *Much* worse! The English provinces —nothing could ever be more disgusting than that rat hole infested with cockroaches she had dressed in while appearing at the Alhambra Theatre, Basingstoke, in 1968. Compared to that, this was a palace.

Too restless to just sit, Chloe stared out of the tiny window. She found she could almost see into the window of the large trailer with "Makeup" stenciled in lipstick red on the door. She wished she could see what was going on in there.

Makeup was a hive of activity. Although it was already seven-thirty, Sabrina's face was not yet finished. Ben was applying peach blusher on her lids and cheeks, while Barry, the third assistant, fretted in the doorway.

"How much longer, Ben?" he asked the bearded giant with the delicate fingers.

"As long as it takes, Barry."

"And how long is that—*pray?*" Barry fumed. Ned, the first A.D., would jump on him if the actors weren't ready on time. Today with all these divas and old-time stars coming in to test, it was an assistant director's nightmare. He realized that a one-and-a-half-hour makeup and hair call, which when discussed at the production meeting had seemed ample time to get each actress ready, was not nearly long enough. The youngest and most beautiful of all, Sabrina—every time he looked at her he swallowed hard, she was so gorgeous—spoke to him sweetly.

"I'm ready now, Barry." She flashed him the world's most breathtaking smile and Barry inwardly swooned. Having just recovered from a year-long crush on Jackie Smith, which had caused him many sleepless nights, he did not want his eager heart to plunge again. Barry continued to worship from afar.

Robert Johnson, the actor known as "A.N. Other" on the call sheet, had been hired today to play opposite all six of the leading ladies. He had been a minor TV star in the fifties in Steve McQueen's TV series "Wanted: Dead or Alive," and his conversation was peppered with references to "Steve and I," as in "When Steve and I went cycle racing in 'fifty-two...When Steve and I went sailing...When Steve and I pulled those broads in Acapulco...." He leaned against the door, trying, unsuccessfully, to engage Sabrina in some sexual eye contact.

Sabrina wished that this good ole boy would stop undressing her with his hot eyes, but she was too polite to say so. She smiled pleasantly as he rambled on about his adventures with Steve.

In the next chair sat Rosalinde, her hair in soft pink rollers, a black-and-white-striped cover over her shoulders, while Nora, the other makeup person, deftly applied frosted eye shadow to her lids. Nora did not approve of frosted eye shadow. It looked common, and it caked into the crinkly crevices of the eyelids of anyone over twenty-five. Certainly it looked wonderful in the current Revlon ads, on their eighteen-year-old models' flawless baby skins, but on Rosalinde it looked hard and old.

Rosalinde held a hand mirror while she applied lashings of thick black mascara. She hummed gently to herself along with the samba music from the radio she had brought along. She had also brought boxes of chocolates for all the hair and makeup crew and a magnum of champagne for the director of photography, which she had given him with a kiss and a sly "Now, darling, you promise you'll give me the key light only directly *above* the camera, *yes?* And don't forget the eye light too, darling."

Lazlo Dominick, who had lit every top actress in Hollywood since Fay Wray, knew all the tricks in the book. He winked at her and agreed. He would have lit her that way anyhow, but the champagne was a nice thought, so perhaps he might give her a little more care than the others. He whistled inwardly when Sabrina Jones, dressed in a pale peach satin negligee, drifted onto the set. What a looker, he thought as did the rest of the crew, who all stood a little taller and watched their language. Sabrina's innocence, freshness and niceness brought out the best in men. The director, another old Hollywood hand, Marvin Laskey, discussed the scene with her and tried to put her at ease. Since she was already at ease, secure in her beauty, fully aware that since she was completely wrong for this part she would not get it, Sabrina gave him her dazzling smile and her full attention.

"They're ready for you in makeup now, Miss Carriere," said Debbie brightly. Chloe walked the ten yards from the tiny shoe box to the vast shoe box that housed the makeup department. The rain had stopped, and a rainbow shimmered in the lighten-

153

ing sky. A good omen, she thought as she stepped into the room. The first person she bumped into was Rosalinde.

"Chloe—*chica*—Chloe, how are you doing?" Rosalinde noted that Chloe didn't look bad, considering her face was totally nude of makeup, and she had pulled her hair straight back. She looked severe, somewhat sexless. No wonder Josh had strayed, thought Rosalinde.

Chloe tried to be polite as she slid into the black leatherette chair and let Ben examine her face. She observed that even though everything was muddy from the rain, Rosalinde was wearing high-heeled black strappy sandals through which her toenail polish showed chipped and discolored. She recalled Sissy's sneering at "the Mexican trash basket," and smiled to herself.

"Hurry *up*, for Christ's sake. We're late enough already," Sissy yelled to her chauffeur. Harry merely shrugged. If they were late, it certainly wasn't his fault. He had been told to be at the Sharps' Bel Air mansion at eight, and he had been there on the dot. Madame had appeared at eight twenty-five, cursing like a truck driver, expecting him to get her to the studio in the pouring rain in five minutes. Well, he wasn't about to risk life and limb to do it—neither his nor the old cow's. He kept to the 35 mph speed limit and to his usual careful driving in spite of her furious shrieks to get a move on.

Having read and reread the call sheet the night before, she had hardly been able to sleep, so enraged was she that there were now no less than *six* actresses testing. SIX!! It was ridiculous. Although she had used every contact she had in this town to get this test, she was filled with bitter rage that she was actually lowering herself to do it.

"Do you realize how *demeaning* it is for me to test—especially with that Mexican slut in the running?" she had spat at

Sam as he relaxed in his armchair attempting to watch a ball game on TV.

"Yes, dear, I do," said Sam, imperceptibly pressing the up volume on his remote. "But you wanted to test, Sissy. You used enough pressure on Abby to get this test. You can't back out now, dear. You will look foolish."

One thing Sissy Sharp did not relish was looking foolish. She glared at her husband, who was totally involved in the Lakers game, and flounced off to bed in quest of an early night; but sleep eluded her in spite of three Valium and eventually a Mogadon taken in desperation at three o'clock. She tossed and turned all night, her mind in a whirl about the test and her competition. At half past six she eventually nodded off.

Bonita, her maid, had brought a spartan breakfast on a white wicker bed tray into her bedroom promptly at seven. *"Buenos días, señora,"* Bonita whispered, drawing the drapes to reveal the sodden palm trees, which dripped relentlessly over the six-acre estate.

Sissy mumbled, turned over in bed and, ignoring the glass of hot water with lemon juice and the sliced pineapple, continued to sleep.

Only when Sam, leaving for his twice weekly squash game, woke her for the second time did Sissy jump out of bed, overturning the wicker tray onto the Porthault sheets and screaming blue murder at everyone in sight, including her Pekingese dogs.

Now, swathed in a new sable cape, with matching crepe de chine blouse, gabardine trousers and polished boots, an Hermès silk scarf covering her hair and immense Ray-Bans covering her bloodshot eyes, she perched on the edge of the backseat of her Rolls and yelled at the driver to hurry.

"Yes, your name?" said the cop at the gate. Sissy glared at him venomously through the smoked glass of the Rolls.

Peasant, didn't he go to the cinema? If she got this part, he would be fired immediately.

"Ms. Sissy Sharp, testing for 'Saga,' " said Harry deferentially, with a wink at the cop. Sissy gritted her teeth. Harry was in the firing line now.

"Oh, of course. Hi, Sissy." The cop smiled familiarly, waving them on.

Sissy gave her dressing quarters a sharp inspection. Knowing that most TV actors are given cubbyhole dressing rooms or tiny trailers, she had insisted on borrowing her husband's lavish motor home, supplied by the studio, for the test. It was fully furnished with a bed, a stove, a television set and a makeup mirror surrounded by flattering pink lights.

Sissy had been used to making films in the days when stars were given the delicate treatment they expected—treated like hothouse orchids, fawned over by everyone. The age of television had spawned a new bunch of overly young and eager, or over-the-hill but grateful, stars, who didn't care a hell of a lot if they had to dress in a garage, they were so thrilled to be working. Then, if their show became a prime time hit, they became excessively demanding. They would then insist on every sort of perk from a cellular telephone to a private sauna, and, in the case of some female stars, on days off for their menstrual periods, and breastfeeding privileges for the infants they often insisted on bringing to work with them.

Each season, network executives observed with a mixture of dread and greed the rise to stardom of obscure actors or actresses. Eager to work initially for a reasonable salary, they soon become complaining, dissatisfied autocrats who, believing their own publicity, wielded their newly gained power over the studio, the producers and the network. The networks liked to create stars, but not superstars. "The bigger the stars, the more the public loves 'em, the bigger the monsters they all become," Abby said ruefully. This happened a couple of times each season.

The public's obsession with new fresh faces on the box guaranteed that new TV stars were born each year.

"We've *got* to keep them in their place, dammit," cried Gertrude. "I *insist* that we make everyone on 'Saga' equal—equal salaries for all."

"Impossible," Abby interjected. "We've got young kids and established stars. You can't give 'em all equal salaries—don't be a fool."

"Well, we must *try* to keep equality in other things then," said Gertrude implacably. "There will be no fancy-shmancy dressing rooms, Abby. No free gowns, no unlimited phone bills. No privileges other than the privilege of working for *us* on 'Saga.' "

"Try it, Gert." Abby smiled cynically. "Just try it, hon. It'll never work, you know it. We've already set a precedent with Sam Sharp. He's getting a goddamn limo, a massive motor home, Doug Hayward flying from London to make his fucking suits. It's a wonder we don't have a unit cocksucker in his contract to keep him happy on his lunch hour. God knows what else. Do you *really* think our other stars aren't going to want the same?"

"Sam Sharp is a highly respected motion picture star. He has *earned* his place in the sun," insisted Gert. "He has a 'favored nations' clause in his contract. No one can get a salary within fifteen thousand of his."

"Yeah, we're not paying him peanuts, thanks to you, Gert," said Abby, angrily lighting his third cigar of the day. "Fifty grand an episode for a new show for an over-the-hill actor is *steep*, baby, it's *steep*."

"Abby, the character of Steve Hamilton is highly important to the success of 'Saga.' You *know* that," Gertrude said stiffly. "If he is not the quintessential patriarch with inbred qualities of leadership and a dynamic force, *we have no show*. In Sam Sharp we have all of these qualities. They are built into his character throughout the years of playing all of those fine Yankee gentlemen. Plus of course his TVQ is tremendous. His last three films did at least a Nielsen forty share in prime time."

"Yeah, and bombed at the box office," said Abby flatly.

"He's a major star," insisted Gertrude.

"He's a has-been," sighed Abby.

"We *need* him," persisted Gertrude.

"O.K., O.K. Maybe you're right, Gert. Maybe he *is* a star, but he's also a fucking faggot. How are we going to keep *that* out of the garbage magazines?"

"Very easily," said Gertrude. "Since he has pulled the wool over the public's eyes for thirty years, there is no reason he cannot continue to do so. *Particularly* if we cast Sissy as Miranda."

"What? Sissy? That shriveled cooze? Oh, c'mon. She's *wrong*, the wrong woman for Miranda. I'm only testing her as a favor to Sam. She could never play Miranda. Miranda is sexy, feminine, voluptuous. Sissy's too—too—" He fumbled for the word.

"Hard?" asked Gertrude.

"Yeah. Hard, ball-breaking hard. She lacks—"

"Sex appeal?" murmured Gertrude.

"Yeah. Miranda's gotta have tons of the old SA."

"She's a brilliant actress, Abby," said Gertrude.

"Yup—in the right role, tremendous. I don't deny that, but I don't know many guys who would want to get it up for her."

"Well, let's think about her for Sirope, then?" said Gertrude.

"Sirope! For Christ's sake, the woman's supposed to be the fuckin' Virgin Mary. She's Ingrid Bergman before Rossellini, Doris Day with Little Red Riding Hood thrown in. We need a *saint* for Sirope. And there ain't many saints in this city, particularly forty-year-old ones."

"Let's try her," said Gertrude with a wheedling smile. "I think she'll be wonderful. A bitch playing a saint—it's inspired casting, Abby."

"Oh, God, Gert. She's all wrong."

"Abby, Abby—what can we lose? She's a fabulous actress, she still looks good—she's got that tired angelic look. A bit of a pain, I admit."

"A *bit?*" Abby threw in. "I know ten directors who would rather direct the shark in *Jaws* than work with her. But O.K. O.K.—O.K.—if you think it could affect the Sam Sharp situation she'll test. She's testing for both parts."

"Right?" said Gertrude, knowing she'd won. "It's the test that counts, isn't it, Abby?"

Sissy had decidedly mixed feelings about testing for both Miranda and Sirope. She couldn't decide whether the network was paying her a compliment or hedging their bets. She sat on the brown suede sofa in Sam's motor home, looking at the bottle of Dom Perignon in an ice bucket, the six-ounce can of Sevruga caviar and the Lalique dish containing grated egg, brown bread and finely shredded onion.

"Welcome to a star, Love, Abby and Gertrude" was written on the gilt-edged card. A Baccarat vase full of calla lilies and cream roses reposed on the mahogany coffee table with another note: "Rooting for you, my darling, Your Sam."

She grimaced. *Why* did he always send her calla lilies? They were only for funerals. God knows she had told him often enough she detested them, even told his florist, but still they arrived on every occasion where floral tributes were appropriate. Lilies and cream roses. How boring!

The orchid was much more attractive—a cymbidium in a plain stone pot. The card simply said, "Kill 'em." It was from Robin Felix, her new agent—a man who knew very well how to keep his clients, and his temper, unlike her ex-agent, Doug. Sissy as a client was a lucrative proposition, but sometimes without a doubt she was simply the most difficult of any female stars Robin had ever handled. However, he felt she had the inside track to the role of Sirope—which he knew she was right for, and he was going to be right there when the big TV bucks came rolling in.

"Ready for you, Miss Sharp." Debbie was deferential as she knocked at the door of the motor home. Sissy was the only actress testing today occupying one. The others were all in the egg boxes. "Can I get you something to eat or drink?"

"No, thank you, my dear," said Sissy grandly. "I never eat or drink before a performance. Just see that the prop man puts a bottle of Perrier water and a packet of Dunhill cigarettes next to my chair and make sure that chair is right next to the one of the lighting cameraman, Mr. Dominick."

"Right away, Miss Sharp," chirped Debbie, scampering away.

Sissy entered the makeup room by one door as Rosalinde exited the other. Ben was putting the finishing touch to Chloe's face. She looked radiantly exciting. This was a completely different face from the pale, washed-out visage of this morning. Witchy, bitchy, sexy, exotic, yet soft—Ben had done his work well, although Chloe had the basic beauty to let his craft express itself.

She looks common, thought Sissy, who believed any woman weighing over one hundred pounds, with a chest measurement of more than thirty-three inches, common. Common and overweight. The ladies nodded briefly and then ignored each other as De De, the body makeup girl, dabbed Beige Blush pancake onto Chloe's cleavage.

When Chloe finally walked onto the set at ten-thirty, her palms were sweating. Sabrina and Rosalinde had finished their tests and had left. The crew was taking a coffee-and-doughnut break. Robert Johnson came up and smilingly reintroduced himself.

"Last time we met was at a party at Steve's, when he was married to Ali. I was the guy that went on the cycle race over the

Trancas dunes with him. You were cheering us on like crazy—remember?"

Chloe didn't, but she made all the right noises.

The director came in to discuss the scene.

Chloe half-listened. She had her own ideas about this character—definite ones. And she was going to play it her way.

Pandora King strolled into the makeup room to give Chloe a quick hug and an effusive "Hello, darling!" Pandora was sharp, a good trouper, with no side to her. Except for her enormous makeup case, which went with her everywhere, she was just like a rather acerbic woman next door.

"Darling, darling, we *must* have lunch and discuss this *insanity*. I'm testing for both roles—isn't it a riot?" She laughed, showing strong white teeth and too much gum. Even though she hadn't been made up yet, she wore a light layer of base, lip gloss, blusher, eye liner, and a tousled blond wig. She was not a beautiful woman, but she made the best of herself and would never be caught dead without her face on. "Ready, Miss Carriere?" Debbie popped her head around the door. "As soon as you're dressed, they'd like you back on the set."

Chloe stood in the center of the magnificent set, feeling more relaxed. Milton, the test's director, had staged the scene much the way she had envisioned it. Now it was time for her to perform to the ultimate. Robert stood behind the camera ready to give her lines off. "O.K., ready, darling?" asked Milton. "Yes, fine. I'm ready." Ben dusted her cheeks with a puff, Theo fluffed out her thick dark curls, Trixie fussed with the lace around her shoulders, Hank brought a tape measure to her nose and called out a number, Lazlo held a light box to her face and called instructions to a shadowy figure twenty feet up in the gantry. Big John and Reggie rearranged lights behind her head.

"O.K., Chuck, take it down a tad," called Lazlo to the figure in the gantry.

161

"Right," called Chuck. Now they had all left. Chloe was alone with the camera to record her emotions, her passions. Alone even though seventy-five men and women stood idly by observing her—judging her. Alone. It was time to show them.

"AAAAAND—ACTION," yelled Milton.

" 'I never loved you, Steve,' " said Chloe to Robert calmly, feeling the fire of Miranda building inside her. She remembered the last time she had talked with Josh. *The last time*. She used the emotion that came welling out of her. " 'To me, you were someone to be used, because you always used me. Someone who could get me what I wanted—what I needed.' "

" 'I don't believe you, Miranda,' " said Robert quietly, with dignity.

" 'It's true, Steve. As God is my witness, it's true. How could I love you when I *knew* you killed Nicholas?' " Her eyes were filling with tears now. Real tears. She felt her throat aching, and she had to use her actor's control to stop the tears from carrying her away.

" 'That's a damn lie and you know it.' "

" 'Oh, no, Steve. I have the proof. You see, I was there that night, when you thought you were alone with Nicholas.' " Chloe took a step toward the camera and started to build her intensity. Her nerves felt raw. For two pages she gave the scene everything she could, every nuance, every emotion. Her experiences of life added to her fire. She berated Robert, scorned him, declared that her love for her dead lover, Nicholas, would never end, and that she would hate Steve until her dying day and would do anything to destroy him. Throughout the scene, she thought of Josh. It was Josh she was pouring out her heart to. Josh who had destroyed a part of her that was hollow now, empty—miserable. She thought of how she had loved him with so much passion, of how she could love him again if only . . . if only . . .

When she finished the scene, sweat was dripping down her robe and tears down her face. Milton yelled out in delight, and several crew members broke into spontaneous applause. "And *print!* That was fabulous, darling, absolutely *fabulous.* You're great! We don't need another one."

"Check the gate," yelled Hank.

"It's O.K.," the operator, Bill, said. "Thank you, darling, thank you," Milton enthused. "You were wonderful, you brought tears to my eyes." He bent his head and whispered, "I hope you get it."

Gratefully Chloe walked off the stage. Her coterie of helpers had deserted her and gone off to attend to the next testee. She got out of the lilac negligee herself, combed her hair free of the sticky hairspray and ripped off the false eyelashes. As she finished dressing, she saw through the mirror that Emerald and Co. had arrived.

Emerald never traveled light, never alone, and never on time —a reaction to her childhood as a baby star, when she had had to get up at five each day and live her day by the call sheet. When she was thirty and her contract finally expired after twenty-seven years of living by the clock, Emerald vowed she would never do it again.

She was forty-five minutes late, which for her was almost punctual. She looked great. Her blond hair was freshly bleached, framing her chiseled, newly tucked face, and her figure was as curvy as it had been in the fifties. Behind her marched a battalion of her troops: her personal assistant and man Friday, Rick Rock-Savage, her manager and agent, Eddie De Levigne, and her public relations man, Christopher McCarthy. Eddie was large and nasty, and Christopher was small and sweet. Together they balanced each other out. Christopher's main job was fending off the dozens of calls and inquiries that still came into his office each week for Emerald's availability to do interviews, talk shows, attend openings, appear at charities and attend premieres. Public interest in her had never waned, although she could not get a decent movie job in the States.

Emerald greeted everyone in makeup and hair like an old friend; she had worked with them all through the years, and they adored her.

"I *want* this job, Ben," she said seriously to the bearded giant. "Make me look better than any of them."

"I'll try, darling. I'll do my very best," said Ben, looking at her with professional objectivity.

"How was the English girl's test?" asked Emerald a mite too casually.

"Oh, er, good. She was very good." Ben didn't have the heart to tell her that Chloe had been great; it could affect her performance. "But I gotta tell you, darling, we had a gal in here this morning prettier than Lana in her heyday. We can't beat *her*, 'cause she's just a baby, but I guarantee we'll beat the others."

"I need this job, Ben." Emerald looked into her old friend's eyes. "Do your damnedest for me, you hear?"

She smiled the dazzling smile that had graced a thousand magazine covers and sank into the black leather chair.

12

For the six women, the following days were not easy. Only Sabrina banished thoughts of the role from her mind. She had been offered a feature movie in which she would play a seventeenth-century virgin transported by time warp to a modern-day college campus. She was more interested in that. The part would pay her two hundred thousand dollars, and could make her a major movie star. Then she would be ready to play opposite Al Pacino or Richard Gere, she hoped. She was continuing with her acting classes, while her nights were filled with love and Luis.

"TV is for old actors," she confided to Sue, her agent. "Movies are where it's *at*, and that's where I wanna be!"

Each of the six women had her own individual method of getting through the agonizing waiting period, since it was going to be at least three weeks before the network executives made their decision.

Pandora went to Las Vegas to visit her current boyfriend, a young Borscht Belt comedian, where she spent her time in bed with him or engrossed at the blackjack table.

Chloe stayed at the beach house. She took long walks along the coast, contemplating her future if she failed to get the part. The marriage with Josh was over. Lawyers had taken over the question of the divorce settlement. When necessary, she and Josh spoke by phone; the conversations were like those of casual acquaintances. He told her about his new record; he said he was working hard on the new scenario for his London play.

After dinner she went straight to bed, restlessly switching channels, comparing herself to Farrah, Jackie, Cheryl, Stefanie and Angie, which only made her more depressed.

One day Johnny Swanson called to invite her out. What the hell? she thought. He seems like a nice guy. Who cares if he's ten years younger than I am? The older woman-younger man couple is all the rage these days.

Johnny came to the beach house in a black Porsche 911 Turbo. Of course he *would* have a black Porsche, thought Chloe. It was the ultimate phallic symbol. As she climbed in and looked around the sleek car, she was amused by the way Johnny had fitted it out like a mini-office. Next to the driver's seat was the latest-model cellular phone with automatic dialing for twenty-five numbers. A microphone above the sun visor assured Johnny that he could always hear and be heard on the phone, even while going through tunnels. A highly complex stereo system with four speakers installed in strategic spots amplified Chloe's own mellow voice as she heard a recording of herself singing "From This Moment On."

She smiled, flattered in spite of herself. He certainly knew how to charm. He'd then put on her own favorite recording—an old album of Cole Porter and Gershwin classics. He was definitely very classy, very smooth, and as she looked at his profile, blond hair artfully curling over a black polo neck, very attractive.

In the back of the car was a small TV set, attached to the back of one of the seats, and a well-stocked bar plus a miniature fridge.

"Drink?" offered Johnny, turning left on the Pacific Coast Highway.

"No, thanks—it's illegal in the car," Chloe replied, remembering Josh's recent trouble. "The police are tough on you if you're caught."

"No sweat, sugar, my uncle's the chief of police down here." Johnny laughed. "Here, have one of these instead." He offered her an expertly rolled joint.

"No, thanks," said Chloe, feeling rather old-fashioned. In spite of her years around musicians and rock stars she still hated druggies.

She hadn't been out on a "date" in a long time—since before Josh—over ten years. She felt strange. Strange and archaic. Johnny didn't seem to be fazed that she didn't want a toke, and he chatted amiably until they arrived at a picturesque restaurant nestled in a tiny street behind Topanga Canyon. The owner knew him well, greeting him effusively, and Johnny seemed at home there, even knowing the names of most of the waiters.

Throughout dinner Chloe felt herself warming to him. Despite his brash exterior he was delightful. Witty, charming, lively, handsome—a veritable cornucopia of male goodies. His sense of humor reminded her of Josh—a youthful Josh. So he was young—so what? thought Chloe, feeling abandoned and young herself after they had drunk two bottles of champagne. Twenty-nine wasn't *that* young.

Arm in arm they walked into the cool California night.

"Look—stars. Maybe the world is coming to an end," Johnny said. "I haven't seen stars in California for years."

"Where's the smog? L.A.'s not L.A. without it." Chloe laughed. She felt ebullient, as if a weight had fallen from her shoulders. She liked Johnny more and more, even though she knew his reputation with women. Well, she was a mature adult now, not a naive young woman as she had been with Josh. She was not going to be hurt, whatever happened.

This they would play by *her* rules.

As the black Porsche pulled into her driveway, she invited him in for coffee.

"Never touch it," said Johnny, as he opened her door in his gallant English public-school manner. "I'll take a cognac though. Or an Armagnac if you have it."

They sat before the flickering fire, sipped Armagnac and talked. She had turned the lights off, and through the big picture window the sky was filled with a million stars. They started exchanging pieces of the jigsaw puzzle of their lives that might one day, if their relationship progressed, form a complete picture.

His lips eventually touched hers, and she found herself responding. His mouth was insistent, seductive, sweet. His hands touched her face, then fluttered to the buttons of her silk blouse. It had been a long time since Chloe had been caressed. It was all too sweet, all too tender.

She tried to draw back as a vision of Josh came to her.

This was wrong, wrong, wrong. Johnny was too young for her. It was too soon after Josh. She wasn't ready. He would tell the boys at Ma Maison. He would boast about her. *Josh,* her inner voice screamed silently. Josh, oh, Josh, I don't want this. I don't. I want you. She tried to put the brakes on, then realized how ridiculous it was. A forty-year-old woman acting like a girl. Necking like an adolescent. Smooching as though she were sixteen again. "No, I can't. I'm sorry, I just can't, Johnny." She pushed his tender, insistent mouth away, and his hands, which were expertly but gently pulling on her skirt now.

"Why *not?*" His voice was hoarse; he became more insistent. He kissed her again and again. He seemed to know where she wanted to be kissed and his lips were there, turning her into a furnace against her will.

She had no answer. She felt weak. She wanted him. She hadn't been with Josh for months now. This, their third separation, looked as though it would be their last. She certainly wasn't in love with Johnny, but he was attractive and she found him sexually appealing.

Why not? She felt surges of desire building within her. She wanted him to take her now. She felt the hunger of her sexual need.

Suddenly it didn't seem worthwhile to fight him any more. Go with it, she thought. To hell with tomorrow. To hell with Josh. To hell with what people think. With thoughts of Josh filling her head and her heart, she let Johnny Swanson take her to bed.

During the difficult weeks of waiting, Emerald went on a social whirl. Ever popular, she accepted every party, every luncheon, every premiere. She emptied her diminishing bank account on dozens of new outfits. Her business manager despaired, but she smiled deliciously and continued to spend.

Sissy punished her body religiously. She lost three more pounds on a magic new diet of Chinese seaweed, rice cakes and kiwi fruit. She spent her mornings jogging, doing yoga and exercising, and her afternoons on the phone with Daphne and Robin Felix, her agent, discussing her chances.

Rosalinde Lamaze spent a great deal of time in her sunny little kitchen indulging in two of her favorite pastimes: cooking and watching soap operas on Channel 8, the Spanish station. At the moment she was preparing refried beans and rice, which smelled delicious. She couldn't wait to devour them with her young niece, Angelica, and later devour Angelica. The two of them sat in the breakfast nook eating beans and rice as, enthralled, they watched Lolita Lopez, great Mexican star of the fifties, emoting in *Mis Niños y Mis Hombres,* a favorite of the Spanish-speaking community of L.A.

Rosalinde was happy just pottering in her house. She was a simple woman at heart. Simple in everything but sex. She had become bored by the sexual embraces of her numerous lovers over the past few years. The weight of their thick bodies, their heavy breathing, their sweating hot flesh, their smells of alcohol and tobacco had started to repel her.

Recently, each time she had let a man make love to her, she had tried to feel *some* sort of excitement and had felt nothing. When she failed to respond, she impatiently sent them away, finding sensation with her fingers. That too, soon began to pale. When Angelica, her cute little eighteen-year-old niece, came to stay, she found to her delight that they had a lot more in common than a love for refried beans and Channel 8 soap operas.

These days nothing could compare to the enthralling nights she spent exploring and being explored by the delicate body of the young Angelica.

When Chloe's agent called and said that Dionne Warwick had suddenly been taken ill and couldn't perform at the Las Vegas Empire Hotel, Chloe jumped at the opportunity to fill in for her. She would be getting away from Johnny, who was pestering her now, wanting what she didn't have to give him. She realized that her attraction to him was diminishing more rapidly than she even dreamed was possible. What had been for her a minor fling to get her over Josh had meant more to him, and he was insistent on seeing her more than she wanted to see him.

"Singing again will get your mind off the waiting, duckie," said Jasper soothingly.

"You're right, Jasper, this waiting is too much even for my nerves of steel," Chloe said gratefully.

"Can you leave the day after tomorrow?" He sounded anxious. "Be ready for a nine o'clock show."

"What?" gasped Chloe. "Jasper, I know we're both British and can do anything, of course, but *darling*, I haven't rehearsed. I haven't even sung a note since the last tour ended."

"That was only two months ago, my dear," Jasper chimed in smoothly. "If you can take the company plane from Burbank on Thursday at one o'clock, you can be rehearsing in the Copa Room at three. You can sing your little heart out for four hours. Surely that's enough for a silver-throated talented nightingale like you, my love?"

"Bullshit, Jasper!" Chloe smiled in spite of herself. "Actually, though, it could be rather exciting; at least it will give me something to do to take my mind off that bloody *test.*"

"Good girl, clever girl." Jasper's voice was soothing. "I have the hotel over a barrel moneywise, darling. Not quite what Dionne was getting, naturally, but forty-five grand a week, how does that grab you, my love?"

"It will keep the wolf from the door and help me at Valentino for a while." Chloe was mentally going through her wardrobe. "O.K., Jasper, I'll see you at the airport. I must pack now."

Chloe filled her suitcases swiftly and efficiently. Twenty years on the road had enabled her to pack what was necessary in minimum time. She surveyed her rack of beaded evening dresses critically as she skimmed through other racks, selecting and eliminating with an expert eye. She packed a red bugle-beaded Bob Mackie slit to the thigh, with a "Merry Widow," also beaded in red, and another in black lace, a silver lace and nude chiffon Nolan Miller, accented on the broad padded shoulders with exquisite appliquéd flowers, went in along with a sleek black silk jersey Chanel, the flute-shaped sleeves trimmed in black fox. A white lace Valentino dotted with pearls and rhinestones, his masterful cut accenting the simplicity and purity of the long, slightly fitted gown, completed her selection of stage gowns. Chloe surveyed them while waiting for her maid to bring her black wardrobe skips and tissue paper.

Next she surveyed her two racks of short, informal evening outfits, dresses and suits that she changed into after the show, when she would either go out to dine or cut a swath through the casinos of the Vegas strip. Three Saint Laurent suits and three Bruce Oldfields, two or three Coveris, one Donna Karan, and her favorite dress, a black lace point d'esprit, designed by herself and made by Freddy Langlan. Was that enough for two weeks? God forbid she should ever be seen offstage in the same outfit more than once. Suppose Sinatra was performing at Caesar's? Barbara would certainly be there, too. Las Vegas was a small community. They would all be at the same parties every night. Be prepared. Better too much than too little.

She hastily picked out two more short dresses, a Karl Lagerfeld and an Anthony Price, and gave instructions to Manuela to pack the correct accessories, which were neatly stored in appropriate boxes under each dress. Chloe was exceedingly organized about her clothes. Each outfit she considered an investment, and she took great care of them.

She scooped up an armful of assorted sweaters, shirts and skirts, threw them on the bed and went to her jewelry drawers. An entire chest of small drawers contained her extensive collection of costume jewelry. Not for her the responsibility of real jewels. With the exception of her sapphire-and-diamond ring and a diamond Boucheron watch, she only wore faux jewels. Her collection was fabulous, extremely expensive, and much admired.

Manuela had finished packing the theatrical gowns and acces-

sories in the black skips, and was now filling her burgundy ostrich suitcases.

Johnny had called this morning murmuring something about
meeting Richard Hurrel at the gym, then lunch with "the boys"
at Ma Maison.

As Chloe rolled her hair and rapidly applied makeup, she
tried to ring him at the gym. He was not there. Ma Maison
expected him at one-thirty. She left a short message with his
secretary.

"Where you going?" Sally appeared at the door without
knocking, as usual. She was sporting a new punk hairdo and her
usual sarcastically belligerent attitude.

"What are you doing here?" Chloe asked as evenly as she
could.

"I'm picking up some more of my things. Dad bought me an
apartment in the Wilshire Towers. I'm decorating it myself." She
fingered one of Chloe's Gallé vases carelessly.

"I'm doing it modern, of course. State of the art. High tech."

"How nice," said Chloe pleasantly, wishing the girl would
stop touching her things and leave.

Sally's hair had been shaved two inches above her ears, and
what was left had been dyed into jet-black and silver stripes and
sprayed with a lacquer so strong that seven- and eight-inch
spikes stood up all over her head. Her lipstick was purple, as
was her eye paint. She wore an incredible outfit—a purple vinyl
skirt, barely covering her pubis, silver thigh-high leggings over
silver crocheted tights, and an immense lavender mohair sweater
which almost covered the skirt. Around her neck was a five-inch
statue of Christ on the Cross attached to a tarnished silver
chain, and she appeared to have pinned what looked like black
bats in her hair. From one ear hung a black rubber snake, the
kind sold at toy stores for fifty cents, in the other was one of
Chloe's most expensive Dior rhinestone earrings. She seemed
high, although it was barely 11 A.M.

173

"Where are you off to then?" Sally opened and closed the drawers of Chloe's lingerie cabinet, picking up and discarding some of her stepmother's most intimate apparel as she spoke.

"Vegas." Chloe gritted her teeth in disgust, determined not to rise to the bait that Sally always threw to her.

"Got a gig then?"

"Yup, two weeks at the Empire, in Vegas." Chloe concentrated on combing out her hair, observing Sally opening her bathroom cabinet and casually inspecting the contents. She seethed, but she could hardly throw a teenager into the street.

"Oh, well, I suppose you better get on with your singing career," Sally said with a sneer. "It doesn't look like you're gonna get the part, does it?"

Chloe was calm as she finished her face, ever determined not to let this snotty kid get to her. "Why do you think that, Sally?"

"It's in the trades today, haven't you seen it yet?"

"No. Why don't you tell me what it said, dear? I have a plane to catch."

"It's in Army's column—he said that Rosalinde Lamaze is a shoo-in." She left the room and returned with the paper. "Here."

Chloe glanced at it briefly, her heart sinking.

"It's just conjecture," she said briskly, checking in her Hermès alligator bag for her lucky mascots.

"Sure." Sally grinned, revealing a small diamond inserted in her front tooth. "Well, good luck in Vegas then, Chloe. See ya."

Chloe noticed that she had appropriated a vial of Valium, a mauve chiffon scarf and four silver bracelets before she left.

"Limo's here, Miz Carriere." Manuela buzzed her. "He's comin' up now for the bags."

"Send him up," said Chloe. "I'm ready." And with a deep breath she walked swiftly down the stairs.

* * *

Rosalinde read the piece and smiled. Her new press agent had proved his point.

She had agreed to sign with his firm at three thousand dollars a month if they got her into Army Archerd's important trade column within the week. Well, they had done it. They were worth the three grand. She called her business manager and told him to send the check.

She glanced at the other side of her bed. It was empty. Angelica had gone to visit her sick mother in Mexico City for the weekend. Three days to work on a tan, thought Rosalinde, luxuriating in her crumpled flowered sheets. And who knows, maybe I *will* get the part. God knows she had said enough Hail Marys, confessed to sins she could barely remember, and lit an extra thirty candles to the Virgin Mary and baby Jesus last Sunday in church. If religion and superstition could guarantee it, she should get Miranda.

Calvin read the item in the gossip column again and again. Cold rage gripped him. What kind of people were these Hollywood morons? Didn't they know a true star when they saw one? How could they *possibly* pass over the most beautiful, talented actress in the world? How could they even *consider* that trumped-up Spanish tart, Rosalinde? It was an outrage. A slur and an insult to Emerald.

Calvin was out every night now with the amateur and professional paparazzi, who hung around outside Spago, Morton's and Chasen's like a pack of wolves, whenever they heard through the grapevine that a party, an opening or a premiere was going on.

He had seldom been disappointed in the past two weeks— Emerald was having one of her social bouts. Desperately insecure about the results of the test, she was hitting the high spots of Tinsel Town with a vengeance.

Emerald had gradually started falling off the wagon. She was furious with herself for her lack of willpower, but she simply couldn't help it. She needed to forget about that damn test. Forget how much she needed that part. Forget the fact that in spite of her mansion and the fabulous jewels, she was almost flat broke. Forget she was well along in her forties and not good marriage material after so many failures. She threw herself into social life with gusto, yet was completely unaware of the slight, sandy-haired, pale-eyed man who watched her every movement. Each restaurant, each party, each opening she attended, Calvin was there, looking through his lens at Emerald, holding his breath at her beauty, capturing her flesh, her blond loveliness forever with each click of his shutter.

His room now was a positive shrine to her. Every wall was covered with posters from her films. More than two hundred plastic frames contained her image, many of the pictures taken by him. Huge scrapbooks also filled with her pictures were piled in the bookshelves, along with seventeen of the books that had been written about Emerald's movie career and her even more exciting private life.

He even had one of the Emerald dolls that had been so popular with every little girl in America in the 1930s when she was a baby star and box-office champion. The doll was three feet high, with big round sausage-shaped flaxen curls and huge green saucer eyes fringed with thick auburn lashes. The little painted mouth formed a perfect Cupid's bow, and tiny porcelain hands had fingernails that were painted pale pink. The doll had come in a white carrying case, complete with three changes of costume, from a lime-and-white striped bathing suit with a tiny rubber cap and a miniature terry-cloth robe to a frilly green party frock. There was also a little green enamel mirror with comb and brush which could be used to comb the Emerald doll's curls.

Sometimes Calvin sat and did his doll's hair. He would talk to her as he manipulated the nylon curls with his rough hands. "You *are* Miranda, my lovely girl," he would croon to the painted face as he turned the curls around his fingers. "No one, but *no one,* can be her except you." Lovingly he would change her clothes, pausing often to examine and stroke the smooth, sexless body of the doll. He would put the tiny cotton socks on her perfect feet, then the little black patent-leather Mary Jane shoes.

He loved this doll. But he loved the real Emerald even more.

13

Rosalinde glanced again in the rearview mirror of her BMW. It seemed stupid to be paranoid about this car that appeared to follow her from La Scala to her home on the summit of Mulholland Drive. The car pulled ahead of her and vanished around a corner at high speed. Stupid, but all the same, the voice of reason warned her, as she drove up the long, winding canyon: "Watch out, *querida*."

John Lennon's sweet voice poured forth "Imagine" from her tape deck. She thought about his death—so recent, so sudden, so... It could happen to *me*, she thought—it could happen to any of us. To Robert Redford, with his notions about solar energy and conservation. Or to Jane Fonda, with her radical ideals and impossible exercises. To anyone some fanatic became phobic about. To *her,* for no reason at all except that she was a star. She shivered, despite the warmth of the car, as she drew up outside her Mulholland mansion.

Why did I buy a bloody mansion? she asked herself as she sat in the car staring at the ominous outlines of her home. And *why* wouldn't I even consider having a bodyguard? Everyone was getting one these days.

The house looked like something out of Edgar Allan Poe on this windy night: a gray stone facade, thick black clouds, winds of fifty mph. There was a Santa Ana blowing, and the palm trees swayed violently in the gale. Strange objects—birds? leaves? debris from some unknown holocaust?—scudded around the house. Her house. Wrested from the fangs of a crazed ex-husband and his ravening Beverly Hills lawyer. Court fights, acrimony, tabloid headlines. Thanks to some brilliant legal manipulations, eventually it became *her* house. Was it worth it, though, this big pile of pewter-colored brick, ersatz nineteenth century, with the latest twentieth-century plumbing?

She cut the engine. It was suddenly still. The wind had dropped with characteristic California suddenness. It was a silent night all right, but far from holy—a silent and venomous night. She felt suddenly fearful.

Calvin sat in the attic observing Rosalinde's hesitation from the tiny window.

He heard her close the car door—her footsteps had a deceptively casual sound—and insert her key into the front-door lock. He heard her call out halfheartedly, "Rosa, are you back?" proving she had given her housekeeper the night off. The door closed. She was inside. Inside the house with him. Just the two of them, he thought, locked in together....

179

Soon the TV clicked on in her bedroom. He heard her flushing the toilet as he crept down the stairs and put his ear to the bedroom door.

"Hi, Angelica." She was talking on the phone. "I know this is crazy, but I'm spooked tonight." Calvin smiled to himself. "I miss you, *querida mía*. Come home to me soon."

Rosalinde was smiling as she hung up the receiver and popped a chocolate into her lush mouth. As Calvin pushed open the door of her sanctuary, she looked up, startled.

"What do you want?" Suddenly her voice was a dry rasp. The pupils of her beautiful brown eyes dilated to points of fear, and her hands brought the creased comforter up to her body as if she could protect herself with it.

Calvin could sense the animal terror in her as he stood at the door. He felt himself controlling the situation. Controlling her with his presence.

"Nothing," he replied slowly. "I don't want anything at all." He stood very still, taking in the surroundings. Everything was pink. She sat cross-legged, a crumpled pink comforter pulled up to her waist, a flimsy silken wrapper barely concealing her abundant body. Behind her dark nimbus of curls were piles of pillows embroidered with sayings: "A hard man is good to find"; "Happiness is having you for a friend"; "I come alive at five." Stuffed animals cluttered the bed, even an old Snoopy.

Calvin jumped as he felt a silken ghost brush his legs and saw a white Persian cat spring off its mistress's bed. The cat crouched under the dust ruffle, peering out. The two of them stared at Calvin with eyes of dread.

Rosalinde swallowed. She thought of what she had read in magazine articles about rapists. How to talk them out of it, be assertive. The stories she had read had said to be ballsy, tough, let him know she was stronger than he, that he could not get the better of her.

"Get the fuck out of this room, you creep!" she shouted in a voice that called upon all of her acting ability. "How *dare* you come in here? You're trespassing. I'm calling the police."

Frantically she tried to remember where she had put the panic button. Bel Air Patrol had been absolutely specific when they installed the latest fail-safe burglar alarm. First and foremost, they had instructed her, *always* turn on the alarm when leaving or entering the house. She realized she had ignored *that* advice tonight, as she had ignored the second warning: *Always* keep the panic button on your person while in the house. When activated, it would send a signal straight to police headquarters, and help would arrive within eight minutes. So they said. She knew it was more like fifteen or twenty minutes because she had pressed the panic button by mistake a couple of times. She *must* keep this maniac talking! Where, oh *where* was the damn panic button? she cried silently to herself.

One hand clasped her robe around her throat as the other crept beneath the rumpled sheets, magazines, pillows and scripts in search of the alarm.

She looked at her bedside table. The pink marble top was obscured by the paraphernalia of her bedtime pastimes. A half-empty wineglass, two coffee cups with congealed contents, an apple with one bite out of it, piles of letters, fan mail, photographs of herself, baby oil, ashtrays overflowing with butts, even, she noticed, a roach. What she would give for a puff now!

This wasn't, *couldn't* be happening to her! Suddenly, she caught sight of the panic button, half hidden under the pile of mail. Time to talk. Time to deal with this madman—for he looked mad, his face soaked with the perspiration that flowed down his forehead, his eyes dilated. He's even more frightened than I am, she told herself—but it didn't help.

Calvin licked his lips. He could taste the warm salt of his sweat. The bitch was talking. It was hard to understand what she was saying, the pounding in his head was so intense, like a hammer. Her lips were moving but he couldn't hear her. As she spoke, her robe parted more. He glimpsed her breasts, her navel, and that other thing. The thing that disgusted yet excited him. Her hand stroked a stuffed teddy bear. He wanted her hand to stroke *him,* but at the same time the thought repelled him. He loathed her femaleness. Hated her moist red mouth, her high, brown-tipped breasts. As she talked, her hand was moving to the bedside table. What was the bitch doing? She had something in her hand, now what was it. A radio? A tape recorder? She continued talking to him. Smiling, looking pleased with herself. Bitch. Cow. Whore. She almost looked as if she were tempting him as she sat on her satin sheets, robe open, stroking her bear and trying to smile.

Suddenly he heard her words: "You know you're quite a good-looking guy. What's your name, honey?"

Honey! She was calling him "honey"! What kind of disgusting slut was she? When a man breaks into her room she calmly invites him to seduce her! She was a slut, a tramp. That the network was even *considering* her for the same part as Emerald was an abomination. *She* was an abomination, he told himself. He walked toward her slowly. The pounding started in his head again. He saw only her actions—her seductive smile, her calm voice. As he came close to her her smile faded. A whimper escaped her.

"Don't hurt my face, please," she said in a feeble, little-girl voice.

"Your face?" The fact that she cared so much about it made him want to smash into it. "What face?" He picked up a large bronze statue and brought it down with all his force on her upturned, pleading face.

"No, please, no!" Blood streamed from her forehead. "I'll do anything. You can take me, do what you want, but please, please don't kill me, don't, don't, I beg you."

"Whore!" he screamed as his hands encircled her white

throat, slippery now with her blood. "Bitch!"

The cat jumped fearfully away, its back arched as it tried to get out of the room, but the door was closed.

When Calvin had finished with her he gazed at her voluptuous nude body splayed on the satin comforter. In spite of himself the urge to ravish her was so strong that he hated her even more for this feeling she aroused. She was stretched out in such a way, her blank celluloid stare and limp flesh curiously erotic, that he could not help himself. The white cat cowered in fright, low yowls emanating from its throat as it watched Calvin perform the ultimate horror. As Calvin finally drew away from the still body he heard police sirens in the street.

By the time the police reached the house he was gone. Only the white cat hiding under a sofa was witness to what had happened.

Chloe stared horrified at the headline: "ROSALINDE LAMAZE SLAIN—RAPED." She put down the paper, shaking her head in disbelief: Rosalinde dead, horribly murdered. It was unbelievable. What was even more horrible was the message scrawled obscenely in lipstick across the body: *"You won't be the last."*

Chloe shuddered, pushing away the poached eggs and grapefruit juice the hotel waiter had placed before her.

The TV set was tuned to the local Las Vegas news program. She switched channels with the remote to hear more. After every program there was another news flash with more reports about Rosalinde's death. Clues, inside information, close friends and family, fans with tear-stained faces talking to the TV cameras about their dead darling.

Chloe was genuinely upset. Although she had not known Rosalinde well, the woman had been a guest at her house only a few weeks ago. She wished she could call Josh to talk about it. He had always been her best friend. They had always been able to laugh, to cry, to discuss everything. . . . But Josh was now the past. She looked at the Cartier clock next to the rumpled burgundy sheets. Not rumpled by passion—just by yet another sleepless Las Vegas night.

It was 1 P.M. It would be 9 P.M. in London. Even if she did call Josh—which she shouldn't anyway, her lawyer had forbidden it—he would be out. He'd be down at one of his haunts, the wine bars in Chelsea or Soho, hanging out with the boys, his drinking and womanizing buddies. No doubt he'd contacted them all again, started up where he'd left off before he married Chloe. He'd be buying them champagne, getting drunk, telling jokes—and all the boys would be hanging on to his every word. After all, he was a star. But he loved the camaraderie of his own sex, the jokes about women, the drunken anecdotes.

Forget Josh, she sighed to herself as the phone rang. It was Johnny Swanson with the latest Hollywood gossip. He wanted to talk about Rosalinde's murder. "They found a book of matches, apparently from some bar in downtown L.A., someplace Rosalinde would never go. Must be the killer's."

"How do you know?"

"Uncle Van. He's a buddy of the L.A. Chief of Police. He says they'll find this nut case soon."

"I hope so." *You won't be the last.* It had an ominous ring to it. Chloe shivered.

"Anyway, sugar pie, I miss you, and I'm thinking of you," said Johnny affectionately, not mentioning the evening of fun and frolic he had indulged in the previous night with a sultry Brazilian actress in town overnight to plug her new movie. "I'll be up to see you next weekend, sugar, O.K.?"

"O.K., Johnny, I'll look forward to that." She sat on the rumpled bed and looked at her heart-shaped face in the mirrored canopy above it. Would it always remind her of Josh? *Damn him!*

She picked up the phone and gave the hotel operator a Lon-

don number. Time to talk to Annabel. Darling Annabel, her
baby, who always made her feel so good....

Rosalinde's sister Maria held the wake at her Beverly Hills
mansion. Maria had married a successful movie producer,
Emanuel Siegal, taking immediately to Beverly Hills like a duck
to water. The wake lasted five days. Chasen's catered continually at a cost of over ten thousand dollars. Chuck Pick supplied
valet parking from noon to midnight, three hairdressers from
the Beverly Hills Hotel were in constant attendance, servicing
Maria, the young, grief-stricken Angelica and a host of Rosalinde's cousins and aunts who appeared from Mexico and
downtown Los Angeles.

Practically every major producer, director, agent and star in
town came to pay homage to the woman at whom they had
often sneered when she was alive, although, to be fair, they had
grudgingly admired her indisputable spirit and the box-office
pulling power that had made millions of dollars for many of
them.

Rosalinde would have been proud to know who attended her
wake. Many of the same people who would barely have crossed
the commissary to say hello to her in life cried crocodile tears
and mouthed platitudes about her. Despite her on-screen success, Rosalinde had never been socially accepted. There had
been something a little tacky about her. Certainly truck drivers,
blue-collar workers and college kids had adored her, but in spite
of her sister's efforts, she had never made a social impact. Not
that she needed to. Her richly varied sex life and her career had
been all-consuming. She had merely shrugged when Maria had
tried to get her more socially committed.

As the turnout at Rosalinde's wake showed, Hollywood still
loved to mourn its celebrated dead in style, as though to make
up for the long-gone wonderful parties of the thirties, forties and

fifties; with each decade, Hollywood's sparkle had dimmed. Nevertheless, a carnival atmosphere prevailed in the Siegals' antique-filled yellow living room featured only last month in *Architectural Digest*. Manny had never stopped moaning about the cost, but he wasn't moaning now, Maria said to herself, proudly watching Hollywood's famous at her groaning buffet.

Comedian Buddy Bridges, with a week off between Vegas dates, was a daily visitor, regaling everyone with a stream of patter so blue that he would not dare to do it on Carson, or even in Vegas. The word had spread that the Siegals' was *the* place to be—that week.

Even Sissy, crocodile tears, crocodile shoes and matching handbag, went to the wake. She made her entrance complete with tiny pillbox hat with point d'esprit veil on Friday evening, the day before the funeral. She had been informed by Daphne, who had hung out at the Siegals' daily, receiving the juiciest gossip she had obtained all year, that *"tout* Hollywood" was there. Indeed it was, and Sissy had herself a productive time culminating in a discussion with Menahem Golan of a possible three-picture deal with Cannon.

The funeral at Forest Lawn was a frantic mix of hysterical fans, munching junk food and snapping stars with their Instamatics, and eager paparazzi, heedless of the immaculate grass and flower beds, pushing and shoving for their respective tabloids. Sweaty cops, boiling in ninety-degree heat, tried to keep order. A small group of soberly clad mourners, Rosalinde's closest friends and family, attempted to retain dignity in the face of the pandemonium. Four burly TV camera crews pushed heedlessly through the gaping crowds, their cables tripping up those too busy gawking to look where they were going. A few blocks down the tree-lined boulevard, four TV trucks manned by efficient technicians recorded the scene for the jaded appetites of their nightly news viewers. The only thing that mattered to them was getting the best footage. To that end, people were pushed, lawns were mangled, tempers frayed. Celebrity funerals rated at least fifteen or twenty seconds on prime time news and garnered good ratings, particularly if there was an interview with a major name.

Chuck Waggoner, anchorman from CBS News, an old and experienced hand, had covered most of the major Hollywood funerals of the past twenty-two years. He looked serious and trustworthy, wearing a somber gray suit, as he stood to the side of the chattering crowd, while the cortege and coffin came slowly out of the church and up the hill to Rosalinde's green and sunny final resting place. It was her wish not to be cremated. She had been shocked when the loveliness of Marilyn Monroe was incinerated nearly twenty years ago. Although barely seventeen at the time, she had told Maria that when she died she wanted to be buried in a beautiful sunny place, Maria had remembered, and as the big oak-and-bronze nine-thousand-dollar coffin was lowered into the ground, and cool earth covered it, she wept for her little sister who had loved the sun so much.

Calvin, wearing a Universal City T-shirt and bermudas, and sucking on a frozen Kool-Aid, stood outside the church with the rest of the paparazzi and fans. He was filled with a strange joy, a feeling of euphoria. He smiled and chatted with the other photographers, who were a bit surprised at the gregariousness of this usually reticent little man.

He felt almost godlike. He had done it! He had paved the way for his idol to get the part. Surely the network would pick her now! Emerald. His goddess.

He pretended to photograph the other stars as they drew up in their mourning clothes, posing briefly for the photographers. Sabrina Jones came with Luis Mendoza. They looked stunning together, arm in arm, both dressed in charcoal gray. Her blond unteased unpinned unbleached hair blew in the warm Pacific breeze. Luis's curls fell darkly over his forehead, accenting his brooding Latin eyes. The photographers surged forward to snap them. Calvin stayed back. He was waiting for *her* to arrive. He knew she would. And she did.

Emerald looked exquisite clad in a silk jersey dress of such a dark green it was almost black, a demure inch below her knees; she wore black hose with seams and a large black straw hat on her platinum hair. She was escorted by Sol, hastily summoned from New York for escort duty. Sol was more than happy to oblige, as the torch he carried for her still burned brightly.

"You'll get that role, Emerald my love," whispered Calvin to himself. "Miranda *is* you! Only you can play her." If only she could know what he had done for her, he thought. But he wasn't finished yet. . . .

Sissy watched the news coverage at six o'clock, grudgingly admiring Emerald's stunning yet sober outfit. She sneered at Luis, Latin-smooth as ever. What a prick, she thought, sipping Perrier and chewing a sliver of lemon peel.

She had just finished her massage. Her skin felt taut and tingly. She was always relaxed after Sven's hard Scandinavian fingers manipulated her bony frame.

A few years ago Sven's hard Scandinavian cock had manipulated her too. It had been an erotic experience, especially exciting since her door had been left slightly ajar and she knew that Sam was on his way back from the studio and might discover her at any moment, flat on her back on a portable massage table, covered with baby oil, legs in the air, a large blond Swede installed between them.

That had been the first and last time Sven had gifted her with the pièce de résistance of his famous Swedish massage. Not that he wasn't good at it, but Sissy preferred toy-boys, and Sven, at thirty-seven, was too old for her taste.

"The best stud in town, dear, is the silent Swede," Daphne had confided to Sissy at Ma Maison one day at lunch as they became nostalgically drunk on champagne supplied by Patrick Terrail while celebrating one of Daphne's many birthdays. "Ten years ago, dear, more or less, I never remember dates, we had a little thing, or rather a big one." She giggled as Patrick poured more champagne and threw in a strawberry for good measure.

"Darling heart, he was divine, truly divine, and what is more, he doesn't *talk,* no ceaseless chatter about business, politics or *golf!"* The dreariness of masculine conversation had never appealed to Daphne. Masculine company was important, men were important, too, for their proper functions, which for Daphne were money and sex, but she preferred the company of her own sex to share her most intimate thoughts, and the thing she adored perhaps even more than sex—gossip!

The fact that Daphne had now been able to parlay her considerable talent for the innuendo, the whispered secret, the rumored affair into a lucrative syndicated column had also given her some new influence in town, which she was beginning to relish.

Now, snuggled in a white terry-cloth robe from the Ritz, Sissy read Daphne's latest column. She owned a selection of terry-cloth robes taken from every major hotel in the world, a habit she had developed when the studio picked up the tab.

"Vivacious and free-loving Rosalinde Lamaze will be sorely missed by her scores of loyal friends and millions of fans. Our town honored the sexy raven-haired spitfire at the fabulous mansion in the heart of Beverly Hills of her sister, Maria, and brother-in-law, Emanuel Siegal. Emanuel told me confidentially that Dustin Hoffman will definitely play Toulouse-Lautrec in his remake of *Moulin Rouge,* which Manny will film in Paris next spring. His lovely and grieving wife, Maria, confided in spite of her sadness that they were looking forward to their vacation on the Côte d'Azur at the fabulous Voile D'Or Hotel, where they would be meeting their good friend Adnan Kashoggi on his gorgeous boat, *Nabila,* and attending Lynn Wyatt's annual birthday bash. And reed-thin, divine-as-ever Sissy Sharp, elegant in Bill Blass black, lamented the loss of the talent and beauty of Rosalinde. Sissy had just returned from a sneak preview of her new picture, *Lady Be Bad,* which opens nationwide next week, and is tipped to be a big one.

" 'Luis Mendoza will be a major star after this film is released,' confided the ever-generous Sissy.

"They sure don't make 'em like Sissy any more. A true star in the old Hollywood mold. Glamorous, talented and considerate. And one of the leading contenders for the most coveted and talked-about role of Miranda in 'Saga.' "

Sissy reread the article, pleased that Daphne had been so kind to her. That's what friends were for. She picked up her Sony cassette recorder and left a message for her secretary to send a basket of orchids to Daphne.

And then there were three, she mused. Three actresses who would be right for Miranda Hamilton.

Poor old Rosalinde, you will not be missed by me, she thought spitefully.

The amateur British bitch and that talentless, passé Hollywood celebrity ex-baby star, Emerald, were her only remaining competition. There surely could be no contest in the minds of the powers that be at the network that she, Sissy Sharp, acclaimed actress and Academy Award-winning star, was the only right choice to play Miranda.

14

The day after Rosalinde's funeral Emerald woke up feeling sad. She had liked Rosalinde, who, although younger, had been a close friend in the early seventies.

Emerald remembered the smoldering summer when they both had found themselves staying at the Byblos in St. Tropez. Emerald was between husbands and recuperating from filming in Spain during which time she had not only fucked her two leading men but also the lighting cameraman—a good trick that guaranteed to get a girl great closeups. Rosalinde was on the prowl, taking her pick of the dozens of tanned, gorgeous young men who strolled the beaches, bistros and discos looking for distractions.

The two women had fun together. Emerald's sexual appetites were not as eclectic as Rosalinde's, but when Rosalinde, flushed from lovemaking with some Gallic stud, regaled her with the stories of her exploits, she would get hysterical with laughter as they ate croissants and drank café au lait on Emerald's tiny balcony overlooking the Mediterranean.

Emerald had been her idol since she was a schoolgirl in Mexico, and it thrilled her to have her idol right there.

Emerald enjoyed playing the sophisticated older woman, dispensing advice and wisdom with the breakfast croissants. "There's nothing wrong at all with having a passion for men. I've loved a few myself, but I married or lived with most of them. Your mistake, my darling, is you're just too open about it."

"I know." A frown creased Rosalinde's pretty face. "I hear what they have called me sometimes. The Mexican Open! What an insult! Did they call Errol Flynn or Warren Beatty such names? They loved women like I love men. Oohh! Look at him!" Rosalinde suddenly leaned over the crimson bougainvillea to observe a young man bouncing on the hotel diving board. He had rippling muscles, a deep tan and a more than respectable power bulge. "Mmm, *very* nice. What do you think, Emerald?"

"Sure is, why don't you go get him?" Emerald laughed. "And I will see you at the Tahiti for lunch." When they met at lunchtime, Rosalinde, as always, had caught her prey. She was twenty-six years old, gorgeous, and a movie star few red-blooded males could resist.

Emerald sighed, remembering those days. She was sad. When she was sad only two things could cheer her up—shopping or a visit to Bekins.

She phoned good old Sol, and he drove her to a large ugly building on Western Avenue. Emerald had told him about Bekins Storage but he had never been there with her.

The staff knew her well. "Good afternoon, Miss Barrymore," the man at the desk said respectfully. "Everything is ready for you."

In an ancient freight elevator they ascended to the third floor and walked down corridors lined with cardboard, metal and wood crates and containers of every possible size.

"Here we are," said the guard as they came to a large padlocked door. "Shall I leave you, Miss Barrymore?"

"Yes, please," said Emerald.

The man left, bowing deferentially.

Sol couldn't believe his eyes. The room was lined with dozens of cardboard dress cartons. The lids had been removed and the contents were revealed, glittering and sparkling in the harsh neon light.

Emerald's dresses. Her costumes. Every outfit she had ever worn onscreen and off was stored there, each carton neatly labeled. "Isn't it wonderful, darling?" Emerald's eyes lit up with an ecstasy that was almost evangelical. "Aren't they beautiful?" she whispered as she caressed silks, chiffons, satins, ginghams, every possible fabric ever created.

Sol nodded, amazed. Emerald had mentioned that she kept a "few things in storage," but the extent of her collection was incredible.

"Look, darling, look, my first movie," she breathed.

The box was labeled *"Little Miss Marzipan. 1940. Columbia."*

Emerald took out some of the tiny spangled dresses, almost in a trance. "I was six years old," she breathed. *"Six* years old." She sighed. "Look, here I am with Mr. Douglas and Miss Goddard. Look, wasn't I *adorable?"* She took out a few eight-by-ten stills from a cardboard folder taped to the inside of each carton and showed them to Sol. She had indeed been a little cutie—her hair a mass of golden curls, chubby dimpled cheeks, Cupid's-bow mouth. In the photo she wore the frilly white spangled dress she now held and stroked. Her mind drifted back over forty years as she gazed at the smiling faces of Melvyn Douglas and Paulette Goddard, who had played her aunt and uncle.

"They wanted me to be a musical star in that, and I *was*," she said softly. "I sang and danced, and no one could ever *believe* I was only six years old. They thought I was a twenty-five-year-old midget, can you *believe* it, Sol?" Her laughter rang out, and, looking at her, Sol could almost see the tiny sweet little girl she had been.

"Miss Goddard was *so* wonderful to me," whispered Emerald. "She showed me how to put on eye shadow and rouge. She used to let me use her perfume. It was so strong, so sexy. 'Je Reviens' it was called. She had it sent from Paris, bottles of it. She even gave me my own little bottle."

"Do you still have it?" asked Sol, his brash New York manner slightly subdued by this new strange Emerald.

"Of *course* I do." She flashed her jade eyes. "Look, come with me." She took him into the next room, which was filled with smaller cartons similarly labeled. She opened the first one. It contained dolls, teddy bears, tiny tap shoes.

"Look!" Triumphantly she retrieved a tiny navy blue bottle, empty now. She held it to her nose and sniffed deeply.

"I can still smell it. 'Je Reviens.' I wore it for ten years after that. Paulette, I mean Miss Goddard, was *so* kind to me. I loved her, really."

She went back into the first room to a carton labeled, *"Daisy Did It,* Fox. 1951." Out came crinoline gowns like those then worn by teenage prom queens. "Janet Leigh and I were the stars of that." She carefully opened the manila envelope. "Look at this *coverage!* We made the cover of every single fan magazine at least three times in 1951. Look Sol, *look!* Every teenage girl in America wanted to look like us."

Sol looked at the two blond smiling girls wearing sneakers

and shorts, windblown at the beach, and another shot of them in matching strapless formals standing beside a young Robert Stack.

"See, I even made the cover of *Life*." She showed him a black-and-white cover of a laughing young Emerald kneeling in a white two-piece bathing suit on the beach, head thrown back, yellow hair blowing, not a care in the world.

"There's another one—*Look* magazine—now *that* was *hard* to get on. Milton Greene took this picture." A serious, pouty young Emerald gazed thoughtfully from the cover of *Look*, wearing a chaste high-necked blouse and a thick leather belt that gave the illusion of an eighteen-inch waist.

"Jesus, why do you keep all this stuff, Emerald?" Sol was confused. A man of simple tastes, he was of the disposable generation—if you don't use it, throw it away. He thought it strange that Emerald kept all this. "It's junk, honey."

"Junk? Junk! You stupid son of a bitch! This is Hollywood history! No one has this, *no one*. Mary Pickford, Gloria Swanson, Greta Garbo, Joan Crawford, Liz Taylor, Lana Turner, *none* of them kept their things, none of them cared enough about this wonderful business of ours to keep their clothes, their accessories, for posterity. Do you realize what this will all *mean* to film historians in a hundred years, Sol?"

Sol nodded, humoring her. He couldn't understand the fascination of a bunch of out-of-date gowns and old movie magazines and stills. Who'd want 'em?

"1962. Look, Sol. I made *Les Amies de Montmartre* in Paris. It was my first French film. With Alain Delon. He was unknown then, of course. I was the star. I was the biggest star in France then. Wasn't I gorgeous?"

"You still are, hon," said Sol, gazing in fascination at a 1960s copy of *Paris Match* where Emerald, teased platinum hair, high white boots, a black micro-miniskirt and fishnet stockings, was leaning on the balustrade of the Pont-Neuf over the Seine next to a glowing-faced dark-haired beautiful young man whom Sol recognized as the young Alain Delon.

"I played an English rock star." Emerald laughed. "Just look at the stuff we wore then. I bought it all on Carnaby Street and Kings Road. Oh, it was such *fun* in those days, Sol. The Parisians hadn't seen anything like my clothes. I wore the shortest miniskirts in Paris—in the whole of France, in fact. Look!" She brought out a hanger on which hung six or eight small skirts made of leather, felt and denim. Each one of them was no longer than thirteen inches and contained only about half a yard of fabric.

"Jesus, you wore those?" Sol swallowed. "They must have seen your cooze every time you crossed your legs."

"Sol, really. I had matching *panties,* look!" Under each skirt hung a pair of pants the same color as the skirt. "With Courrèges flat high-white boots, I looked like a teenager, even though I was nearly thirty. See." She shoved another bunch of eight-by-ten glossies into his hand. "London and Paris in the swinging sixties. *God,* did we have fun."

There was Emerald with Brigitte Bardot on the quay in St. Tropez, both of them in gingham shorts so short that the cheeks of their round brown derrières were almost revealed; there was Emerald sitting with Belmondo in Paris, wistfully sipping coffee at a Left Bank café. Emerald had long blond bangs and she wore a French beret. There was Emerald in London with Mick and Bianca, with John Lennon at a Bob Dylan concert, both of them in identical flat black leather caps and granny glasses, and with Michael Caine, Terence Stamp, and England's most famous model, Jean Shrimpton, dining at Club del Aretusa. They all looked young and eager and joyful. "The sixties." Emerald sighed fondly. "The best of times—and the worst of times for me." She picked up another batch of photographs.

"Here's me and my Lord." She laughed, showing him a formally posed black-and-white wedding picture. "Lord Lichfield took the pictures. Princess Margaret came, so did the Duchess of Argyll and the Duke of Westminster. All the English aristocrats came. The crème de la crème of England. It was at St. Mary's church in Mayfair. I was Lady Haverstock for, oh, at *least* two or three years."

Sol laughed. Emerald always joked about her many marriages, filled with delight and expectation as each nuptial day approached. She always started out as a devoted, dutiful wife, until her expectations were unfulfilled and the husband turned out to be a human being after all. None of Emerald's six marriages, other than to O'Herlihy, had lasted longer than three years, but, ever the optimist, she continued to walk blushingly down the aisle.

"Didn't you marry *twice* in the seventies?" queried Sol.

"Yes, the English lord and my Italian count—'the cunt,' my friends all called him." Emerald smiled and went to a carton marked 1971, which was filled with lacy, flowery garments—floating sleeves, embroidery, and ethnic trimmings. "In 1971, I became La Contessa Calimari for seven and one half magic months—which I spent mostly lying in the sun in Franco's marble villa in Ibiza, while he cruised for young boys. And when I say young, darling, I mean *young*. He married me as a cover-up. Let's face it, an American movie sex goddess is about the best cover-up you could have for a practicing Italian homosexual. We were annulled. The Pope did it, of course."

"Of course," Sol said. "Who else?"

"Sol?"

"Yeah, hon."

"I don't know why I'm doing this. I never brought anyone here before. Maybe you think it's strange, but—" her voice started to break, but she controlled it—"it's all I *have*, really."

197

"You got *me,* hon. If you want me, of course," said Sol, who would have remarried her in a flash if she'd have him.

"No, Sol. You're sweet, but this place, these boxes of possessions, *they* are my real life, Sol. They are more real than any of the men, any of my marriages. This is the *real* Emerald Barrymore. This warehouse is where she lives."

She sat down on one of the cartons, sobbing violently. Sol felt helpless. She had never opened up like this to him before. Emerald Barrymore, Movie Queen Supreme for over forty years, had a heart just like any other broad. He didn't know what to do.

Up to now, theirs had been a friendly marriage and divorce based on physical attraction and convenient availability. Emerald often needed an escort. She liked going out, was bored being "walked" by gay men friends. For Sol, it was a dream come true when he finally met the gorgeous girl whose picture he had pasted on the wall of his locker while he fought the Koreans. But that dream had lasted considerably less time than her others. She had worn his Van Cleef and Arpels emerald-and-diamond wedding ring for only three months. But thank God, they were still friends. Now he could be the strong shoulder she needed to cry on.

And cry she did. "If only I could have had children," she sobbed, as mascara ran down her cheeks in blue rivulets. "Sol, I wanted to have kids more than anything in the world, when I was thirty."

"What happened?" he said, stroking her fine platinum hair, the roots showing grayish brown.

"Between the abortions the studio insisted I have and the damn fucking *pill*—too many years on that goddamn pill, Sol, that's what happened. I stopped when I married his lordship. I really wanted to give him an heir, someone to play with Princess Margaret's son when they grew up."

She dabbed her wet lashes with a tiny hanky trimmed in lace.

Sol didn't know anyone else who carried a hanky, let alone a lace one.

"So, go on, hon."

"I got pregnant by his lordship three times in two years. I lay flat on my back, hoping, but each time I lost it. Finally his mother gave him an ultimatum. Emerald can't have children, get rid of her. You must have an heir to the title. Well, anyway by that time, I was bored to tears with that horsy 'Hooray Henry' British crowd, but I was sad. I was so sad, Sol." She blew her nose on the tiny hanky violently.

"So then?" asked Sol. He couldn't believe what she was telling him. She never had confided in him during their marriage.

"Oh, so then, I bought the dogs!" She laughed hollowly. "I had the dogs, and I got fucked a lot, and I fell in love a lot, and I got engaged a lot, and I kept getting pregnant, and I kept losing them until my gynecologist took me into his office the day before my fortieth birthday, by which time I'd been pregnant *eleven* times in ten years, and told me I could *never* have a child, and to stop fooling myself. Forty was too old anyway."

"Nonsense," Sol said kindly.

"For motherhood," Emerald said bitterly. "I was an aged primipara every time I got pregnant. Cute, isn't it? An aged primipara! Ugh! So I got rid of all the equipment."

"What equipment?" Sol was bemused.

"The *female* equipment, darling. The tubes. All the stuff that makes you moody and unpredictable twelve or thirteen times a year, and which arrives unexpectedly as you've put on a new white skirt and you're sitting at a formal dinner with the Ambassador of God-knows-where and the host is gay, so you know you can't find a tampon in *his* bathroom, just Vaseline and amyl nitrate."

She smiled sadly. "So that's when my career packed up. My gyno must have told *tout* Hollywood I was no longer a *real*

199

woman." Anger crept into her voice. "No more offers for poor little Emerald. And I still had my 'fabulous' life style to support. That's when I did the pornos."

"They weren't *pornos,* for Christ's sake, Emerald. They were fuckin' *art* films, and you know it."

"To you they were art films. To me they were pornos."

"So you showed your tits," he argued.

"And my ass, too."

"You got a great ass, kid," he said, affectionately squeezing it, wondering if she might consent to a quickie among the crinolines.

"They *were* great photos though, weren't they, Sol?"

"Yeah, oh, yeah, babe." He remembered, as had thousands of men, her revolutionary pose for the exceedingly serious yet erotic Italian film *L'innamorata.*

"There's the picture, Sol. It's five years ago now. Do you think I look any different?"

She was holding up an eleven-by-fourteen color photo from *L'innamorata.* She wore a Gestapo officer's hat set at a rakish angle on cropped blond curls, and a black Nazi uniform, the jacket of which was open to reveal a medium-sized but perfect bosom.

It was a sensational photo, more so because Emerald had been forty-three years old at the time. It had got her the cover of *People, Newsweek* and a spurt of new movie activity, mostly in Spain, Germany and France.

"Now you know why I must play that part in 'Saga,' Sol. I *swore* I'd never do TV, swore it on Momma's grave, but time is running out, and my only assets are my face, my body and my fame."

"You're still beautiful, hon, beautiful," Sol soothed.

"I have exactly two hundred and fifty thousand bucks in the bank, which, with *skimping,* will last me a year, if I'm clever. I have the house in the hills..."

"That's worth a couple of mil," Sol said, "easy."

"Maybe *one,* tops. I have furs galore, loads of fabulous jewels; if I sell those then maybe I can get by for another year, and then what? *Then what,* Sol? What does Emerald Barrymore do for an encore?"

"Marry me again, sweetheart. Marry me."

"No, I can't. I'm sorry but I don't love you, honey. You're adorable, funny, sweet, but I *must* feel passion. I've always had to feel passion, and I can't pretend. You know it, and I can't fake it."

Amidst the paraphernalia of Emerald's forty-year career, they gazed at each other sadly. "Now you know why I *have* to have that part, Sol," she said, gripping his hand. "I've been an actress for forty years. I don't know how to do anything else. I *want* this role, I want acceptance in this town by my peers. I want the money, the fame, the magazine covers again, Sol. If I don't get them, I'm on the scrap heap forever. I'm too tired. I'm too old..."

"No, hon, you're not."

She stopped him. "If there's one thing I know, it's Hollywood. Yes, I'm still a star to the public, but everyone in the business, every goddamn producer and agent in this whole stinking, rotten town thinks I'm a washed-up has-been, Sol, and, damn it, it's not going to stay that way. I'm going to play Miranda if it kills me. I'm going to do everything I can, and I'll be a *real bloody* star again! I can't and I won't settle for anything else."

He nodded sadly. It was only too true. "Let's get the hell out of this place, kid," he said.

15

Nothing had changed in Las Vegas, Chloe realized, as she surveyed her companions in the casino elevator. Fat thighs in tight shorts, shriveled old ladies whose hair had been permed so often it looked like gray-blue cotton wool, hookers and businessmen. Chloe never failed to wonder at the beefiness of the Vegas visitors. Maybe they had too many milk shakes and doughnuts, too many snacks. Certainly the fattest were the ones who drank diet soda with their food. A woman sucking an ice-cream cone dripped it onto Chloe's suede shoes, and she grimaced.

Her suite at the Las Vegas Empire was as lavish as ever, even though the "damask-and-silk" hangings on the wall and windows were 100 percent polyester and felt like glazed cardboard to the touch, and the "velvet" sofa was hard as a rock. The black acrylic bathtub with ersatz gold faucets was wide enough for two; it had a thin black plastic pillow at one end, in case two wished to sample the delights of the Jacuzzi. She sat on the eight-foot-wide burgundy crushed velvet-covered bed and looked up at her lonely reflection in the beveled mirrored ceiling. She remembered the last time she and Josh had played the Empire, how they had shared this suite, the shiny black tub, the same bed, watched themselves in that same mirror. . . .

Josh always loved looking at their two bodies entwined together on wine-colored sheets, her ivory legs encircling his bronzed ones. He was never more aroused than when they were together in Las Vegas, and he took her sometimes three or four times a day, his ardor fired by the sight of their bodies in the mirror. She sighed as she removed her De Fabrizio suede pumps. Stop thinking about Josh, she admonished herself. Stop thinking about what was. Get yourself together, girl—you've got a show to do.

In a cramped motel room in downtown Las Vegas, Calvin unpacked his canvas holdall and regarded the contents. There it was. The knife. Its flat bluish metal reflected his flat bluish eyes, which gazed blankly out the window at the high blue Nevada sky. They didn't see the bare sandy vista shading into the distance, interspersed with a few sickly palm trees and shaggy bushes. All they noticed was the sign that dominated their view. A huge billboard announced:

CHLOE CARRIERE

JULY 16–27

$25 EARLY SHOW $20 LATE SHOW

For show reservations call 732-8800

THE LAS VEGAS EMPIRE

AMERICA'S #1 ENTERTAINMENT SPOT

Slowly Calvin picked up the phone and dialed 732-8800. Under the name John Ryan he booked a booth for the following night. It was time to get her.

Later that evening, as she sat in the dressing room, her hairdresser fixing white sequinned flowers in her dark hair while she painted her face with trembling hands, thoughts of Josh tormented her. She could hear the crowd out front, laughing at the opening act—Shecky Greene.

She remembered four years ago, in this same dressing room, begging Josh to stop taking the drugs that were destroying his career and their marriage. The bouquet of medication he needed for support had become a nightmare. He usually awoke at four or five in the afternoon and got a vitamin shot for his voice from the local Vegas quack. Then he took three uppers, a large snort of coke and a Coca-Cola. He'd stop at the crap table for a couple of hours if Chloe was having a massage or a manicure. If she was around, he'd want to have sex. In spite of his drugging, he was still incredibly virile. He was her husband, and she adored him in spite of everything. An hour before their show he would get another shot for his voice, swallow a decongestant with codeine, two uppers, and take another massive snort of coke. Just before he went onstage he took a Dilaudid, a legal drug twice as powerful as heroin. His beautifully tanned and muscular body in a white silk shirt open to the waist and black pants showed off his tremendous sex appeal. He still had "it" for the female Las Vegas patrons. Old and young, they found him wildly attractive. After the show, in which he sang for the first forty minutes, she for the second forty, they then harmonized and vocalized together for fifteen more minutes. They gazed into each other's eyes, singing ballads, love songs and point numbers with sophistication and sexy undertones that drove the audience wild. Afterward, his trusty doctor took his blood pressure, and if it was over 140 gave him a pill to come down, after which he'd take another snort of coke. Fortified by the applause, by the onstage empathy and rapport with each other, they then received visiting friends, acquaintances and business associates in their dressing room with the mirrored bar and wood-burning fireplace.

Later they would go to dinner with friends in the Rib Room; then he would hit the tables until dawn. Before he went to sleep, Josh took two Quaaludes, a blood-pressure pill and a Demerol.

It was too much. Much too much. She had lectured him long and often, but he maintained he was not addicted, he could handle it, he needed it to work. "Cut the crap, Chlo," he'd say. "It's not hurting me."

The extraordinary thing was, it didn't seem to—then. But gradually his habits began to erode his performances, then his life.

The owners of the Vegas casinos soon got the message. He was becoming irresponsible, unreliable. Slowly the Vegas gigs, the years of the big money—seventy-five, one hundred grand a week—started to drift away, and then they had to start doing the tours. Oh, those tours! Numbing. Soul-destroying. Milwaukee, New Haven, Idaho, Atlanta, Connecticut, Kansas. Weeks, months of one-night stands.

It was a killer. It had killed his career and their marriage. Now she only had herself to take care of. She looked at her face, finished now. The matte complexion, the fuchsia-gloss lips, the smoky eyes. Her black lace over nude chiffon Bob Mackie original clung to every contour of her thoroughly toned body. She looked in fighting form.

The band was playing her intro now. She heard applause for the well-known songs—*her* songs.

It was time to perform.

Although Chloe hadn't played Vegas for four years, her opening was a huge success—she still had many fans. To her surprise and delight, Sammy and Altovise Davis, Milton and Ruth Berle, and Steve Lawrence and Eydie Gormé had shown up the first night to wish her well. Pandora had been there too. Her romance with the young comedian was on the wane. He spent more time at the tables than he did with Pandora. She was philosophical.

"Honey, romance is like a bag of groceries, the more you put in, the heavier it gets."

Chloe laughed as the two of them lay by the pool at the Empire the next morning, watching the constant action.

"Another ship will cross my horizon, honey," Pandora drawled, rubbing Bain de Soleil on her slender legs. "Men are like buses; if you wait long enough, another one will come along."

"The way you look, darling, it won't be long either," said Chloe, admiring her friend's slim body in her white maillot.

"Phone for you, Miss Carriere," trilled a tiny page as he plugged a phone into an invisible outlet and handed it to Chloe.

"Hello, darling, it's Jasper," he said in his impeccable English accent. Chloe smiled.

"Hi, Jasper, what's happening?"

"I think you're the number one front-runner for Miranda, my pet. I spoke to Abby and Gertrude this morning. They *and* the network feel that you gave the best test. They feel certain that they want you for Miranda."

"But they're not completely sure yet, right, Jasper?"

"Right, petal. You know how it is. So stay calm, dear, do the show, and I'm sure by the end of the week we'll have a firm answer."

"Good." There didn't seem much else to say.

"Oh, and Robert Osborne has you as his lead item in the *Reporter* today, said that you were the main contender for Miranda. Just thought I'd let you know."

"Thanks, Jasper, keep in touch, love." Chloe hung up feeling elated.

Pandora was deep in conversation with the straight half of the magic act that was currently breaking all records at the hotel. "You know The Great Geraldo, don't you?" she breathed, her eyes alight with new found interest.

The Great Geraldo inclined his head with European gallantry, revealing dyed black roots and an inch of flab hanging over green Ralph Lauren trunks.

"*Enchanté, madame.*"

"Excuse me a second, I'm going to buy the trades." The Great Geraldo bowed in gallant Continental fashion, as Chloe, avoiding oiled mahogany bodies, walked into the cool darkness of the lobby.

She was indeed the lead gossip item in the *Hollywood Reporter:* "Abby Arafat and BCC network seem to agree that the perfect choice for Miranda Hamilton on Abby's new series, 'Saga,' is Chloe Carriere, now headlining *sans* Joshua Brown at the Las Vegas Empire until July 27th. Catch her if you can, folks: this gal is hot!"

Chloe was pleased. This was no public relations plant. She didn't have a press agent. Maybe the item was true.

> "*It had to be you*
> *It had to be you*
> *I wandered around*
> *and finally found*
> *somebody who—*"

Chloe was in good voice, relaxed and confident. The nerves of the first few nights had evaporated, and she was surprised at how much she was enjoying this gig.

She looked radiant in a silver lace Nolan Miller gown. The spotlight sparkled on the tiny rhinestones scattered on it, and her face seemed to reflect the glow. The house was packed. The audience liked her, and appreciative applause greeted the end of each number.

In a back booth, huddled alone with an unaccustomed whiskey to bolster his courage, Calvin watched her every move.

Bitch. Where did she get that confidence? How *dare* she flaunt herself in that gown, that silken dress so sheer that the audience could see the outline of her breasts and twat. She was an English whore; she would pay dearly for it. He swallowed the whiskey, feeling the unfamiliar taste burn his throat. He stared at her malevolently as she came down into the audience singing her signature tune, "Everyone's Gotta Love Someone," weaving gracefully through tables full of polyester-clad tourists who reached out to touch her radiance. She took their hands, looking warmly into their faces, sharing her joy with them.

"Cunt." His lips tightened as his hand tightened on the knife in his pocket. His fingers itched to slash the bitch's face. He groaned. He was getting hard. Why did this happen *now?* When he hated this woman so much, why did his body betray him?

He tried to distract himself by observing the faces of the audience, eyes glued to her glittering feline figure as she threaded her way through the packed tables in the moving spotlight.

"Get a load of the guy in the booth," Jake Walker whispered to his partner, Hank Gillis.

A plainclothes security man, with fifteen years in the casino business and ten years as a state cop behind him, Jake prided himself on his instincts. But Hank wasn't listening to him. Jake nudged his partner again.

"Ssh!" Hank hissed. He was mesmerized by Chloe, gazing at her as she slowly advanced through the audience. Maybe she'd reach out and touch him. Oh, boy! "Shut up, Jake, I'm in love," he said.

Chloe was getting closer now. She paused at a table of excitable Japanese tourists. *"Everyone's gotta love,"* she breathed, clasping the hands of a young Japanese girl, who blushed with excitement.

Calvin's breath caught in his throat. He'd planned it brilliantly. This booth was next to the exit. One quick move, and even before the blood could come spurting out of her throat, before anyone realized what had happened, he would be in the casino mingling with the crowd. It was almost midnight on a Saturday, and the room was packed. He could disappear easily into the crowd. He was disguised in a red wig and horn-rimmed glasses, which he intended to dispose of later.

She was edging nearer. Would she come to him? Yes, of course she would. Last night he had observed both her shows. She always performed to the last row. The time was nearly ripe. The knife was burning on his lap. His hands were soaking wet as he wiped them on the red linen napkin. Red, the color of the blood that would soon be splashed all over that silver dress. He hadn't had an erection like this for a long time. He groaned. He needed relief.

Chloe was so close now, he could almost smell the scent she wore. It was pungent, musky—in spite of himself he liked it.

All eyes were on her except for the pair that was fixed on Calvin.

As Jake watched him with instinct honed by years of experience, he knew something was very wrong with this man. *"You gotta love, love, love..."* Chloe sang, thrilled by the love and happiness the audience brought to her and she gave back to them.

"Love, love, love," the audience sang back happily. All except Calvin, his eyes glazed, and face sodden with sweat. Jake watched his eyes, then his hands, waiting for any move that would tell him his suspicions were correct. When Chloe was only yards away Calvin's hand reached for the knife. Jake moved into the booth next to him. Calvin froze.

Jake flashed his badge. "Freeze, motherfucker," he said, as, with expert pressure on the man's hand, he extracted the knife. It was certainly a lethal weapon, a deer-hunter's knife, eight inches long, five inches past the legal limit. Sharp as a bayonet.

"This is a concealed weapon. You planning on going hunting?" he snarled to the trembling Calvin, as Chloe sang her way past the booth on her way back to the stage. Terror gripped Calvin. Sweat dripped from his brow onto Jake's hand, which held his wrist in a viselike grip. No one noticed the two men. All eyes were on Chloe's undulating figure. As thunderous applause rang out, Jake's attention was momentarily distracted.

With an animal cry and a madman's sudden strength, Calvin whipped his left arm into Jake's face, leaped over the table and sprinted toward the exit.

"Stop him!" Jake yelled to the uniformed guards at the entrance. "Stop that man!"

Calvin screamed in frustration and pain as the hefty guards grabbed him and tussled him to the ground. His wig fell off, his glasses crashed to the floor. Chloe's reprise was forgotten as the audience, distracted by Calvin's screams, got up to see what was happening.

Chloe froze in fear as the chattering crowd thronged around her, pushing her in their panic. The same people whom she had enthralled only seconds before now shoved her out of their way. As she started to move up the steps to the stage, she lost her footing and tripped. A hand reached out from the crowd to steady her and helped her onto the stage. The band was playing another tune now, the bandleader having signaled the orchestra to play something upbeat.

"Are you all right, Madame?" Chloe looked gratefully into the eyes of a tall, dark man, who put his arm around her protectively.

"I'm fine...no, I'm not. I...I feel faint. What's happened, do you know?"

"Come with me," he said, leading her backstage, past gossiping bare-breasted showgirls in ostrich feathers who were oblivious to the commotion out front.

In her dressing room, Chloe sat on the couch as he poured her a glass of water. Then, silently, he half-filled a brandy snifter with cognac and passed it to her.

"Do you know what happened?" she asked again.

"Drink, don't talk. Drink the brandy," he commanded.

Chloe felt a surge of gratitude to the stranger who obviously understood how disoriented she was and wanted to help.

"Oh, God," breathed Chloe. "What was that man *doing?* Who was he?"

"I don't know." Chloe recognized an accent. French, Italian? She couldn't tell.

"Thank you for helping me. Please excuse me, I'm a bit rattled."

"Understandably so, Madame. May I introduce myself? I am Philippe Archambaud, *à vôtre service.*" He made a slight but formal bow and gave her a smile that enhanced his attractiveness.

"Las Vegas is a long way from France." Chloe felt better as she sipped the brandy, felt it warming her.

"I'm here on a working vacation, to experience and write about what we call 'The American Scene.' I'm doing a series of articles for *Paris Match.*"

A *journalist!* Chloe groaned inwardly. She never trusted journalists. They were her *bêtes noires.*

Her maid came in and said the police would like to talk to her. Philippe stood up. "I shall go now." Philippe pressed her fingers swiftly to his lips. *"Tout à l'heure, Madame Carriere."*

"Au revoir, et merci," Chloe said, admiring his physique, his impeccably cut dark suit, beautifully knotted, subtle tie, and noticing that he had written something on a book of matches which he now put into her hand.

"I shall be here for the rest of the weekend. If you would like, perhaps we could have a coffee together. If you are free, of course."

He bowed again, in the manner of a cultivated Frenchman,

and left her dressing room as two policemen entered.

The interrogation was short. Although the officers seemed sympathetic, there was an edge to their concern that made Chloe feel almost guilty, as if the incident had been her fault. She was glad when they left. There was nothing she could say to help them. She had only seen the man for a second or two. She had no enemies.

Her maid bustled about. Would madame like another drink, a cigarette? No, madame would not. Madame knew what she needed tonight.

She felt lost, lonely, cold. She wanted to be close to someone. She picked up the match book that Philippe had left, and looked at it. "Philippe Archambaud. Room 1727."

What an attractive name. What an attractive man, she thought. And opening her handbag she put the match book firmly inside.

She would spend the night as she had spent the last forty nights—alone.

Part Four

16

Chloe looked at her watch. This was the day. Jasper Swanson had promised to call her with the news as soon as Abby called him. It was three o'clock. He should be back from his Friday lunch at Ma Maison. It's gone to Sissy, thought Chloe, staring at the ocean. Better accept the offer to tour Europe for three months. It was preferable to doing episodic TV guest shots on "Charlie's Angels" and "Policewoman," both of which she'd politely declined in the three weeks since she had been back from Vegas. Were they *ever* going to make a decision? It was almost the end of summer. "Saga" would start shooting in two weeks—what were they waiting for?

She pulled on a black one-piece swimsuit and a white terry-cloth robe. To hell with waiting. To the ocean—a long swim, a glass of iced tea, then off to the Bill Palmer Salon to have Tami give her a manicure and Dino give her a new coiffure. *Forget* about Miranda! The phone rang. Twice. Three times. She picked it up on the fourth ring.

Chloe heard Jasper's excited tone. "You have it, my love, you have it!"

The excitement in his voice infected Chloe. "Oh, Jasper, I can't believe it! Are you sure? Are you positive?"

"Yes, yes. Of course I'm sure, my love. The network *adored* you. They said there really was no contest. Your test was by far the most exciting. Gertrude said you *are* Miranda!"

"Oh," bubbled Chloe, "Jasper darling, you're a magician. How could they have chosen me over Emerald, who is such a huge star...and Sissy, such a great actress? I simply can't believe my luck. Why did they wait so long?"

He laughed. "They received a million dollars' worth of publicity by stringing it out. Dear girl, the network isn't stupid, you know. You have a quality, Chloe. You may not even understand what it is. If you start to realize what it is, and if you start to analyze it, you may lose it, so don't think about it, that's my advice, dear."

"What do you mean?" asked Chloe. The enormity of what had happened was just beginning to penetrate.

"I mean you have got *star* quality, toots." His British voice became more serious. "Abby and Gertrude knew it right after your test. They just had to convince that bloody-minded network that you were the right woman for the part."

"And they did. Oh, God, Jasper, I'm so excited I could scream! We must celebrate."

"All right, we'll hit the town tonight. Put on your best bib and tucker." Jasper had been in the business for nearly thirty years but he had rarely heard a performer so happy to get a job.

"Spago, Chasen's, Ma Maison—what is your pleasure, Mi-lady?"

"Oh, all of them!" Chloe laughed. "Spago for champagne, Chasen's for chili and Ma Maison for dessert."

"You're on, toots." He added knowingly, "Now you must watch out, my love. Watch out for the woodwork people—the ones who didn't want to know you before, who will try to become your best friends now. You will be *swamped,* dear, with new 'best friends.' "

"I will watch out, darling, of course I will. By the way, how much will I be getting?"

He paused. "Weeell, my love, that's a *teeny* bit of a problem. I mean, let's face it, we *know* you're a cabaret star. For a singer you're quite big."

"Bottom-line it for me, Jasper darling."

"Fifteen an episode."

She was astonished. "Fifteen! Oh, Jasper, that's *peanuts.* I don't mean to sound ungrateful but I know that Sam Sharp is getting fifty, why only fifteen for me?"

"My dear, you know this business. They want you, but as far as the U.S. of A. is concerned, you're an unknown."

"I just sold out the house in Vegas," remonstrated Chloe.

"For goodness' sake, Chloe, be reasonable! After all, we are *both* British. We know you did well in Vegas, but they've got ten other cast members to pay. You are not a star yet. Oh, by the way, they've cast Sissy as the other wife, Sirope."

"Sissy! How odd, when she tested for Miranda. Why?"

"Well, Abby needs star power for this role. And Sissy needs a decent job. That is why they can't pay *you* what you deserve, dear. Sissy is still a star, and she will be paid like a star. In this town, my love, a star is a star is a star."

"O.K. You know how much I wanted this part. And I'm certainly glad I got it. But what happens if I become a big star too, Jasper? Will I get a raise?"

217

"My love, the sky will be the limit then, no question about it, I'll see to it that they triple your salary if you get a high TVQ, I promise you, my love. *Triple* it."

"Fine." Chloe beamed. "Then I accept. Not that there was any question, really. You knew I would."

"That's my girl. You've always been smart, Chloe. My limo will pick you up at eight. Don't forget, watch out for the wood-work people."

"I won't forget, Jasper, I promise."

"No—no—no! I *can't believe* it!" screamed Sissy to her agent. "How dare they give it to that no-talent saloon singer? How *could* they?"

In spite of herself, large black tears rained mascara from her eyes. She clutched a towel around her nonexistent breasts and signaled to Sven, the Swedish masseur, who had been doing his best with the kinks in her neck, to bring her a cigarette.

"Shit! Shit! Shit!" she screamed in frustration and rage as she sat up on the portable massage table inhaling smoke deeply into her lungs. Screw cancer, she thought to herself bitterly. "I'm fin-ished, *ruined* by this foreign *cow.*"

Sven lit a Camel and stoically sat studying the latest issue of *Body Building* he had taken from his briefcase. His calm Scandi-navian features betrayed nothing of the pity he may or may not have felt for Sissy—sad sight that she was, with her overtanned skin, overdieted body, and overdyed hair, sobbing in rage on the telephone.

"How can I hold my head up in this town ever *again?*" she yelled to Robin, her hapless agent, on the other end of the phone. "How? Tell me?"

Robin was obviously trying to placate her because she re-mained silent for a while. "Well, I'll think about it," she mut-tered. "That wife is nowhere near the role that Miranda is, but if

I did accept, of course they *would* build the show around me more, wouldn't they?"

She listened again, dragging heavily on her cigarette. Sven observed the lines etched deeply above her thin lips, the result of thirty cigarettes a day, which no number of face-lifts could erase.

"Forty thousand an episode? Hmmmm." She was getting visibly calmer. The lines in her face softened a little.

Sven looked up from his magazine.

Sissy finished her phone call with an "I'll think about it. I promise I will. Call me tomorrow," and hung up. She smiled. The deep wrinkles and the bitterness in her face seemed to vanish. When she smiled she lost ten years, and could look almost girlish. "Come here, Sven," she commanded in a husky, sensual voice.

The beauty of Sven was that he was terribly discreet and definitely heterosexual. None of the ladies who had partaken of his munificent Scandinavian charms had ever had cause for complaint. He aimed to please, and he did. He also never passed up an opportunity. If the lady wanted it, he could and would supply it. In spite of his total lack of interest in Sissy as a person, her body or her sexuality, Sven uncapped a bottle of baby oil and, slowly removing the towel from her body, commenced work on the famous pièce de résistance of his repertoire.

When Sue Jacobs told Sabrina that she hadn't gotten any of the roles, Sabrina had been pleased, and she signed for a new movie immediately.

But Emerald, Miss Tricky One, was something else, and she had to be placated.

Emerald was upset when she had lost Miranda to Chloe— very upset indeed. She had spent one entire morning weeping alone in her bedroom, her hysteria mounting along with her insecurities, then called Eddie back.

"Why Chloe? Why not *me?*" she demanded. "Who is she anyway? Can she act? Is she a megastar? I *still* am!" she yelled, looking closely into her superstrong magnifying mirror to see if the tiny scars from her jaw job were visible.

Fast Eddie sighed. The bigger the star, the harder they fell, and the more difficult it was for them to accept it.

"They *loved* your test, kiddo. Abby and Gertrude thought you looked fantastic, and your performance was great—magic, kid."

"Terrific!" spat Emerald, catching sight of yet another line under her wide green eyes. "But Eddie, dear—if it was so fucking magical, why didn't I get the fucking part?"

"Chloe fits the role better, that's all, kiddo. They wanted a new face, they always do." Eddie was right. They wanted someone they hadn't seen for years with their morning coffee in every gossip column and on their TV screens with another newsworthy scandal, marriage, engagement or divorce. It was obvious that the American public, although they still admired Emerald, found her a larger-than-life character. They could never disassociate the persona of Emerald Barrymore, superstar, from the character she played. This was Abby's, Gertrude's, and the network's opinion. Emerald would off-balance what they wanted to be an ensemble piece.

Eddie tried to explain this to a furious Emerald, but in the middle of the conversation, Emerald hung up on him with a harsh "Fuck you and your fucking agency! Eddie, I'm firing you!"

Emerald took a deep breath and a long, harsh look at her own assets. She still possessed beauty and sex appeal, and she was famous. She hired the best agent in town—Jasper Swanson— who, never one to let a star fall by the wayside, immediately found her a low-budget movie in Australia. It was directed by the very hot, very up-and-coming young black filmmaker Horatio George Washington.

"Australia? Again? Why not?" Emerald said. "I want to be as far away as possible from Chloe Carriere when she becomes a star."

17

P erry brought Josh his breakfast along with a copy of
the *Hollywood Reporter* which he had thoughtfully highlighted
in red for his master to read.

CHLOE CARRIERE TO PLAY MIRANDA IN SAGA

Josh, in L.A. to record a hopeful new single, read the piece
with a mixture of elation and sadness.

She'd done it. His little Chloe had the role she craved. He
wanted to congratulate her, send her her favorite flowers, a little
note. He picked up the phone to call Perry, but then out of habit

punched in their private number at the beach house. It hadn't changed.

She answered on the third ring.

"Chlo, I'm so happy for you, luv. I just heard the news. Congratulations."

"Thanks, Josh." Chloe couldn't keep the happiness out of her voice. He had called—and in spite of her denial to herself, she still cared. "It's sweet of you to call."

She had heard it in his voice. He cared too. In spite of his other women, his boozing, his drugging, his newfound bachelor freedom, his voice brought such happy memories flooding back. He wanted to see her, wanted to hold her close to him again.

"Well, I'd like to buy you a bottle of champagne, babe. I don't suppose you're free for dinner tonight?"

She hesitated for a moment, then, "Yes, I am. I think I'd like that, Josh. Where shall we go?"

Possibly as a result of her getting the part, Josh and Chloe reconciled again, for the fourth and—Chloe hoped—final time. Her lawyer had groaned in annoyance, saying he had never in thirty years of practice known a woman who changed her mind as often as she. Josh had said he was definitely going to go to a psychiatrist and solve his problems.

For the last two weeks everything had been more or less rosy, thought Chloe as she surveyed herself objectively in a tiny spotted mirror of what was laughingly called a star's trailer.

Ben had done a good job. Good old Ben. Discreet makeup, excellent hairstyle, chic, definitely *non*-Hollywood. Simple black Chanel suit, expensively elegant enough to make the other actress's clothes look like those of a hausfrau. It was Chloe's own suit. Last week she had categorically rejected in disgust the studio's safe little tweed suits with mink collars and rhinestone buttons. Asserting her dramatic rights, she had requested a

223

high-fashion look. All the actresses on most of the other prime time soaps wore silk blouses, gabardine trousers or skirts. For evening scenes, they dressed in low-cut silk jersey dresses with spaghetti straps from Holly's Harp or Strip Thrills. Chloe was determined to create a look that no other actress had featured since the glamorous days of Dietrich, Turner and Crawford.

She had stressed the glamour image in all her interviews. "I am *not* the woman next door," she insisted over and over again. "Miranda is a mysterious woman of the world, and that's what I shall look like. She wears couture clothes and lives a jet-set lifestyle."

There had been some flak at the front office when Abby and Gertrude heard about the way she wanted to portray Miranda, but after viewing some tests, they were ecstatic.

"Gorgeous, she looks simply gorgeous," glowed Gertrude, congratulating herself for having had the strength to reject Sissy's frenzied pleas of longtime friendship, reminders of all the things *she* had done for Gertrude when they had been starting out in New York together a century ago.

"Fabulous. I *love* her. She looks mean and bitchy and evil, but underneath it there's something about her that you can't help liking," Abby said.

"You're right, and she's a good actress too," said Bill Herbert, "Saga's" executive producer. "She'll be big, very big. What are we paying her, Abby?"

"She's a steal, a *steal.*" Abby was excited. A bargain always appealed to him. "Only fifteen grand an episode, and by looking at these tests she's worth at least twice that."

"Don't let her get too full of herself," warned Gertrude, ever the pragmatist. "This is an *ensemble* piece, remember, everyone's equal."

"Bullshit," said Abby, getting to the point as usual. "She and Sam will be the stars of 'Saga'—I can see it."

"Any actor or actress is dispensable," Gertrude continued. "Don't let us *ever* forget that, fellows. If we do, we let the inmates run the asylum. Look what happened to the movie business!"

They all took a moment to think regretfully about how the movie business had been disrupted by upstart actors and actresses who had started their own production companies, taking over the reins and the power. Redford, Beatty, Reynolds, even Goldie Hawn, had taken off and, in control, were calling themselves producers. And, of course, some of them had become successful, which made it even worse.

"Well, it'll never happen in TV." Abby broke the silence.

"Oh, yeah? What about Lucy? She owned a frigging *studio,* for Christ's sake! How about Mary Tyler Moore?"

"Mary was a figurehead. Her husband was the power. TV is safe. Actors act, producers produce, directors direct, and that's the way it's going to be in *my* company, all the way down the line. On 'Saga' no one is more important than the producer and the product." Abby was adamant. They nodded in agreement.

"Run those rushes again," he ordered. They watched earnestly as Chloe's face filled the tiny screen.

"She's got it," breathed Gertrude. "I just hope she doesn't realize it too soon. Once she does, we won't be able to hold her back."

Chloe walked onto the set of "Saga" exuding a confidence she did not feel. She was exhausted; she had spent half the night— when she should have been preserving her looks for the camera that never lies— in screaming arguments with a drunkenly abusive Josh.

His new single, "Rainbow Girl," instead of gliding slowly but surely up the charts, as he and his advisers had predicted, had failed to make even the Top 100. It was received coolly by DJs from Coast to Coast.

His hopes of making a three-minute video of the song, an innovation still in its infancy, had been dashed when Polygram's president brushed him off. "I gotta be brutally frank: The rock-video market is aimed at kids—and by kids we mean eleven to twenty." He shrugged. "Josh, these are the *children* of your fans, y'know what I mean?" he added, with a hint of malice.

Josh had taken his fury out on Chloe, and now sat in front of the giant TV in their "playroom" off the master bedroom drinking brandy from a tumbler and flipping channels every few seconds. The volume was on full blast, and the constant changing of the channels was driving Chloe mad.

She tried not to get rattled as she busied herself with the myriad details she had to attend to before going to work the first day on what was probably the biggest career move of her life.

She puffed furiously on her twentieth cigarette, trying to study dialogue already committed to memory. Her hair was wrapped in a towel while the conditioner worked, and she tried with shaking hands to give herself a manicure.

She had dieted and exercised for weeks now, and was down to a fighting weight of one hundred and ten pounds. Ideally she would have wanted to rinse out her hair, dry her nails and fall asleep by nine o'clock with a glass of wine, which beat sleeping pills *any* time. That would give her eight solid hours of beauty sleep before she had to arise at five to get to the studio by six.

Perfect. Simply perfect. To make this break work for her, she had to be prepared. Mentally, physically and emotionally. TV was a tough, competitive arena. There were several prime time bitches out there, waiting for Chloe to come out of her corner; they were sharpening their claws, ready for battle. "I'll chew her up and spit her out in little bits!" one of her TV rivals had sneered to Daphne Swanson, who couldn't wait to print it in her column. "After all, I *am* ten years younger and four inches taller." Chloe had smiled at the insecurities of this actress, obviously terrified she was going to slip in the ratings. The truth was, Chloe planned to give them all a damn good run for their money. She would make Miranda unforgettable. She hadn't spent the past twenty years of her life singing to and observing the jet set in their natural habitat without getting a head start on the character of Miranda. Witty, scintillating, glamorous and naughty—Mirandas were everywhere in the *haut monde,* the international jet set.

"Chloe, Chloe, when's dinner, for Christ's sake?" Josh yelled from the playroom, interrupting her reverie.

"Well, darling," she placated, "you said we didn't need a live-in cook any more after Manuela left. Can't you find something in the fridge?"

The old row about having a live-in housekeeper was about to start. Chloe disliked cooking, and certainly did not intend to learn on the eve of her new job. Josh had always tried to instill a bit of old fashioned prefeminist guilt in her by insinuating that a "real woman" always cooked. His mother cooked. His sister cooked. Even Sally cooked. Why couldn't she?

"What kind of a wife *are* you?" He was still clutching the brandy bottle as he lurched into the room. He tried to smile in a winning way—the way that always warmed her heart.

"Ha, indeed, and what kind of a husband are you?" She tried to banter with him. "Don't start, Josh, darling, please," she said calmly, trying to ignore him as she unwrapped the towel from her hair.

He grabbed her, twisted her around to face him. The brandy was strong on his breath and his pupils were dilated. Her heart sank. Brandy and cocaine. A bad mix. He was out of it. She had seen it before, and it was not a pretty sight.

"I've got to rinse this off. If it stays too long on my hair, the hairdresser won't be able to work with it tomorrow." She shook herself free and escaped into the shower.

"I don't care. I want dinner, and then I want you." He loomed in the doorway, yelling over the noise of the shower. "C'mon, Chlo, let's open up a coupla cans of beans and fry some eggs like the old days. Chloe, c'mon, luv." His tone had changed to flirtatious charm, hinting of romance, a prelude to what had once been their mating call in his voice. In spite of herself she found him exciting. In spite of a six-o'clock makeup call and first-day nerves, the residue of their long-time passion still stirred her.

She stepped out of the shower and wrapped herself in a terry-cloth robe. What the hell. She returned his embrace. Two poached eggs and a can of beans didn't take long to fix, she decided. If we make love, he'll fall asleep instantly, and then I can get some rest....

Afterward she snuggled against him trying to recapture old feelings of satisfaction and comfort, and longing for sleep. But he started complaining again. He moaned about his career being on the wane while hers was taking a turn for the better.

She let him ramble on about his frustrations with show business, about the unfairness of a record industry that failed to appreciate his talent, and about the stupidity of his fickle fans.

"Darling, please go to sleep," Chloe mumbled, her glass of white wine having done the trick. "I've *got* to sleep, Josh."

"Damn it, Chloe, you don't *give* a shit, do you?" he accused. He sat up in bed, snapping on the lights and the TV at the same time. "You just care about yourself and *your* bloody career, not about mine. You're a selfish bloody bitch."

There was no stopping him. Chloe closed her eyes, trying at least to rest them, and resigned herself to a bumpy night. Finally she went to the chilly, narrow bed in the guest room.

The final separation was easier than Chloe had expected. She had returned unexpectedly one day from the studio and found him making love to another fifteen-year-old girl. They were in the Jacuzzi, no less, using *her* foaming bath oil and with *her* favorite Lalique champagne glasses balanced on the edge of the tub, massaging each other with *her* one hundred and fifty-dollar-an-ounce body lotion.

She couldn't even be bothered to fight any more. Numb with

pain, shock and disappointment, she locked herself in the guest room, swallowed two Valium and went to sleep in spite of Josh's night-long crying outside the door.

There was a limit to anyone's endurance, and Chloe had reached hers. The next day she called her lawyer. It was the end—absolutely. Reluctantly he agreed to take on the case again.

Josh didn't fight her. He moved to his favorite suite at the Wilshire. Tactful Perry arrived, quickly packed twenty suitcases of clothes, tapes and electronic equipment, and Josh was out of her life. "No sweat, babe," Josh said with a smile as he kissed her goodbye—kissed eleven years of their life goodbye.

"Still mates, O.K., Chlo? We'll always be mates, won't we?"

She nodded dumbly. Her throat hurt with the effort of trying to stop the tears from running down her cheeks. Damn him, how dare he be so cool, so casual, so chummy. Would she *ever* get over him completely?

She slammed shut the heavy Aztec-carved doors and walked out onto the balcony. It was a sensational beach day. Seagulls swooped, joggers jogged, the cobalt seas washed the seaweed-encrusted shoreline. A perfect Trancas Sunday. She was alone: her marriage ending, a TV career beginning, big things ahead. But she was now forty, an age considered scrap-heap ten or fifteen years ago. Thank God for Jane Fonda's changing so many people's attitudes about aging women. They should build a shrine to her.

But today she felt her age. Felt old, washed-out, sad.

Sunday stretched ahead emptily. So, for that matter, did Monday, Tuesday and the rest of the week. The months and years seemed to lie ahead of her with nothing to fill them, except "Saga." Was a TV career that important to her? So many of her recent years had been dedicated to just being with Josh. He had filled her life, fulfilled her for much of the time, too. And now it was truly over. Dammit, *why* couldn't she stay happily married?

229

Not for her the bed-hopping and assignations that filled the lives of so many of her acquaintances. It didn't thrill her. Her thrill was being with one person. All she wanted was one guy. One faithful man to be with, to share her life with. Why couldn't she have it?

So now what? She had the TV series, but she did not have— would never have—what she wanted most. A child. A baby to hold and hug and be Mummy to. A bit late now, sneered her inner voice. Your biological clock has ticked itself out. Her baby, Annabel, her best-kept secret, was now a long-legged, independent eighteen-year-old, living happily in London with an equally independent boyfriend, blissfully unaware that the famous Chloe Carriere was her mother. Chloe wrote to her every week, called her as often as she could, and thought about her every day. Annabel suspected nothing. Chloe felt such love for the tomboyishly beautiful girl so like herself at the same age. Independent, enthusiastic, ambitious. God, she prayed she wouldn't get hooked on a man like Matt or Josh.

"Good to see you, Auntie Chlo," Annabel beamed whenever they saw each other. She was always rushing somewhere, long auburn hair flowing, guitar thrown over her shoulder, off to some rendezvous to play her music with her friends. "Must dash, luv, see you *soon,* promise." Oh, yes, Chloe's sister-in-law sympathized with her, but if Chloe had been stupid and ignorant enough to get pregnant by Matt in the days when it was such a stigma, she must now bear the consequences of her actions. Besides, Annabel was Susan's child—legally adopted, much loved. And no one would ever know the truth.

Part Five

18

*I*n the late fall of 1982 "Saga" went on the air. Sam Sharp played Steve Hamilton, the gruff, manly patriarch of the Hamilton clan. Chloe played Miranda Hamilton, his silkenly sexy ex-wife. Pandora King played the cool, sophisticated Judith Hamilton, ex-wife number two, and Sissy Sharp played Sirope, the saintly current Mrs. Hamilton.

With assorted young actors playing a variety of sons, daughters, nephews and nieces, mistresses and lovers, within six weeks the ensemble soap opera became the biggest hit of the 1982–83 season. And Chloe Carriere was well on her way to becoming the household name that everyone had predicted.

•   •   •

"It's a total bummer," confided Larry Carter, over a year later, as they sat in the studio commissary at a quiet corner table. He ate an Abby Arafat Sandwich, while Chloe munched on sliced apple and avocado to keep the pounds off.

"I mean, how do you think I feel taking over from Alex? It's a break, I know, but, hell, he's one of my best friends."

"Yes, but he didn't conform to the system, darling," said Chloe. "He bucked the system, Larry. You know he was always giving interviews, knocking the show, making fun of it on Carson and Merv. They won't stand for that. You know it."

"True," he said gloomily.

"Saga" had been on the air for one and a half seasons. It had become a gargantuan hit, greater than any other prime time soap opera in history. It had catapulted Chloe to stardom and fame she had never believed possible. Now there were Miranda Hamilton dolls, Miranda Hamilton makeup, Miranda Hamilton T-shirts, greeting cards, and even car-bumper stickers with "Let Miranda Live!"—referring to the courtroom scene in which Miranda had pleaded for her life after being wrongfully accused of killing one of her many lovers.

Magazines were clamoring for Chloe. So were gossip tabloids desperate for any skeletons in her cupboard to reveal to their readers. She started with diet and beauty magazines, fan magazines and fashion spreads. But soon she graduated to interviews in *People, US* and prestigious foreign publications like *Paris Match* in France, *Holá* in Spain, *Oggi* in Italy, and the Sunday *Times* Magazine in England. After that she started getting covers. Over an eighteen-month period, she was on the cover of more than two hundred magazines worldwide. "Saga" had done great things for Chloe and for its other stars. All except Alex Andrews.

He had played Steve and Judith's evil son, Cain, in the first thirteen episodes, but he had become deeply embarrassed by some of the clichéd dialogue and situations his character was involved in. He had started to bad-mouth the show in every interview he'd done, and he talked disparagingly on the set and in the makeup room about how stupid TV viewers were to be interested in such a puerile piece of crap.

It didn't take long for his bad-mouthing to reach the ears of Abby and Gertrude. He was called on the carpet in their palatial suite of offices—offices which could easily contain the living spaces of all the actors' trailers in "Saga"—and told to cool it or else he would be replaced.

"We simply will *not* tolerate disloyalty to our show." Gertrude's normally high color dramatically increased, and her normally placid voice had turned shrill.

Abby said little. His huge bulk seemed totally in proportion with his massive imported black onyx desk, bare except for a color photograph of him and Maud with President Nixon, one of his closest friends. It was tacitly understood that Gertrude was the spokesperson for the show when dealing with difficult actors, the schoolmarm telling off the naughty little boys and girls. Spank their bottoms, scold them sternly, and tell them to run away and behave. Alex was embarrassed. At twenty-three, he considered himself intellectually superior to both of these doddering relics who knew absolutely nothing about art, whose idea of cultural fulfillment was watching a Bertolucci movie at Sue Mengers's house. But he was also an actor who had to eat, and he had not bankrolled himself sufficiently to relinquish the role of Cain.

Gertrude's diatribe lasted twenty minutes, in spite of three phone calls from a panic-stricken Ned, who needed Alex back on the set.

"So don't let it happen again," hissed Gertrude, her face now as flame-colored as her frizzed red hair. "We're a family here—a happy, productive family. We support each other, we *don't* bite the hand that feeds us."

235

"Yes, Gertrude, of course. I'm sorry, it won't happen again," he promised, hating his hypocrisy.

"Well done, Gert," Abby said after the actor left, tail between his legs. "Mustn't let them get away with it."

"We never will," she said strongly.

Two weeks later, while in New York for the weekend, Alex found himself drinking with some newly acquired Actors Studio friends at the Russian Tea Room. They were all unemployed, all secretly jealous of his prestige and the bread Alex was making, but they goaded him about what crap "Saga" was, told him it was demeaning for a serious actor to be on it.

"The worst thing I have *ever* seen; it's an insult to the intelligence," said the small wiry-haired actress with a cast in one eye whose lack of talent and looks guaranteed that she would remain unemployed in her chosen profession forever. "Doncha get sick to your stomach when you have to say those ridiculous lines?" said Tiger Lily, a beautiful Oriental actress who was having a tough time getting a job performing in anything other than porno films.

"The acting is the pits, man. The motherfuckin' *pits,*" groaned Mack, who washed dishes at Sardi's at night and auditioned in vain during the day. "Quit! Become a *real* actor, man. Cut the crap. Come and live in New York where the action is, where an actor can have respect for himself. Where real talent is appreciated. Get back on the boards, man—the theater. The real thing..."

Gertrude was in the middle of watching "Saga" when the call came in.

"Fuck you—fuck your motherfucking shit show—it stinks. *You* stink. Let me out!" screamed drunken Alex.

She wasted no time. Without taking her eyes off the screen and Chloe's lovely face, while making a mental note to tell the hairdresser that Chloe's bangs were getting too long, she dialed Abby's house.

The news was on the street by the next afternoon. Alex had been dropped like used Kleenex. His scenes had been canceled and new scenes with other actors substituted. A scene was written in which everyone wondered about his disappearance, then discovered that he had gone to Australia on a quest for his real father.

Two weeks later, Larry Carter was cast to replace him.

There was no explanation to the viewers as to why Cain had a different face, was ten years older and spoke with a British accent.

Larry's hair, dyed black, was the only concession that the producers made to the public. Such was the popularity of "Saga" that viewers bought it without a murmur and the show continued from strength to strength each year.

Her message service called Chloe with a wake-up call at 5 A.M. "Good morning, hon, it's five o'clock. Are you up?" said the sympathetic voice of Gloria.

"Mmm, yeah—I am." Chloe groaned, glancing at the digital clock on the bedside table. She slipped out of bed and into her lavish bathroom/dressing room, where she plugged in the electric coffee-maker which sat on top of a small fridge next to her "Who Says Life Begins at Forty?" mug. She did ten minutes of fast sit-ups and push-ups while the water heated and her bath was running, and she watched the news on CNN. Twenty minutes later, scrubbed, showered and shampooed, and wearing a comfortable velour track suit, she jumped into her Mercedes and drove to "The Factory," as the cast and crew affectionately called the studio.

MCPC Studios was a dull gray windowless building on the less attractive part of Pico Boulevard in Los Angeles. It bore about as much resemblance to the public's idea of a movie or TV studio as a prison did to a nightclub.

In her tiny dressing room, Chloe switched on Channel 5 to

watch the local news, listened to the messages on her answering machine, and, sitting before the lightbulb-framed mirror, applied her TV makeup with swift, practiced strokes. She preferred doing her own makeup when it was feasible. It was a little bit of time she had totally to herself—the only time she would have during the long twelve-hour day ahead.

Theo, her hairdresser, put hot rollers into her thick, dark curls, as she studied the scenes for the day. Debbie, the second assistant, brought her breakfast on a Styrofoam plate, with plastic fork, paper napkin and apple juice in a can, the whole covered by aluminum foil. At seven o'clock she went down to Stage 11 for the first rehearsal of the day. Gina, her secretary, arrived with a clutch of eight-by-ten fan photos, and they discussed Chloe's schedule of social events and interviews for the next two days.

Today they were shooting a party scene in which all the cast were present. Sissy and Sam huddled together in a corner as usual, talking their heads off privately. For a married couple whom everyone knew had no sex life they certainly spent enough time gazing raptly into each other's eyes and having in-depth conversations. Today both wore designer jeans and plaid shirts and great wads of Kleenex were tucked into their collars to protect their clothes from the orange makeup the TV cameras required. Sissy's behind was so flat now, it looked as if it had been cut off by a bacon slicer. Her thin blond hair was uncombed. It had suffered from the strong TV lights and from constant setting with hot rollers of the past seasons so she now wore a soft blond wig while shooting.

Chelsea Deane, Chloe's favorite director, was directing this episode. The thirty-fifth. There were only nine episodes left before the end of the year. Ratings couldn't have been higher, nor could the spirits of everyone involved in the show. " 'Saga,' Prime Time Hit Show," the assistant director cheerfully answered the stage phone, which rang constantly. There were eighty extras today, dressed in 1920s costumes for a costume ball. Three cameras were being used for the opening shot of the Hamilton mansion in which Sam, as Steve Hamilton, and Sissy, as the third Mrs. Hamilton, stood in the doorway to greet their guests. The crew sat around desultorily gossiping, munching bacon-and-egg sandwiches or doughnuts, sipping coffee. There was a hum of conversation as the actors rehearsed the first scene of the day. Chloe, Pandora and Sam usually referred to the script while they rehearsed, as they had not yet memorized the lines. Sissy was always word perfect, not only with her own lines but with everyone else's too. Woe betide any actor who dried. She had no patience and would blow her top.

After rehearsal Chloe went back to her dressing room. A heavily beaded gold flapper dress that had been designed for her by Rudolpho, "Saga's" resident designer, was hanging in the wardrobe.

"God, this is heavy," she gasped, as Trixie, her dresser, helped her into it. "It must weigh at least twenty pounds."

"Thirty," said Trixie laconically laying out long chandelier earrings, diamanté bracelets and golden shoes. "We weighed it. It's broken two hangers already."

"Great," said Chloe. "My shoulders already feel like I've been pulling a plow."

"You must suffer to be beautiful," deadpanned Trixie, as they heard the sound of Sissy yelling down the corridor, "Trixieee, where the hell *are* you?"

"Ah, the dulcet tones of our divine diva." Trixie smiled and winked at Chloe. "Maybe I'll catch that skinny ass of hers in the zipper. That'll *really* make her yell!" Sissy was generally detested by cast and crew alike, but seemed oblivious to it.

In the hairdressing room, Theo combed out Chloe's hair and fixed golden ostrich feathers into it on a tight beaded band across her forehead. In the next chair sat Larry, while the other hairdresser, Monica, applied a layer of black pancake makeup to the bald spot that had started to appear recently on his scalp.

"Great, huh?" said Larry ruefully. "My only consolation is that Prince Charles has one too."

"And he's younger than you," Chloe teased.

Larry grimaced. At thirty-five he was playing twenty-five, and it was becoming more difficult. He had to watch his weight constantly, as did all the actors to maintain their youthful appearance for the camera that never lied. Most of the crew gained several pounds each season, due to the long, boring hours and the ever present trestle table loaded with snacks and coffee that the producers laid on for them all day long. But the camera added five to ten pounds to an actor's appearance, so the cast tried to keep away from the junk food that was always on display. Often, however, at the end of the day all willpower lapsed, and to Pandora's and Chloe's dismay their tight-fitting costumes now and then would have to be let out in the waist or hips. This never happened to Sissy, however. Dieting was her religion.

"Ready, Chloe?" chirped the ever cheerful Debbie. "Stage eleven, mush, mush, woman."

On the stage, eighty extras were being organized by Ned, the first assistant director, as Chelsea Deane painstakingly rehearsed a scene in which Chloe and her latest lover, played by Garth Frazer, arrived to greet Sissy and Sam.

It was a short scene but difficult to shoot because the extras, or "atmosphere" as they preferred to be called, had to move around in front of the principals without blocking the camera when the actors spoke their dialogue. The extras had to look animated, talk and laugh, yet were only allowed to mime so that the sound operator would pick up only the principals' dialogue.

After five takes Chelsea yelled, "Cut and print." The performers sat in a semicircle in their green director's chairs amidst a tangle of cables and arc lamps, relaxing for the eight to fifteen minutes it took to relight the scene for each of their close-ups.

Theo and Ben fussed around Chloe's hair and face and Trixie worried about the bugle beads that kept falling off Chloe's bodice. She tried to sew them back on but finally gave up with a sigh. "I don't think it'll show on camera." Chloe tried to remain cool, calm and collected even though at 10:30 A.M. the temperature outside was hovering in the mid-nineties and the studio wasn't much cooler. According to weather expert Doctor George on Channel 7, it was due to hit a hundred today.

Chloe felt her face sting under the heavy makeup. The strong lights washed out the performers' features to such an extent that excessive makeup was necessary to give definition to their faces. Sissy sat fanning herself with an antique fan she was convinced had once belonged to Lily Langtry. Garth, Chloe's TV lover, sat next to her, sweat pouring down his orange-tinted face.

Garth Frazer had blond, thinning hair and was only five feet nine, short compared to the other actors, most of whom were at least six feet. He had to wear high lifts inside his shoes, which gave him a curiously tipped-forward look, as though, if pushed, he might tumble over like Humpty-Dumpty. Chloe surreptitiously inched her chair away to escape his breath. Garth had obviously indulged the previous night in a fine Italian dinner laden with garlic. Little thought had he given to the fact that he would be locked in passionate embraces today with Chloe. But the more she moved her chair away to escape his breath, the closer he leaned, explaining to Chloe, as if she didn't know, the finer points of the scene they were going to perform.

Chloe was amused by his pomposity as he informed her what *her* motivation in their scene should be. Certainly he had been the star of two or three reasonable Movies of the Week, and had done a fairly respectable long-form series on prime time, but Lord Olivier he was not. She was beginning to resent his condescending attitude toward her and the rest of the cast and crew.

"I know you've only been acting for three years, darling." He smiled, revealing the most awful capped teeth she had ever seen. How much longer could she tolerate this buffoon? Her "beauty crew"—Trixie, Theo, De De and Ben—sat nearby, observing, containing their amusement. Gina came over with a pile of mail to try to help Chloe escape as he droned on.

"So you see, darling, *that's* how I see Miranda and Charles's subtext in the scene, don't you agree?" said the blond actor earnestly.

"Mmmm, yes, of course," muttered Chloe. She knew her character better than he knew his, and she certainly knew her lines. He had been having serious trouble with his dialogue for the last four episodes. This was becoming a problem, as they were falling behind schedule. It cost them money, and if there was one thing the producers hated it was spending extra money. But Garth was seemingly unconcerned; he was a boorish puffball, a conceited egotist, in short, a fairly typical example of a mediocre prime time TV actor who had hit it lucky and whose success had gone straight to his head.

Mumbling "Excuse me," Chloe let Gina lead her away.

Several hours later the time had come to do their love scene. Chloe groaned inwardly.

"Ready for you, Chloe," said Ned, as Ben packed Max Factor powder onto her face to stop the shine.

"O.K., my darling, let's go for one, shall we?" said Chelsea, still as hearty as a sailor on leave.

The lighting cameraman instructed the gaffer to move the lights more to the left. The sound man instructed the boom operator to adjust the proximity of his mike to the two actors because he was picking up too much echo. The camera assistant whisked a tape measure up to Chloe and Garth's noses and did some computations in his head, which he jotted down. Trixie fussed with Chloe's beads, Theo fussed with the feathers in her hair, which were starting to molt and fall onto her eyelashes. Ben outlined her lips for the fifteenth time that day with peach lip gloss. Bobby, the second makeup man, with a sigh of resignation mopped Garth's face with a wet chamois dipped in witch hazel, then mopped it with Kleenex before adding a thick coat of powder.

One of the secretaries from Bill Herbert's office arrived on the set with her entire family from Arkansas. They stood, mouths agape, directly in Garth's eye line. One of them fiddled with an Instamatic camera, and they whispered loudly among themselves with excitement.

Chloe signaled to Ned to have them moved, but before it could be done Garth blew his top.

"Get those people out of my eye line, *please,*" he yelled. "What is this, feeding time at the fucking zoo?"

"Calm down..." Chloe started to say.

"We're trying to do a goddamn scene here, not be stared at like monkeys in the motherfucking zoo, for Christ's sake."

In unison the crew silently raised their eyes to the heavens. They had been suffering Garth's overbearing airs and graces in silence for months. Sissy they tolerated. Sissy was a big star, a central part of this show, their bread and butter. Garth had no such clout. This was basically Chloe, Sissy and Sam's show, in spite of the constant insistence by Abby and Gertrude that it was an ensemble piece.

Garth's makeup man once more attended to his sweaty face, and Chloe wondered if he was on coke. She had never seen so much sweat.

"O.K., kids, let's 'ave a go, shall we?" Chelsea Deane was calm on the surface, but seething inside. This ignorant poofter was getting to him. "What a no-talent numbnuts," he had confided to Chloe the previous week, after directing a scene in which Garth blew his lines no fewer than eight times.

"I know, I know, darling, he's a pain. Why they cast him instead of Colin Bridges I'll never know."

She and Chelsea exchanged glances of understanding. "O.K., kids, *action!*" Chelsea stood next to the camera watching intently as Chloe and Garth started the scene. Garth immediately blew his first line.

"O.K., we go again," said Chelsea, as the beauty crew trotted in to mop up. Ned called for the red light. The third camera assistant brought in the clapper board. "Thirty-three take two," announced the sound man. "Rolling."

"Action!" yelled Chelsea.

"I love you, Miranda," breathed Garth/Charles as he gently bent his blond head to Chloe's dark one. They were seated together on a chaise longue in the Hamilton mansion.

"I've never loved anyone as much as I love you." Chloe felt nausea assail her at his garlic-laden breath.

"Oh, Charles, why do you say one thing, yet mean another?" Chloe moved her head away as far as she could without getting out of the careful lighting setup. There was a pregnant pause. Chloe tried to fill it with a girlish sigh. Garth had dried again.

"Sorry about that, love," he said calmly. "Heat's got to me."

Chloe gritted her teeth. Trixie and Gina threw her sympathetic looks. The crew tried not to look affected.

"Thirty-three take fourteen," cried the camera assistant briskly an hour later, as he snapped the clapper board exceedingly close to Garth's nose. The crew were seething inwardly now, and they felt sorry for Chloe, who was extremely uncomfortable. It was over a hundred degrees on the set. The heavy beaded dress, the molting ostrich feathers, this ghastly actor with his awful breath and the sweat that poured from his brow onto her upturned face were a nightmare. Chloe had had enough. She had really had her fill this time.

They finally finished the master scene, and after Chelsea covered it with medium shots and close-ups, Chloe went to her dressing room and called Gertrude's office. "I need a meeting with you, now," she said. "And it can't wait."

After seeing the abysmal rushes, Abby and Gertrude realized they had to find a new love interest for Chloe, and soon. She had rebelled for the first time in three and a half seasons. She told them she needed a strong, assertive man for her character to play opposite, a real macho man with strength, masculinity and sex appeal. They knew she was right.

An emergency meeting was called with Bill Herbert, Chloe and Jasper Swanson in attendance. Sitting in Abby's oak-paneled office they discussed the possibilities. Who was available, who wasn't. Who would do TV, who would think it was demeaning.

"Burt Reynolds," suggested Chloe optimistically. "There's a real man, and his movies haven't done well recently."

"Ha!" said Abby. "He's features, honey, *features*. He won't do TV."

"Timothy Dalton," suggested Jasper, ever one to get a fellow Englishman a job.

"Timothy who?" rasped Gertrude. "Never heard of him."

"He's good. He's an excellent Shakespearean actor. He's going to be hot," insisted Jasper.

"Well, not on 'Saga,'" said Abby. "I saw him in that Mae West film years ago. Nah—next."

"You'll be sorry," said Jasper. "Timothy's going places, he'll be big."

"Let him be big somewhere else," said Gertrude. "We need a macho guy with a name."

For two frustrating hours they played the casting game. Then Jasper played his ace. He'd been waiting for the right moment. The moment when Tom Selleck, George Hamilton, Robert

Wagner, James Farentino, Alain Delon, Michael Landon, Peter Strauss, Martin Sheen, Jeff Bridges and Gregory Harrison had all been considered and, for one reason or another, dismissed.

"How about Luis Mendoza?" he suggested.

Luis sat across from Jasper at Ma Maison twiddling his thumbs. It had been three years since his movie with Sissy, a bomb if ever there was one. The producers couldn't even sell it to cable TV. Movie offers since then had been thin on the ground for Luis. If it hadn't been for his passion for Sabrina, he would have gone back to Mexico, where he was a superstar and his records still outsold Julio Iglesias's. In spite of his looks and his belief in his talents, Hollywood refused to take a singing Mexican seriously. He had hired the best public relations firm in town to promulgate his image as a serious but sensual actor. He had fired Klinger and hired Jasper Swanson as his agent. He had been considered for movies with Bo Derek, Kim Basinger and Kathleen Turner—but he had had no firm offers.

He was now nearing thirty, and, with his black lustrous curly hair and slanting, heavily lashed brown eyes, handsomer than ever. He and Sabrina were the most beautiful and photogenic couple in Hollywood; the paparazzi went wild whenever they went out publicly, which was not often. They preferred to stay at the beach making love, lying in the Jacuzzi that was fitted into the deck outside their house, drinking wine and talking about their future.

Recently, though, the charms of Sabrina had begun to pall for Luis. Sabrina, gorgeous and loving as she was, had become a tiny bit boring. Occasionally, to his horror, he found that he was unable to respond to her amorous advances. Pretending head-aches, exhaustion or lines to learn, he would retire to his study, where he sat pondering why his libido, of which he had always been justly proud, seemed to be deserting him. He recalled hear-ing the macho men of his youth discuss their *amigos* who "couldn't get it up"; now he, too, seemed to be joining their ranks. Although it had only happened a couple of times in the past month, it was enough to turn Luis's hot Latin blood cold.

In the nearly three years he and Sabrina had been together, he had been more or less faithful to her, which for a Latin man was unusual. They had made love at least once or twice a day. Now his equipment was letting him down, a fate worse than death.

Preoccupied with his troubles, Luis was barely listening to Jasper.

"I think you should do a series," Jasper was saying as he expertly slipped the band off a Davidoff cigar, lighting it with a kitchen match from a Victorian silver box he carried.

"A series? *Ay, mamá,* I was offered a series last month. The stars would be me and a talking car. No, thanks."

"I don't mean *any* series." Jasper was impatient. "I'm talking about 'Saga,' the series of the moment, the hottest show in town."

"So what? It's already cast with Sam and Sissy—ugh!" He grimaced remembering their ill-fated movie and even more ill-fated short-lived affair.

"What do you think of Chloe Carriere?" asked Jasper, puffing on the huge cigar with enjoyment. At his age, a cigar gave more comfort and pleasure than sex.

"Chloe Carriere, she's a dish, a bitch too, I hear." Luis laughed. "I hear she cuts off her leading men's balls and fries them for breakfast like *huevos rancheros.*"

"Not true, Luis," said Jasper gravely. "Not true at all. Chloe is actually a very nice girl who has become a victim, of sorts, of her own publicity."

"But she's gone along with it, hasn't she?" persisted Luis.

"Dear Chloe, she is a wonder, I'll admit," laughed Jasper. "She's waited a long time for this break, so she's making the most of it. To get to the point, Luis, Abby Arafat and Gertrude have made us an offer that is hard to refuse."

"What is it?"

"Two years on 'Saga' with an option for a third. Twenty-five thousand an episode for the first year, forty thousand for the second, and the third negotiable, of course."

"Hmm, I can make more than that on a tour of Spain in a month," said Luis.

"Luis, old boy—" Jasper was more serious now—" 'Saga' is a hot show this year, next year too. If they're lucky, they may even go to six or seven years. Chloe Carriere is a hot actress. They want you for her lover, husband, boyfriend, whatever. This will make you the household name in America you've been dying to be. Let me tell you something, old boy, about the film scene. Nicholson and Redford find it hard to get the right roles and stay up on their movie pedestals today. TV is making the stars now. Take this part, Luis. Make every woman in America cream in her knickers when you come on the screen, and you can write your *own* ticket in two years' time. Look at Selleck—he made it on TV, and now he's got more movie offers than he can handle."

Luis considered the Englishman's advice. It was true. TV was where it was now. With a few exceptions, there were no big movie stars any more. TV stars were the current royalty of show business, invited to the White House, curtsying to the Queen, on the covers of major magazines.

"Maybe I should do it. Let me think it over."

"Do that, old boy. You have twenty-four hours to make up your mind; then they will go in another direction."

Luis frowned. "Don't threaten me."

"I'm not, old boy, I'm not. I simply believe this is a major career move for you."

"I told you I'll think about it," said Luis.

It didn't take Luis long to accept the offer, and a few weeks later, locked in a passionate embrace with his new on-camera lover, Chloe, it didn't take him long to become a macho man again. He felt his manhood rising against the filmy chiffon of her nightgown. They were entwined under lilac Frette sheets on the set. Dozens of men and women barking orders and busying themselves with the thousand and one duties necessary before the camera could roll on the love scene unfolding in front of them milled around the bed. Luis started to sweat, something he normally didn't do. How *could* he be aroused by Chloe? She was far too old for him, and he hated her crisp British manner. She seemed always to be secretly laughing at him, and although she was friendly and charming, he hated her coolness and her lack of deference toward men in general.

Chloe looked startled at the feel of Luis's normally lackadaisical cock twitching against her thigh.

She looked into his eyes as they lay together while the camera assistant brought the measuring tape to each of their noses, and gave Luis a conspiratorial wink. Luis managed a weak smile as he willed his defiant member to subside.

Why, for God's sake, why now with Chloe? Why not with soft, adoring, gorgeous young Sabrina?

"O.K., kids." Chelsea Deane beamed his cockney charm. "I'm givin' you a lot of space here to really 'ave a go at it. I really want you to melt those TV screens. We've got a lot of leeway, so let me see if all the stuff they write about you in the papers is true, eh, luv?" He grinned at Chloe and she smiled back. Chelsea had a great sense of humor, something sadly lacking in most of the producers and directors of the show. He and Chloe insulted each other outrageously on the set, sometimes joking and kidding around until the crew broke up and Chloe had to go to her dressing room to try to recover from the giggles.

"*Aaand* action!" shouted Chelsea.

After the passionate love scene was over, there was silence from the crew. Trixie gave a terry-cloth robe to a stunned Chloe. Luis had been amazing. His ardor, inflamed by his sudden unexplainable desire for Chloe, had almost caught her up in the passion of the moment.

"Blimey, kids, that was *hot!*" said Chelsea admiringly. "Print it—we don't even need coverage. Hey, Luis, you were great, man. Like just great!" Proudly Luis accepted compliments from various crew members and retired to his trailer as lunch was called.

Debbie Drake, the pretty young second assistant director, brought him his usual chef's salad, iced tea, and apple pie with ice cream. "Anything else you want, Luis?" she said brightly, standing silhouetted against the bright California noonday sun in the doorway of his trailer, her taut breasts outlined by the simple white T-shirt she wore. She had a cute rear end enhanced by faded blue jeans. Her face, unadorned by makeup and framed by long blond hair caught up in a ponytail, was pretty in a wholesome all-American way.

"Yes, *querida*—I want you," he said huskily, giving her the benefit of the famous dark eyes that had caused maidenly hearts to flutter throughout Latin America.

"Oh," gulped Debbie, having witnessed the love scene earlier. Oh, well, uhm, why not? she said to herself. Let's see if it's true what they say about Latin lovers. With a sharp kick of her sneakered foot, she pushed the door of his trailer shut and, pulling her T-shirt over her head, joined Luis on his sofa bed.

The following week Luis fucked Pandora. Although he had never been interested in older women, Pandora's brisk manner, coupled with a truly magnificent bosom, captivated Luis's imagination. His conquests seemed to improve his ardor for Sabrina. He found himself able not only to have some of the most interesting lunch hours he had ever had, but also to achieve new heights of passion with Sabrina. It was clear it couldn't last. All of a sudden Luis Mendoza was having his cake and eating it too.

His sudden fame astounded even himself. After appearing on the TV screen in "Saga" only twice, he had received tons of fan mail. Women found his macho, slightly cocky good looks a total turn-on. He was suddenly the flavor of the month throughout the whole United States. Editors besieged Christopher McCarthy, the PR man for "Saga," with requests for cover stories, photo sessions, interviews, anything and everything to do with Luis.

Before he knew what had hit him, Luis was on the cover of *US, People, USA Today, GQ,* the *American Informer,* the *National Enquirer,* the *Star,* the *Globe* and even the corner cover of *Newsweek.* It was heady stuff. Intoxicating. Luis had never been modest, and his Latin pride swelled even more at the sudden attention and admiration he was receiving.

Sabrina didn't like it. It wasn't that she was jealous. With her wholesome all-American beauty, she was in demand herself, building a solid foundation for a film career that she hoped would flourish for years. But she didn't like Luis's preening himself all day long, constantly combing his shiny black hair, working on his rippling muscles and admiring them from all angles in the three-way mirror in *her* dressing room. This was when he wasn't lying by the pool obsessively working on an already perfect tan, a sun reflector handy to catch every last ray. Their love life was still good, but there was something missing in their relationship now, and she didn't know what it was.

19

In a weathered house on a small cul de sac in Santa Monica lived Sam Sharp's very good friend, Freddy.

A designer of ladies' clothing, Frederick Langlan was not in the class of Bob Mackie or Nolan Miller—his Hollywood gowns were more in the seven-hundred-dollar price range than the seven-thousand—but he had a loyal show-business clientele of not only wealthy, frugal women, but also of young TV starlets on the way up who wanted to look fabulous but couldn't afford Bob's, Nolan's or even Neiman-Marcus's prices. Wives of B-picture actors on a tight budget but with a full social schedule, girlfriends of studio executives, older actresses who did occasional guest shots on "Love Boat" and "Magnum" and wanted to look their best, all were habitués of Freddy's rococo salon by the sea.

He painstakingly designed an "original" Frederick Langlan for each one, an original that bore more than a passing resemblance to the exquisite creations of Valentino or Jacqueline de Ribes in the current issues of French or Italian *Vogue*.

To the ladies, it didn't matter. They were secure in the fact that there was no chance of the catastrophe that had happened recently at a Beverly Hills charity ball. The wives of two of "Saga's" producers, who had each blown nine thousand dollars on a gorgeous Galanos gown, appeared at the ball wearing the same dress. If looks could kill, Mr. Abby Arafat and Mr. William Herbert would have been widowers. Hollywood chuckled with delight when the *Beverly Hills Tattler* ran front-page photos of the two women side by side wearing the identical dresses.

As they waited for Freddy, Sabrina Jones and Daphne Swanson sat in cozy chairs in his anteroom flipping through the *Beverly Hills Tattler* and laughing at the photographs of the two women.

Freddy drew aside the silver lamé curtains to his anteroom and swept in, followed by a cloud of pale gray organza and a torrent of the latest gossip.

"My dears, have you *heard* about Emerald's new boyfriend?" he said, giggling, as he lowered the neckline an inch and a half on Sabrina's creamy silk jersey to reveal more of her fabulous bosom, a sight guaranteed to get her, if not into the "People" section of *Time* magazine, at least into "What the Stars Are Wearing" in the *Beverly Hills Tattler*.

"I thought she was still seeing Solomon. Who is it?" Daphne interrupted her inspection of a box of Cadbury's milk chocolates which Freddy's flight steward friend had brought him from England. Daphne prided herself on being the first to know who was sleeping with whom—often stale news by the time the couple in question finally did it. With her network of spies in every restaurant, studio, boutique and hotel between Palm Springs and L.A., she usually knew, before the fact, the first time the eyes of potential lovers locked.

"My dear, it's *too* camp," Freddy said through a mouthful of the pins with which he was outlining Sabrina's bosom. "You *know* she's doing that movie in Italy?"

"Yes, yes." Daphne impatiently lit a Dunhill, ever true to all things British.

"Of course we all know it's a turkey, if I ever heard of one, and she's playing opposite that has-been Italian star, what's his name?"

"Fabiano Frapani." Sabrina whispered the name reverently. A has-been indeed! The greatest actor ever to come out of Italy. So what if he was pushing sixty—with talent like his, who cared?

"Weell," said Freddy slyly, enjoying drawing out this scrap of gossip. "You *know* who's directing, don't you?"

"Ouch!!" He had inadvertently pierced Sabrina's priceless left nipple with a pin.

"Oooh, *sorry,* dear, mustn't tamper with the merchandise. Do you want me to kiss it better?" He giggled, though both women noticed he was somewhat less effervescent than usual.

"It's all right, *go on.*" Even Sabrina, usually bored by gossip, as those who whose lives are full mostly are, was intrigued by tales of Emerald's escapades. Almost three generations had now been titillated by them, yet interest in her private life still persisted.

"Horatio's directing, right?" Daphne was offhand. Although she knew who was fucking whom, minor details like who was directing whom usually escaped her.

"Yes indeedy. Horatio George Washington." He stopped, becoming involved with the extent of the slit in Sabrina's skirt.

"To the thigh or to the crotch, dear? What do you think?"

"The thigh, please. I'm *not* Cher."

"So what about Horatio George Washington?" Daphne was impatient. "He's married to Edna Ann Mason, they just had a baby. Oh, dear, I *must* send her flowers."

"Dear, he and Emerald have been at it like rabbits ever since they met when she went down under nearly three years ago."

"How do you *know*, Freddy?" snapped Daphne, annoyed that her sources from Italy had not filled her in on this one.

"It's been in the English papers. Dempster's column, as a matter of fact. Now you've *got* to believe Nigel Dempster, haven't you, darling?"

"Not necessarily," Daphne snapped. "How do you know this for an actual fact?"

"Sorry, dear, can't reveal me sources." Freddy leaned back on his heels, surveying the perfection of Sabrina in his copy of a Halston. "We all know Emerald has always liked a touch of the tar brush, and Horatio *is* a famous colored man, isn't he?"

"Black," corrected Daphne. "We say 'black' now, Freddy dear, not 'colored.'"

"Black, shmack, he's no more *black* than you and me, dear," sniffed Freddy. "More the color of those chocolates, I'd say. But that doesn't matter at all. I think the fact he's married makes it a bit, well—"

"Tacky, darling?" finished Daphne.

"Yes, I suppose."

"Well if the American papers get wind of this, *if* it's true, of course," said Daphne unzipping her dress and struggling into her organza, "she will be in a lot of trouble with Middle American backlash."

"I don't understand," said Sabrina during the conversation as she threw on a faded denim shirt. "He's married to Edna. *She's* white, *he's* black, no one cares about that, so why should it be such a scandal if Emerald sleeps with him? I mean DCOL: *Doesn't Count on Location,* right, Daphne? Isn't that what you told me once?"

255

"Absolutely," said Daphne breathing in for dear life and pressing her flesh over her rib cage as Freddy attempted to zip her into the new dress. "Dammit, Freddy, why did you make it so *tight?*"

"Duckie, face it, you've gained," said Freddy, patiently opening up the seam.

While Freddy worked, Daphne explained. "Edna is a, well, *proper* actress. I mean no one is really interested in what she does and with whom she does it. She could stand naked on the Empire State Building jerking off King Kong and it wouldn't even rate a mention in the trades, let alone the tabloids. She's too boring, too good, too mumsy. So the fact that she's married to a black director, even if he is only milk-chocolate-colored does *not* interest the public. Edna is Edna. Solid, dependable, dull. But Emerald is Emerald, and *everything* she does, even if she sends back an overdone steak at Hamburger Hamlet, is of enormous interest to the public because of her *charisma,* darling. . . . *Aaah,* that's better, Fred." Daphne breathed a sigh of relief as Freddy finally managed to do her up.

"Telephone, Meester Langlan." The maid came in tentatively, in awe of Sabrina's beauty and Daphne's assertiveness.

"Who is it? I'm busy." Freddy was fussing with the frills around Daphne's still appealing cleavage. Daphne was determined to outdo Lady Sarah in the frills department at next week's gala dinner in aid of cancer research. Her gown was an exact copy of the latest Zandra Rhodes.

"Eet's Meester Smeeth," the maid said hesitantly.

Daphne looked knowingly at Sabrina.

" 'Scuse me, dears, be right back." Freddy disappeared into his tiny cubicle of an office.

"Now you *know* who Mr. Smith is, don't you, darling?" Daphne said smugly.

"No," said Sabrina. She was wondering if she should take out a full-page ad in *Reporter* and *Variety* when the sequel to her college movie was released. Her press agent wanted her to, so did her agent, but her boring business manager said she couldn't afford it. What a drag. She was making over two hundred thousand a movie, and he said she couldn't *afford* a measly nine hundred bucks for an ad to enhance her flourishing career. Where did all her money go, for goodness' sake? she wondered. Nobody in Hollywood ever seemed to have the "fuck-you" money they craved.

Her rented furnished house at the beach cost three thousand a month, the cost of which she shared with Luis. Her car was leased. She had few good clothes; those she had were made by Freddy, who always gave her a good deal because she was the freshest, most beautiful of all his clients. Where *did* the money go? Her reverie was interrupted by Daphne's whispering, "If you don't know who Mr. Smith is—I shall tell you, dear."

Sabrina neither knew nor cared. Her interests were mainly limited to her career and Luis. Both were full-time jobs, especially Luis, who seemed distracted these days. They certainly weren't making love as often as they used to.

Daphne went on, "He's Sam Sharp, of course. They've been having a thing for *years.*"

"Oh." Sabrina looked at Daphne, who was obviously pleased with imparting this bit of spice to one of the few who didn't know about it. "How interesting." Golly, she was bored by gossip.

"What's going on?" said Freddy to Sam, who almost never called during Freddy's work hours. They met, when possible, twice a month in Freddy's art deco-filled apartment above his shop.

"I haven't been feeling well, Freddy, and I'm working late. I can't make it tonight. Thought I'd let you know because we're on location and the damned cellular phone doesn't work when we get beyond a twenty-five-mile radius of L.A."

"Never mind, poppet," said Freddy, slightly relieved to be on his own tonight. Now he could meet that pretty young sailor who was on leave for a week, and who drank at the King's Head in Santa Monica every night. They had locked eyes a few times, and Freddy thought it time to move in before the others did. "Next Tuesday, O.K.?" Sam asked.

"Of course, luv."

"Later, then." Sam was terse on the phone. Terror at the possibility of his gay lifestyle being discovered became stronger with each passing year.

After Sam hung up on Freddy, he stretched and surveyed himself in the bathroom mirror of his luxurious trailer, which was now proceeding at a brisk clip down the Ventura freeway.

Not bad, not bad at all. He was fifty-three now, a vigorous, athletic, macho-looking fifty-three. If only he didn't feel so weak...maybe it was time for a checkup.

20

"What do you think of them?" asked Emerald
shakily. The emerald-and-gold bracelets winked on their dull
black velvet bed.

"Beautiful, simply beautiful," Vanessa Vanderbilt breathed. "I
must have them. How much?"

"Well, a bargain at thirteen thousand," Emerald said tentatively. "Don't you think?"

Thirteen thousand dollars. Vanessa mentally calculated the
profit she could make from Emerald's bracelets. "Too much, luv.
Nine thousand, take it or leave it."

And Emerald had to take it. It had been more than three years now since she had failed to get the role of Miranda. In that time things had gone from bad to worse. Everyone knew who she was, but as usual no one wanted to employ her. She still spent money as though it were 1957 and tried to live the way she had then.

But it wasn't 1957. She was no longer in her twenties and America's favorite sweetheart, with suitors galore, a lucrative contract and money to buy enough gems to fulfill all her girl-hood fantasies.

It was 1985, and in spite of the face-lifts, the other plastic surgery and the celebrity, she was in big trouble.

The six films she had made in the past three years had been worse than B. They were F—F for Failure. Emerald would now go anywhere for a movie. Anywhere she would be paid at least twenty-five thousand, anywhere they would agree to pay for an expensive suite at the best hotel near the location, anywhere she would be assured of five hundred a week in expenses, anywhere she would get to keep her wardrobe.

She didn't care if the movie was good, bad or indifferent. She had to keep up her lifestyle; she could not drop her standard of living.

Although she had traded her Beverly Hills mansion for a smaller house, it was still a little jewel in the hills of Beverly. But it cost. It cost her every penny she made. Unable to cope alone, without a steady man in her life, she took solace in vodka. Lots of vodka. Vodka with orange juice in the morning, vodka with ice on the set in a water glass; then bottle after bottle of Dom Perignon throughout the afternoon and night, whether she worked or not. And then after dinner, 90 proof Armagnac. Her drinking pattern would make strong men reel.

As the movies got worse, she hid her pain with other substitutes. The occasional odd joint at first. Then the snort. The blessed white powder that gave her such a lift. That made her feel young, successful, full of life and love again. It was expensive, and she was now selling her jewelry to get it.

Vanessa Vanderbilt sounded tougher than she looked. Underneath her hard business exterior, she was generous and sympathetic. But dog will always eat dog, as Daddy had taught her. Only the most cunning survived in this world. There was no room for compassion in business. "There's a bunch of fuckin' barracudas out there, me luv!" Daddy had instilled this dogma in her from the time she was four. "Watch that little arse of yours *all* the time, darlin', otherwise the sharks will have it for their tea—mark my words."

Vanessa, dutiful daughter, did just that, soon becoming more cunning and manipulative in business than Daddy ever had. Oil-rich sheiks, Arab arms dealers, superstar entertainers, American politicians—Vanessa knew many, and she used them before they used her and abused her.

"*Everyone's* a user. Don't ever forget that, my little love," Daddy had said. "If they're not a user, then they're a loser, and you're bloody well better off not havin' doin's with 'em, darlin'." Thus spake Luke Higgins, the oracle of Petticoat Lane, as he cheerfully dispensed cockles and whelks from his stall every Sunday, worked in his secondhand furniture shop Monday to Friday, and Saturday taught his brood of eager kids the facts of life. Every Saturday morning in his cluttered shop off Petticoat Lane, a stone's throw from the Elephant and Castle, where Vanessa attended the local comprehensive school, Luke Higgins wheeled and dealed. This enabled Vanessa to grow up not only knowing the value of a pound, but also that of a dollar, a yen, a franc and a ruble.

Perhaps "fence" was too strong a word for Luke, as he managed to stay a hair's breadth away from the law by dealing only in property stolen from another country. Interpol, although often hot on a scent, never managed to trace it to Luke, who was in his own words "a crafty bugger" who always looked out for number one. Possessing a streak of Robin Hood's philosophy, he was a good-looking cheerful chap, with ginger wavy hair, matching mustache, and rippling muscles in his wiry body, and he always gave the poorer of his clients a break when they needed to sell something legitimately. But to those from Italy, France and Germany who passed their stolen goods to him, he showed no mercy.

The jewelry, cameras and other objects he received were the fruits of petty thievery on the French Riviera or the ski resorts of Gstaad and St. Moritz—also minor baubles that ladies had not bothered to put into their safes when they locked away their forty-carat diamond rings and half-million-dollar diamond necklaces. This was daytime jewelry, fun jewels: gold chains, Cartier or Piaget watches, one-carat diamond earrings, the odd charm bracelet. So wealthy were these women that they usually didn't even report these losses to their insurance companies, since it would only increase their premiums. A five-thousand-dollar Bulgari gold chain can easily be replaced, so can a Cartier watch—and it's *so* much fun to do it.

Through Luke's capable hands had passed some up-market, not overly expensive merchandise, which he managed to dispense via dealers in the antique markets of Portobello Road, Bermondsey and Kensington.

Luke had an enjoyable life, a pretty Jamaican wife who adored him and didn't give him a lot of lip like some of those uppity black women from Nigeria and Uganda. In return, he was a good father, a good provider and an excellent teacher, and his four children learned well from him.

Vanessa broke away from the family fold at eighteen to become a model. Having seen photographs of a gloriously elegant Gloria Vanderbilt in American *Vogue,* and becoming intrigued with all that her family represented, she changed the name Higgins to Vanderbilt, Vera to Vanessa. Higgins was too evocative of the East End to suit the lifestyle she craved.

In the 1960s Vanessa, a bubbly cocktail of her father's red curls and Irish charm and her mother's warm brown Jamaican skin, black eyes and sweet personality, became a minor success as a model, but a major one on the London social circuit.

Modeling was soon behind her, as she accompanied princes, rogues and rock stars on their travels. A diamond earring here, a Buccellati bracelet there, mink coats and fox wraps galore, Vanessa was in heaven. The Jet Set life was hers. Gloria Vanderbilt, watch out, she mused, here comes Vanessa Vanderbilt snapping at your heels.

She was courted and admired and made love to by wealthy and powerful men, but none of them ever fell in love with her. She sailed in their yachts, cruising in extravagant 180-foot vessels. She drove in their Ferraris, their stretch Mercedes, their antique Bentleys. She pocketed their crisp dollars, pounds, or francs and shopped—as much as her heart desired. Vanessa was desirable, an alluring toy for rich men to play with. Year after year she flaunted her pert café au lait body on luxury yachts in Portofino and Monte Carlo, basked by the pools in marbled villas in Marbella and Sardinia, grazed the boulevards of the Rive Gauche, Fifth Avenue and Rodeo Drive in search of ever more outrageous clothes to add to her vast wardrobe. She was a happy woman. So happy in fact that she celebrated this happiness with her favorite pastime—eating.

Vanessa would rather make a reservation than make love. Often during the act of love, she would think excitedly about the snack she would order after this tiresome tussle was finished. As the rich and powerful of the world buried their heads and their members in her fragrant alcoves, aroused by her moans of ecstasy, they never imagined that her lust was not for them, but for food.

Usually Vanessa kept a little snack next to whatever bed she happened to be occupying—perhaps a biscuit tin with a picture of the Queen on it, full of Mars Bars or Swiss milk chocolate, on which she would happily munch afterward, while her lover lay spent beside her. Soon, as she ripened like a watermelon in the noonday sun, she started to lose her lovers. The Americans went first, then went the English, then the French left. Soon the Italians and Germans lost interest, until eventually the only men left who desired her were Arabs.

Vanessa didn't care, so happy was she with her life of luxurious opulence and the friends she still had in abundance. Friends of both sexes adored her. She was fun, the first to make fun of herself, including her battle with the bulge.

In vain Vanessa tried to diet. Jane Fonda videotapes littered her rooms, but she had absolutely no willpower. She simply could not resist caviar with sour cream, veal chops with *pommes frites, mousse au chocolat,* everything delicious—not to mention the wines that accompanied her feasts and the liquor-filled chocolates, mints and savories that followed.

To her current beau, an Arab sheik, she was manna from Allah. A Western woman who loved to eat was as rare as teeth on a hen in London. Most of the "models" and starlets he entertained ate like birds. Vanessa was more than just a hearty eater. She matched him in gluttony.

"Another baby lamb," he would roar with delight as they squatted on the floor of his suite at the Dorchester Hotel, while his personal chef from Kuwait prepared delights from the Sinai desert, desserts the like of which could not be found in any cosmopolitan restaurant in the Western world.

Vanessa leaned her plump little cheek on Samir's big plump shoulder, and, spooning pâté into a piece of pita bread, popped it affectionately into his mouth. It was so wonderful. Such a wonderful life. Samir was so generous with money and presents, so attentive when she needed him—which was not often, as she was far happier eating and shopping. Unlike many Arabs, he had charm, manners and, thanks to a Harvard education, the cutest American accent.

Sex bored her, and she found "The French Way" positively repugnant. The only way she could tolerate it was to pretend she was eating an ice-cream cone. When Samir had to go to Kuwait, he left Vanessa in his permanent suite at the Dorchester with a generous supply of money and his company's American Express and Visa cards made out in her name.

She heard about his murder on breakfast television news in bed one morning as she devoured her fifth croissant with raspberry jam and Devonshire cream.

Things did not go well for Vanessa after that. Since she was not mentioned in Samir's will, his money and estate went to his three wives and eleven children in Kuwait. All that Vanessa possessed, apart from clothes and jewels, were two company credit cards. Her father's teachings having had good effect, she immediately went to the Bond Street antique shops and art galleries and bought as many objects of value as she could until the credit dried up. Although she still had a pretty face, Vanessa's weight now hovered around the 200-pound mark; she no longer appealed to any of the eligible rich or powerful men in London or Europe. They preferred their women sleek, like their boats, their planes and their automobiles. Pretty butterballs with cheerful personalities did not interest powerful, eligible men, not even as temporary arm decoration. For the occasional one-night stand, maybe—but most of the men of her acquaintance were not interested by Vanessa sexually at all.

Vanessa had to face the unhappy fact that her days of using her looks to earn a living were over.

She was thirty-two. She had enjoyed *La Dolce Vita* to the hilt. Now it was time to go legit.

She started selling her own jewelry and the paintings and objects she had acquired after Samir's death. She had an abundance of items from fourteen years of grateful donors. Her father gave her a few pieces and she started attending auctions and estate sales in England. She had a clever eye both for a bargain and a good jewel, and in three years she had built her traveling jewelry emporium into a lucrative business. Often she did business with many of the men she had bedded, and since she was such a likable and loyal friend, her business prospered, and now she was on a trip to L.A.

"Would you like the box?" Emerald asked Vanessa. Looking at the red leather Cartier container with the embossed gold edging, Vanessa nodded. "Yes, but I'll wear them," she said, scribbling a check. "I like them so much, I'm keeping them for myself—temporarily, that is."

Emerald looked longingly for the last time at her bracelets. She loved them. She adored all her jewels. If a man wasn't buying them for her, she bought them for herself. Now they were going. And no one, it seemed, would be buying any more for her. Ever.

After selling her bracelets to Vanessa, Emerald headed for a bar she knew in West Hollywood. She ordered vodka stingers. Five in a row.

The barman looked at her curiously. She looked vaguely familiar, but he knew better than to engage in conversation anyone who obviously had a lot of problems in life. This woman looked as if she had more than most. Obviously she had been quite a looker in her day. Now the blond hair had gray roots and hung in uncombed snarls around a face devoid of makeup, but in which he could see vestiges of what might once have been aristocratic cheekbones, a sculptured nose and luscious lips. Her eyes were hidden behind tinted glasses, and she wore a shapeless tweed jacket and sweatpants that hid her body. On her feet were scuffed high-heels. She smoked Luckys, lighting each one from the last, rejecting offers of a light from the men who occasionally looked at her, perhaps catching the animal scent of her former glory. She stared straight ahead, barely moving except to lift the glass to her pale mouth.

Draining her fifth stinger, Emerald motioned shakily to the bartender for another.

"Lady, I think you've had enough, don't you?" The bartender tried to be kind. He had observed her coming back from the ladies room. This broad could hardly walk.

"I'm fine. Give me another," she snapped.

"I can't, lady. I'm sorry."

"Screw you, buster!" snarled Emerald.

"Look, lady, there's a law in this town. I can't serve drinks to a person who's obviously had too many. I don't want to lose my license."

"Fuck your license," mumbled Emerald, getting up from her stool and lurching to the door. "Fuck your license and your crappy bar." She looked around the bar at the dozen men staring at her. None of them recognized her. "Fuck you, all you bastards," she exclaimed and, slamming the door, staggered onto Olympic Boulevard.

The next day, when she came to, she pulled herself together and went to visit Daphne Swanson.

"To be frank, love, I need a job—any job. I'm not proud. I'm down to my last few trinkets. I sold my favorite bracelets yesterday, the ones Stanley gave me for our wedding. You know how much he meant to me."

"I know, dear, I know. I remember it well, even though it was thirty years ago."

"Twenty-eight," said Emerald crossly. "And I *was* only twenty."

"Of course," Daphne agreed, smiling inwardly. Why did they all try and lop off the years when the town knew to the month what year they were born—and to the thousandth how many bucks they had in the bank?

"You know everything that's going on, Daphne. There must be *something,* somewhere, coming up that I would be right for. I mean, I *am* Hollywood royalty." She laughed lamely.

"I know, duckie, you were—I mean, of course you are," soothed Daphne. "But dear heart, you must realize that movie stars of your generation are, well, a bit *passé.*" She bit into a marron glacé, grimaced at the sweetness of it and fed it to the Pekingese nestled close to her on her pink down comforter.

Emerald bit a hangnail and lit up a Lucky Strike. God, she'd love a drink. She'd love a snort, too. What time was it? 11 A.M. Oh, well, it was 7 P.M. in London—cocktail time, civilized time. Her friends in Eaton Square and Chelsea would be drinking martinis now, or champagne.

"Do you want a drink, dear?" asked Daphne, reading her mind.

"Oh, I don't think so, yet...well, maybe just a Bloody Mary."

"I'll join you," said Daphne, graciously coming down to her level. "Then we'll have lunch at the Ivy. Burt Hogarth is lunching there today."

"What is Burt doing these days?" asked Emerald.

"Darling, *really!* I know you've been away, but don't you know anything that's going on in this town?"

"No," said Emerald vaguely. "I've been in Italy for the past five months, remember."

"You'd better wise up, dearie, or get off the merry-go-round," said Daphne, accepting the Bloody Mary from her maid. "This is 1985, dear. If you want to stay in this business, you better get into television fast, because *that* is where it's all happening today. Even Burt Hogarth knows that—that's why he's doing TV after all those hit movies."

Emerald drank her Bloody Mary, feeling the quick buzz vodka

always gave her, the false sense of hope and optimism it in-spired.

Daphne continued, "Burt Hogarth is producing a prestigious and *very* ambitious series, darling. Not the usual potboiler schlock. It's called 'America: The Early Years.' I think the title tells the story, dear. I know they are casting now, major names, darling, major. They've already signed Sir Geoffrey Fennel and Olivia Grosvenor from the National Theater—remember her Juliet? God, she was wonderful! But if Burt could see you, see how good you still look..."

In fact, Daphne didn't think Emerald looked good at all. The face-lift had not been much help, though her glamour was still there under the bloat, the bags and the gray roots. Having read the script, Daphne realized that actually Emerald might be a long shot for the part of Evelyn, the lusty, adventurous pioneer woman who comes from the old country to a new frontier town in the America of the 1880s. Against all odds she makes herself and the new town a force to be reckoned with throughout the nation. It was going to be the most important new series on prime time for the 1985–86 season—the most talked about series, in fact, since "Saga."

The fact that Burt Hogarth, film *Wunderkind,* was taking a temporary leave of absence from his dazzling film career as writer, producer and director of seven worldwide box-office blockbuster movies was a major and unprecedented event for television. Already all the rival networks were concerned enough about "America: The Early Years" to be approaching top talent from both film and theater to prepare projects to pit against it.

"So, shall we lunch or shall we not, dear?" Daphne asked. Emerald nodded. Daphne picked up the phone and made a res-ervation.

"Now go home and change into something glam and sexy, darling," Daphne instructed. "I'll meet you at one and you'll work your magic on Mr. Hogarth. He'll be entranced, I'm sure of it."

It hadn't worked out quite that way. Emerald had gone home and taken several Valium washed down with vodka to calm her nerves. In her muddled state, remembering Daphne's "glam and sexy, darling," she had chosen a highly unsuitable lime-green lace cocktail dress, too *décolleté,* too short, simply too much, in fact.

She was late, as usual, as she pulled up outside the Ivy, and instead of hitting the brake, her foot slipped onto the accelerator, smashing her Mercedes into the open door of Abby Arafat's brand-new maroon-and-black Rolls-Royce Corniche—all in full sight of the amused lunch bunch and a couple of cops.

When her agent, Eddie—she'd come back; he'd known she would—finally bailed her out, the media had a field day. Her secret life of drugs and booze was openly discussed in newspapers, on television and in every drawing room and office in Los Angeles. Tongues wagged, and what they said was not complimentary.

"You've fucked up royally, kiddo," said Eddie in no uncertain terms. "You have *blown* your career. No studio, no network, no producer will ever touch you now."

Emerald wept. She couldn't help it. Forty years of stardom! Is this how it ended? "I'm not a lush, Eddie, I'm not an addict either, you know I'm not," she sobbed into a lime-green hanky.

"Do I?" He looked cynical as he peered at her through his giant magnifying spectacles. "You certainly looked like one, kiddo, when I sprung you from that vile prison." He shuddered at the thought of seeing Emerald in her ridiculous short lace dress, facing the harsh California sunlight and the hordes of press and paparazzi. "You looked the pits, woman."

The photos had not been pretty. They had made the front pages of every tabloid from Tokyo to London—a weary, disillusioned, bloated and blowsy woman looking older than her fifty years. Over the hill. Used up. No use to anyone anymore.

Calvin had been in jail for nearly three years. Most prisoners doing time for possession of a deadly weapon were paroled sooner, but Calvin had blown his chance for that by his uncooperative behavior and attacking a guard who had tried to have sex with him. He sat in his cell and reread the article in the *American Informer* for the umpteenth time.

"As Chloe Carriere soars to superstardom on the hit prime time show 'Saga,' so the sad, once superstar, legendary actress Emerald Barrymore fights the twin battles of depression and dope. Picked up for drunken driving in Hollywood last month, the once-beautiful star is now practically destitute and unable to get a decent job in Tinseltown. How different would her life have been if *she* had won the coveted role of Miranda? Chloe Carriere now queens it in Hollywood while Emerald Barrymore is a broken woman."

His Emerald. *His* beautiful, indestructible Emerald, was being ruined by this English bitch! He looked at the calendar again. The date was engraved on his memory. April 24, 1987. That was the day he finally would be paroled. That was the day the bitch would die!

Burt Hogarth studied the clippings his assistant had placed on his desk.

Certainly the woman looked awful. In that short low-cut dress she looked ridiculous. Booze and drugs had finally caught up with her as they do with everyone who abuses them. Her skin was stretched too tightly across her neck, and her cheeks were bloated, but there was an undeniable strength beneath the vulnerability there—a softness underneath the tacky veneer that appealed to him. "Let's test her," he said to his assistant.

"*Test* her!" The young man looked at Burt in amazement. "You can't *test* Emerald Barrymore, she's a superstar—a legend in her lifetime, even if she's the town joke this week."

"She tested for 'Saga,' didn't she?" Burt knew his Hollywood like a great white hunter knows the plains of Africa. "'Saga' is schlock, we know that, but she wanted it. Badly, I hear. That was three years ago, and she's done nothing decent since. From what I hear she's hungry."

"Maybe we should take a look at that 'Saga' test?"

"No. I want to shoot my own. As far as I'm concerned, Emerald Barrymore is an over-the-hill aging *ex*-star who *could* be right for this role, and if she is, it will be the best thing that happened to her since Rin-Tin-Tin rescued her from the train track. So get her fucking agent on the phone and set up the test. The network is trying to ram Angie Dickinson down my throat, but as much as I like Angie, she's not right. So we test Miss Barrymore, and hope for the best."

"*Another* test! Oh, Eddie, why? I mean, I've made fifty-two fucking films for Christ's sake. I tested for 'Saga' and lost. Can't they look at *that* test?"

"No, kiddo," Eddie said coldly, looking straight at her. He was tough with his clients when they got out of line; hence they respected him all the more. Apart from Emerald no client had ever left him, was his boast, but he had dropped several.

"The 'Saga' test was over three years ago, dear. Hollywood has a short memory. As far as the network shooting 'America' is concerned, you are a convicted drug addict and a drunk."

"No, Eddie, that's not true!" cried Emerald.

"It's the truth that hurts, kiddo. Face it, my dear, you were the family favorite of the forties, the flavor of the decade of the fifties, the sexpot of the sixties and seventies. But it's 1985 now. You've been around a long time. It's time to get your act together or get out of the rat race."

"I love this business. It's my *life,*" cried Emerald.

"Good. Then test," said Eddie bluntly. "Test and you'll get the part. Trust me." The tiny man suddenly smiled a rare smile. "The ironic part, kiddo, is that the network is throwing all of its biggest guns into 'America,' they are going to pit it head to head against 'Saga' next season. They're sick and tired of having 'Saga' the number one prime time show week after week. This is war, toots, total war."

"I've always loved a battle." Emerald smiled, beginning to feel more like her old self.

"I know you do, duchess, and one of the things that is going to make this battle even more interesting is that if the series succeeds—which it will, of course—you will be Chloe Carriere's main rival on television. 'The Battle of the Bitches!' I can see the headlines now." His elderly eyes twinkled mischievously behind the huge glasses.

"I thought you adored Chloe, Eddie."

"Of course, kiddo. I *do* adore her. She's my friend even if she isn't my client. She's made it big, and it hasn't changed her. I wish she could be happier in her personal life, though. I think she's still carrying an ember for her ex. That's the trouble with all you girls." He looked scoldingly at Emerald. "Unless you have a man in your life, you don't seem to be complete." Emerald shrugged. "But competition is healthy, kid. Makes the juices flow. Emerald Barrymore versus Chloe Carriere. For this event *I* want to have a front row seat. And so will the public, I guarantee it."

21

Chloe awoke at six o'clock. It was still dark outside, and "cold and damp," as Lena Horne sang it was in California. She staggered down to the kitchen to make a strong cup of Nescafé with three teaspoons of honey for energy. She showered, jumped into jeans, T-shirt, shirt, sweater, jacket, scarf and woolly hat. Despite what the world thinks, it really is *icy* in California in the early hours. Since the temperature changed from forty to eighty-five degrees during the day, she always dressed in layers.

The teamster driver waited for her in the minibus for the seventeen-minute drive to the studio. While he drove, she tried to study the scenes for the day, a total of eleven pages of dialogue—mostly a diatribe by Miranda.

After more than three years, the dialogue had begun to bear a dreadful similarity to the dialogue of last week's episode, and those of the weeks and months before. The actors seldom changed, the sets didn't change, only the costumes were different, which represented the only proof that this was another episode. In her tiny shoe box of a trailer, identical to those of the other ten actors, the makeup man had laid out the tools of his trade. The trainee A.D. brought her another cup of coffee. She turned her radio to FM KJLH (Kindness, Joy, Love, and Happiness—*the* survival station) and to the songs of Al Jarreau and Lionel Richie applied her makeup while studying lines, drinking coffee and eating an orange.

At 7 A.M. Debbie, the second assistant director, summoned her to the set. Half made up, hair in rollers, script in hand, lines still fuzzy and only half-learned, she, with Sissy and Sam, blocked the first scene of the day.

Then it was panic and rush to finish hair and makeup and run lines with Ostie, the dialogue coach.

Trixie, the wardrobe assistant, entered the trailer carrying six outfits in plastic hanger bags and a large Neiman-Marcus shopping bag full of shoes and purses.

"Rudolpho thinks you should wear the black, but the director says that the set's too dark and you'll fade into the woodwork, so I brought the red for the first scene, hon."

"O.K." Chloe squinted at her face in the three-way mirror. Losing a pound or two wouldn't hurt. Weight always went straight to her face, and then her cheekbones disappeared.

"What do you want for lunch?" Debbie popped her head in the door. Chloe grimaced. Lunch! How could she know at 7 A.M. what would titillate her at one in the afternoon?

"Give me a tuna on rye and apple juice, darling," she said, turning to Trixie, who was rummaging through a four-foot-high black chest of drawers—Miranda's jewel box—which stood on the floor.

275

Pearls, diamonds, rubies, emeralds and gold baubles trickled through her fingers.

"I think the Chanel pearls would look hot with this outfit," said Trixie, critically laying them on the elegant suit. "Or do you want to wear that Kenneth Lane gold chain?" "Anything you say, luv," agreed Chloe. She trusted Trixie's excellent taste in accessorizing the nine or ten outfits she had to wear each week.

"How about the Givenchy earrings? They look fabulous."

"Don't you think they're too big?" said Chloe distractedly, working on her lashes.

"Hon, nothin's too big for 'Saga,' surely you know that!"

After Chloe put on the tight red suit, Trixie stood back surveying her handiwork and tugged at Chloe's skirt, which was beginning to feel uncomfortably binding around her waist.

"Got a little extra there today, huh?" Trixie was used to her female stars' fluctuations in weight. Even two pounds made a difference when each outfit was fitted like another skin.

"Thanks, darling. You're not exactly Twiggy today either." They smiled at each other, used to the banter that kept them sane at 7 A.M.

Chloe bumped into Pandora on the short walk to Stage 2. Pandora was wearing a gray flannel Thierry Mugler suit, the shoulders of which were so exaggerated that she looked like a football player. Her red wig was styled in a 1940s page-boy, and she wore fuchsia lip gloss and gold eye shadow. She looked hard and chic.

"Hi, there. What did you think of the show last night?"

Pandora was a friendly soul with no ax to grind with anyone. She was no great shakes as an actress, but she was sweet and professional, and knew that she was lucky to be pulling down twenty-five grand an episode in one of the hottest shows on prime time.

"I thought your courtroom scene was excellent—really good." Chloe never praised unless she meant it.

"Thanks, honey, it was a well-written scene. What did you think of *her?*" She gestured toward Sissy, already sitting upright in her director's chair, Kleenex folded down the neck of her turquoise suede dress, smoking the first of her eternal cigarettes through a holder and dispensing a stream of invective to all who came her way. "Watch out, someone got out of bed on the wrong side today," Pandora said.

"What else is new?" Chloe laughed.

Sam stood on the set sipping coffee from a Styrofoam cup and chatting to the crew. He was popular with all of them, making genuine efforts to communicate, to joke, trying to make up for the bitchiness of his wife. The crew felt sorry for him. "No wonder he's a fruit," Maxie, the teamster, muttered to Chloe one day. "With a cow like that for a wife, I'd like boys too."

Like everyone else, Chloe despised Sissy and adored Sam. She gave him a peck on his heavily made up cheek, which was becoming alarmingly thin these days, she noticed.

He was not looking well. His normally luxurious brown mustache looked unkempt and bedraggled. The thick brown toupee he always wore looked strange and lopsided, as though it was too big for him. Maybe it was because he was in pajamas and a dressing gown and made up to look ill that he didn't look good. They were shooting a scene in which Sam/Steve was in a coma in a hospital bed, while his three wives, one current and two ex, stood around his bed willing him to live.

"Here's your coffee, darling."

"Hi, Vanessa." Chloe smiled at her new personal assistant.

Since stardom had been hard to handle with just a secretary, she had started to look around for a personal assistant to help her with the hundreds of requests for interviews and personal appearances, to sift through the thousands of pieces of fan mail and to read some of the torrent of scripts that were sent.

Vanessa Vanderbilt had become vaguely bored with her jewelry business. Fine jewels at the price she could afford to pay were not easily available these days, and Vanessa had been looking around for something more stimulating. One day she and Chloe had found themselves seated next to each other on a flight from London after one of Chloe's visits with Annabel. Chloe complimented Vanessa on her beautiful emerald-and-diamond bracelets, and Vanessa replied that they were for sale. Surprised and thrilled, Chloe wrote out a check for twelve thousand dollars, in defiance of her business manager, and slipped Emerald's lovely jewels on her wrists. The two women toasted the transaction with champagne, and after the third glass started to let their hair down. They discovered they had tremendous rapport. They laughed, told intimate stories of their lives, and found they were soul sisters. Before the plane landed, Vanessa had agreed to a trial run of three months as Chloe's personal assistant. So far it had been a success. The two women got along like a house on fire, much to the envy of Sissy, who could never bear to see happy business relationships around her, particularly between two women. She was unable to keep any assistant, and few of her domestic staff, longer than a few months.

"O.K., let's try a rehearsal," called Ned, the first A.D.

The four actors walked onto the "Saga" set. Sam stripped off his dressing gown and gratefully lay down in the bed. Thank God he had nothing to do in this scene except groan. He felt he could do that realistically enough. Last night had been ghastly. Sissy had been in one of her more vile moods. Her jealousy of Chloe was fueled each day by various items in magazines or gossip columns. Last night her fury was released when she read the piece in Army Archerd: "Chloe Carriere's career goes from strength to strength. The hottest female on TV has been signed to produce and star in her own miniseries 'Ecstasy' in conjunction with Hammersmith Productions. Shooting will commence in London and Madrid during Chloe Carriere's third hiatus from 'Saga.'"

"Damn that woman!" Sam barely had the strength to duck as Sissy threw the trade paper across the room with such force that the tropical fish swimming lazily in their five-thousand-dollar aquarium, tastefully set into the polished granite above the authentic wood-burning fireplace, hastily disappeared behind their painted rocks.

"Damn that bitch. *Why*, why does she get her own fucking miniseries? What's *wrong* with my agent?" she railed, pouring a generous shot of Smirnoff into a Lalique tumbler.

Sam lay on a tan leather sofa quietly trying to watch a video of a John Wayne movie and feeling weak and ill.

Now Sam lay in a hospital bed on Stage 2, feeling worse. During a break in the shooting the three women couldn't stop talking about an item in today's Army Archerd column about "America: The Early Years." The columnist waxed enthusiastic about the new prime time series and the excitement in the industry about Burt Hogarth's masterminding of it.

"I heard he was interested in Emerald Barrymore for Evelyn," said Pandora, tolerating having Theo comb out her red wig for the umpteenth time.

"Really!" sneered Sissy, dragging on her cigarette holder. Her brown birdlike hands were tipped by scarlet claws that matched the slash of her thin lips. "Are they going to be able to get her out of bed and off the bottle long enough to get her in front of the cameras?" She laughed maliciously.

Pandora and Chloe ignored the remark, but Sam managed a weak smile. He was not feeling good. He *must* find time for that checkup.

"Now, now, honey," he remonstrated to his wife. "You know Emerald's had a run of bad luck. Let's hope she gets that part. She's a nice gal. She needs it."

Hmmm, Sissy calculated to herself, if Emerald *did* get it, there might be some advantages. Emerald might knock that snotty British bitch off the front pages and the magazine covers. Chloe's success was beginning to become more of an irritant every day. Chloe was becoming an obsession with Sissy. An obsession of hate. Only one person felt that hate more strongly.

Calvin lay on a rough gray blanket in his cell trying not to listen to the disgusting conversation of his cellmates. They were talking about sex as usual. That was all they ever talked about. Occasionally baseball or football was discussed, now and again a new inmate would cause a brief flurry of interest, but basically every man in that jail was obsessed by one subject. Sex.

Calvin's cellmates were discussing in intimate detail the merits of the current *Penthouse* pinup. The woman's legs were spread wide, showing a view only a gynecologist usually saw. The men were turned on. Calvin knew what would happen next. After three years he knew only too well. They would do things to each other, pretending it was the woman in *Penthouse*. Sometimes they would do it to Calvin, even if he resisted. He knew that. It had happened the first day he arrived in this jail. With sickening regularity it had continued. Calvin was not classically handsome, but he was reasonably young, had fair skin and a firm body. The rest, the men's imaginations took care of.

Prison was a seething cauldron of the suppressed sexual desires of nine hundred potent men cooped up in the prime of their life with nothing to do except fantasize about sex.

Calvin tried to feign sleep but it was no good. Kolinsky, the big twenty-three-year-old Pole with the dark hair, bad teeth and huge thing, came over to him.

"C'mon now, Calvin, old buddy. Time to have a good time with yer ole friend here."

Calvin knew if he rebelled he would get beaten. The guards turned a blind eye. Sometimes they themselves sampled some of the tastier young "virgins" first. As he braced himself for Kolinsky's onslaught, he blanked out his mind until all he could think about was his hatred for Chloe Carriere, how she was to blame for this, and that he had only fifteen more months of this horror.

22

Since her final split with Josh, Chloe's love life had become a topic of great interest to the supermarket tabloids and gossip columns, and they printed every bit of dirt they could on her.

More than a casual chat with a man at a party, and she was reported to be having an affair with him. More than two dates with the same man, and she was engaged. More than six, and elopement and marriage were imminent. Since her split with Josh she hadn't been serious about anyone. She and Johnny spent the occasional night together now and then and dated on and off, but it was not a deep relationship. He had plenty of women on his string. With the AIDS threat hovering uneasily on the horizon, she was not about to risk her life for a casual encounter, however attractive that encounter might be. Three years of stardom and celebrity were beginning to take their toll. She was becoming snappy, irritable and uninterested in anything except "Saga."

"You need a man, dearie," observed Daphne at lunch one day. "A *good man.*"

"Yeah, and they're hard to find around these parts," Vanessa added.

Chloe, tight-lipped, was drinking Perrier on the rocks and picking at her cuticles.

Daphne was insistent. "You don't look happy."

"I don't need a *man* to make me happy," snapped Chloe, lighting a cigarette and wearily signing another autograph.

The table at which she sat with Daphne and Vanessa was in a corner of the studio commissary, but it was still the focus of all eyes. Fans came in droves to do the studio tour. The top draw was a visit to the "Saga" set. It didn't matter that the actors were filming scenes that required concentration. Abby and Gertrude, realizing they had a gold mine in "Saga," allowed tourists to roam free on the lot and provided a friendly studio tour guide to accompany them.

"You know, Vanessa, I don't mean to be paranoid but do you see that woman with the Instamatic over there?" Chloe said. Vanessa looked over to where a nondescript woman, dressed in a drab gabardine pants suit, sat looking around the commissary, her eyes too often returning to Chloe.

"What about her?" asked Vanessa.

"She gives me the creeps. I *swear* she's press. I've seen her here several times. She was even lurking on the set listening to me talk to Annabel on the phone last week."

"You're joking?" Vanessa was alarmed. She was very protective of Chloe.

"No. She was hanging around by the coffee machines chatting

with the craft service guys and the teamsters. I thought she was a hairdresser from the cop show on the next sound stage; then I saw her make notes in a book. Check her out, Van."

"O.K., Boss Lady," said Vanessa. She glanced at the woman, who looked away quickly. Chloe was right. She did look like press. British press, too, probably from one of the scummier daily rags.

Magazines and tabloids had now printed every major and minor detail of Chloe's past life ad nauseam. They had interviewed her school friends, teachers and co-workers. Rick, her old lover from her provincial touring days, had sold his "kiss and tell" memoirs of their "stormy affair" to the *Sun*, and reporters constantly called Richard, Susan *and* Annabel for any scraps of trivia on Britain's by now most famous actress. Chloe lived in terror of the press's discovering that Annabel was really her daughter. One of the gutter tabloids had gone to Somerset House, the British register of births and deaths, and had printed her birth certificate, so that none of its readers could have any doubt how old she was. What was to stop them from snooping around and finding out that on January 15, 1964, a baby girl, father unknown, mother, Chloe Carriere, age twenty-one, occupation singer, had been born in a nursing home in Plymouth? Chloe had nightmares about how it would affect Annabel's life.

She hated the fact she was becoming cynical and paranoid, but the relentless onslaught on her personal life, by both the media and the fans, had clouded her normally sunny disposition. The work was hard. Just the act of keeping her hair, makeup and clothes pristine twelve hours a day, while the crew sweated in T-shirts and sneakers, was an effort.

It was tiring to smile all the time at the fifty or sixty visitors a day who plucked up courage to speak to the Queen Bitch in person. God forbid she slough one off. Every fan lost was multiplied a hundredfold in viewing audiences, scolded Gertrude.

"Offend one fan, and they'll tell ten friends who'll tell ten more."

"Be nice to them on the way up," warned Jasper. "You may be the flavor of the month now, but they'll all be there waiting on the way down—and there *will* be a way down, luv. That's for sure. Every actor has his shelf life. With some—the Cary Grants, the Katharine Hepburns—it's fifty years or more. With others—*especially* TV stars—it can be fifty months, or weeks, even days. The public is..."

"Fickle! I know, Jasper. You've told me a million times. I *know* they are."

"Good girl. Remember it now. Don't become bigheaded."

"I won't," she almost screamed. "I'm just trying to be *me*."

She had no time for men in her life. On a rare day off she was involved in interviews and photograph sessions. And fittings with Trixie and Rudolpho took hours of thought and concentration. She had to know lines, have script conferences, have a weekly manicure and pedicure, she had to exercise regularly, she had to have facials, keep up with current fashion trends. All in all, there wasn't enough time in the day even to read a newspaper or get a decent night's sleep, let alone get involved with a man.

"If only the public realized what a bloody grind this so-called glamour job is," sighed Chloe, acknowledging the signal from Ned that her fifty minutes for lunch was up.

Lunch gave her indigestion. Everything was always rush, rush, rush. By the time she left the set, exchanged the beaded décolleté gown or some other fashionable outfit for a track suit, walked to the commissary, waited for a tuna salad and Perrier to arrive, exchanged a few stories with Vanessa and Daphne, who sometimes came by, it was time to return to the set. "Heigh ho, heigh ho, it's off to work we go. Just like the seven dwarfs." Vanessa laughed.

285

"I think, dear, you need a man, for therapeutic reasons if nothing else, and I happen to know just the one. Perfect for you, and *very* handsome, darling." Daphne never let up; she kept pushing the subject each time they had lunch together.

Vanessa giggled. She adored romance and intrigue. "Who is he, anyone we know? I'd like her to get laid too. She's becoming a pain in the neck to me." Vanessa smiled at Chloe teasingly. She adored her, even though they sometimes clashed. And Vanessa had become indispensable to Chloe for social arrangements, business meetings, clothes problems. Vanessa was Chloe's confidante and doer—a far cry from her days as an Arab potentate's mistress, but more interesting, certainly.

"Laid! What's that? I can't remember that experience. Isn't it something mortals do?"

"Next Saturday night, darling, dinner *chez moi.*" Daphne loved playing Cupid. "This man is French, and he is seriously sexy."

"Oh, an import!" Vanessa beamed at Chloe. "Someone who hasn't fucked all your friends. Ain't *that* good news?"

Chloe recognized him as soon as he walked into Daphne's living room. Although she hadn't thought about him in more than three years, she remembered the chemistry she had felt that awful night in Vegas. She shuddered. She still had nightmares about it.

Philippe Archambaud smiled his Alain Delon smile, revealing perfect teeth. He looked romantically Continental in a dark blue suit and a conservative tie, in sharp contrast to Daphne's beau, Richard Hurrel, who was a sartorial disaster in a cyclamen blazer with matching ascot, and to Luis Mendoza, who hadn't really bothered, because when every woman in America wants your body, all you need is a black silk shirt, tight white pants, and a tan. Philippe was handsome, tall, with brown wavy hair, dazzling eyes. He was also quiet. Not your actual comedian, thought Chloe, having sat through his rather pedantic discourse on French politics during dinner.

She remembered Josh's colorful English charm—how he had entranced her with his wit and humor. There had been so much passion and togetherness between them in the first seven or eight years. Where had it gone wrong? Why? Forget about it. She pushed those thoughts from her mind and concentrated on Philippe. Yes, he was extremely handsome. Yes, he was exceptionally charming. Yes, he certainly paid her attention and was very flattering. And why should he not be? She was at this moment the biggest female star on TV. For how long, of course, no one could predict....

"When can I see you again, Chloe?" Philippe's hand traced a tiny path down her spine. She suddenly felt the remembered stirrings of desire—absent now for so many months. "Tomorrow?" His eyes—what color were they? Gray? Green? Blue? Chameleon eyes—they sent a clear message of ardor. In spite of herself she was interested.

"Well, tomorrow is Sunday. I have *tons* of dialogue to learn, a new script to study, and..."

"Darling!" Vanessa interrupted, reddish curls bouncing, cleavage brimming over her creamy antique lace blouse. "*No* excuses, I think you should take him to the beach house," she whispered through gritted teeth, her tiny satin pumps giving Chloe a sharp dig in her shin.

"And Richard and I will come too. Don't *worry*," said Daphne joining in as she saw Chloe start to demur. "I know you don't have staff on Sunday and you *hate* to cook. Richard will stop at Nate 'n' Al's tomorrow and get their Scottish smoked salmon, bagels and cream cheese. We'll have a picnic on the beach. Won't that be fun, dear? Just like England."

Richard groaned. At sixty-five he felt a mite too old for picnics on the beach, let alone hopping down to Nate 'n' Al's on Sunday with the Beverly Hills jet-setters. But Daphne was the boss in their relationship, so he tried to muster a smile.

"All right," said Chloe, seeing Vanessa's enormous grin. "We'll *all* have a picnic."

"With champagne!" Daphne added.

"*Naturellement,*" Philippe said with a smile that was definitely beginning to affect Chloe. "I will bring it."

"Dom Perignon," Vanessa warned. "One *only* drinks D.P. on a picnic."

"Of course, it will be my pleasure." He bowed slightly, his eyes not leaving Chloe's.

Here we go again, she thought.

It was a short, fast courtship. Philippe's physical charms captured Chloe so quickly she didn't know what had hit her. For a woman who had always insisted on wit and conversation in her relationships with men, suddenly it didn't seem to matter this time.

They started seeing each other every weekend, then every other night, then every night. Soon he had moved many of his things into Chloe's houses at the beach and in Beverly Hills. After a couple of months they decided it was foolish for him to waste money renting an apartment he hardly used, and he moved in.

Philippe still wrote stories for *Paris Match, Jour de France* and an occasional article for *Oggi* or *Tempo*. That kept him reasonably busy during the day. Since he was good with figures and a dab hand at analyzing the stock market, Chloe let him invest some of her money. He did so well and made her such consistent profits in the market that finally she fired her business manager and let Philippe handle her finances full time.

"Darling, he *is* adorable, but he is, well..." Vanessa tried to warn her friend a few weeks after her whirlwind affair with Philippe had begun.

"Dull? Boring? Opinionated?" Chloe laughed. "I *know*, Vanessa. I'm not so stupid. I realize that he isn't Einstein. I don't know what it is—he seems to have my number, though." She thought of last night and the passion they had shared until she had wearily risen at five to leave for the studio.

"Well, whatever it is he's doing to you, it seems to be doing you good," said Vanessa. "You haven't looked so well in a long time."

Chloe blushed. Her nights, mornings and afternoons with Philippe had been amazing. The man was a fountain of energy. When he wasn't making love, he wanted to hold her in his arms, stroke her hair and tell her how wonderful she was. It was unusual for a man of thirty-nine to be so openly affectionate. And Chloe *liked* it, and liked him. More and more.

She still thought about Josh. Occasionally he phoned her from England or wherever he was. The first play he had done had been a disaster. Then he had disappeared for a year, and she had no idea where. One rumor was that he had emigrated to Australia, another that he was living with a pair of seventeen-year-old twins. Writing music. Entertaining in piano bars, men's clubs. Finally, out of the blue he'd called her.

"Hello, Chloe, my little love. How are you?"

She couldn't believe the way her heart still fluttered when she heard his voice. Like a stupid schoolgirl, she scolded herself, after their short but sweet conversation.

He told her he'd been working in Australia, touring the outback. There was no mention of teenage twins. And she didn't ask. He was working on cruise ships now. It was fun, he said. He had a lot of fans still. Middle-aged matrons and their paunchy consorts who remembered the young Joshua Brown of the 1960s. Remembered his songs. Gave him the applause he craved. He was off to sing his way around the Caribbean for the next few months on another cruise ship.

"Is it really fun?" Chloe had asked, feeling in some bizarre way guilty about her own immense success and his slide down the ladder. "Are you enjoying it, Josh?"

"Sure, it's great," he lied. "All the fun of the fair, darlin'. Lots of booze, lots of laughs, lots of birds." Chloe couldn't suppress a wince. The thought of Josh with another woman in his arms still gave her a jolt.

"Hopeless! You're *hopelessly* old-fashioned and out of date," said Vanessa after Chloe recounted her conversation with Josh. "I don't think you really know anything about men, do you, Chloe?"

Vanessa, having spent eighteen years studying them, was somewhat of an expert and was often amazed by Chloe's romantic naiveté.

Chloe changed the subject. Talking to Josh had rattled her. She wanted to hear from him again. Their divorce still wasn't final. It had been dragging on for two years now. Her lawyer kept trying to get her to sign the final papers. Then, when Josh disappeared, even his own lawyer couldn't find him.

Philippe was now pushing Chloe to get the divorce finalized. He wanted to marry her, but Chloe wasn't at all sure. She was mad about Philippe physically; it was almost as if he had put a spell on her. But the communication she'd shared with Josh was missing.

Perhaps she expected too much, she told herself, as she drove down drab Pico Boulevard to MCPC Studios. Oh, well, you can't have it all. You can. You can. You can, her inner voice whispered back. You *can* have it all, Chloe. You can and you *should*.

"Saga's" success had been so immense and extraordinary that every TV company and network had jumped on the bandwagon to imitate it. One rival network had put out an imitation, "Abraham's Family," a near-clone of "Saga," another had tried with "Arizona Empire," but both had fluttered briefly and then expired.

"Imitation is *still* the sincerest form of flattery," beamed Gertrude at a meeting with a worried Abby. "We have nothing to fear, Abby. Just look at our ratings." She was right. "Saga" had consistently been one of the top five shows for the past four seasons. Saga clothes, Saga jewelry, Saga dolls, Miranda and Sirope dressed in tiny facsimiles of Rudolpho's beaded gowns, were everywhere. The world was aglow with Sagamania. The world loved Chloe and Sissy. And Sam and Pandora. They loved them all. Saga bedspreads, plates, candles, shoes, blouses and ties—department stores bulged with them.

"About the only goddamn things they haven't put the Saga name on are condoms," laughed Pandora to Chloe on the set as Christopher, the diminutive public relations man, approached Chloe with the blueprint of the new advertisement for two Saga perfumes she, along with Sissy, would endorse.

One would be called "Wicked" and feature Chloe looking provocative on the package. The other would be called "Woman," and would feature Sissy looking as warm and sincere as her talent would allow.

In the four years the show had been running, Sissy had indulged in two mini face-lifts, one eye job and a breast implant. She still dieted relentlessly and looked like a hawk in real life, but she was a good enough actress to breathe life into the saccharine role of Sirope. She personified Mother Earth: sweet, long-suffering and kind, putting up with the problems of her TV children and the machinations of her TV husband's ex-wives. Chloe, on the other hand, personified the wicked, manipulating, sex-hungry bitch.

The public had taken the two women to their hearts, never quite sure if they were in reality the characters they played on the screen.

291

"You're sitting in my chair," snapped Sissy to Chloe. "Oh, sorry," said Chloe eying the three empty canvas chairs that Sissy could have parked her scrawny behind on if she had chosen.

What Sissy did choose to do was to needle Chloe and the rest of the cast at every possible opportunity. With her newfound success, she had become impossible. Even faithful Sam, who had been loyal to her for years, found it hard to swallow her arrogance. She was rude to the crew, who loathed her. She was envious and spiteful to the cast, refusing to rehearse, abusing any actor who forgot his dialogue, and never deigning to read off-camera lines even for Sam. She hassled the producer to get better story lines for herself, she changed her dialogue constantly, confusing the other actors, and then became furious with them because they couldn't understand what she was doing.

Recently she had started snorting a line of coke first thing in the morning to get her through the tedious days, another line at lunchtime, and one more halfway through the afternoon. At home each night she complained bitterly to Sam about the fact that the lighting cameraman preferred Chloe and Pandora to her, that the director was an untalented ruffian, her trailer not as big as Sam's. Sissy overreacted to the merest slight. Cocaine was turning her into a paranoid schizophrenic. If the public that admired her so much had known the truth, she would have been standing in the unemployment line on Sunset Boulevard.

"So what do you think of the new script?"

Chloe was surprised Sissy bothered to ask her opinion. She never had before. "It's O.K. What do you think?"

"Trash, fucking trash. They keep writing like this, we'll be off the air next season." Sissy was nervously running her fingers up and down her satin-clad thigh. "Doris, bring me a cup of coffee —for Christ's sake, *hurry up.*"

Chloe felt sorry for Sissy. She couldn't really hate a woman whose insecurities were so obvious, and she often defended her while the rest of the cast tore her to pieces and mocked her. It didn't really help, because Sissy hated Chloe more than anyone else in the show.

If Chloe made the front page of *USA Today*, Sissy would scream at the network public relations people until they got the same coverage for her. In fact, the women got an equal number of national magazine covers. With a show as hot as "Saga," the magazines knew a good way to sell copies was to put Sissy, Chloe or Pandora on the cover.

"Oh, did you see this?" Sissy had a glint in her eye as she passed Chloe the latest copy of the *American Informer*.

"CHLOE CARRIERE IN LOVE CHILD MYSTERY," the headline blazed.

Chloe almost fainted when she read it. She pretended a casual glance, aware of Sissy watching her with a glint in her eye.

"Interesting, isn't it?" Sissy smiled her cobra smile. "Any truth to it, Chloe *darling?*" She attempted a confidential girl-talk tone, which Chloe found even more offensive than her bitchy needling. "You can tell *me.*" She leaned closer and Chloe saw the deep crow's-feet under her eyes and around her lips that even three face-lifts hadn't managed to erase.

"The usual pack of lies, Sissy—you know that." She couldn't resist a dig. "You remember the story they had about Sam being gay a few months ago? Ridiculous, isn't it?"

Sissy's jaws clamped shut and her flat gray eyes gave up their pretense of charm. "Doris, where's that fucking coffee, for Christ's sake. Hurry it up."

Chloe moved away. The story she had dreaded had finally appeared. She saw Sissy display the tabloid's cover with waspish glee to several of the crew and groaned inwardly.

At home Chloe studied the tabloid article with mounting horror.

"Secret Love Child Chloe Hasn't Seen In 20 Years," blared

the headline. "Chloe Carriere—superstar of the soap opera 'Saga'—has a secret that will haunt her to her grave. Twenty-one years ago she gave birth to an illegitimate child. The *Informer* can exclusively reveal that this young girl, Annabel, lives happily in the English countryside with Chloe's brother, Richard, and his wife, Susan, unaware that her real mother is television's most famous bitch."

"Oh, my God—Annabel!" She threw the offending scandal sheet onto the floor and picked up the phone with a shaking hand.

"Hello, Daphne—Daphne, darling, I didn't wake you, did I?"

"No, no, of course not, dear, I'm wide awake. What's happening in your life?" Daphne pushed Richard aside, and brought out the tape recorder she kept next to the bed.

It was not often that she received a call for help from Chloe. Chloe received so much unfavorable personal publicity that she rarely bothered to do anything about it except shrug it off.

"Have you read the *Informer* yet?" Chloe asked desperately.

"Yes, dear, I have."

"It's a bunch of lies, Daphne, you *know* that."

"Of course I do, dear. Everyone in town who reads that revolting garbage knows it." But they love it, Daphne thought, *everyone* reads it at their executive desks, at their hairdressers', or borrows it from their maid, avidly reading the lies and innuendo about everyone else. "Stop it, Richard," she hissed. Being rejected had excited him more than usual, and he was exploring Daphne's abundant thighs with his tongue.

"Daphne, people are actually beginning to believe all that stuff about me being a bitch. I don't mind that, but this story is terribly upsetting for my niece."

"I know, dear, I know it's a pack of lies. Ignore it, you're bigger than all of them, don't you ever forget it."

"I always ignore it—maybe that's the trouble."

"So what can an old friend do, dear?" said Daphne, having slapped Richard away and tried to settle him comfortably in the crook of her arm like a big floppy doll.

"Tell them to print a retraction as soon as possible."

"I'll do what I can for you, I promise, dear," said Daphne, her attention distracted by Richard's halfhearted administrations as she hung up.

Chloe picked up the vodka and poured a generous slug into her orange juice as the phone started to ring. She let the answering machine pick up, listened, heard the nasal tones: "Hello, it's Mike Russel here from *The News of the World*. I'd like to speak to Miss Carriere about..."

Wearily she switched it off. Tomorrow this American tabloid story would be in all the English papers. Annabel would see it. Uppermost in Chloe's mind was how her daughter would react. Her darling Annabel, who thought of Chloe as her aunt. What would she think? How would she feel, knowing she had been lied to all her life? She had to be devastated.

Whatever her reaction, Chloe had to see her face to face. *Now.* There was no putting it off. She had to tell her the truth.

She called Gertrude. "You've read the story?"

"Yes, of course. Is it true?" rasped Gertrude.

"It is, Gertrude. As far as I'm concerned I don't give a damn what the press write. But this has to be the most ghastly shock for Annabel. She had no idea that I was her mother, that Susan and Richard were not her real parents. I *must* go to England, Gertrude, immediately. Can you shoot around me? Please. It's urgent."

"Darling." Gertrude's voice was cool. "You *know* we can't. We're coming to the end of the season, you're in *everything*. This has to be the best cliff-hanger ever, because 'America' is starting up against us next season. Can't it wait?"

"No!" Chloe was desperate. "No, it can't. It's my daughter's *life,* Gertrude. Isn't that more important than the show, for heaven's sake?"

"Frankly, honey, it isn't. I have every sympathy for you, I promise we'll get the publicity people to do the best they can to help you out of this mess, but we simply *cannot* and *will not* cater to the whim of an actress in this way."

"*Whim!*" Chloe almost wept. "Gertrude, this is the most important thing in my life!" She started to tell her the real story, but Gertrude cut her off.

"I'm in the middle of a dinner party, honey—now don't you worry," Gertrude tried to soothe her. "I don't think bad publicity will harm you. After all, you *are* a bitch."

"I'm not!" Chloe screamed. "I'm an actress and a good one too, which is why they all think I'm a bitch. Please let me go, Gertrude, please, just for the weekend. I must sort it out. Annabel needs me—I have to explain everything to her myself. I *can't* do it on the phone."

"I'll have to speak to Abby," Gertrude said crisply. "I'll see what I can do. I've got to run now, my guests are waiting." She hung up.

"*Damn* you!" yelled Chloe, tears welling up. "Damn you all! I'm bloody going anyway." Lifting the receiver, she called Vanessa. "Get me on tomorrow night's British Airways flight to London, Van, and call a meeting here tonight with Christopher. I've got to face the music."

"I'm going, Abby," she said calmly the next morning, as she sat across from the huge man in his immense office.

He had been more sympathetic to her than Gertrude. "We're going to let you go so that you can sort this unfortunate story out," he said. "It makes you look bad in the public's eye. If you just ignore it, the public will think you're a bitch. So although there really isn't a stigma about the illegitimate aspect, I think the public have got to know the truth. You owe it to them, if not to the girl." He chewed on his cigar and surveyed her kindly. When the chips were down, Abby usually came through for his stars. He liked Chloe and he knew she was nothing like the hardhearted vixen she portrayed.

"Go, sweetheart. Give a press conference in London for the media, that's important, but more important is the kid—how's she taking it?"

"I don't know," said Chloe, fighting back the tears. "I can't get through—they've taken the phone off the hook, and I can't reach her at college. It's really hard, Abby. This girl is the most important person in my life." Tears started to flow down her cheeks. Abby, a sentimental man in spite of his hard exterior, felt his throat tighten and hastily passed her his handkerchief before he started to bawl too.

"Now, now, sweetheart," he said gruffly. "No tears, please, you'll only hold up production while they fix your makeup. Go back to the set; we'll release you by four-thirty so you can catch the flight to London and sort things out."

Before the story broke, Annabel had been a well-adjusted young woman at college, studying to be a musician. She had been outgoing and happy, as well, in her home life in a secure family atmosphere. This did not stop the Fleet Street vipers, who fell upon the scandal like vultures. Anything about Chloe was news. This was huge, and they would play it up to the hilt. The glaring headlines shrieked their news daily.

"Chloe Abandons Love Child," screeched the *Sun*.

"Selfish Soap Queen Gives Baby Away," the *Star* squawked.

"Oh, Chloe, Chloe, how could you be so heartless? Where is your sense of moral virtue, your motherly instincts? Foolish woman. Do diamonds, furs, Hollywood mansions, and swimming pools make up for a child's life? For a baby you bore, and then gave away to your relatives while you pursued your career, chasing shallow fame and the frivolous good life and leaving your own flesh and blood to be brought up living a lie?..." Every tabloid drooled on. It was a hot story and they milked it for everything it had. It was nauseating, thought Chloe.

She read the articles on the plane to London, more horrified at each one as she wondered how Annabel would take all of this. Vanessa was with her, excited about going back to London. Some of Chloe's fame had rubbed off on her and she had become something of a celebrity in Petticoat Lane, where her family still lived. Philippe was there too, sitting next to Chloe, asleep and snoring. He had been supportive of her when the news broke, and had insisted on coming along.

"What does it matter, sweetheart, what they say about you?" he had asked. "They all think you're a bitch anyway." He had infuriated her with his French pragmatism, and they had finally had a tearful argument.

The press were out in force at Heathrow—dozens of them including TV cameras and news. As soon as she stepped off the ramp, they were all over her, pushing, yelling and snapping her as she strode down the drafty Heathrow corridor, head held high. She wore a simple tan cashmere overcoat belted snugly against the London chill. A smooth-tongued BBC reporter thrust his microphone into her face, demanding a statement. The woman from ITV insisted on a quote too. NBC and ABC were there, as well as her parent network BCC, and news crews from Europe and Australia.

"Wait a minute. *Wait a minute* everybody!" Christopher, "Saga's" diminutive press agent, was flushed scarlet with the effort of trying to control the excited crowd and the press. "Miss Carriere is *not* going to make any statement at this moment. As you all know, we have called a press conference at the Ritz Hotel at four o'clock. Miss Carriere will then talk to all of you in detail about—recent events."

Chloe smiled through clenched teeth as three policemen, two officials from the airline, Vanessa, Philippe and Christopher tried to force a way through the throng of photographers, journalists and rubberneckers.

This was going to be tougher than she had expected. They had stayed up late the previous night planning their strategy. Make it work, please God, breathed Chloe. Make it work.

23

Annabel's protected private world had suddenly become a public nightmare. Her face was splashed over the front pages of the tabloids. Her fellow students gossiped about her at college. Why hadn't Auntie Chloe—no, it was Mummie Chloe now, wasn't it?—told her the truth?

The gutter press started bombarding the neat terraced house in Barnes with phone calls, and Annabel's family went into shock. It became unbearable. When they were "door-stepped" by dozens of journalists and photographers from all over the world, they turned the house into a fortress. They took the phone off the hook, kindly neighbors brought in food, and the family waited and prayed it would all be over soon and that the media circus outside would go away.

But it wouldn't. The reporters dug themselves in, waiting for action, and soon it arrived in the person of Chloe as they knew it would. When she arrived at the house she was inundated by a thousand intrusively crude, curious questions. Flashbulbs popped so rapidly in the afternoon gloom that she was almost blinded. Christopher, his diminutive height no barrier to his strength as he maneuvered her through the jabbering throng, was red-faced by the time the door was opened by a pale, worried-looking Susan, who hurriedly ushered them into the narrow hall.

She, Richard and Chloe exchanged affectionate greetings and muffled words of encouragement, then Susan took Chloe aside, motioning toward the closed door of the living room. "She's in there," she whispered, as Richard took Christopher through to the kitchen.

"She's taking it very hard, Chloe. I've tried to tell her it wasn't your fault, that it was the way the world *was* then and that you did your best, but it seems that the more I say, the more upset she gets."

"Thanks, Susie." Chloe smiled at her sister-in-law and squeezed her arm appreciatively, remembering those long-ago days when they were schoolgirls, remembering the whispering, the giggling, the sharing of such delicious secrets when they were twelve and "best friends" forever. And now here they were whispering secrets again. "I told her you were coming," said Susie, "but she didn't say anything."

"It's all right, Susie. I have to talk to her, I know how difficult it must be for her." Chloe pushed the door open.

Annabel sat in the living room slumped on a flowered chintz sofa. Mother and daughter looked at each other. This was the moment Chloe had been dreading. Her throat was so tight she had difficulty swallowing, and she had developed a nervous tic in one eye, probably because she had not had a wink of sleep in the barely three days since the story about Annabel had broken. She looked at her daughter with love, but Annabel's eyes were cold, flat and detached.

A fire crackled in the grate. It was a cold March afternoon, and although only four o'clock, it was almost dark outside. The green velveteen curtains were drawn and the windows tightly closed, but even so, the hubbub and chatter of the press outside could still be heard.

Chloe had come straight from Heathrow, and as she stood in her tan suede boots and matching cashmere overcoat, she felt horribly Hollywoodish and overdressed in this simple, cluttered living room. On the piano and mantelpiece were photos of her and the family. In one corner sat a ficus plant Chloe had sent Richard for his birthday, in another, a plastic trolley held bottles of whiskey, gin, vodka and liqueurs. How she would love a drink, she thought fervently, but this was not the time.

Her daughter, her beautiful, joyous daughter, had turned away from her, her eyes hard.

"I suppose you expect me to fall into your arms and all will be forgiven," Annabel said sarcastically in her clear young voice.

"No, of course I don't, Annabel, I would never expect that of you. You deserve an explanation, and I'm going to do the best I can to explain everything."

Chloe took off her coat, tossing it onto an armchair opposite the sofa on which her daughter was curled up, her normally cheerful expression a hard mask. Her curly dark hair was caught up with a bright yellow plastic comb, which matched the yellow sweater she wore over worn blue jeans torn at the knees, and cowboy boots. She was truly a lovely young girl who looked so uncannily like the young Chloe that an outsider seeing them together would have known instantly they were mother and daughter.

Susan had left a tray of tea and shortbread biscuits on the walnut table in front of the fire. There were two cups and an earthenware vase with a few early daffodils from the garden. The silence seemed endless. Annabel glanced at Chloe, then turned away again, drawing deeply on her cigarette and gazing into the fire.

Chloe tried to swallow. She knew she couldn't speak, say any of the thousand and one things she needed, wanted, to say until she had a sip of tea. Her throat was so dry it hurt. "Would you like a cup of tea, darling?" Her voice sounded too bright, theatrical, her newly acquired transatlantic accent all wrong in the calm Englishness of this room. "No, I wouldn't," the girl's voice was low. "What I *would* like is an explanation, *Auntie. Now.*" Sarcasm didn't become her. She was unused to problems; hers had been a happy life, full of laughter and fun.

"I know, darling, I know and I—I want to explain. I really do. But I'm a bit dry from the plane." Chloe managed a wan smile as she poured the tea with a shaking hand.

"Go ahead," Annabel said coldly as she looked away from Chloe again and into the fire.

Chloe sipped the scalding liquid gratefully. "Annabel, you must realize this is not easy for either of us."

"You bet it isn't. God, how I despise liars." She looked at Chloe defiantly. "I hate the fact that you *all* lied to me all my life—every one of you lied. Mum lied, Dad lied, *you* lied. Why couldn't you have told me the *truth*, for God's sake, or at least told me I was illegitimate when I was old enough to understand what that meant?" she said bitterly. Chloe noticed that her nails were bitten to the quick, and she was clenching and unclenching her hands as she twisted a damp handkerchief in her palms.

"I want to know, *why* didn't you tell me? *Why?*" Her voice was accusing.

"I'm going to be honest with you," Chloe said with a calmness she did not feel. "But the events I must tell you about belong to a different era almost, a totally different morality, a period of time I know may be hard for you to comprehend, darling, but please try."

The girl looked challengingly at Chloe. "I'm *all* ears—" that sarcasm again. Her hostility was a barrier, she prickled with rage. This was harder than Chloe had thought it would be.

"I was twenty-one years old, about the age you are now, so I'm sure you can understand maybe a tiny bit what that was like," Chloe began slowly.

"Of *course*," Annabel said coolly.

"I fell in love for the first time in my life," Chloe continued. "He was married, but I didn't care. I was completely infatuated with him—totally besotted. I couldn't think about anything or anyone else. He became an obsession." Chloe stopped, lit a cigarette, her hand shaking.

"*Please* don't smoke. Mummy hates people to smoke in the house." Annabel's voice was icy, and now her face seemed even more full of hatred for her mother. Chloe started to protest that Annabel had just extinguished a cigarette, but decided that was not the issue here. She swallowed. Her foot started to twitch; seemingly it had a life of its own. The tic in her eye flickered madly. She had to tell her everything. Annabel was her child. Even if it meant the end of the relationship they had had up to now, she would tell her every detail, all the reasons. Painstakingly, haltingly, Chloe described her bittersweet affair with Matt. Her hurt feelings when he had suggested an abortion. Her pain when he rejected her. "I couldn't destroy that part of us that we created together. I simply couldn't, it was too precious. If ever there was a true 'love child,' it was you, darling." Annabel didn't answer, but at least her attention had turned away from the flickering fire and to Chloe.

"It was a different time then. The world had just come out of the moralistic fifties," said Chloe. "Women were still second-class citizens; it's hard to believe, I know, but it was years before the sexual revolution. Before the sexual equality we have now. It was a time when nice girls didn't have sex, didn't take lovers. I was in show business, which had a different morality to most people's, so those attitudes never really applied to us. But Matt told me he was through with me when I became pregnant, and I simply didn't know what to do. I was at my wit's end. The only way I knew to earn my living was to sing. I had to support myself because my father was dead and my mother made very little money working in a shop."

"I see." Annabel leaned forward, her eyes still cold, and took a sip for the first time at the tea that Chloe had poured for her. "Go on."

"I wanted to have you, Annabel. I wanted to have my baby so much. I couldn't do what some of my girlfriends did when they became pregnant, go to some butcher on a back street, get it cut out, destroyed. I simply couldn't. I wanted you, Annabel. Can you understand that, darling?"

Annabel didn't answer and Chloe continued, trying to be as factual as possible. Trying not to get too emotional, trying to hold back her tears, both for the memories and for the hostility emanating from the girl she loved so much.

"There was no doubt in my mind, Annabel, that I couldn't destroy that life. Your life. My agony was knowing that an illegitimate child in 1964 would have ruined what little chance of a career I had, and that the child would grow up living with the stigma of 'illegitimate.' And it was an enormous stigma then—it really was.

"It would have been a nightmare trying to bring you up properly. It was difficult enough being a young single girl on the provincial nightclub circuit in England, what with one-night stands, bus and truck tours, standing in railway stations for hours in the middle of the night waiting for milk trains to take you to Wigan or Sunderland or Skegness. Having a baby along to look after would have been absolutely impossible. Singing was my only way of making a living, and if I'd kept you I would have had to give that up. Can you understand that?"

Chloe's eyes were blurred with tears, but Annabel's expression did not soften.

"Whatever your cheap, self-serving excuse, Mummie *dearest*, nothing can change the fact that you *didn't want me*, you didn't have a place for me in your life. You abandoned me. You simply didn't care, and you didn't have the *guts* to tell me before, when you could have. You had to wait until some *rotten* newspaper spilled the beans. Don't give me all that crap about loving me. You never loved me—you never cared at all. All that mattered was your bloody *career*. The limelight—the bright lights." She looked as if she was going to cry; all the pent-up hostility and anger of the past three days came bursting out as she let loose a tirade of fury at her mother.

"What kind of a woman *are* you?" she screamed. "Selfish, thoughtless—you never gave a thought to what might happen when you went jumping around in bed—a married man's bed," she said in disgust. "While his wife was away. I think that's nauseating.

"Oh, I *know* all about the sexual revolution of the sixties, women thinking they could fuck around like men. We're not like that today," she said accusingly. "Young women today think a bit more before we jump into bed, we *try* to be responsible, we take precautions, we have a bit of a social conscience. We are not promiscuous bitches in heat." Her voice was rising now in evangelical fury. She was the new generation of sexually educated young women—the AIDS generation. Look before you leap, and don't leap unless you're very sure it's safe.

"Annabel, I was *not* promiscuous, so stop it, stop it *now*." Suddenly Chloe was very angry. "I've had enough of this."

Annabel looked up, startled at the change in her mother's attitude.

"Stop being so judgmental. It's no good your going on at me, telling me what a terrible, lousy person I was. It's too late for that now, Annabel. We have to understand each other and to accept the past—make the best of it."

She lit a cigarette in spite of Susan's "no smoking" ban and continued, calmer now.

"I'm not going to excuse my behavior in 'abandoning' you, as you say, to be brought up by my brother and Susan. It's a fact that I *cannot* and *will not* apologize for any more. I did what I had to do. I still believe that it was the best thing for you too, whether or not you think so now. You have had a very happy life. They adore you like one of their own. They think of you as their child—can't you realize that?"

Annabel looked at Chloe, her green eyes unfathomable, but Chloe thought she saw a spark of understanding.

"I've come six thousand miles today, Annabel, to tell you the truth. Yes, it's painful. Yes, it's horrible. Yes, it's unfair. I know these last days have been difficult for you; they've been no picnic for me either. But think about this—" She put both hands on her child's shoulders and she could feel her trembling under the thin yellow sweater—"I *could* have aborted you."

Annabel shuddered and moved angrily away from her mother. "Thanks for that," she said flatly. "I suppose I should be thankful, but knowing you now, you were probably too much of a coward to do it."

"Damn it, Annabel, don't *be* like this," Chloe exploded. "I love you. I have *always* loved you and I have never gone to sleep at night without thinking of you—but I needed to make a success of my career. I *wanted* to be a singer. It was my life. If I had acknowledged you, I would have had to live with the scandal of having given birth to an illegitimate child. That would have meant *no career*. I would have been finished. I would have had you, yes, but I would have had to give up my dreams, *my life.*"

"I understand dreams," said Annabel quietly—no trace of sarcasm now. "They make life worth living."

"I want you to remember, I *chose* to have you." Chloe was calmer now. "Susan and Richard were wonderful parents to their children and they welcomed you as one of them. I knew you would be in a loving home with a devoted family, two big brothers, that you would have a stable, happy life. So I made that decision—a decision I've thought about every single day of my life since."

She paused. The memories were so painful: Matt's rejection of her and their baby, the agonizing sleepless nights when she found out she was pregnant, the frenzied discussions with Susan and Richard, the constant tears, trying to contact Matt, hearing his voice telling her he wouldn't see her again, he didn't want any "aggro." She was a big girl who knew what she had been doing. It was her problem. Hers alone. Yes, it *definitely* had been; he had done nothing. He considered it had nothing to do with him, so Chloe had dealt with it alone.

Annabel leaned her dark curly head on the back of the green sofa and bit into a shortbread biscuit as she looked at Chloe. She still felt angry, but her rage and turmoil were softening with comprehension.

"What are you thinking, Annabel?" Chloe asked, trying not to sound too eager.

"Oh, just a saying the kids are using at college." A faint smile illuminated her sweet face briefly. " 'Life's a bitch—and then you die.' " Chloe smiled tentatively. Oh, how she wanted Annabel to understand and accept what had happened. She wanted to comfort her, wipe the unshed tears that must be shed from those clouded eyes. She remembered holding her at the hospital when the nurse first put her in her arms. Remembered the funny wrinkled little face, the warmth of that tiny body close to hers. Remembered how with a fierce primal urge she had wanted to keep this infant with her forever. She remembered cuddling her daughter for hours in that stark hospital room with its acid-green, peeling paint. Annabel had rarely cried. Sometimes when she awoke and gazed up at Chloe with wise infant eyes, Chloe had felt the purest love she had ever felt for another human being.

Now Chloe looked into Annabel's eyes, so troubled now, and longed to hold her again, to stroke her hair, to tell her how much she loved her. But this was not the time. Not yet. Maybe tomorrow. Maybe next week. Maybe, God forbid, it would never happen; maybe Annabel would never forgive her, never accept what she had done.

Chloe had said what she had to say, done what she had to do. Now it was up to her daughter.

"Ladies and Gentlemen—" Chloe cleared her throat. This was *terrifying*, probably the most difficult audience she had ever had to face. No, she thought, telling Annabel had been worse. A battery of microphones and cameras was massed in front of the podium where she stood, palms damp, sweat rolling down her back, drenching her simple beige crepe de chine blouse. A sea of hostile faces confronted her. God, there must be at least one hundred of them! She panicked. Could she pull this off? A great deal depended on it. Most important were her daughter's feelings, but the public's opinion of her concerned her too. She was sick of their thinking of her as an inhuman bitch goddess.

Out of the corner of her eye, she observed Annabel giving her a tremulous smile and a "thumbs up" sign. She began:

"Twenty-one years ago..." then—Oh, my *God,* who was that? In that sea of journalists, she recognized a face. It couldn't be—it couldn't! She took a deep breath and looked at him. He was staring at her with a vestige of that sexy smile she had found so irresistible so many years ago.

Matt Sullivan! Her selfish, sexy, self-absorbed lover, Annabel's father. Her first real love. Chloe was shocked, mesmerized into immobility. His black eyes, still remarkably sparkling, gazed mockingly into hers, as though the people around them didn't

309

exist. He still exuded sexual confidence, amazing in a man of his age; he must be over sixty, she thought. He had lost most of his hair, but there was an animation about him that made him still attractive. A cigarette clung to his lower lip, as it always had—and what was that in his hand? A notebook! How could he? He was taking notes—he was obviously still a reporter. Apparently he didn't have what it took to become the editor of one of those sleazebag rags. At his age he was still just a hack, competing with twenty-five-year-olds. She felt sorry for him. For what gutter tabloid did he work now? Chloe tried desperately to pull her thoughts together and continue her speech. He must *know* that Annabel was his baby. Their love child. This was sick. The last time they had met, twenty-one years ago, he had told her to get lost. How could he be here now?

She swallowed, directing her attention to another part of the room and the other journalists.

"Twenty-one years ago, I was very naive," she began tentatively. "I was starting a career as a singer, and singing was my life. At least I thought it was." She glanced momentarily at Matt, who was looking at Annabel with an unfathomable expression.

"One day I fell in love, for the first time." The press scribbled wildly—oh, the headlines tomorrow!

"He was a married man, much older than I. I know it was terrible to have an affair with a married man, but I fell in love—very much in love." The truth was the only thing that could save her. This was tough, but she couldn't stop now. "Don't let the bastards get you down, dear," Vanessa had warned her before she had walked to the microphones.

Chloe told them the full story. How she hadn't been able to bring herself to have an abortion—to kill a life born of love. How her brother and sister-in-law, a secure and lovely family unit, had agreed to take the baby and bring her up with their own. How her career had meant so much to her and how, in

1964, giving birth to an illegitimate child could have wrecked her career and hurt the child irreparably.

Chloe realized she had their rapt attention now. Some of the more emotional sob sisters of Fleet Street were almost teary-eyed as Chloe finished her speech. She noticed Jean Rook giving her an encouraging smile.

"I know that many of you believe I have sinned, but my transgression was one of innocence and ignorance and love for my unborn child. Later I realized it would be terribly upsetting for my daughter to find out that her parents were not who she thought they were. I didn't want to upset her. She had a stable family, she was adored by her parents and her brothers. I kept the secret for the sake of my daughter's happiness, not for mine, and I sincerely hope you will all believe me."

They all seemed to. But first they had to ask their nosy Fleet Street questions. How did she feel when she found out she was pregnant? Did she feel guilt about having an affair with a married man? And, finally, who was he? Who was the man whom Chloe had been so passionate about? What was his name? Where is he now? They were really curious about this—desperate to know. She told her only untruth then, but she knew that if she did not tell a lie the investigative reporters would go to work. It wouldn't be too difficult to find some bartender, one of her musician friends, somebody who had seen her and Matt together in Liverpool, Manchester or Newcastle back then. So she lied. "He died," she said simply, "in a car crash in Marbella, just before the baby was born." They seemed satisfied with that, although Annabel looked sad. "And now, ladies and gentlemen," she said, her voice tight with emotion, "I would like you to meet my daughter." As Annabel joined her mother on the podium, the press went wild. Annabel's resemblance to Chloe was unmistakable. The same walk, the same cheekbones, the same eyes, the same dark curls. They posed for the cameras for five minutes until Christopher had to beg them to stop.

311

Later, Chloe, answering questions, surrounded by a group of female writers from the more conservative women's weeklies, suddenly felt a tap on her shoulder. "Good girl, I'm proud of you, Chlo." Matt spoke to her as if they had last met yesterday, instead of twenty-two years ago.

She looked at him long and hard. Strange—even though he was almost old now, the feelings he had created in her could still flicker faintly. "Thanks, Matt," she whispered. Memories came flooding back.

"She's a beauty—just like her ma." He gave her a wink, then drew her aside, brushed his lips against her cheek and whispered. "I loved you, Chlo. I didn't realize it then. Too young, too ambitious—too selfish, I suppose."

Too drunk, too often, Chloe thought without malice. "I don't think you loved me, Matt. You never told me you did. Please—don't say it now. I know it's not true," she said.

"I, well—you were just a kid, I was married. Still am." He was rueful now. "I'm a fucking grandfather. Can you believe it, Chloe? A grandfather!"

She could believe it. He was old enough. Still, her heart wondered, "Why did he desert me when I loved him so much?" For years she had thought about him. His memory had never been fully erased—not until she met Josh.

"I'd like to see you again, Chlo." His whisper was urgent. "I'd like to get to know her, too. Spend some time together."

"No, Matt. No." This time it was Chloe's turn to reject him. She remembered the endless phone calls to his office, a secretary telling her he was out to lunch, off, away, not in, not available—all of the stock secretary's lines.

Not that revenge was sweet—that had never been Chloe's way—but seeing him again had closed their chapter forever. "Goodbye, Matt," she whispered, brushing his old man's cheek with her well-preserved one. "Take care."

"Goodbye, darlin', and good luck. You did it, Chlo! You made the buggers do you right this time!"

She watched him go, and to her surprise saw that he was crying.

Within the month the whole incident was forgotten when Prince Charles and Princess Diana announced that she was expecting again.

Emerald had tested well, she decided. Banishing her usual glamour, she had thought of herself as just a working actress, and got on with it. The crew applauded when she finished. Afterward she went straight home to her penthouse in Century City, took off her makeup, told the answering service to ring through only if Eddie De Levigne called, and went on a bender.

For three days she lay on her bed drinking straight vodka. If she didn't get this role, she was determined to drink herself to death. What would be the use of going on? It was difficult enough to survive in this business. She couldn't *not* continue to enjoy her lavish lifestyle. She had sold all of her jewels that were worth anything, except one necklace. This she wore, with a tattered white terry-cloth robe, for the three days she lay in bed mindlessly switching TV channels and drinking vodka from the bottle.

She didn't talk, she didn't cry, she didn't think about anything. She was in limbo, waiting to be put out of her misery forever—or to rise to new heights.

The call came on Wednesday morning. "Eddie De Levigne on the line," said the voice of Gloria at her service.

"Hi, Eddie. What's up?" The actress in her managed to banish any hint of drunkenness from her speech. She didn't even slur her words.

"You've got it, kiddo," he said excitedly. "God knows, Emerald, you're a lucky woman, after the fool you made of yourself.

Jail and all. But Hogarth loves you. He's had to practically suck cock at the network to get you for this."

"Why?" she demanded. "I'm still a big star."

"Christ, Emerald, the truth, kiddo, *is* you've been in the game too long. The network knows it, the studio knows it, even the great unwashed public knows it."

"I'm big—*huge* in Europe," Emerald said proudly. "I get mobbed when I walk down the Via Condotti."

"So does Pia Zadora, dear. So what? Listen, Emerald, Europe is a *very* small piece of the action, and frankly, I don't see Zeffi-relli banging on your door—even if you are big on the Via Condotti."

"He couldn't," she giggled. "He doesn't like girls."

"You are not a *girl* any more, kid. Face it, Emerald, however many studs you take into your bed, you are a middle-aged woman who is rapidly losing her pulling power—on *and* off the screen."

"You don't have to rub it in, Eddie," she moaned. "I can still look good, though, and you know it." She understood he was being harsh to her as a warning. This was her last chance.

"They want you in wardrobe next Tuesday. Eleven o'clock. Be punctual, toots—for a change. And they start shooting in a week. You're a lucky woman, Emerald," he added gently. "Don't screw it up."

She knew he was right. In the intervening five days, she stopped drinking, cold turkey, lost eight pounds, spent two hours at the gym every day, bleached her gray roots back to their golden glory, and arrived in wardrobe punctually on Tuesday morning, almost as good as new.

Nobody else, she told herself, could have done it.

Part Six

24

*J*osh yawned, stretched, and threw out his arms.

" 'Ere, watch it," the little redhead with the thin frizzed hair groaned sleepily.

Not again. Self-disgust flooded him at the memory of last night's performances, on and off the stage. The opening night. The party. The people.

The Manchester Hippodrome was a far cry from Broadway and Las Vegas, where he had once done sellout business.

Show business was brutal, as all who chose it as their profession knew. Ultimately no one gave a shit. Every cliché was true: dog eat dog; jealousy thrives; adulation on the way up, indifference on the way down. Josh was on the way down, and he knew it. Self-pity and nausea attacked him simultaneously, and he groped for the paraphernalia to prepare his first fix of the day.

He lit the match under the spoon and watched the white powder dissolve into brownish syrup. After it hit him he turned to inspect the tiny girl by his side. Christ, this one was *really* young stuff. He lifted the sheets up. No more than fourteen or fifteen by the look of her. Even for him, this was younger than usual. He liked them in full bloom, just past puberty, in their first flush of womanhood—sixteen or seventeen was usually the age he preferred. Once he had been lucky enough to find sixteen-year-old twins. They couldn't do enough for him, unlike this little creature, who had lain back uncomplaining while he tried to whip up a fever for both of them. He had failed miserably. Maybe he was getting too old. But the forties weren't old these days. Tom Jones was still around, so was Julio Iglesias, and Jagger—Mick, the idol of all of them—was creeping up the old 4–0 ladder. Not to mention McCartney, Rod Stewart and David Bowie. Forty wasn't fatal—or was it?

" 'Ello," the little thing said. God, she was *tiny*. Maybe she was even younger than fourteen. Innocent gray eyes gave him a tentative smile. She hurriedly skipped out of bed, hoping he wouldn't try and do again what he'd done so boringly last night.

Why did I do it? she wondered. He's old enough to be me dad. No, on second thought, he was possibly old enough to be her granddad. Her dad was thirty-two—Josh must be at least fifty. She dressed quickly, rehearsing tales with which to regale friends at school. Joshua Brown, big stud, big star. Her mum's favorite crooner. She had grown up to the sounds of his plaintive ballads on her mum's stereo. Her mum had had a real thing for Josh. Used to talk about him for hours. Boring old fart, she thought. Couldn't fuck his way out of a paper bag. Had a hard time even getting it up. Uncle Fred was much better. She struggled into black lace tights, green Lurex socks and, mumbling something about being late for school, skipped away.

Josh was relieved. Now he must get it together. Meet the press, then face the cast at rehearsal, discuss the reviews. Oh, God, the reviews. He was in no hurry to do so. During his final ballad last night, he had observed a steady trickle of customers edging out the exit doors. The applause had been meager at the final curtain. The stage manager had been hard-pushed to milk two curtain calls.

After the show last night, a supercilious pockmarked journalist from a down-market tabloid had cornered him at the party. Josh, conscious of the power of the press, was always ready to fraternize with them. He needed them now, if this show was to succeed, but basically he loathed their guts. Maybe this reptile could serve a purpose, though. Josh bandied wisecracks and charm for four full minutes before the reptile asked him the oh so familiar question he dreaded. "So what's Chloe *really* like?" Josh played dumb. The hack plodded on. "You were married to her for over ten years—is she *really* like Miranda?"

Chloe. That woman was ruining his life with her goddamn TV series and her "over forty" fame. Some kind of fucking Joan of Arc for the blue-rinse brigade. She thought she was hot stuff now. Showing off her body in those magazines, bragging about how women over forty were just as sexy as twenty-year-olds. Balls. How could she know? She wasn't a man. Young, firm flesh was what most men were interested in. They were wrong, these feminists with their "Look at us, we're over forty and aren't we wonderful" crap. Didn't they *know*, didn't Chloe realize, for Christ's sake, forty was *past* it?

It was pathetic. It was O.K. for him to be over forty—he was a man. But everywhere these days were these ball-breaking broads with their diets and exercise books, their hit records and their box-office pulling power. Tina fucking Turner, Jane fucking Fonda. And now Chloe.

To add insult to injury, only yesterday she had been on the front page of the *Daily Mirror* with Macho Man Luis Mendoza.

"SOAP'S HOTTEST LOVERS" screamed the headline, and the story chronicled how Chloe and Luis were making the screen ignite with their passionate love scenes and volatile chemistry.

"Not since Petruchio tamed Katharina the shrew have a pair of lovers excited audiences so much," drooled the article.

"Luis Mendoza is the sexiest, most electrifying leading man to hit the TV screen since Tom Selleck. Already movie companies are standing in line to offer him contracts. All America is at his feet, thanks to 'Saga' and the combustibility of Luis and Chloe Carriere."

Josh had smiled bitterly, trying to hide his jealousy from the reptile. "Oh, Chloe... Yeah... Great... She's a great girl. Deserves her success. Yeah, really. I'm happy for her." Bullshit. The words, uttered for the umpteenth time, stuck in his throat, and he had to excuse himself to go to the men's room for a snort.

Sally had looked after him worriedly. He was too pale. The show had not been good. She had seen the audience's glazed faces as the subtlety of *The Private Life of Napoleon and Josephine* went over their heads.

Poor old Dad. She had tried to cheer him up in the way she knew he loved—had looked around and seen the tiny redheaded teenager gazing admiringly into the space her father had recently vacated. She wandered over to her. "How'd you like to meet him?" she offered casually. "Ooh, not 'alf," squealed the girl. It was easy for Sally to succeed in anticipating her father's wants and needs—though "thanks" was not a word that was featured in his vocabulary these days. But Josh should certainly see that Sally cared very much for him.

Josh, relieved that the girl was gone and feeling better as the cocaine took effect, dressed and left for a press luncheon at the Metropole Hotel.

A Fleet Street hag, invisible venom dripping from her ballpoint pen, pretended to give Josh her rapt attention. She was asking the inevitable questions again about Chloe. The practiced answers flowed easily from Josh's lips as he tried to hide his chagrin. Would they never stop interrogating him about her?

"Phone, Dad." Sally was at his elbow, steering him away. The hag seemed satisfied. She had her story. She would make up the rest. She always made it up. That was why she was called "The Barracuda of Fleet Street."

She had already written the story before meeting Josh today. It was titled "The Fallen Star."

"He was once a superstar in America and all over the world. Now he ekes out a meager living playing suburban theaters in Britain. Joshua Brown, once the idol of millions, is now a broken man—a broken man full of broken dreams. His beautiful ex-wife, Chloe Carriere, has become a mega-soap star on American TV while Josh barely makes ends meet touring in mediocre musicals." The article continued in this vein. This was tremendous stuff. The public would eat it up. They adored a rags-to-riches story, but when it was rags to riches and back to rags again, they loved it even more. And Josh was a natural, with his bouts with drugs and alcohol, jail sentences, drunken rages, affairs with young girls—they all made great copy. The public longed to see him fall on his face.

The female barracuda had the perfect set of photos to accompany the story. Josh in 1965, all white teeth, tumbling black locks and shiny satin trousers, holding the mike as if it were his cock, and giving the camera his wildest, sexiest look next to a recent photo of Josh hunched up in an overcoat and scarf, pale face, graying hair, spectacles, glancing suspiciously over his shoulder, surprised by the camera's flash and, hanging on his arm adoringly, a girl easily young enough to be his daughter. Before and after. How the mighty have fallen. Eat it up, all you readers! Two nice photos of Chloe. Chloe in 1962—wide-eyed innocence, black hair in neat bangs, a chaste miniskirt and knee socks. And there was Chloe now—sheathed in Rudolpho bugle beads, white fox and diamonds, lying seductively on a satin chaise, with a knowing and successful look on her painted face. Perfect. The hag cackled. She had never liked Josh anyway. Too bigheaded by far. He had reaped what he had sown.

Chloe read the piece on Josh a week later. In spite of herself she felt sad for him. Why had he allowed himself to fall so far? He had had it all. If he found himself a decent agent, went to a psychiatrist, gave up drugs and bimbos and really concentrated on his work, on his music, he could have it all again. Maybe. Maybe not. Nothing in this business was easy.

She sighed and looked at Philippe, who lay next to her in their huge bed with the art deco padded satin headboard and lilac silk sheets. He was watching MTV, his favorite station.

Chloe thought it odd that a man of forty could become so hooked on the gyrations of Madonna and Michael Jackson. But he watched Music Television all day long when he wasn't working on her accounts or writing an article for *Paris Match*.

Philippe was always in the house. He was on a marriage kick again after seeing the article about Josh in the British tabloid.

"When are you going to get the final papers signed, *chérie?*" he asked, massaging her shoulders in the seductive way she loved. "Why don't you get them? Then we can be married. Get rid of Josh, *chérie,* it's time."

Oh, no, here he goes again, thought Chloe. Not wedding talk again. They had been living together for a year, but he kept going on about marriage. It was unusual for a man. And much as she adored him, she didn't feel like making a lifelong commitment. Josh was always at the back of her mind.

As tactfully as possible, Chloe gave him once again her anti-marriage speech. It didn't placate him and he sulked for the rest of the day to the sound of MTV turned up full blast.

• • •

Chloe left for the studio attempting to forget Josh's predicament and Philippe's sulks. She called Jasper from her car phone. "What is the decision?" she asked. "Has the network come up with the raise for next season, Jasper? We're on our last episode of the season. We've only got another five days to shoot."

Jasper had met with Abby in the big man's sumptuous office at the beginning of the season. Abby's reputation as a producer who couldn't tolerate insubordination in actors and others who worked for him was legendary. To the world he played Mr. Always Understanding, but in reality he was ruthless if anyone dared step out of line. Several members of the company had been fired for demanding more money.

Jasper had transmitted Chloe's discontent with the fact that after four years on "Saga," contributing to its success in the ratings, and having become one of the most copied, admired and hated women on TV, she was still receiving far less salary than Sam and Sissy. Abby would not hear of an increase for Chloe. Through gritted teeth he spelled it out: "Tell her if she wants to continue working in this town she'd better not make waves. If she doesn't conform, if she gives us *any* trouble, she'll be *out*. We'll kill her off; write her out. We won't be blackmailed, Jasper, not by her nor any of them. She's making forty thousand a week—that should be enough for an ex-nightingale from provincial Britain."

He added with a shark's smile: "Tell Chloe I'll expect her at my 'Man of the Year Award' dinner at the Beverly Hilton next Tuesday, Jasper. She's seated at my table. She'd better be there."

A command from the emperor. Abby wore his power easily. It confirmed his self-worth. God knows his wife, Maud, didn't care about it, unless it was his *net* worth. Abby was not going to let any actor, producer or director get the better of him, and he was not above deliberately humiliating any of them. Chloe would never forget what he had done to Pandora King last season.

Pandora had been late on the set too many times, made fun of "Saga" too often on talk shows, and complained and moaned on the set about the poor dialogue she was getting and how her costumes were not as expensive as Chloe's and Sissy's. Abby and Gertrude were becoming thoroughly sick of her.

Pandora, along with the rest of the cast and crew, had attended the wrap party at the Beverly Hills Hotel for "Saga" to celebrate the end of shooting. Everyone was in an "up" mood, and it should have been a joyful occasion. Nine months of hard work were over. A three-month hiatus lay ahead of them. They could all do what they wanted. For the crew, this usually meant getting another job as quickly as possible, since they couldn't afford to be out of work for that long. For the three best-paid actors, Sam, Sissy and Chloe, it meant they could choose from the fat pile of scripts that their agents had waiting on their desks or go on an extended vacation. The rest of the cast were at the mercy of whichever producer or network chose to give them a job.

After dinner and the gag reel—a twenty-minute compilation of actors and crew doing inadvertently funny things, breaking up, tripping, choking, giggling or generally making fools of themselves—Gertrude and Abby went to the podium and introduced all the cast, each of whom was invited to the stand and to say a few words.

First Sam, as the most senior member of the cast, made his usual charming speech. He sounded good, even though he was beginning to look old without his thick orange makeup.

Vanessa whispered to Chloe, "He's lost so much weight, his teeth seem to be getting too big for his mouth!"

Sissy flounced on, thin as bone, brittle as glass, wearing a gray taffeta strapless dress that made her shoulder blades look like chicken wings.

Then came Chloe, looking strained after another petty row with Philippe. He had refused to come to the wrap party, so she had to ask Ostie, her dialogue coach, to escort her.

Abby then called upon Pandora:

"And now we are going to hear from a lovely lady and a talented actress who, regrettably, will not be back with us next season. Please all give a great big round of applause to Miss Pandora King."

Pandora's blood froze. *Not be back next season?* They couldn't. They wouldn't. Not after she had just turned down a firm offer from Disney for a half-hour sitcom. She had suspected for some months that her days on "Saga" were numbered. That was the way the cookie crumbled in TV Land. Her fan mail had been getting sparser, and it seemed that the fewer letters she received, the fewer lines she had to learn. She was a realist and had been excited about the Disney series, looking forward to the challenge of a new project. However, after speaking to Abby, her agent had told her that she would definitely be back on "Saga" next season with a hefty raise. Abby had assured him they all adored her. She shouldn't have believed a word of it. Now the sitcom at Disney had gone to another actress, and the bastard was firing her in front of the entire cast and crew. She swallowed her pride, aware that her face was aflame, and went up to the podium to say the few words she had carefully prepared but which now seemed horribly inappropriate.

After her speech, Chloe squeezed her arm sympathetically as they stood next to each other on the podium. It could have happened to any of them. In their hearts, all of the cast breathed a sigh of relief that this season, at least, they had escaped the hangman's noose. During the shooting of thirty episodes of the third season, Chloe had tried to remain calm and not get upset when highly paid guest stars were brought in for seven or eight episodes to "bolster the ratings"—which were already high. Neither the network nor Abby nor Gertrude had any qualms

325

about paying these often fading stars twice the amount they paid Chloe.

"It's my fault for coming in so cheap at the beginning," Chloe told Vanessa bitterly, having just played a scene with a "famous name" who had blown his lines fifteen times in a row and who was getting sixty thousand dollars an episode.

Two days before shooting ended, Chloe received Jasper's news that her raise had once again been denied. Backed by Philippe, she grimly decided she had to take a stand before the next season began. Since she had not received the twenty thousand-a-week increase she felt she warranted, she informed Jasper that she would quit the show.

"I mean it, Jasper," she said. "I'm off to the south of France and I'm not coming back unless you can get them to change their minds."

They didn't.

Although the network wanted Chloe to remain on the show, Abby and Gertrude were adamant. No raise. In their eyes, Chloe had committed the cardinal sin. Self-righteously they announced that Chloe had attempted to blackmail them. People who would cut each other's throats for a project, who lied, cheated, schemed and manipulated, were up in arms over Chloe's deed. During the hiatus, which had been shortened from the usual three months to six weeks by the network's desire to have "Saga" back on the air in late October, Jasper tried to negotiate a compromise with Abby, Gertrude and the network executives. To no avail.

They dropped her. They wrote her out of the first episode, giving her dialogue to other actors, and they sent her the news by cable.

Cold rage gripped Chloe when the cable arrived. "The producers of 'Saga,' MCPC, and the BCC Network hereby inform Chloe Carriere that, effective today, her services as a performer in the television series 'Saga' are no longer required." It was signed "Abby Arafat, President of MCPC."

She had been lying by the pool, basking in the warm Mediterranean sunshine, when Philippe handed her the cable.

"How *can* they even consider doing this to 'Saga' even if they don't care about me?" said Chloe, amazed at how they would cut off their nose to spite their face.

"It's suicidal," Philippe agreed. "Everyone knows how popular Miranda and you are. You're the only reason anyone watches the damned trash in the first place." It was four o'clock on the Côte d'Azur. It would be 7 A.M. in L.A., Chloe thought. The cast would be rushing to finish their makeup and hair to be on the set for rehearsal. Sissy would be putting her wig on while gulping down her vitamin pills and protein drink for the grueling day ahead. Sam would be resting. The younger actors would be gossiping in the hair and makeup rooms.

Chloe felt a touch of melancholy. The view of the Mediterranean from the house was more beautiful than any in Beverly Hills or Malibu, but the thought that she might have blown her hard-won career made her worse than melancholy.

"Drink?" Philippe asked. She nodded and he went to the bamboo bar, poured cassis and Dom Perignon over ice into a tall glass and brought it to her.

She drank it gratefully. "All I did was ask for what I deserve, Philippe. No more, no less."

"I know, *chérie*."

"They all think I'm really a bitch," she said bitterly, a sliver of self-pity in her voice. She gazed at the turquoise waves, oblivious to the semi-naked flesh that paraded unself-consciously up and down the *plage*. Young and old, perfect and not so perfect, downright ugly—it was of no importance on the French Riviera. They all showed it off. "Don't brood, *chérie*," he said, leaving her to go surfing.

Her eyes scanned the bay. White yachts rocked gently on their

327

moorings as their owners sat sipping cool drinks and watching speedboats piloted by tanned young men and bare-breasted girls dart between them. Floating on the waves like multicolored butterflies were the gaily hued striped sails of the wind-surfers. It was a view Chloe never ceased to admire as she lounged in her beach chair luxuriating in the laziness of watching other people hard at play.

The telephone rang.

"Chloe, my dear, you *must* be back for the second episode or you will never work in television or movies again." Jasper's long-distance voice was faint. "They mean business, Chloe. You cannot fight them. I have done everything I can, dear, *everything,* but I must tell you that I have never seen Abby so resistant. He's *very* angry with you."

"I thought he loved me," sighed Chloe. "He told me so often enough."

"He does, in his way, he does. But I think it's more than resistance to you and the raise. It's Sissy's influence. I think if you come back, though, you just may get your raise, my darling."

"What do you mean?" Chloe was puzzled.

"I found out that Sam has points in the show. It's supposed to be a deep, dark secret, but I found out. He originally signed only a two-year contract, and when it was up, the only way he'd agree to stay was if he got a financial interest in the show."

"Ah!" cried Chloe. "All is clear. It *is* Sissy, then."

"Right, darling, Queen Bitch herself. She *will not,* as part owner of the show, allow you to have a raise, and she will rip Sam's balls off if he agrees to give you so much as one cent more."

"Damn her," said Chloe sadly. "Why does she hate me so much?"

"Jealousy, my pet. You get more fan mail, more attention. You're more popular, your role is more exciting *and,* of course, you're better-looking. Don't fight it, toots, jealousy is a fact of life in this town. And don't take it personally, either. If it wasn't you playing Miranda, Sissy would loathe whoever it was. She's that kind of woman."

Chloe sighed. "I know, I've worked with her all these years. She's not a lot of laughs, believe me."

Jasper continued, "The network told me in deepest confidence that if you come back, *they* will give you the twenty thousand out of their own pockets. But Sissy and Sam must never know.... Ignore the cable, Chloe dear. Come back Tuesday. I promise you within two months you will have your raise."

"All right, all right, Jasper—I'll come back. Just as you knew I would, darling."

Jasper was pleased. He liked Chloe. The fact that she hadn't saddled herself with the usual slew of personal managers, business advisers and tax-shelter specialists meant she had probably saved more of her earnings than most actresses in her position. Clever girl. Not only that, but she steered clear of booze, dope and the swingers scene. By Hollywood standards she was almost square.

Chloe hung up, her feelings still unsettled. She felt ill-used. The tone of the cable, the way she had been so swiftly written out of the premiere episode, gave her a sense of mortality that made her uneasy. I'm dispensable, like Kleenex, she thought.

She watched Philippe on his wind-surfer as he maneuvered the small craft across the waves, brown curls clinging to his head. His body was tanned, lean and athletic, although he did little exercise. Emotionally he had been a rock, a difficult rock sometimes, but a rock nonetheless that she could lean on. And he handled her finances and her business affairs, and most of the time she was content with him, although he could be stubborn, and he had incredible mood swings which turned him from Prince Charming into male chauvinist pig. His conversation was quite limited, too. She sighed. The more she knew Philippe, the less substance there seemed to be in him. But the more the fabric of their psychological relationship weakened, the stronger the physical side became.

She shivered in spite of the Mediterranean sun. He pushed her so often for marriage. *Why?* She was extremely wary. The pain Josh had inflicted on her had not gone away completely.

Josh. Poor Josh. Brilliant, funny, self-destructive, complex Josh. Where was he now? And what was he doing?

25

*E*merald was the first big name to be cast in "America." She would play Evelyn Alexander McFadden, the female lead, the lusty, beautiful proprietress of a hotel saloon in the little Midwestern border town. But Burt Hogarth was having trouble casting the male lead. He had approached some of the most prestigious actors in England for "America," with no success.

The network was anxious to start production by early July. They wanted the series ready to start airing in October of 1986. They had decided to program "America" opposite the so far invincible "Saga," which had been the ratings winner practically every week for the past four years.

331

It was generally agreed by the producers of "America" that the competition between Emerald Barrymore and Chloe Carriere would excite the viewers' interest. And they had shrewdly cast Pandora King, recently dumped by "Saga," to play the second female lead.

The only problem that remained was finding a strong English leading man to play opposite Emerald—a man who would not be overshadowed by her star power. Sir Geoffrey Fennel had bowed out in favor of doing Mercutio at the National. They approached Pierce Brosnan, Roger Moore and Michael Caine. All turned it down. The part of Malcolm McFadden called for a forty-to-fiftyish actor to be the heroic, tough and sardonic husband of Evelyn/Emerald. He had to be strong, sexy, masculine, have a sense of humor, ride a horse, fence, and be in peak physical condition.

Ten days before shooting commenced, the producers, having interviewed and tested dozens of actors and watched hundreds of miles of videotape, were still no closer to finding their male lead. Shooting was set to start the day after Independence Day. July Fourth was "America" Day, but no suitable leading man had been found.

Josh lay in bed sweating. Pulses he never knew he possessed hammered in his skull and his tongue was a slab of decaying meat. The phone wouldn't stop. It kept on interrupting his dream—or was it a nightmare?

He and Chloe—young again. In love again. Kids, in the 1960s walking down King's Road laughing like teenagers. He never failed to have her in gales of laughter. She laughed a lot, and he wondered if she still did. He wondered if Philippe made her happy.

In his dream, he was hugging her so tightly he could feel his hardness against her thigh. Then people started to tug at him, pulling her away, as her expression of joy turned to fear. "Chloe,

Chloe—" he tried to call her name, but the words wouldn't form. "Josh," she screamed, as hands, eager, excited hands, grabbed at her body and hair, tearing at her clothes. Then hysterical voices started yelling her name. "Chloe! Chloe! Miranda! Miranda! We love you! We love you!" Faceless fans pushed Josh away. He staggered and fell to the pavement, watching as they overwhelmed Chloe, pulling at her clothes, pulling them off, grabbing chunks of her hair and her flesh, tearing at her with their fingernails and teeth, huddling over her now as she lay bleeding on the pavement. She was screaming for help, but Josh couldn't move.

As the dream continued, he saw her body supine on the ground. Fans crawled over her like ants: kissing, biting, ripping her flesh, sucking her everywhere as she screamed with horror. He couldn't stop them. "Fuck off, Granddad," yelled a punk with green hair who was about to plunge himself into Chloe. "Fuck off or I'll ram this up yer arse." He shoved Josh viciously and he fell against the wall watching helplessly as the fans ravaged his Chloe.

He woke up screaming her name. Finally he heard the sound of the ringing phone echoing Chloe's cries.

"What? Who is it?" he yelled hoarsely, needing liquid, anything to ease his throat. The voice on the phone was friendly.

"Josh, dear boy, it's Jasper Swanson. How are you, old boy?"

"Fine, fine, just great, Jasper. How's yourself?" He tipped a half-empty wineglass to his cracked lips and felt the sour liquid moisten his parched tongue. "What's up, Jasper?"

"Well, dear boy, I don't know whether you'll be interested or not because I know the tour is going so well. . . ."

Fucking liar, thought Josh. The fucking *world* knows it's a flop. What's the old fart going on about? "Not that well, Jasper." He might as well be honest. "I mean, if another gig came along I could be tempted."

"Naturally, dear boy, naturally, which is why I'm calling you at this unearthly hour. You've heard of the book, *America: The Early Years?*"

"Yeah, of course, who hasn't?" He sat up, dying for a smoke. The ashtray was full of butts, the pack empty.

"Well, it's going to be a very important series. I think I have convinced them that you would be perfect for the part of Malcolm McFadden—the lead opposite Emerald Barrymore. Would that interest you, old man?"

There was silence as Josh digested this.

"Hello, hello, Josh? Are you there?" Jasper's time was money, and he was always impatient. He was a great agent, and he knew it. Some said he could sell the Vatican to the Pope, so good was he at his job.

"Yeah, yeah, I'm here." Josh lit one of the butts. The smoke seemed to clear his fuddled brain. "It's a soap opera, isn't it?"

"Well, I suppose you could call it that, but it's a very prestigious series. Burt Hogarth is the producer, and he is one of the most important men in Hollywood, let's face it, and of course Emerald Barrymore is still a major star."

"She hasn't worked in a while, has she?"

"Neither have you, dear boy." Frost crept into Jasper's voice. "I think you should face the fact, *young man,*" he said with a hint of sarcasm, "that Hollywood is not clamoring for the services of fifty-year-old English ex-pop singers."

"Hold on, old boy, I'm nowhere near fifty," said Josh, "and I was *never* a pop singer."

"This role could make you an important star again, Josh. Everyone knows you have talent, but we all know your—well —your problems. I've had a damn difficult job convincing the network that you don't drink now, and are certainly *not* doing drugs." Disdain colored his tone. Jasper despised both drug addicts and alcoholics. "They have bought my idea of Joshua Brown as Malcolm. It's a hell of a role, old boy, and a stupendous break for you. They will pay twelve thousand an episode this year, and twenty-five thousand next season. They will supply you with two first-class tickets from London to L.A., and first-star billing after Emerald. And they want you in Hollywood for costume and camera tests the day after tomorrow. We'll go through all the other details then."

Josh's mind reeled. "My musical—what about the show? We've got another week here, then Leeds and Manchester, all the provinces."

"Your show is a flop. You know it. I know it. Even the British public knows it. The network is prepared to discuss a payoff with the theater owners. They will spring you, in fact. What do you say, Josh? This could be a major comeback for you, something you cannot turn your back on."

"Of course I'll do it," said Josh excitedly. "I have to—you know it. Book me into my old penthouse at the Wilshire. Can you get three plane tickets, first class?"

"No." Jasper was cool. Starting his demands already, was he? "If you need to bring two other people we can exchange the two first-class into three club. Remember, Josh, you are not a star in Hollywood. You cannot make demands—yet."

"Yeah, well, O.K. Change the tickets. It's just that I need to bring Sally, and Perry, my valet."

"Done, dear boy, done. Now, congratulations. I know you are not going to regret this. I'll be in touch tomorrow."

Josh lay back on the bed feeling euphoric. Hollywood! A major TV series with a major star! Emerald Barrymore. Publicity. The studio machine in action for him. The big time—it could be the big time for him again. It could be. It *would* be.

He leaped out of bed, energized with excitement, not needing the fix he'd been subconsciously thinking about.

"Look out, Chloe, babe, here I come!" he yelled.

Chloe went back to work on "Saga." Due to pressure from the network, Abby and Gertrude had relented. They had wanted to make an example of Chloe, show the rest of the cast and actors in their other shows what would happen to a star who demanded more money. Although they had bragged that they could do without Chloe's contribution to "Saga," they hadn't considered the network's reaction.

"Get her back on this show," Irving Schwarzman, president of the network, told Abby. "Give her the fucking raise—she deserves it, for Christ's sake. *Get her back.*" Despite Abby and Gertrude's protestations that the inmates would end up running the asylum, they were overruled. Chloe came back twenty thousand dollars a week richer.

But her life with Philippe was becoming somewhat confusing. He had often been loving and affectionate; at the same time he was constantly arguing with her about getting married. His own bourgeois ideas and his even more bourgeoise French mother were pushing him. His mother thought that at forty he was too young to be living with a forty-three-year-old woman. She wanted grandchildren. He was her only child and she was nearly eighty.

Philippe hoped he could persuade Chloe to get married and then persuade her it was still possible for her to have a child. Now that he had seen her with Annabel, he realized how maternal Chloe could be and was determined to have a baby with her.

That was his plan, but it clearly wasn't Chloe's. Marriage to Philippe and babies at her age—ridiculous.

"Ursula Andress did it," he sulked. "She had a child at forty-four. Many women do; it's possible, you know, *chérie,* and you would be a wonderful mother."

"Why, Philippe? *Why* do we need marriage and a baby? We're happy the way we are—why spoil it?"

"You treat me like a stud," he replied sulkily. "You use me like men used to use a woman. You pick my brains and use my cock. You're just a user, Chloe."

"That's not true and you know it," she said angrily. "Look, we're together, we live together. I love you. Please, darling, *don't* make me get married. I've done it once. It doesn't work for me."

Annabel was living with them for the summer in the guest house. Both women were happy with each other. Their relationship was excellent and they spent hours together in deep conversation. Philippe felt annoyed and left out, and was sulking more than ever. Annabel swam in the pool, tended the rose garden, and scattered the pillows she beautifully embroidered all over the house. Making them was her hobby, that and playing her guitar.

Having Annabel around was good, the show was doing well, but Chloe often awoke in the night with nightmares. Sometimes in her nightmare she would see the face of the man with the knife whom the police said had wanted to harm her that night in Las Vegas. She wished they had never shown her his picture, that blank, emotionless face. When she awoke in the middle of the night, Philippe's strong arms and calming voice enfolded her. She needed him to fend off the demons that haunted her.

There was no question Sam was not feeling up to par. He had lost an alarming amount of weight and couldn't seem to force himself to eat anything. During the day's filming he often became exhausted and had to lie down to rest. He first noticed the ugly red patch when he felt an itching on his chest. Forcing himself to look in the mirror, he saw with a sinking dread what he had feared, what he had tried never to allow to enter his conscious thoughts—a red patch, scabby and swollen, the size of a quarter.

Bile rose in his throat. It couldn't be. It *couldn't*. Since the wild days of his youth, he had indulged in very few homosexual affairs. He had been more-or-less faithful to Freddy. Good old dependable Freddy. They were almost like a married couple—

except a married couple who only do it occasionally have a tendency to do it with other people. He remembered Nick. He groaned. What about Freddy? Had he been with anyone else?

While the cat's away, the mice go down to the nearest gay bar. Did Freddy do that still? With AIDS the latest scourge? A rapping on the door announced that Sam was needed on the set in four minutes. He went back to the set, convincing himself it was all in his imagination, but he told his secretary to make a doctor's appointment as soon as possible.

He sat opposite Dr. John Willows, who looked grave.

"I'm sorry to have to tell you this, Sam." The doctor coughed. He was embarrassed. He'd known Sam for thirty-five years, but his homosexuality was a topic they had never discussed.

"What? What? Tell me for Christ's sake, John. Is it AIDS?"

The physician nodded. "I'm...I'm afraid so, Sam. We tested your blood twice to make sure there was no mistake. I'm very sorry." The doctor looked down at his mahogany desk, at the framed photograph of his wife, his grown-up children and his grandchildren. He thanked God he had always been faithful to her—for more than thirty years now. Thank God he hadn't given in to the temptations that had occasionally crossed his path. But what could he tell this aging TV superstar whose gaunt, lined face suddenly looked much older than fifty-five? How to help him?

"I'm afraid there's no cure just yet, as you know." He twiddled with the pencils on his immaculate desk.

"We can, of course, treat the carcinoma with ointments and antibiotics, but eventually the patches will get worse, I'm afraid."

Sam felt the room swimming before him. His career was in ruins. He had caught the plague—some likened it to the bubonic plague—the Black Death. And as with the plague there was no cure for this scourge of the eighties.

"How long." He gulped for air. "How long do you think I have before it'll be obvious?"

"Hard to say—months, maybe years. I'm not an expert, Sam. You know we've only been really aware of this disease for a few years, but it's spreading. My God, it's spreading."

"Will people have to know from you? Do you have to tell them?"

"Of course not, of course not." The doctor's voice had a heartiness he didn't feel. God, Sam was the seventh person he'd seen this month who had contracted the virus. It was terrifying.

"Listen, sport, if you need counseling about this, there are experts who know how to deal with the problem."

"Christ, no!" Sam was shocked. "I can deal with it myself. My career will be shot if a word of this gets out. You do understand that, don't you, John?"

"Of course, of course I do. Don't worry, Sam. No one will know, but..." The doctor looked at his watch. He had a waiting room full of patients. "You better check your contacts, your recent ones, that is."

"Damn it, John, I've only had one contact."

"Yes, yes, of course. Well listen, sport, come in next Tuesday and we'll get you set up with all the right stuff." He was desperate to end this. Nothing he could do. He was just a doctor seeing these pathetic men, trying to help them. He managed a sympathetic smile as he walked Sam to the door.

Only eight more months left. Eight months before he was out of this fucking hellhole. He had made no friends. No one in jail wanted to be friendly except when they abused him sexually.

In his cell each night, Calvin took out the magazines he'd accumulated. *Penthouse. Playboy.* All the magazines were old issues, but he didn't care.

He looked at them, gloating with excitement. In these magazines, the full-bosomed girls in their black lace underwear, with their open legs, all had one face. Emerald Barrymore's. Calvin had cut pictures of his idol from other publications and carefully pasted her head onto the bodies of the lush young creatures in his magazines. His Emerald. His queen.

He had been upset when he had seen the photographs of her in the tabloids emerging from jail. What infuriated him even more was the piece written at the time in the *American Informer*.

"If the part of Miranda Hamilton in prime time's hit series 'Saga' had gone to Emerald Barrymore, who lost the role to British singer Chloe Carriere, would Emerald have come to this pathetic end, living like a down-and-outer and with no trace of her former beauty left?"

Calvin had scrunched the paper up into a tight ball and thrown it into a corner of his cell. It was all *her* fault, that black-haired witch, that no-talent nonentity. It was because of Chloe Carriere that his Emerald was in this state. All because of her. She would suffer for it. When he got out of here she would really suffer for her sins.

Sam stalked into Freddy's workroom and went directly to the bar. Satin and lace, half-finished beaded frocks for fashionable starlets littered the sofa and table. Fashion magazines from Italy, France and England were piled on the floor. An orange cat lay on the windowsill basking in the hot Santa Monica sunshine. Outside, Sam could see suntanned teenagers oiling themselves, surfing, eating hot dogs and laughing. Laughing. Ha! Would he ever laugh again? Could he?

"Who've you been fucking, you lousy little faggot?" he demanded, as he knocked back a whiskey and poured another.

"No one, no one, I *swear*. My love—I've been faithful."

"Tell me the *truth*," Sam screamed. "Who? *Who?!* I know you did, I know it. I've got fucking AIDS, for Christ's sake, and you've given it to me, you bastard."

"Oh, God, no, no, you can't—oh, my good Lord. How could it happen?" Freddy threw himself onto the pile of fabrics on the couch and burst into tears.

"Don't fucking give me the fucking tears routine, you mother-fucking queer." Sam could not contain his rage. The cat looked up, decided this was the wrong place to be and padded to the kitchen with dignity.

"Only once," Freddy sobbed. "Only once, darling."

"Don't call me darling." Sam's voice was hoarse. "Where? When? Who with?"

"Oh, God, Sam, I love you, you know I do. Oh, my God, I don't know why, I swear I don't know how but..."

"Yes, go on." Sam's lips tightened into a thin line. There was so much anger in him he thought he would explode. His face was crimson and his heart was beating so fast he thought he might have a heart attack.

"It was two years ago." Freddy wiped his bloodshot blue eyes with a scrap of one-hundred-dollar-a-yard Fortuny silk. "At the bathhouse."

"The fucking bathhouse! Shit! Go on, who with?"

"I don't remember," whined Freddy.

"Remember!" Sam grabbed him by his mauve cashmere sweater and leaned his face close to Freddy's. "Fucking *remember,* or I'll fucking kill you."

"Oh, Sam...Sam. It was awful, awful. I couldn't help it. I was drugged. God knows why I did it. It's you I love. You know I do."

"Shut up, shmuck. I want *details.* All the details."

Gulping back his tears, Freddy tried to explain.

His friend from the airlines had arrived one night from Acapulco. He had brought a new kind of dope with him.

"Acapulco gold is a Marlboro compared to this," Hugh had told him, grinning from ear to ear.

341

They had smoked two joints, becoming so high that they didn't know what day it was—which was when Hugh suggested they visit the bathhouse. Since Sam had become Freddy's lover, bathhouses were strictly off-limits. But the dope had taken effect—Freddy no longer cared.

The place was jumping with the usual Saturday night insanity. The two men had showered and gone into the sauna room. Freddy, a handsome short blond man of thirty-nine, was usually highly sought after. Although he had saved himself exclusively for Sam for the past few years—except for a very occasional and discreet fling, that is—the dope had made him feel not only high but also extremely sexy. He was approached by the three gorgeous young studs he had observed oiling themselves on the beach this morning. He lay back as the boys attended to him expertly. It was mind-blowing. Ecstasy. Three or four other men stood around watching.

"Don't stop," begged Freddy. "I want more." By this time the other men were excited too. The first one rolled off Freddy and another took his place. Then the next, then the next. Freddy couldn't get enough of this incredible feeling. He felt like a satyr. The dope had made him insatiable.

"More," he begged, and they were only too eager to oblige.

Freddy's joy continued into the morning hours. But his shame lasted considerably longer.

"So that's it, my love," he said sadly to Sam. "That's what happened. I couldn't help it. I'm sorry. It won't ever happen again, I promise you."

"Too fucking late." Sam was weary now, disgusted with Freddy's story. "I've got AIDS. And you've probably got it. We're both going to *die,* Freddy, you know that, don't you?"

"Oh, God, what can we do?"

"Nothing." Sam sat heavily on the sofa, his anger spent. "There's nothing we can do now, Freddy, except wait."

• • •

Sam lost more weight each week. He had cleansed his system as much as possible, cutting out red meat, sugar, alcohol, salt and preservatives. He lived on the healthiest possible diet, slept ten hours a night, exercised, prayed, thought positively—and was terrified.

The hideous red scabs were gradually spreading all over his body until he could no longer bear to look at his flesh. He refused to allow his "Saga" dresser to help him when he changed. He lived in constant fear of being found out. He couldn't even confide the dreaded secret to Sissy. He didn't trust her—he didn't trust anyone.

His private line rang one lunch hour when he was restlessly trying to nap in his trailer.

"Sam, how are you. It's John Willows."

"Oh, hi, John. I'm ... I'm fine." He tried to muster a cheerfulness in his tone.

"Well, Sam, I've got some good news and some bad," the doctor said, trying to sound heartier than he felt. "Which do you want first, old man?"

"The good," said Sam.

"Well, old man, it looks like we've arrested the virus—in your case. I wouldn't say you were in remission exactly, but the tests we did on you last week showed a slight but definite improvement. I think this new experimental drug from France could be working."

"Great, great, that's wonderful news, old boy. Wonderful!" He felt instantly better. Arrested the virus! That meant he could maybe last for years, decades even. He smiled a genuinely happy smile for the first time in months.

There was a pause as John Willows cleared his throat—an embarrassed silence.

"And so what's the bad news, old man? Nothing could be *that* bad after what you've just told me."

"Well, old boy, I've just had a call from the clinic."

"What clinic?" asked Sam.

343

"The clinic where we sent your blood to be tested," said Dr. Willows, treading carefully.

"So—so what, what's so bad about that?" barked Sam.

"I have to level with you, Sam, this is terrible for you, I know, but when we sent your blood in to be tested, I told my assistant to put a phony name on it."

"Yes! Yes!" Sam sat bolt upright, almost screaming now. "So what happened?"

Silence.

"She did it, didn't she?" His voice rose to such a crescendo that Sissy, trying to nap in the trailer next door with earplugs in and eye mask on, sent her maid over to tell him to shut up.

"Fuck off!" Sam screamed at the woman as she knocked tentatively on his trailer door.

"I'm sorry, Sam," continued the doctor. "She didn't. She goofed. She's new, it was her first week here, fresh out of nursing school. Your name was on the blood sample we sent to the clinic. And there's a problem now. The problem is—"

"*Whaaat*—tell me what the fuck the problem is. I'm making a fucking series here, I can't shilly-shally around listening to you all day. *Tell me!!*"

"O.K., O.K., calm down, please. This is pretty embarrassing for me."

"Embarrassing?" Sam shrieked, out of control.

"I'm very sorry to tell you, Sam, that the clinic's confidential log book containing the names of all the individuals carrying the virus has been stolen."

"Stolen. *Stolen.* Who the hell would want to steal it?" Suddenly Sam thought he might black out. He groped for one of the cigars he hadn't touched in three months and tipped a bottle of Evian water to his lips.

"They think it's been stolen by blackmailers," the doctor said quietly.

344

"*Blackmailers!*" Now he knew he was going to faint.

"In fact, the police are pretty sure of it."

"Oh, my God, I'm ruined. I'm fucking ruined!"

"Well, if it's any consolation to you, old man, there are hundreds of others on that list who could possibly be ruined too. Prominent lawyers, politicians, doctors and actors. You're not the only actor in town who has AIDS, you know. It's rampant here. In San Francisco it's a nightmare. It's bankrupting the city."

"Jesus Christ, Jesus Christ, Jesus H. Christ," Sam kept repeating.

"I'm sorry, Sam. Look, I'll talk to you tomorrow. I—I have a few more calls I must make. You do understand?"

"Sure, John, sure, sure." Sam hung up and, head in hands, sat stonily until Sissy walked in.

"What is it, darling? You look positively *vile*. And why have you started that filthy habit again?"

Sam didn't answer. Sissy was wearing a fawn 1930s fitted suit, with a beige fox collar and muff, and a ridiculous Cossack hat. Her blond hair, teased to within an inch of its life, fuzzed out around the hat. Her eyes were shaded by eyelashes like awnings, her lips a thin crimson slash.

"Sam. Answer me, Sam," she snapped, used to his jumping to attention when she spoke.

He looked at her—at her angular hard body, her bony sparrow's face.

"Get out of here, Sissy, right now," he growled.

"Sam—I—"

"Get out, you cunt," he screamed. "Out, *out,* out of here. I don't want to see your bloody face again. Get out of my dressing room." The uproar caused two assistant directors and a couple of stand-ins to come over and gape at the normally charming, even-tempered star.

345

"Mr. Sharp, Mr. Sharp, calm down, *please.*" Debbie Drake shooed the others, including a furious Sissy, out of the trailer and slammed the door behind her.

"I'm sorry, sir. Is there anything I can do for you?"

"Nothing, dear, nothing. I'm sorry. Give me half an hour, Debbie, and I'll be back on the set. Tell Chelsea to shoot Sissy's close-up first. I just need a little time to myself, dear."

"Of course, sir, of course. We will give you as long as you need," she said, and tactfully left him, closing his trailer door quietly.

26

Horace Reid, editor of the *American Informer,*
flipped through the pages of the thin book with mounting excitement. What a coup! This list was dynamite. It was mind-
blowing. And to top it all it had come into his hands
anonymously. He hadn't had to pay a brass farthing for this
unbelievable and incriminating item. It would have cost at least
thirty thousand dollars if he had had to buy it.

"Six actors, three of them household names, four politicians,
two writers. It's *dynamite.* The hottest thing we've ever had.
We'll have the sellout issue of all time when we print this list.
We're gonna take TV ads, the works." The ugly little man
smirked with glee at his assistant, as he wondered fleetingly who

347

hated someone on the list enough to do this.

"We'll leak it a little bit at a time, I think," said Horace, picking his teeth with a paper clip. On the walls behind his desk were framed some of the more memorable best-selling front-page stories of the past decade:

"Marilyn Monroe a Lesbian." That had sold over eight million copies.

"I was Elvis' Love Child." Close to eight and a half million there.

"President Kennedy's Assassination: Masterminded by His Own Family." Another biggie.

Since leaving Australia and becoming editor of the *Informer* ten years ago, Horace Reid had turned the tabloid into a gold mine. He left no stone unturned to obtain the most intimate, degrading and damaging stories on celebrities: stars, politicians, British royalty. His assistant shook his head. "It's definitely an original. If anyone else *does* have it, we go to press first, don't we?" He smiled, revealing jagged yellow teeth.

"Look at these names," Horace said gleefully. "Look at 'em. It's a dream come true! I don't even know which name we should devote the bulk of the story to."

"I think it's obvious, don't you?" the other man said crisply. "Sam Sharp's the one. I mean...Star of 'Saga' Has AIDS. What a story! We'll sell ten million."

"You bet your bollocks, sport," chortled Horace Reid in his thick Australian accent. "That poor old poofter is finally going to pay for his sins, and we're going to have our best-selling issue ever. Whoopee!"

"Saga's" diminutive PR man, Christopher McCarthy, called Sam in his trailer a few days later.

"Sam, I'm a little worried."

"Why, what's up now?" Sam replied irritably. He was like a

cat on hot bricks these days, even taking to snorting a touch of cocaine each morning to get him out of his terrible black depressions.

"I've heard a rumor," began Christopher tentatively. "I know it's ridiculous, it couldn't *possibly* be true—and you can sue the arse off them, of course—but I've heard that the *Informer's* cover story for next week is the most disgraceful they've ever had. And I'm afraid it's about you."

"Me? About me?" Sam's words were a whisper. This couldn't possibly be true. So *soon?* It was impossible. "What about me?" He sat down. He felt nauseated.

"Well..." Christopher was embarrassed, but he was a good press agent so he had to get it out. It was his job. "They say you've got AIDS. I *know* it's ridiculous, Sam."

"It *is* ridiculous, it's disgraceful. Outrageous." Sam summoned up all his theatrical talent to make his outrage believable.

"It's disgusting," sighed Christopher. "They're unscrupulous bastards, those supermarket rags, absolute scum. Nevertheless we've got to fight this all the way, Sam. I think we should set up some interviews immediately: Oprah Winfrey, Carson and the morning news program. Then *People,* I'm sure, will do a cover story. I'll call Suzy, Liz Smith and the trades. We'll kill this whole thing. Defuse the story right away. Show them how great you look. This is a vicious smear campaign and we *cannot* let those bastards get away with it, right, Sam?"

"Right," Sam said wearily. He had slumped onto the couch, shakily trying to pour whiskey into a tumbler, but his hand was trembling so much that he dropped it.

"Are you *sure* about this story, Christopher? Are they *really* going ahead?"

"I'm afraid so. In fact, I'm positive," said Christopher grimly. "It's unfair, Sam. It's the pits. I'll keep you posted. Don't worry about anything. I'll set up the interviews, and prepare a statement for the press to go on the wire service immediately."

"Do that, Chris," said Sam softly. "Do that. I'd appreciate it."

Chloe and Sissy were having a heated argument on the set with Luis Mendoza. He stood arrogantly, arms crossed, in his black silk shirt and white linen trousers, gold chain adorning his neck, challenging the two divas of soap. It was rare for Sissy and Chloe to agree about anything, but in this case they had no choice. Luis was becoming a conceited oaf. His astonishing success had swelled his head and ego to such an extent that few people could handle him any longer.

This argument, about Luis's motivation in the scene, raged while the crew stood around watching. When the shot rang out, everyone thought it was from the cop series on the next sound stage. It was only when Debbie Drake, calling Sam's trailer, didn't get an answer, and so went to investigate, that they discovered what had happened. The hero of the United States, the actor who had so brilliantly portrayed Lincoln, Eisenhower and FDR—America's "real man"—had killed himself.

Calvin was glued to the television set in the prison common room. A second celebrity funeral in four years, and he was missing it. Soon there would be a third—and he'd be there that time. His lips parted in an animal snarl as he saw Chloe, escorted by Philippe, descend from a black Mercedes, dressed in dark gray and looking sad.

You're next, *madam!* he said to himself. Trumped-up bitch. She *deserved* to die.

"It's a nightmare, a fucking *nightmare*," ranted Abby, stomping up and down the Aubusson carpet in his football stadium of an office. "What the hell are we going to do?"

Gertrude's cuticles were picked to the quick. Her normally

well-groomed frizzy hair hadn't been combed for twenty-four hours, and the network was in a furor. Sam's suicide was tragedy enough; but when the *American Informer* came out with its AIDS cover story on him, it was crisis time.

Hate mail for Sam started pouring into the offices of the producers, and especially to Sissy.

The grief-stricken widow had retired to the seclusion of her Holmby Hills mansion for ten days, emerging only for the funeral, a fragile ninety-five-pound figure sheathed entirely in Oscar de la Renta black, wearing a veil as thick as a beekeeper's.

She had cried herself to sleep for ten straight nights. She missed Sam more than she had ever thought she could. But there was something else. So little was known about AIDS—could he somehow, even though they had not had sex together for years, have given it to her?

To those privileged to see the early rushes, "America: The Early Years" looked as if it was going to become a gigantic hit. The chemistry between Emerald and Josh was electrifying. Both were vibrant, dynamic and attractive. Sparks sizzled in their scenes together.

Emerald became seriously attracted to Josh, completely infatuated with his intelligence, his masculinity, his sensitivity and his fabulous sense of humor, listening to his anecdotes and jokes for hours. Josh loved having such an appreciative audience, but unfortunately he did not feel the slightest desire for her. He liked her—she was a competent actress and still a looker. Yes, she was in peak condition, all traces of the blowzy hag leaving jail just a few months before obliterated by a strict regimen of early nights, no dope, no alcohol and lots of exercise. But she was not his type, and he was going through a period of celibacy.

Emerald was happy in her work. She enjoyed "America," enjoyed being Queen Bee again, but she needed, wanted a man, and her luminous green eyes were firmly focused on Josh Brown. They spent a great deal of time together both during and after work, but however much Emerald practiced her feminine wiles on him, Josh was simply not biting. He did not want to become involved with her. She was a man-eater, an extremely demanding female in her relationships with men. He liked her but was not prepared to be her next man. He didn't want or need that. What he *did* need was to concentrate on his career, on keeping fit, steering clear of booze, broads and drugs, and making this the best damn show on prime time. In everyone's mind was the desire to beat "Saga" in the ratings. The network, the actors and the producers were all doing their utmost to make their show the best. And it was.

Long before the first episode of "America" aired, those who had seen some of the rushes were raving about the quality of the production and the performances of the cast, particularly Emerald and Josh. Emmy talk was bandied about. Eventually Chloe heard about it.

On Chloe's instructions, Vanessa had visited the set of "America" to check out the rumors and see what was going on. Vanessa had made a lunch date with Pandora King. Standing on the sidelines, watching Burt Hogarth direct, Vanessa realized this wasn't the usual hurried TV direction—this was feature time.

Each episode of "America" cost twice as much as "Saga." The network executives were tearing their hair out, but Hogarth had been given carte blanche on this production, and only if he failed to deliver in the ratings could they change anything. Until then, they realized they had a gem on their hands even if it cost a fortune. They would not rock Burt Hogarth's boat. "America" had more class than "Saga." It was masterly, artistic, stylish yet with a rugged outdoor realism depicting pioneer America. They were banking on the fickleness of the viewing public to switch gradually from "Saga" to "America."

Vanessa stood quietly in a dim corner of the set watching

Emerald and Josh rehearse. The rumors of their magnetism together were obviously true. Not only did Josh look more attractive than ever, but Emerald was as ravishing as she had been at
thirty-five. It was astonishing, since she was fifteen years older
than that, give or take. Granted, face-lifts and other plastic surgery and platinum hair can do a lot for a woman, but Emerald
had an undeniable glow about her, particularly when she was
close to Josh and looked at him with the eyes of a woman in
love. As a screen pair they sizzled.

Vanessa knew that she would have to report this news to
Chloe, who still cared for her ex-husband in spite of their separations. The rumors that Emerald and Josh were having a passionate affair and were crazy for each other were upsetting her
in spite of herself. Neither Emerald, Josh nor the network publi-
cists denied the story. It was great publicity for the show. From
the look of the two of them together on the set, Vanessa was
pretty sure the rumors were true.

Poor Chloe. Vanessa sighed. She disliked Philippe, and Vanessa knew that Chloe was becoming bored with him, despite
her assurances that their love life was as good as ever.

Wait until Chloe sees the "new" Josh, thought Vanessa. He
was a changed man: more at ease, more in control, more manly
and wittier than she remembered. He really was quite wonderful. His potential had come to fruition. Mmm, thought Vanessa.
If I still liked men, I might even go for him myself.

There was no point in telling Chloe she had any chance of
getting him back. He was obviously as crazy about Emerald as
she was about him. Vanessa watched them as, arm in arm, they
strolled toward the coffee machine, deep in conversation.

Chloe listened to Vanessa and died a little. So it was true. Oh,
well, she thought regretfully, how could Josh help but fancy
Emerald? According to Jasper, she was as beautiful and desirable as she'd ever been. Josh knew that Chloe was living with

Philippe. She hadn't even called him in the months he'd been back in California.

Stop thinking about Josh, she chided herself. Think about *Emerald*. If her looks and acting are as stunning as Vanessa, Jasper and half the town says they are, and the series is as brilliant as people think, "Saga" could be in serious trouble, and Chloe's reign as Queen of Prime Time could soon be over.

"Saga's" ratings started to slip badly three episodes into the new season. It was as though the public's love affair with the show had ended with Sam's death. As "Saga's" ratings dropped, "America: The Early Years," which had come into the Nielsen poll with a 20 share in the first week, started to accelerate. As each week it picked up one or two more ratings points, "Saga" dropped a couple. "America" was on the way up as "Saga" was on the way down.

At a meeting in the offices of Gertrude and Abby, the creative forces of "Saga" had come together to try and devise some new angles and clever story lines *fast*.

"Who got the most fan mail last month?" barked Abby to Bill Herbert.

"Chloe," replied Bill, consulting his notes. "Between ten and twelve thousand a month. That's more than any other series star, and she's been holding that average for over four years now."

"Who's next?" Abby was impatient. He already knew Chloe got the most.

"Well, it used to be Sissy, but since Sam...er...left us, it's dropped considerably. Actually, Luis Mendoza's mail has increased tremendously, especially after his first love scene with Chloe."

"We should definitely feature him more," murmured Gertrude.

"Make him more important. Now we've lost Sam, we need a

strong male character. You know it was Sissy and Sam who stopped Luis from getting a meatier story line. So let's build him up, make him our main male focus."

"He's strong all right." Bill grinned. "I've never seen so much erotic fan mail from women. You can't believe the things they say they'd like to do to him."

"Give him more screen time," said Abby curtly. "More love scenes, strong emotional scenes with Chloe."

"Make him the male lead," said Bill.

"Exactly," Abby replied. "Build him up. We've got to regain our ratings from 'America.' They're fucking destroying us. The network is pissed. They want to see some action." He turned to the show's three scriptwriters. "Now get to work, boys, write some juicy scenes, for Christ's sake. Otherwise we'll *all* be out of a job by the end of the season."

Josh looked at the magazine Perry had brought him. "From Has-been to TV Stardom." The cover of *People* magazine heralded the favorable article inside.

Josh's smiling face was on the cover. It was the face of a handsome, sexy, confident man in his forties. His hair, showing few traces of gray, was pushed casually forward to disguise the fact that his hairline had receded slightly. His tanned face had a few lines around the eyes, and wrinkles here and there, but they suited him. They were the lines that appeared on a face that laughed a lot. It was the face of a man at peace with himself, who accepted his age, was comfortable in his own skin.

Josh had gone through many changes since his latest comeback. He had learned from his past mistakes. In addition to giving up drugs completely, he had cut his drinking to a minimum and no longer chased young girls. With a newfound success in middle age, he lost the need to prove himself between the sheets with women young enough to be his daughters. A psychiatrist had helped, too.

He had the occasional girlfriend—usually a woman over thirty, but lovemaking now was secondary to what he wanted from a woman. Conversation, wit and humor, shared values, friendships were his requirements now. He looked for these in the women he dated, but although they had some of the qualities he admired, none had them all—he realized he had found them all together only in Chloe. Often he dreamed about her— about their life together before his career had started to go foul, before little dollybirds had loomed too large in his life.

In sessions with Dr. Donaldson, he realized what a shit he had been to her, how wonderful she had been to him.

Why, why did I screw it up? he often asked himself. The best goddamn woman I ever had and I fucking ruined it. Shit!

He sometimes fantasized that he and Chloe had reconciled, were together again as they once had been. He had never met a woman with whom he had enjoyed life so much, whose humor was on his own wavelength, who so completely understood him. God, what he'd put her through. How many reconciliations had they had? He couldn't remember. He'd been too heavily into nose candy and nymphets at the time. Trying to bolster his flagging career. Sticking his prick into whoever asked for it, and some who didn't.

And Chloe had known. But she had been there for him until it had become unbearable for her.

He heard she was happy with Philippe. He was glad for her, although it gave him a pang every time he saw pictures of them together. Occasionally they bumped into each other at a social or industry function—the People's Choice Awards, the Emmys, or a Beverly Hills screening room. She was always on Philippe's arm, smiling and friendly. Chloe was not one to bear a grudge, and she was genuinely happy for Josh's success.

If it was a scientific principle that no two objects can share the same space at the same time, then Chloe knew there was not enough room for Philippe in her life. She still thought subconsciously about life with Josh, although conscious thoughts of him were banished from her mind with military precision. But her dreams were peopled with images of their life as it had once been. Her weekdays were filled with "Saga" work, "Saga" minutiae, time-consuming problems with script revisions, dialogue changes, costuming, set politics. The public could never imagine what a hard, unglamorous drudge grinding out a prime time TV series could be. Her weekends were spent in a mindless daze drifting about the house without makeup, in a track suit, lazing, with Philippe ever attentive nearby.

Philippe's idea of a fun-filled evening was to watch three videos back to back, make love a couple of times and dine on takeout pizza in bed. Chloe, exhausted from her unrelenting pressure of work, enjoyed this at the beginning of the relationship, but she soon began to realize that culturally and conversationally Philippe was dull. True, he filled the present need in her life for companionship without effort, intimacy without commitment, closeness without true emotional involvement—and she was fond of him. He demanded little of her except her presence, and since she was usually so exhausted after work, for a while this was welcome.

But on the rare occasions when they made the social rounds of the Bel Air circuit, he often succeeded in embarrassing her by his lack of depth and obliviousness to anyone other than himself or Chloe. It was, nevertheless, flattering to be so adored, thought Chloe as she observed Philippe lolling sleepily on a Regency satin couch at one of Daphne's star-studded soirees. Around him thronged two dozen of Hollywood's most famous and scintillating individuals, the women resplendent in designer dresses, designer jewelry and designer cosmetic surgery, the men all distinguished, whether they were six feet four and hirsute or five feet two and bald.

Chloe's friends had all made genuine efforts to conduct a civilized conversation with Philippe during the eighteen months that

357

he and Chloe had lived together. All had eventually decided that it was a waste of time. He had little to say, no opinions to speak of, and other than his obsession with Chloe and his dashing good looks, none of them saw what she could find remotely interesting about him. Chloe found herself thinking the same thing as she touched up her makeup in Daphne's powder room. They had often quarreled about his lack of enthusiasm and his lack of interest in her friends, but he refused to compromise, making no attempt to ingratiate himself, leaving Chloe embarrassed by his dullness, and her women friends changing place cards in desperation at dinner parties so as not to sit next to him.

Chloe sighed as she adjusted the sleek lines of her black silk Donna Karan dress. The thought of sitting on the sofa attempting to talk to Philippe, who would try to make an early getaway so that he could watch another video and try and jump on her for the third time that Saturday, was not enthralling. The man was insatiable, and she was wearying of his incessant sexual demands and lack of communicativeness and empathy.

"Bored, let's face it, duckie, you're *bored stiff* with him, aren't you?" Daphne interrupted Chloe's reverie, red curls springing animatedly around her chubby Cupid's face, as she entered the room with her usual gusto.

"I mean, he really *is* dull as dishwater, dear. Good-looking or not, I know you can do so much better. Don't you think it's time to dump him? I know this *divine* Italian marquis who is coming to town next week. Dying to meet you, duckie. If not you, then Linda Gray is his second choice. What do you think?"

She plucked off a few loose beads on the bodice of her old, but still serviceable, Norman Hartnell frock, and squinted at her abundant curves with satisfaction. At well over sixty-five, she was still a good-looking, sexy woman. She knew it and it had been proven many times throughout the past four decades by the number of stars who had shared her bed.

The walls of her tiny guest loo were decorated from floor to paisley-tented ceiling with photographs of Daphne in the company of many of Hollywood's and Europe's most famous celebrities. There were over one hundred framed pictures dating back to the late 1940s when Daphne and Jasper Swanson had descended to the shores of Malibu and the hills of Beverly fresh from their respective successes in England—his at Gainsborough Studios, where he had starred in a dozen swashbuckling adventure films, and hers initially through a contract wihh Sir Alexander Korda, who had tried unsuccessfully to turn her into a clone of either Vivien Leigh or Merle Oberon. When the realization hit Sir Alex that red curls, a perky smile and a thirty-nine-inch bust cannot compete with alabaster skin, smoldering black hair and a sylphlike body, he sold her contract to Ealing Studios, where she did rather better in black-and-white comedies with Alec Guinness and Jack Warner.

Chloe looked at the attractively saturnine face of thirty-six-year-old Jasper and vibrant thirty-year-old Daphne laughing arm in arm with the Oliviers and Sir Ralph Richardson on the lawn of Highgrove one long-ago summer afternoon. In another photo, Daphne gazed fondly into the faces of a handsomely togaed Richard Burton and a Grecian-draped Jean Simmons on the set of *The Robe*, a CinemaScope epic in which Daphne had played a small part. Daphne was smiling and laughing in many other photos in the company of what were, the gossips said, some of her many lovers. Errol Flynn, Gary Cooper, David Niven, William Powell—Daphne had been rumored to have bedded them all, but would neither confirm nor deny to even her closest chums which, if any, of those illustrious lads she had tumbled with.

"Let's just say all my lovers have been well-endowed," she would laughingly reply to anyone inquisitive enough to ask. "Both *above* and *below* the belt, I require the utmost stimulation. Big cocks are not enough. I need big brains too.

"Take a look at him, duckie." Daphne pointed with a long vermilion fingernail at a photo of herself with a young, very handsome blond boy taken on a film set in about 1950.

"That's the sort of man you should meet, dear heart." She sighed. "Dusty Lupino. He was a big star and one of the best lovers I ever had. I taught him a great deal too—even though he was eighteen and I was—ah—eh—over thirty. He's rich as Croesus now, duckie, and *still* only fifty-six. His business manager got him out of the movie business and into real estate when you could still buy half of Rodeo Drive for under a million. He's never looked back, and still looks divine, even if he is a bit of a recluse."

"Darling, darling! *Stop*. I *know* what you're saying. Philippe is not right for me. I'm aware of that. I'm not as much of a fool as everyone thinks, Daphne darling. Yes, we squabble. Yes, he's not very stimulating or entertaining. But for *now*, Daphne, dear, I'm living with him, and when we end it, which, as you say, and as I *know*, is inevitable, I shall then cast my eyes further afield, but *not yet*, my dear." She bent and kissed Daphne's Coty-perfumed cheek. "Not yet. I can only handle one man at a time."

"What a quaint, old-fashioned girl you are," sighed Daphne in mock exasperation as they went back to the party. "But remember, dear, when you *are* ready to dump him, all your friends will be rooting for you."

"O.K., creep, time to get the fuck out of here." The guard picked at a boil on his chin. "Better not try anything again, creep. You'll be in a lot of trouble if you do. Now git!"

Calvin ignored the man. He was free. Free at last to go where he wanted—do what he wanted. He had to find her now. Track her down. Make her suffer, as he had suffered over the years.

Although he had read in the tabloids that Emerald had the

lead in the new series, "America: The Early Years," it continued to infuriate him that Chloe Carriere was such a huge star in "Saga," which was still a phenomenal success. He couldn't stand Chloe. He loathed her arrogance in that part. He detested her trumped-up English accent. He despised everything about her. Most of all he hated her because she was the reason his beloved Emerald had hit rock bottom. She had to be punished.

27

"And now, ladies and gentlemen, it's America's Favorites!" The crowd applauded frantically. Whistles and shrieks of appreciation greeted the master of ceremonies as he announced the nominees in each category.

Chloe and Philippe had arrived late. They smiled for the phalanx of fans and paparazzi who were gathered like a flock of sheep outside the Santa Monica Civic Auditorium. She held his tuxedoed arm, looked into his smiling face, smiled for the cameras—Mr. and Mrs. Togetherness, a portrait of bliss, even though they weren't wed.

Tonight was an important night. These January awards, both

for films and TV, were considered the harbingers of the Emmys and the Oscars later that year.

Chloe wore a magnificent Christian Dior white taffeta dress, which cinched her waist and pushed up her bosom. Her black hair was piled high with diamanté combs, and around her neck was a beautiful Georgian rose diamond necklace that Vanessa had found for her.

As she and Philippe settled themselves, with whispered apologies, at the "Saga" table, where Sissy, Luis, Abby, Gertrude and Bill Herbert were already seated, Chloe glanced around the auditorium. Josh was smiling at her. She smiled back. After all, he was her ex-husband. "We must be polite, dear," said Sissy snidely. She was dressed from shoulders to toes in yellow bugle beads that matched her hair. The six-month period of mourning was over and she was playing the merry widow with a good-looking young actor on her arm.

"Pour me some wine, darling, will you?" Chloe murmured to Philippe. "You drink too much," he whispered too loudly. Surreptitiously she looked over at Josh again. He was with Emerald, who looked dazzling in a mint-green silk jersey Empire gown, the bodice embroidered in four-leaf clovers.

"How cute!" sneered Sissy. "She needs all the luck she can get: Tyne Daly is the hot favorite tonight."

It was a night of extreme competition. "Saga" and "America" were competing with "Hill Street Blues," "Dynasty" and "Cagney and Lacey" for best dramatic TV series.

Chloe, Sissy, Emerald, Tyne Daly and Sharon Gless were up for best actress in a dramatic TV series. Josh and Luis, Daniel Travanti and Larry Hagman were nominated for best dramatic actor.

The tension was palpable as one by one glittering stars of screen and TV paraded their finery onto the stage either to present an award or accept one.

Chloe, having won the past two years, was less concerned than the others about the coveted crystal statuettes. She felt that Tyne or Sharon Gless definitely deserved one for their consistently fine work in "Cagney and Lacey."

Emerald was desperate for the award. "America: The Early Years" was only in its first season, but it was a huge success— now neck and neck with "Saga." Winning would be a major step for her and complete her comeback.

Josh didn't really care. He had quickly joined the rarefied ranks of mature TV leading men and it would not mean anything to his career one way or another. What *did* mean something to him, although he was reluctant to admit it, was the beautiful black-haired woman in the white gown sitting two tables away.

Goddamn it, Josh, he said to himself for the hundredth time, why did you mess up that relationship? How the hell could you have let that woman go? You loved her, she adored you....

Emerald pulled at his sleeve and whispered animatedly into his ear, but he hardly listened. He was watching Chloe out of the corner of his eye, across a room filled with some of the most beautiful women in the world. His Chloe. His forever lover, gone now forever. He watched her bend her dark head to Philippe's brown one, smile at something the Frenchman said, and put her pale hand on his arm in the loving gesture he remembered only too well. She raised her hand to Philippe's hair and ruffled it. She used to do that to me, thought Josh fiercely. They certainly looked happy, gazing into each other's eyes, fingertips touching. There was something about the tall Frenchman that Josh didn't like. He envied his relationship with Chloe, but there was something else that he couldn't quite put his finger on. It was a quality many people felt about Philippe. He made them uneasy.

Josh came out of his reverie to hear the nominations for best actress being announced.

Emerald had a hand on his knee, which became more viselike as each name was called. She was about to cut off his circulation. He could see her moist cyclamen lips parted in anticipation, longing. She was lusting for this award, this accolade to symbolize her return to the top of the heap.

He glanced at Chloe, who looked cool, calm and collected. Sissy's face wore a fixed smile. She too was dying for this award. She had won it the same year she won the Oscar. It was time again. She deserved it. Hers was a performance—an acting tour de force. She was a wonderful actress; everyone knew it. Certainly for someone of her rancorous nature to bring such believability to the cloying role she played proved she indeed had considerable talent.

The "Cagney and Lacey" actresses looked self-possessed. Their show was a hit, too. This award wouldn't affect it—or them—much. It would just be icing.

"The envelope, please." Don Johnson was presenting this award. "And the winner is..." He paused, looking mischievously at the audience, milking the moment.

"Once again, Miss Chloe Carriere!" A shriek of delight came from the fans and audience high in the gallery of the auditorium. Almost as loud was the cry from Chloe, who threw her arms around Philippe in a bear hug that almost strangled him, blew kisses to everyone at her table and, in a flurry of white taffeta, ascended the stage to make her acceptance speech.

In the gallery, Calvin's fury turned his face scarlet. It was Emerald, the Goddess, who deserved this honor. She truly deserved it. Not this second-rate British bitch. How *dare* she take Emerald's award?

His binoculars focused on Chloe's slim figure as she addressed the audience and the millions of TV fans. She expressed her happiness, thanked the cast, the crew, Jasper, blew a kiss, wept a little and was escorted triumphantly off the stage by Don Johnson, holding the statuette high above her head.

Calvin turned his binoculars on Emerald. She had removed a tiny lace hanky from her rhinestone Judith Leiber purse and was blowing her nose. *She was crying!* Chloe Carriere had made his darling weep! Bitch!

Josh was trying to comfort Emerald when the award for best actor was announced. "And the winner is Joshua Brown for 'America: The Early Years,'" Angie Dickinson announced with a big smile. Calvin ignored Josh's hasty departure to collect his award and continued to focus his attention and his binoculars on his lovely Emerald. He hated to see her hurt like this. Chloe, done up like a dog's dinner in virgin white, would pay for this. The time was coming for Miss Carriere. Oh, the time was coming *soon*.

In the eighth week of the fall season, "Saga" was rated the number two show and "America" number one. One week later the ratings were reversed: "America" was number two, "Saga" number one. The following week, "America" held its lead but "Saga" lost a couple more ratings points, dropping to number six.

Panic reigned at MCPC. Advertisers started to cancel the time slots on "Saga," which they now thought were overpriced. They preferred to sell their products on the rival network where, with more viewers tuned to "America," their goods would sell better. The network was giving Abby and Gertrude a hard time. They must make the shows more exciting, more dramatic, meatier, so that they could regain their lost audiences. Gertrude and Abby screamed at the line producer, Bill Herbert, they screamed at the writers, they screamed at the actors and crew. An emergency conference was called with Sissy, Luis and Chloe, to pick their brains for fresh story ideas. Everyone seemed to be becoming desperate to get back their place in the sun.

Chloe was not too concerned. She had always realized that the flavor of the month had to change. She still felt loyal to the show and enjoyed it, but she was looking forward to accepting other offers of miniseries and movies, singing again, making a video for MTV.

Luis hoped "Saga" would be canceled. He was hot for movies now. Jasper had three sizzling offers for him in the spring. In one he could even star with Sabrina. He felt he had done enough TV, although he had been in "Saga" little over a year. He wanted to move on, become a real movie star.

Sissy, perennially discontented, wanted to stay with "Saga." Since she now owned her own *and* Sam's points in the show, she was making a fortune. She would make even more when it went into syndication.

After losing the America's Favorites award to Chloe, Emerald had gone on another bender. Increasingly frustrated and upset by Josh's lack of interest in her as a woman, she had again sought solace in liquor. Try as she might, she could not get him to play her game. He had told her frankly, "Look, Emerald, I think you're great. You're a terrific woman, beautiful, fun to be with. I just don't think of you that way." Emerald bit her lip until it almost bled. Rejection from a man was hard for her—it had happened so rarely. Was this a portent of her future?

They were in Josh's car outside her house, having just returned from a screening and dinner at Corinna and Freddie Fields's house. Emerald had had many glasses of champagne and, feeling frisky, she tried to embrace Josh, but he had drawn away from her.

"Please, Emerald. I want to be your friend, I've told you that so many times. It's better that way."

"Why?" Emerald almost yelled. "Why just *friends?*" She spat the words. "We've got so *much* going for us, Josh. I don't have anyone in my life right now and I don't think you do...do you?"

Josh didn't answer. He lit a Marlboro and stared out at the starless sky.

"Do you, Josh? If you do, tell me and I'll...oh, hell, I'll get over it." A tear slid down her matte-complexioned cheek and dripped onto her green satin Enrico Coveri lounging pajamas. He remained silent, smoking, his strong profile etched against the door of his Porsche.

"Are you in love with someone?" she asked again, so persistently that he turned to her and said quietly, "Yes, Emerald, I suppose I am. I am 'in love,' as you say, with someone else."

"Who is it?" He was silent. She *had* to know. "It's Chloe, isn't it?" She felt bitterness. "It's your ex-wife, isn't it?"

"She's *not* my ex-wife—not yet—and, yes, well, you're right. I haven't quite got over my feelings for her."

"Oh, my God! Have you been seeing her?" Emerald took the cigarette from Josh's hands and took a deep drag.

"No, absolutely not. She's living with Philippe Archambaud. But I'd like to."

"Damn, shit, hell!" cried the diva as she jumped out of his car and ran into her house in tears. *How could he reject her?* Emerald Barrymore. World-renowned beauty, idol of millions. Legendary sex goddess. How *could* he? She couldn't understand it. Not when she was looking so good and was so successful. She realized she was acting ridiculously but she couldn't help it. She loved him. Why couldn't he love her back?

Josh started his car and drove off. No point trying to calm her now. It was a difficult situation. He wanted to keep their working relationship a good one. It seemed that might be a little harder now. Oh, hell, he thought, I'd better send her flowers tomorrow.

His driving away infuriated Emerald even more. "Damn

you," she muttered and climbed into her Mercedes to follow him down the canyon to the bright lights of Santa Monica Boulevard.

The police picked her up four hours later, hopelessly drunk, without a driving license, and weaving her car in and out of the Sunset Boulevard traffic. It took four cops to subdue her enough to get her into the police car, and a passing Japanese tourist with a camera made a fortune from the photographs he took of her and sold to the *American Informer* for a cover story.

Her second sojourn in a jail cell garnered even more publicity than the first. Out-of-control drunken TV actors were not what viewers wanted. Drunken actresses were even more of a turnoff. When the torrent of unfavorable press came out, turn off they did.

The ugly front-page photograph of Emerald fighting the police who arrested her harmed "America's" ratings enormously. Public sympathy turned against her. The ratings started to plummet and soon "Saga" rose like a phoenix from the ashes back to the number two spot again.

Calvin reread the article in *Daily Variety*. " 'Saga' boffo in ratings war once more gains five points." His lips clenched in fury. He had just returned from another fruitless attempt to find out Chloe's new address, having failed to gain entrance to the "Saga" studio where he knew she would be. He had bought a map to the movie stars' homes from a crone sitting under a faded umbrella in the boiling sun on Sunset Boulevard and staked out the vine-covered house on Blue Jay Road identified as hers for two weeks. But he never saw Chloe either coming or going. Three times the police had moved him on. Then, not wanting to arouse more suspicions, he had kept away for a few days. Eventually he struck up a conversation with the young housekeeper after bumping into her "accidentally" at Hughes supermarket one morning. She was pretty, with long blond hair and a cute Scandinavian accent. Casually he had asked what it was like working for Chloe Carriere, the famous TV star.

The girl had laughed at him as she threw packages of frozen peas into her basket. "I vork for Dr. Sidney, the famous plastic surgeon." She giggled. "I don't think he even knows Chloe Carriere, unless he did her face."

Calvin went back to the map-selling hag and screamed at her for selling false information.

She shrugged. "Listen, fella, half the names on that list are dead. The other half has moved. I don't print it, I just sell it. So fuck off, fella, otherwise I'll stick this to ya." She revealed a switchblade gleaming under her torn dress. Calvin backed away from the old witch. He had other fish to fry. He had to find Chloe's address.

On Hollywood's biggest night, Academy Awards night, Mary and Irving Lazar threw their celebrated annual Oscar party at Spago. Every major name from movies and TV attended. The women wore their most gorgeous gowns and the men were equally elegant.

Irving Lazar—"Swifty" to his friends and foes—circulated through the well-dressed throng, dodging TV cameras and paparazzi and having a word and a joke with everyone.

Chloe sat at a corner table with Philippe and Annabel. She was glad Irving had invited Annabel to attend as it was a very insular Hollywood party—superstars and megacelebrities only. Annabel was again visiting from London. She and Chloe had developed a very close relationship.

Philippe didn't say much. Chloe sighed. When you ran out of things to say to each other, it was a sure sign of serious trouble in a relationship. She knew the relationship was more than just sour, yet she didn't have the heart to end it.

Across the room a battery of flashbulbs popped as Emerald and Josh entered Spago. Emerald looked radiant again in a jade-green velvet gown with deep décolletage. All traces of the drunken harridan of last month were erased. She certainly can pull herself together in a hurry, thought Chloe. Emerald was smiling glowingly as she gazed at Josh, who returned her look affectionately.

Chloe turned away. They seemed in love, so happy. She glanced at Philippe, who was eying a new redheaded vamp at a nearby table, brought in to boost "America's" ratings.

Emerald and Josh were being seated at a table in the center of the room. Oh, Lord, thought Chloe, Josh is right in my eyeline. He was indeed positioned in a such a way that when she turned her head to the left she was directly facing him.

He came over to her table as soon as he saw her, gave Philippe a manly handshake, Annabel a hug, and Chloe a kiss on the cheek. She shivered when she looked into his eyes. He was, if anything, more attractive than ever; there was a quality of tenderness and compassion about him now that he had never possessed before.

Soon it was time for everyone in the room to become absorbed in the large TV screens which had been set up at strategic points throughout the restaurant. Chloe could not concentrate on who was winning, on the delicious pizzas with smoked salmon and caviar, on the vintage champagne. She kept sneaking glances at Josh.

This is idiotic, she said to herself. Stupid. A grown woman, a *middle-aged* woman at that, mooning like a schoolgirl.

During one of the commercial breaks, as she and Annabel were in the powder room, Emerald swept in.

The two women eyed each other. Although they had attended a number of Hollywood parties, it was the first time they had been alone together since "America" had begun. The only other person in the room was Annabel, who was now in the cubicle.

"Hello, Emerald." Chloe smiled, extending her hand.

Emerald didn't take the proffered hand. She simply stared, stunned with jealous anger as she realized that the sensational diamond-and-emerald bracelets encircling Chloe's wrist were *her* bracelets. Her favorite jewels, the last to be sold to Vanessa to keep the wolf from her door. Bitch! Chloe now possessed her bracelets *and* her man. It was just as many people said of her in this town—Chloe was a nouveau-riche conniving bitch, and Emerald detested her.

Suddenly she leaned against the door, facing Chloe with a strange expression. Chloe realized she was more than a little drunk.

Fishing a phial of scent from her purse, she turned to the mirror.

"So now I know," said Emerald, her speech slurred. "Now I *really* know."

"Know what?" Chloe applied fragrance rapidly behind her ears, wishing Annabel would exit so they could leave.

"What he sees in you, of course," Emerald hissed.

"Who is *he?*" Chloe said, her voice betraying little of the emotion she felt.

"Josh, of course." Emerald gave a brittle laugh. "He loves you, don't you know that? He's never *stopped* loving you. Aren't *you* the lucky girl?" She staggered to the mirror, pretending to be busy combing her hair but Chloe saw that her eyes were blurred with tears.

"How do you know that?" In spite of herself she had to ask. Was it true? Could Josh still care as much as she did? Nonsense. It was nonsense, Emerald was stoned out of her skull.

"He told me." Emerald looked at Chloe's reflection in the mirror. "He *told* me he loves you. Always has. Big deal. Who cares? *I* certainly don't. We're just friends—good friends—and that's how it's gonna be." She turned away to inspect her painted face, dismissing Chloe with a shrug of jade velvet Giorgio di Sant'Angelo shoulder pads.

Annabel came out and Chloe grabbed her arm as they quickly left the ladies' room.

"I *heard,* Chloe. I heard it all," said her daughter. "Do you think it's true? Do you think Josh is still in love with you?"

"I don't know, darling. I really don't. She's drunk."

"Well I hope he is," said the girl, affectionately squeezing her arm. "You know how I feel about Philippe."

The two went back to the festivities. For the rest of the evening, Chloe tried to avoid Josh's eyes, but as winner after winner appeared on the TV screen and made their speeches, she heard none of them. All she could think of were Emerald's words.

"Give that bouquet of flowers the archer." Chelsea Deane was peering through the viewfinder on the set of Chloe/Miranda's boudoir.

"The what? What is he talking about?" prop man number one asked prop man number two.

"Beats me, Stu, ask him. These limeys sure have a strange way of talking."

"Sorry, Chelsea, what d'you mean?"

"*Archer,* that's slang for Get rid of it," Chelsea yelled with exasperation.

"What the hell's an archer?" yelled the prop man.

"Oh, Gawd, sorry, thought I was at Pinewood for a sec!" Chelsea smiled his captivating cockney grin. "Spanish Archer— El-*bow,* get it?" The two prop men scratched their heads.

"*Elbow* the flowers—get rid of 'em," Chelsea said with an up-and-down movement of his elbow, irritated by the man's obtuseness. Chloe gave him a sympathetic glance from where she sat with Vanessa and a coterie of makeup, hair and wardrobe assistants. She was trying to run through her lines with her dialogue coach, while the girls gossiped around her.

"O.K., first team, ready for you," called Ned.

"Second team can relax."

The couple who had been standing in the middle of the set for

373

the past fifteen minutes while the crew set up the camera and lights went off to the coffee stand. Chloe and Luis took their places. They walked through the scene for marks only. After every move, the camera assistant used his tape measure to judge the distance from their faces to the camera.

God forbid it should be a millimeter out of focus in dailies tomorrow. Gertrude and Abby would scream blue murder, and if it happened more than twice, heads would roll, in particular, the camera assistant's—so he was a careful fellow.

It was freezing cold on the set today. As usual, the heating had gone on the blink. The studio was over fifty years old, freezing in the winter and boiling in the summer.

"That's when they put the bleedin' 'eatin' an' air conditionin' in," said Chelsea acidly. "Fifty bleedin' years ago."

The crew all wore sweaters, parkas and scarves, but Chloe had on a low-cut black chiffon dress. The only thing she had to keep her warm was four hundred dollars' worth of Kenny Lane rhinestones around her neck.

They shot the master. They had to do it four times because once an airplane could be heard on the sound track, the second time a visitor coughed in the middle of Luis's impassioned "I love you, Miranda," and in the third Chloe caught her heel in the carpet.

Eventually Chelsea printed the fourth take. "All right. That's a print. Let's go in for coverage. We'll do Luis's close-up first, Chlo, you can relax, darlin'."

Brad, from Abby and Gertrude's office, came on the set and handed around a piece of paper with last night's ratings score on it.

Chloe was glad to see that last night they had taken their time slot by a good margin and had got a thirty-one share that would definitely put "Saga" among the top ten prime time shows this week.

"How did 'America' do last night?" she inquired.

"They're doing *very* well," enthused Brad, even though they were on the rival network. "Very well indeed. They're a big hit. Of course, Josh winning the award helped. The public have certainly taken to your ex, haven't they?"

Chloe was glad for Josh. She had sent him a cymbidium plant and a congratulatory note after he won. She wondered how he was. She hoped he was happy. She wished *she* were happier and wished she could do something about the information Emerald had drunkenly given her. Trouble with Philippe again. Another ridiculous row over nothing. *Why* was he so spiteful? Recently he had started to ridicule her. He called her "Diva" and "Megastar." What was wrong with him?

"Darling, you'll never *guess* who I saw today!" Red hair hidden by pink rollers, Daphne sat next to Chloe under the dryer at the Bill Palmer Salon, ready for a good gossip.

Chloe put down her magazine and smiled at her friend. She never failed to be amused by Daphne, whom she basically thought kind and funny, although a bit of a chatterbox.

"Joshua Brown, darling—looking, I *must* say, very, very fanciable indeed." Chloe's heart skipped. Jungle drums started beating whenever she heard his name.

"Where?" She casually lit a cigarette. "Where did you see him?"

"At his new house at the beach, darling. I interviewed him for *TV Faces.*"

"How was it? I mean, how was he?" Chloe was interested, intrigued. Damn it, she thought, I wish I weren't.

"Wonderful," gushed Daphne. "Darling, he is *so* divine, full of the old S.A. What a man! I mean, my knees were so all of a tremble I could barely balance my pad in my lap."

"You don't use a tape recorder?"

"Of course I do, dearie. The pad is for background, you can't record *that*. Color of sofa, what he was wearing, that sort of thing."

"What *was* he wearing?" Chloe was curious in spite of herself.

"Blue shirt," Daphne said breathlessly. "Open, very simple. Very sexy. He's got a wonderful body, Chloe."

"I know, dear. I was married to him, remember?"

"How could I forget?" Daphne laughed. "Anyway, darling, we had this terrific *in depth* conversation. He told me *all* about his drinking and drugging—how it destroyed him."

"Did he tell you all about his schoolgirls?" Chloe asked sarcastically.

"I'll get to that," Daphne said crossly. "Don't interrupt, dear. Anyway he told me that *he* was the one who ruined your marriage because of his drug taking. He said what a wonderful woman you are—the best ever." Daphne smiled as she saw Chloe blush slightly.

"Anyway he was going on about you when his valet or whoever came in with a *terribly* important call from South America —something to do with a film he's going to do out there next year, so he excused himself and went and took the call."

"And?" Chloe was more than interested.

"Well, darling, he'd left the door to his inner sanctum open. I absolutely couldn't resist—I peeped in, and *what* do you think I saw?"

"What?" Chloe smiled. She liked this.

"One whole wall, darling, is covered, I mean literally *covered,* with photos of you."

"Come on—you're joking."

"No, darling. I mean it. There must be twenty pictures of you. You alone, you with him, you and Annabel—even your wedding photo." She leaned forward to give Chloe a conspiratorial nudge. "I think he still loves you, dear, I really do. This is obviously his most private room. Oh, and there was also one of your records on the stereo—your last one, the love ballad." She leaned back triumphantly under the dryer as she waited for Chloe's reaction.

"Well, Daphne, what a regular little Sherlock Holmes you are. That *is* interesting, darling, but I'm not interested in him. What's over is over."

"Nonsense," said Daphne. "You never got him out of your system. If you had, you would have signed your final divorce papers *and* you would have married Philippe by now."

"I'm allergic to marriage," said Chloe sincerely. "I'm not good at it."

"You were *very* good at it, dearie, for all the years you were married to Josh. You looked the other way when he was unfaithful. You ignored his drug problems. You put up with a lot of naughtiness from him. You were too easy with him and too forgiving, dear. Treat 'em mean, keep 'em keen!"

"I know, I know. Look, Daphne, don't go on. I told you, it's over, I'm happy with Philippe," she said crossing her fingers. She hated to lie.

Daphne's dryer buzzed. "I must dash now, darling. I'm doing a cover story for *US* on Sabrina Jones."

"Come to dinner next Saturday. Philippe's barbecuing," called Chloe.

"Love to, duckie," said Daphne, aware that she had stirred certain unexpressed feelings in Chloe.

Alone for a moment, Chloe sat very still, one thought continuously turning over and over in her mind. Emerald had told her the truth.

Calvin had finally managed to find a way to get onto the set. He had struck up a friendship with Debbie Drake, the assistant director. He had observed her every day after work, going into the bar across from the studio. She usually sat and drank a few beers with the crew before getting into her little red Mustang and driving home to Westlake. He spent several days sitting at the bar observing her. She was a friendly soul, and it was not difficult to become acquainted with her. He cultivated their camaraderie over the weeks, although it made him feel disloyal to Emerald. Her hair was long and pretty and she had a nice smile and a pleasant personality, but Calvin didn't care about the girl one bit. All he wanted was to win her confidence and friendship enough to gain access to the "Saga" set.

One day he casually mentioned that he would like to visit the set as he was a great admirer of Sissy Sharp. Debbie, ever anxious to please, arranged a visitor's pass for him.

One fine spring afternoon, when the temperature hovered in the nineties, Calvin Foster entered the "Saga" set for the first time.

28

*P*hilippe, his face flushed, stood before Chloe. His cream crocodile shoes contrasted with his immaculately creased dark-brown trousers. He was impeccably turned out, as usual, even though it was seven in the morning and the temperature was stifling.

Chloe, with a slight hangover from the previous night, was attempting to get ready in her dressing room. She was already half an hour late. It was unprofessional to be late, and it threw the assistant director into a flap.

"*Chérie,* we have *got* to talk about this video offer. I thought you *wanted* to get back into singing again." He kept waving the contract in front of her as she zoomed around the room trying to dress, clean her teeth and brush her tangled curls.

"Look, Philippe, I *can't,* I simply *cannot* discuss it now. I'm terribly late, can't you see?"

"We must agree on this deal, *chérie*. You're *always* too busy these days—putting things off, procrastinating. Now, sweetheart—*calm* down—sit down and let's read the contract together for a minute."

"Philippe, listen to me, damn it!" Her rage, the rage she was saving for Miranda's scenes with Sirope today, had built up so much she could no longer control it.

"I have to leave now! I have a hangover. I've had four hours' sleep. *Please,* Philippe, let me go to work." Her face was flaming, the heat and anger making her heart skip several beats. Could women in their forties have heart attacks? she wondered fleetingly. "We'll have to talk later, Philippe. Tonight, I promise you."

"O.K., O.K. You never listen to me, I'm just a dog. Forget the video deal—we'll just forget it, see if I care. I was doing it for you, but you never appreciate my efforts, *Miss Diva.*"

She felt she couldn't bear another day of his sulking. "Darling, look, I know the video deal is important. I don't want to forget it, let's discuss it at the studio after work, before we go to Jasper's dinner, O.K.?" She gave him a fleeting kiss and as much of a smile as she could muster.

"O.K., O.K., we always have to fit in with your plans," he grumbled, semi-placated by Chloe's affectionate gesture.

"Well, I *am* the one who has to be a 'Saga' slave," she said, throwing on a scarf and sunglasses and noticing in her full-length mirror that she needed to lose three pounds again. "Come to the studio about sevenish, darling. It will be quiet then, we can go over the contract thoroughly without being bothered. Bye now, darling, I *must* go."

Shooting went slowly. The sudden heat wave had affected cast and crew alike, and, as usual, the air conditioner was not working properly. It seemed to Chloe that the temperature in southern California was never temperate. It was always either too hot or too cold, and at the ancient studio the heating and air-conditioning units were, as usual, inoperative.

Tempers were frayed. Chloe had even had a tiff with Chelsea Deane, whom she adored. Sissy was more vicious and back-biting than usual, and the crew was glum. But when Bill Herbert brought the overnight ratings to the set, everyone brightened up—they had gained three places in last week's ratings, and now were one place above "America."

Wearily, Chloe sat in front of the portable makeup table and powdered her face for the twentieth time. She looked and felt exhausted, and there were dark circles under her eyes that even the thick TV makeup couldn't hide.

Calvin had been lingering on the periphery of the studio floor all day. A shadowy figure in his reddish wig, baseball cap and sunglasses, he had been observing Chloe's movements intently from the moment she had arrived. He noted how nasty she was when she walked off the set after a row with the nice little English director, phony tears running down her face.

He watched her pack of sycophantic bitches—Vanessa, Trixie, De De—go to her trailer to placate her, listen to her demands, bring her tea, aspirin, cigarettes. Cater to the slut.

He overheard Sissy tell her girl Friday, Doris, what a selfish arrogant cow Chloe was. How she couldn't act her way out of a paper bag, how she only got her role because she had slept with Abby Arafat.

"Ugh, Abby is so gross, can you *imagine* four hundred pounds of heaving flab on your bones," they giggled together in mock horror.

Calvin picked up a discarded copy of the *American Informer* and read that Chloe had simultaneously just been voted by their readers:

A. One of the most admired women in America

B. One of the most hated.

There was no doubt how Calvin would have voted. Those who voted as he would have would thank him when he finally disposed of her.

He had failed before in Las Vegas, but this time, nearly five years later, he knew he was going to succeed. He felt it in his bones. His hands tightened over the handle of the seven-inch switchblade in his pocket. He had experimented on a couple of stray dogs. It had slit their throats extremely efficiently.

This was the third day he had hung around the set waiting for her. He hoped to get her that night in the parking lot. She had given up being driven by a studio driver since she had bought that flashy red Ferrari. He would wait for her in the back seat of her car. She never bothered to lock it. Stupid bitch.

"O.K., it's a wrap," called Ned. "Same time tomorrow everyone. Goodnight." Gratefully, the crew started packing up their equipment. It was 6:45 P.M. and already dark outside. It was not a late day, as TV shooting went, but most of the crew would still have to be back at six the following morning.

Chloe flopped onto the chintz couch of her tiny trailer on the sound stage. Wearily she removed her earrings and necklace. "I'm too tired to dress," she said to Trixie, and sat in her silk robe while Trixie put away her Miranda clothes and Vanessa poured her a much-needed glass of wine.

"Do you want me to stay with you, love?" asked Vanessa protectively.

"Not tonight, darling, Philippe's coming over with a contract to look over. I'll see you tomorrow." She managed a wan smile.

"Bright and early!" chirped Vanessa, who never seemed to get tired. "Don't forget to bring your blue Saint Laurent blouse."

Outside, on the dark sound stage, Calvin waited. He was hidden behind a flat with "Miranda's Bedroom" stenciled on it. He saw the two women leave the bitch's trailer, saw the last of the crew members trundle away their equipment. It was quiet now on the set except for a hint of thunder in the stale air. Stealthily he crept to the window of the trailer and looked in.

She was sitting at the dressing table in a red dressing gown, leafing through some papers. She was sipping wine and smoking. What a whore! He crept to the door. Pushed. It was unlocked. Careless slut.

With a gasp, Chloe turned to confront the intruder. Who was he? He smiled, a horrible grin. "Good evening, Miss Carriere."

"Who are you? Get the hell out of my dressing room before I call security." She felt fear immobilize her.

"Don't you remember me, Miss Carriere?" he mocked as he took off his sunglasses and baseball cap, then slowly peeled off the red nylon wig.

Oh, my God! Chloe almost fainted. It was he, dear God. The man the police said had tried to kill her in Las Vegas. They had let him out. Why?

"What are you doing in my dressing room? What do you want?" Her voice exuded a confidence she didn't feel. Although she was petrified, her hand went to the phone, but he grabbed it first.

"I want to talk to you, Miss Carriere. You remember me now, don't you?"

She didn't answer.

He put his face close to hers. "*Don't* you remember me, bitch?"

"Yes," her voice was a whisper. "I do."

Close your eyes and he will go away. It's a dream, a nightmare. It isn't happening. Where is Philippe? He's supposed to be here at seven. Oh, God, where is he? Why isn't he here?

"We are going to talk now. I want to talk to you, Miss Chloe *Mega*star *bitch*, but first I've got a little *present* for you."

383

He unzipped his jeans and revealed it, an angry red, rigid penis, which he held with filthy callused fingers. In his other hand was a knife, its blade glimmering in the bright lights of her dressing room mirror.

He was inches from her, that revolting object in one hand, the knife in the other. She picked up the glass of wine and in a desperate move threw it in his face. He gave a hoarse shout, blinded momentarily by the wine. His hands went to his face and he dropped the knife. In that split second, Chloe darted between him and the bunk bed in the tiny trailer and escaped onto the sound stage.

It was dark, except for the glimmer of a dim work light high above on the gantry, but she knew this stage like the back of her hand. Knew the location of the four exits. She had to get to one of them, find a guard. She realized it was futile to call out. No one would hear her on this soundproofed stage. Her high heels smashed into the pitted bare floor as she tripped over a cable and fell to the ground. She turned, sobbing, and saw the man silhouetted against the light of her trailer. Animal sounds issued from his throat. She could see the knife and his flaccid penis hanging outside his jeans.

She tried to stand up and, with a sob, realized she had wrenched her ankle. Gasping with pain and fear, she tore off her shoes and limped across the network of cables to the library set of "Saga," trying to reach the Exit sign.

"Bitch. Whore. I'm gonna get you, you fucking *bitch!*" She heard him crashing through the cables behind her as her stockinged feet felt the soft Persian carpet of the library. Only fifty more yards. The green Exit sign was like a beacon. She hobbled past the arc lamps lined up like sentries, past the coffee wagon. Where was the guard? Where was Philippe? She was weeping with fear, unable to move any faster.

Suddenly she felt Calvin's hands clawing at her back. She tried to throw him off, but he had her. She smelled his sweat as he

threw her onto the brown leather couch in the library and strad-
dled her.

It was hard again, that revolting red thing. Her silk robe had
fallen open and she was naked underneath, except for sheer
black tights. He sat across her thighs, his erect penis pressing
into her stomach, the knife at her throat.

"This is it, Miss Carriere. This is the end of the line for you.
You *slut!*" He spat at her as he took his knife and slowly slit her
tights from waist to pubis. Terror engulfed her as she struggled,
but his knife was digging into her chin, drawing blood.

"*Don't!* Don't move, bitch. If you want to enjoy this—and
you *will* enjoy it, won't you, don't you dare move, you ugly slut.
I've read about how you enjoy doing it with everyone—everything—men—dogs—horses—right, bitch! Right? I heard all
the filthy stories about you in prison, you whore." He slapped
her face repeatedly as he tried to force himself inside her.

Death was preferable to this, thought Chloe. Instant death
was infinitely preferable to being raped by a homicidal maniac.
With superhuman strength, screaming for help, she threw Calvin
off her body kicking out at his groin as hard as she could. On
her knees she started to crawl toward the door.

Outside the stage, Philippe thought he heard muffled cries as
he slammed his car door shut. It was almost impossible to hear
anything coming from the soundproofed stage, but he sensed
danger.

He pushed open the heavy doors and stopped in his tracks as
he saw the horrific tableau before him. A nude Chloe huddled
on the carpet, her face a mask of mute terror. Inches from her
stood a man, his upraised hand holding a knife poised to strike.

Calvin looked up at Philippe, startled. For a second the tableau was frozen, then Philippe moved and Calvin's hand sliced
through the air and the blade tore through Philippe's shirt.

Chloe's ears were ringing with the screams, but she could no
longer tell whether they were hers, Philippe's, or the madman's.

385

• • •

They always watched the early-morning news on the tiny portable TV in the makeup room.

Emerald sat in one chair, her lovely new face having a delicate layer of Max Factor base applied to it. She looked at herself in the mirror, seeing again, with eyes that had with the passing years lost some of their clarity, the face of a beautiful thirty-five-year-old.

Josh leaned back in his leather-and-chrome makeup chair, eyes closed, thinking about the next scene while his face "had the polyfiller applied," as he joked to the makeup man.

The TV announcement of the attempted murder of Chloe, and Philippe's death, jolted them out of their respective reveries.

"Christ! I must call her," he cried out, springing out of the chair and into his dressing room. Chloe's phone number, the one he had obtained from Daphne but had never used, was busy— constantly busy. In frustration, he dialed and redialed.

"You are needed on the set." Emerald came in without knocking. "I wouldn't call her if I were you," she said jealously. "The woman has just lost the man she loved. The last person she wants to hear from is her lovesick ex-husband."

Josh put the phone down. He asked Perry to send Chloe a basket of white roses and tulips, and wrote a note of condolence. The next day he left with the unit for a week of location shooting in the San Gabriel mountains.

Emerald traveled in the limo with him. She looked at him coldly as he sat, shoulders hunched in his woolen sweater, deep in thought, ignoring her. She bit her lip and settled back angrily into the fake leather upholstery.

She would try to get him out of her system. She would. She must. She had just met a new man, a stockbroker from Houston. He was rich, twice divorced, gray-haired, but still reasonably attractive. Maybe he was finally the one. The one she had been searching for all her life yet could never find—would never find. She opened her compact to gaze at her face again. Yes, it was still gorgeous. It had not changed in the half hour since she had last looked. She still had "it." Beauty, charisma, fame, power. She was a superstar again. She had the world in the palm of her hand. Didn't she?

The radio was playing soft, romantic music. "The greatest thing you'll ever learn is just to love and to be loved in return," crooned Nat King Cole.

Josh listened to the words. That had been one of the songs he and Chloe had sung together in Vegas in the seventies. It had brought the house down.

He remembered her turquoise eyes, how they had glowed when they looked into his, as they harmonized those words, oblivious to everyone and everything in the smoky saloon except each other.

29

Philippe's funeral made front pages all over the world, getting almost as much coverage as those of Rosalinde and Sam. "Saga" was hotter than ever, even if tragedy was the reason. Abby and Gertrude were ecstatic. They were now consistently ahead of "America" in the ratings.

But Chloe was melancholy and depressed. She lived because Philippe had died. She mourned for him, for the love they had shared. She forgot his sulks, his stubbornness. She chose to only remember the happy times.

It was a hot Saturday afternoon in June of 1987. Chloe walked slowly along the beach at Malibu, her little terrier dog panting at her heels. In two weeks, the fifth season of "Saga" would end. What then? What would she do with her life in the three-month hiatus that stretched ahead of her? Should she accept one of the movie offers she had received? Or should she take a trip round the world with Annabel, who had been such a comfort since Philippe's death? Annabel had flown in from London to be with her mother as soon as she had heard the news, and she had not left her since. She was in the beach house now preparing Chloe's favorite dinner.

Chloe kicked a stone along the water's edge as she contemplated her future; the little terrier bounded joyfully after it.

"Good afternoon, Chlo. What a day, huh? Makes you glad to be a Brit in California." The familiar voice interrupted her thoughts.

"Josh—what are you doing in this part of Malibu? I thought you lived in town." She was thrilled to see him.

The reflection of the sun sparkled in his eyes. His black hair, flecked now with gray, was tousled, a little too long, a little untidy. She had always loved it like that. Her eyes sparkled back at him, drank him in.

"I took a house just down there." He gestured past where toddlers were playing and teenagers were now throwing a ball to Chloe's dog, pointing to a small redwood shingle house. The house had a little chimney from which smoke was rising. It looked cozy, faintly English, and had hollyhocks growing outside.

"What a sweet house," said Chloe.

What a sweet face, he thought as he looked into her turquoise eyes, at the tan freckles dusting her upturned nose. She was wearing jeans and a plain white T-shirt. Her hair was tied in a ponytail and she wore no lipstick on her pale, full lips. He wanted to hold her in his arms, to kiss away the pain that he saw in the depths of those eyes.

"I got your flowers and note," she said softly. "Thanks,

Josh." He squeezed her arm gently. There was no need to say more. The sun was shining, the waves were lapping at their bare feet, and she was here.

"How about a cuppa?" he asked.

"English tea? I'd love some. Do you have Earl Grey?"

" 'Course I do, luv—you don't think I'd drink *American* tea, do you, in *bags* with string hanging out of it? It's revolting. I've even got a new china teapot from Harrods, *and* scones and cream."

"Biscuits?" Chloe smiled as they slowly sauntered across the sand to the little gray house. "Do you have any English bickies?"

"Do I have bickies?—I most certainly do." He looked at her with raised brows and a mischievous smile. "Name your brand, babe, and I've got 'em. McVities chocolate digestive. Custard creams, ginger snaps and Scottish shortbread from Fortnum's." Chloe smiled as he went on. "And brown bread and butter, with the crusts cut off. All your favorites, Chloe, all the ones you've always loved."

"What about sugar?" She liked this. She liked him. She more than liked him, she loved him—she'd never stopped. She knew it. The flame flickered stronger. "I hope you've got proper sugar."

"You bet I have, darlin', none of that saccharin sweetener stuff or brown crystals—turns the tea a funny color. Proper sugar. Lumps, of course. White. Even if it is bad for you, I don't care. I'm English—I like my tea how it's meant to be." They looked at each other for a very long moment, then walked slowly along the wet sand.

The tide lapped their bare feet, and they laughed as they rolled up their jeans. A phalanx of seagulls swooped in the distance in perfect formation. The little dog chased them, wagging his tail, frolicking in and out of the waves. The Malibu ocean was flat, like deep blue velvet brushed the wrong way. The late afternoon sun burnished the gentle swell with golden reflections. "And is there honey still for tea?" she murmured softly.

Josh's arm encircled Chloe's waist, her head folded into his shoulders, and her hand found his and held it very tightly.